Kimberley CHAMBERS

Born Evil

HARPER

This novel is entirely a work of fiction.
The names, characters and incidents portrayed in it are
the work of the author's imagination. Any resemblance to
actual persons, living or dead, events or localities is
entirely coincidental.

Harper
An imprint of HarperCollins*Publishers*
The News Building
1 London Bridge Street
London SE1 9GF

www.harpercollins.co.uk

This paperback edition 2017
1

First published in Great Britain by
Preface Publishing 2009

Copyright © Kimberley Chambers 2009

Kimberley Chambers asserts the moral right to be identified as the author of this work

A catalogue record for this book is available from the British Library

ISBN: 978-0-00-822860-6

Set in Times New Roman PS by Palimpsest Book Production Limited, Falkirk, Stirlingshire

Printed and bound in Great Britain by Clays Ltd, St Ives plc

MIX
Paper from
responsible sources
FSC˙ C007454

FSC™ is a non-profit international organisation established to promote
the responsible management of the world's forests. Products carrying the
FSC label are independently certified to assure consumers that they come
from forests that are managed to meet the social, economic and
ecological needs of present and future generations,
and other controlled sources.

Find out more about HarperCollins and the environment at
www.harpercollins.co.uk/green

Sunday Times #1 bestselling author Kimberley Chambers lives in Romford and has been, at various times, a disc jockey, cab driver and a street trader. She is now a full-time writer.

Join Kimberley's legion of legendary fans
on Facebook/kimberleychambersofficial
and @kimbochambers on Twitter.

Also by Kimberley Chambers

In memory of my wonderful grandparents
Daisy and Charlie Chambers.

ACKNOWLEDGEMENTS

A big kiss to Rosie de Courcy, my partner in crime! Sue Cox, my hands and brains! Tim Bates, my agent and therapist!

Also, a special mention to Trevor Dolby, Lesley Pollinger, Annabel Robinson, Pat Fletcher and my number one fan Jeanette Slinger.

A life is created
A child is born
A beautiful gift
Not one to mourn
A son for keeps
A love to gel
Unless that child
Belongs in hell

ONE

October 1990

'Look, Mum, there's no easy way for me to say this.
You're gonna go mental, so I'm just gonna give it to you
straight. I'm pregnant.'

June Dawson felt bile rise from her stomach and reach
the back of her throat. Dropping the dishcloth she'd been
washing up with, she clung on to the worktop for physical support.

For a moment, she thought she was going to pass out.
Breathing in deeply and blowing out slowly, she somehow
managed to steady herself. As she turned around to face
her daughter, she felt every hope and dream she'd ever
nurtured for her fly straight out of the window.

Trying to speak, June found that her voice sounded
anything but normal. She usually spoke loudly, but her
words came out in no more than a whisper.

'Is Billy the father?'

Debbie stood, hands on hips, staring defiantly into her
mother's eyes.

'Of course he is. I love him, Mum.'

June fished around in the kitchen cupboards and found
the bottle of brandy she kept there for cooking and med-
icinal purposes. She and her husband only ever drank
socially.

June poured herself a large glass and downed it in one,

then immediately knocked back another. She was in that much shock, she could quite easily have swallowed the whole bloody bottle. With the drink going straight to her head, her voice suddenly came back and she decided to say her piece.

'You're gonna have to get rid of it, Debbie. You're eighteen years old, with your whole life ahead of you. Don't sell yourself short and end up with a no-good arsehole like Billy McDaid. He's a wrong 'un love, everybody says so, and far too old for you. He'll run a mile once he knows you're pregnant. You mark my words, he'll be off like a shot. Blokes like him are all the same.'

Blinded by love and obstinate by nature, Debbie glared defiantly at her mother.

'Well, that's where you're wrong, Mum. Billy already knows about the baby and he's over the moon. He's dying for it to be born and can't wait to become a father. I love him so much and I'm keeping the baby whatever you say. You're just gonna have to accept it, or you'll end up losing me *and* your unborn grandchild. As for calling Billy a wrong 'un . . . you'd know all about that, Mother, wouldn't you?'

June looked at her daughter with a mixture of pity and disgust. She needed to talk to her Peter. He would know how to handle the situation.

'Get out of my sight, Debbie. You wait till Peter gets home from work. I'm gonna tell him what you said to me and he won't be very happy.'

'As if I bloody well care! He's hardly me father now, is he?' Debbie screamed, and slammed the kitchen door.

June sat down at the table, put her head in her hands and sobbed. Both her children had now fucked their lives up, and she wondered where she'd gone so bloody wrong.

She'd disowned Mickey, her son, a while back, when he'd got caught hijacking a lorry load of cigarettes with a gang of well-known villains he'd been knocking about with.

Her Peter had gone totally apeshit and demanded she wash her hands of the lad. It hadn't helped that the story was front-page news in the local paper. She and Peter had had to endure the shame, stares and gossip for weeks.

Unbeknown to her husband, though, June still discreetly enquired after Mickey. She'd heard through the grapevine that he was due out of prison in the next few weeks. He'd served his sentence in Wormwood Scrubs and had written to her from here a couple of times, pleading with her to visit him. June had tearfully read the letters that her first-born had sent and felt nothing but love and compassion for the son she still adored. But, after careful consideration, she'd torn them up and severed all contact with him.

It had been the hardest decision she'd ever had to make, but in her eyes it was the only one left to her. She'd had to choose her husband over her son.

Now the same thing was going to happen with Debbie, Peter was gonna go mad when he heard she was pregnant. Unless Debs agreed to get rid of the baby, June knew that he would make her daughter move out of the house.

Peter wasn't an ogre, just a strict, highly regimented man of integrity, with a high opinion of himself and his family. He was also preparing to stand as a Tory councillor in the forthcoming local election and certainly wouldn't welcome any bad press.

June poured herself another brandy, dreading what was to come. Without Peter she was nothing, a nobody. In many ways he'd been the making of her. He'd turned her from a rough East End girl into a respectable member of the community. He'd moved her from a shit-hole house in Poplar to a nice little cul-de-sac in Rainham. He'd taken on her kids as his own and given her a purpose in life, a chance to better herself, and she'd grasped that opportunity with both hands. She couldn't throw it all back in his face by siding with Debbie, she just couldn't. Not when her daughter was making the biggest mistake of her life.

Debbie lay on her bed. She felt like crying with frustration. She bit her trembling lip as hard as she could and drew blood. The pain stopped the tears from coming. She knew there was going to be a showdown when Perfect Peter walked through the door.

Well, he wasn't her dad and she was sick of jumping to his bloody tune. This baby was hers, and she wasn't taking shit off no one. He'd been good to her, had Peter, but his attitude really wound her up. Both he and her mother were shoved so far up their own arses, it was as though reality didn't exist for them. In their world, dinner parties, Masonic events, local politics and golf club meetings were much more important than what was going on in the real world.

Debbie had never had the pleasure of meeting her real father. She'd been only eighteen months old when he'd kicked the living daylights out of her mum and brother and left the house for the last time. Her brother Mickey, who was seven years older than she was, remembered him well and said he'd been an out and out cunt, a total scumbag.

Johnny Fuller was his name and part of Debbie wished she'd had the chance to meet him. Just the once would have done the trick. It would have satisfied her burning curiosity to know exactly where she came from.

She had no chance of that now, though. Six months ago her father had been found dead outside a betting shop in Whitechapel. He'd died of a single stab wound, a homeless alcoholic.

As Debbie heard the front door bang downstairs, she forgot about her real dad. Pulling the quilt over her head, she prepared herself for one of her stepfather's lectures.

Twenty minutes later, there was a tap-tap on her bedroom door, and a surprisingly calm Peter entered her room. Perching himself on the end of her bed, he came straight to the point.

'If you decide to have an abortion, Debbie, your mother and I will give you our one hundred per cent support. I'll pay, send you to the best private clinic available, and your mum and I will accompany you, so you won't have to go through this alone. However, if you are adamant about keeping the baby, then I'm afraid you'll be on your own. Your mum and I will have no option other than to wash our hands of you.'

Debbie took a deep breath as she pulled down the quilt and prepared to stand her ground.

'Look, Peter, I know I'm only young, and I appreciate your concern and Mum's, but I want this baby. I love Billy and he loves me. What can be so wrong about two people in love having a baby together?'

Looking at her disdainfully, Peter spoke slowly, clearly, in his most patronising voice.

'Debbie, Debbie, Debbie . . . you are so young and naive, my dear child. What am I going to do with you? Billy McDaid is not a very nice person, my love. He has a terrible track record with convictions for violence as well as drink- and drug-related offences. Eight years ago he was locked up in Pentonville for a vicious assault on an ex-girlfriend.'

Debbie's eyes were burning with fury as she leaped off the bed.

'I don't believe you – you're making it up! You're only

saying all this so I'll get rid of the baby. I bet my mother's put you up to this, hasn't she?'

Peter slowly shook his head from side to side and looked sadly into the eyes of this strong-willed girl bent on defying him.

'Everything I've told you is for your own good, Debbie. Your mother was so worried when you started courting this lad that I decided to have him checked out. I have well-connected friends, as you know, so getting the low-down on him wasn't that difficult. I can assure you, everything I've told you tonight is the absolute truth. He's also lied to you about his age. He's not twenty-nine, he's thirty-five years old. The ball is in your court now, and the decision is entirely yours. Get rid of the baby and Mummy and I will help you as much as we can. But, I have to be brutal about this, Debbie, if you decide to keep it, I want you out of this house by next weekend. Your mother and I have our reputations and also my standing in the community to consider.'

As he quietly shut the bedroom door, Peter said a silent prayer for the girl he'd brought up as his own and grown so very fond of. He was satisfied he'd done his utmost, his very best. Composing himself, he went downstairs to comfort his tearful, heartbroken wife.

'Wanker,' Debbie mumbled, as soon as he was out of earshot. 'Lying fucking bastard.' She was absolutely seething. Billy wouldn't lie to her about his age, and as for all the other shit . . . she didn't believe a word of it. It was definitely a ploy, just so she'd get rid of the baby. His standing in the community? What a tosser! Well, they could both go and fuck themselves. Perfect Peter and her drama queen mother deserved one another. As for the lies they'd concocted, she'd never forgive them for that.

Pulling her case out from under the bed, she started

to pack her clothes and belongings. They wouldn't have to wait till next weekend to get rid of her, she'd be long gone before then. She crammed in the last of her necessities, zipped the case and slid it back under the bed. She was seeing Billy tomorrow morning and couldn't wait to tell him the whole sorry story. He'd been asking her to move in with him for the last few months, but she hadn't wanted to upset her parents so had said no. Now, though, she couldn't wait to set up home with him.

Billy had a council place on an estate in Barking. The area was a bit rough and his flat was dirty with virtually no furniture. In fact, it was the complete opposite to the clean house and nice area that Debbie had become accustomed to.

All it needs is a woman's touch, a good clean, a bit more furniture and we'll be fine, she told herself.

The last night in her perfectly furnished bedroom with its pink wallpaper, hi-fi system, TV, video, and all her other personal belongings, wasn't an easy one for Debbie. She spent the whole night tossing and turning, unable to sleep. Ninety-nine per cent of her felt sure she was doing the right thing. Moving in with Billy and having his baby was what she wanted, wasn't it? There was only that one little seed of doubt at the back of her mind telling her that her choice could be wrong.

There's an old saying in life: 'Little seeds grow into very big trees.'

Unacknowledged by her, Debbie's little seed had already begun to sprout.

TWO

June sat on a floral-upholstered chair in the conservatory, a thousand thoughts spinning through her mind. She sipped her coffee and stared through the plate-glass window while Peter mowed the lawn. Watching her daughter leave home this morning, suitcase in hand, had broken her heart. She hadn't said a word as Debbie had walked away but kept schtum, to please Peter. What kind of mother did that make her? She should have shaken the girl, made her see sense, cuddled her and begged her to stay. Maybe even sat her down and told her the whole sorry story of her own younger years. Surely that would have been enough to make Debbie sit up and take notice.

Instead she'd done nothing, absolutely sod all, just let her daughter walk down the path and out of her life, with that no-good bastard Billy McDaid standing smirking by the front door. All she could do now was hope and bloody pray that her Debbie's life didn't turn out to be a mirror image of her own.

June Dawson had been only a kid, sixteen years old, in fact, when she'd had the misfortune to meet Johnny Fuller at the local fairground. Ten years older than herself, he was a handsome bastard. He had the clothes, the looks, the chat and the charm to impress a gullible teenager.

June had fallen for him, hook, line and sinker. She could remember the night she'd lost her virginity like it was yesterday. He'd looked so good in his black Crombie, tight trousers and winkle-picker shoes, she'd been overwhelmed with lust for him, putty in his hands.

Her pregnancy had shocked her parents to the core and they'd demanded she go away to a home, give birth to the child and have it adopted. Blinded by a mixture of naivety and love, June had ignored their request and chosen her own path. A brief spell living with Johnny's mother was followed by a council tenancy in a house in the back streets of Poplar.

Overjoyed at having her own home and determined to be a good mother and potential wife, June threw herself into a homemaking role where cooking, cleaning, scrubbing and lovemaking were all part of her everyday duties. Trouble was, as happy as she was in her new life, her Johnny wasn't. Within weeks of their moving in together, he was spending more and more time in the local pub.

The night her Mickey was born would stick in June's mind forever. At just turned seventeen, she knew nothing about having babies. On the night her waters broke, she thought she'd accidentally wet herself. When the contractions started she put it down to an upset tummy, blaming the bread and dripping she'd eaten earlier. For four hours she lay on the floor, crippled with pain, hoping and praying that Johnny would come home. Finally, unable to stand it anymore, she crawled on her hands and knees to old Lil next door.

Lillian Wade had lived through two world wars. After taking one look at June, she grabbed a towel and a pair of scissors, and forty-five minutes later young Mickey Dawson let out his first cry.

Johnny Fuller arrived home five days after his son was

born. Unbeknown to June he'd met some old scrubber, eighteen years his senior, from the Whitechapel area and had been staying at hers. After spending less than an hour with his first-born, Johnny headed off to the pub to wet the baby's head.

Life grew harder for June from that moment onwards. Money was scarce, and as time wore on she was left more and more alone with her son; Johnny was usually nowhere to be seen. But June, being a fighter, learned how to cope on her own with her boy. Her neighbours were wonderful, and whenever her so-called partner stayed away for long spells they helped her out with Mickey, making sure that both of them were okay. Many a cold night June and the boy sat huddled around a neighbour's coal fire for a bit of warmth; the rest of the time, they sat indoors with their coats on and a blanket over them.

As the years rolled by, June and Mickey settled into a nice routine. By now, Johnny hardly came home at all. If he popped in twice a year, he overstayed his welcome. Working up North was his excuse, but truth be told he was living with a bird over in Dagenham, playing Daddy to her two kids.

June's pleasant routine ended on the morning of Mickey's sixth birthday. Lily had baked him a cake, all the neighbours had chipped in to buy him a second-hand bike and a party was planned for him that afternoon. Hearing the front door open and slam shut, June thought it was Lily bringing the cake in.

'I'm in the kitchen, Lil.'

To her horror, it wasn't Lily at all. It was a drunken, unkempt, old-looking Johnny carrying a bin liner full of belongings in his hand.

'I'm home, darlin',' he slurred. 'For good this time, there's no more work up North.'

Life got a lot worse for June from that moment on.

Nursing a broken heart and an alcohol addiction, Johnny drank for England, refused to work, and took out all his frustration on her and the boy.

The beatings started within weeks. First it was just the odd clump here and there, but within months he was knocking seven colours of shit out of her.

June hated him, wished he was dead, but she was trapped.

Due to his drink problem, he'd stopped wanting regular sex but she dreaded the nights he beat her. It wasn't the pain, she could handle that, it was the aftermath. The violence seemed to arouse him and he'd then force himself upon her. It was on one of these nights that Debbie was conceived.

A couple of weeks after June's pregnancy was confirmed, Johnny did another disappearing act. Money was still tight and life was tough, but once again the neighbours helped out and June began to smile again.

Debbie was just over a year old when her father returned from his last jaunt. This time his behaviour was worse than ever and the beatings became more frequent. Things came to a head a few months later when, instead of just knocking his wife about, he started beating the living daylights out of Mickey boy as well. After a particular vicious attack on her son, June confided in her neighbour Lily, who knew exactly what to do. The lad was rushed to hospital and the police were called.

June did not clap eyes on Johnny Fuller again from that day onwards. A year later she met Peter at a wedding and had not looked back since. He had loved her, supported her, and made her financially and emotionally secure. Which was why, whatever happened, she had to stick by him. He had rescued her from a living hell and she would always be indebted to him for that.

'Are you all right, my darling?'

Peter wiped his muddy boots on the mat and sat down opposite his wife. Taking her hands in his, he spoke softly.

'Everything will be okay, June, trust me. Debbie will come to her senses. But meanwhile we have to stick to our guns, be strong. What's meant to be is meant to be, my love.'

June looked into his eyes. He was so sincere, so sure of himself. Squeezing his hands, she smiled. 'I hope you're right, Peter, I really do.'

Her husband kissed her gently on the forehead. 'Believe me, darling, I'm always right.'

Billy carried Debbie's case as they walked towards the tower block on the Gascoigne Estate. Gagging as she stepped into the lift, Debbie held her nose to block out the smell. She had been in the same lift plenty of times before, but the stench seemed far worse now that she was pregnant.

Billy lived thirteen floors up, which gave Debbie plenty of time to study her surroundings. They consisted of graffiti, spit, fag butts and stale urine. Noticing her expression, Billy smiled.

'Aye, lassie, you'll get used to the smell after a bit, you will.'

Debbie pretended to agree, but made a mental note to use the stairs whenever possible.

'Now, make yourself at home, hen. I have to pop out for a wee bit, to pick some money up. I willnae be long.'

Debbie took a good long look at her new abode and felt increasingly depressed. 'An absolute shit-hole' was the best way to describe it. She'd been here before, lots of times, but always after a drink and of an evening. Her mum and Peter had never let her stay out all night, so she'd never had a chance to see the place in daylight. The flat itself was okay, quite big for a council place, it was just so bare and desperately in need of decorating and some furniture.

Debbie looked into the bedroom and found there was nowhere for her to put her clothes. The one small wardrobe was full of Billy's stuff. As she sat down on the mattress on the bare floor, which served as the bed, Debbie started to sob. She would have to have a serious chat with Billy, she told herself. She wasn't coming round here once a week now, bladdered like before. She was a pregnant woman and needed comfort, a proper home.

Billy arrived back two hours later. Listening to Debbie talking between her sobs, he hugged her tightly.

'Shhh, now. Hey, come on, everything will be okay. I've got plenty of money. We'll get some paint tomorrow, spruce the place up a bit. There's a second-hand furniture place down the road – I'll take you there and we'll kit the place out. I didnae bother with all that shit before, living here on my own, but now you're here it's different. Now come on, stop crying, we'll get it sorted, I promise.'

Billy woke up early the next morning. Debs had been tossing and turning all night, she'd kept him awake for bloody hours. He glanced at her, and was surprised to see that she was now fast asleep. He hoped he'd made the right decision, letting her move in with him. Her performance last night, with all the tears and shit, wasn't his scene – dramatics had never been his game. He'd thought Debs was different, a laugh. He'd never seen her cry before, she'd always been so happy-go-lucky. He really hoped she wasn't about to change. For some reason or other, he always attracted nutty women. The last three had been all right until he'd moved in with them. Within weeks they all seemed to turn psycho on him.

Sighing, Billy slung his arm round Debs. 'Wakey, wakey.'

As he rubbed his erection against her leg, he willed her to respond. He was fucked if he was going to stand painting for hours, buy furniture he didn't want, and get nothing in return.

Stirring, Debbie reciprocated his kisses. She'd been silly last night, all emotional. This was her new life now. She loved Billy and was determined to make it work.

Billy was as good as his word. He bought a couple of tins of paint and then took Debbie to a tut shop where she chose a sofa, coffee table, small wardrobe, lamp and a chest of drawers. She refused to sleep in a second-hand bed, which pissed him off as he had to fork out for a brand new one. She also demanded saucepans, utensils and a big shop at Tesco.

'Fucking women,' Billy muttered, as soon as she was out of earshot. Three hundred and sixty pounds today had bloody well cost him! He just hoped Debs was worth it because if she wasn't she'd go the same way as all the others had.

Billy took a deep breath as he fought to keep his temper in check. In the past he'd made the mistake of lashing out at women, but he was determined to put all that shit behind him now and make a fresh start.

He really loved Debbie, but prayed she didn't push him too far. The others had all taken the piss out of him and he wasn't the type of geezer to take shit off anyone, especially a woman. His mum was to blame for the way he was, he knew that. She had fucked him up. He had tried desperately to forget his damaged childhood, but sometimes when women pissed him off, it came back to him. As he terrorised them, all he could think of was his whore of a mother.

Billy put the last of the Tesco bags in the kitchen, then

14

rummaged through them and opened a can of Strongbow. Greedily gulping the cider, he calmed himself down. This was a new start for him and he had to make it work. If he didn't, his evil bitch of a mother would have won.

THREE

Six months into Debbie's pregnancy, the cracks in Billy's resolve began to show. Spending most of her time in the flat alone, while Billy spent his in the pub, had become second nature to Debbie, so she was surprised when he insisted she attend a pal's wedding reception, which was being held in a local pub.

'Do I have to come, Bill? I can't drink, and I feel so fat and frumpy.'

'Aye, I want you to come. All my mates are taking their other halves, so I need you to be there for me.'

As she got ready that night, Debbie felt like shit. She'd made good friends with a couple of the neighbours, Sharon and Donna, and was usually quite happy to spend her time at home with them while Billy was out gallivanting. After powdering her face, she applied blue eye shadow, squeezed herself into the one black dress she possessed, and stood facing the cracked mirror which hung next to the wardrobe. The sight of her reflection didn't do her mood any good. 'Bleeding hell,' she muttered. She'd overdone the bronzer and felt like an orange that had become too big for its skin. Studying herself, she picked holes in her appearance. Her shoulder-length brown hair looked thin and lifeless. Her nose was a bit too big for her face, and her teeth had always been crooked. When she'd been slim her features hadn't bothered her so much, some people had even called her attractive, but now she was fat it was a different story. She felt unsightly.

'You ready, babe?' Billy stood at the bedroom door, looking smart in his light grey suit.

Plastering on a false smile, Debbie pecked him on the lips. 'As ready as I'll ever be.'

To her dismay, both lifts in the block were out of action, and by the time she'd walked down the thirteen flights of stairs she felt absolutely knackered.

The party was awful. The pub was a shit-hole, everyone was slaughtered and the DJ was a blind man. She'd have tried to enjoy it if only she could have had a drink, but standing in the corner on her own all night, with only a glass of Coke for company, wasn't much fun. Billy had introduced her to everyone earlier. He'd even stood with her for the first hour, but now he was drunk and up at the bar with the lads.

Debbie found herself studying him. He looked really smart tonight. Like her, he was no oil painting. Billy was skinny and pale, with light brown hair and sharp features. Attractive in his own way, though. She loved his Glaswegian accent, it made her laugh, and he was always cool and self-assured.

'It's Debbie, isn't it? Debbie Dawson?'

Swinging around to see who was talking to her, Debbie vaguely recognised the short lad with blond cropped hair, but couldn't think where from.

'Darren,' he said, shaking her hand. 'Darren Jackson. I was in your class at junior school.'

Once the penny had dropped the evening flew by for Debbie and she spent the rest of the night with him, discussing their classmates, teachers and old friends.

Billy stood at the bar, seething. Talk about making him look a prick in front of all his mates! With his blood at boiling point, he could stand it no more. Slamming his pint down on the bar, he walked over to where his slut of a bird and the blond-haired dwarf were standing.

'Whaddya think you're doing, you fucking slag?'

Terribly embarrassed, Debbie tried to smooth over the situation. 'Stop mucking about, Billy. This is Darren. He's an old school friend of mine.'

'I couldnae give a fuck who the cunt is, we're going home!' Billy grabbed her arm and dragged her out of the packed pub.

As they walked back to the flat, Debbie felt more and more uneasy. Billy looked furious and hadn't said another word.

'Tell me what's the matter, Bill? Has someone upset you?' she asked him. When he still said nothing, she carried on, 'Surely you're not annoyed because I was talking to that bloke. He's only someone I went to school with.'

Squeezing her arm fiercely, Billy pushed her ahead of him. 'Get home, you slag. I'll deal with you indoors.'

The nearer they got to the flat, the more worried Debbie became. She'd never seen him like this before and his behaviour was intimidating. With the lifts still out of action, Billy shoved her towards the staircase.

'Get up them stairs, bitch!'

Coming down thirteen flights of stairs while pregnant had been bad enough, but going up was even worse. Unable to keep up with his pace, Debbie sat down on the landing on the eighth floor, panting for breath.

'Please, stop pushing me, Bill. I need a rest . . . I can't breathe.'

Billy grabbed her hair and pulled her to her feet. 'You do as I say, you fucking whore! Get up them stairs, *now*.'

The look on his face told Debbie she had best do as he said. Petrified, she tried desperately to calm him down.

She was frightened to go inside the flat with him in this state.

'Billy, tell me what I've done? Please don't be like this. I love you . . . why are you doing this to me?'

Ignoring her plea, Billy dragged Debbie into the flat and pushed her down on to the sofa. He put on a Simple Minds LP and turned it up full blast. He knew Debs was friendly with the neighbours and didn't want the nosy bastards knowing his business. Then he walked into the kitchen, took a can of cider out of the fridge and gulped it down. Taking a deep breath, he ran towards Debbie who had started to get to her feet and pushed her back on to the sofa, using his full body weight to trap her there.

'You acted like a slag tonight . . . making me look a cunt! If you ever, ever do that again, believe me, I'll fucking kill ya!'

Not knowing how to handle the situation, Debbie loudly protested her innocence. 'I've done nothing wrong, Bill. Honestly, he was an old school friend who . . .'

She got no further. Billy stood up, lifted his right foot and kicked her with such force between the legs that it brought tears to her eyes.

'Nooooo, Billy, stop it! Why are you being like this?' she screamed.

Billy snarled at her, 'I can do exactly what I want, Debs, and do you know why?'

Debbie shook her head.

'Because *that* is mine,' Billy said, pointing at her crotch. 'That also is mine,' he said as he gestured towards her oversized stomach. 'And, believe it or not, girl, *you* are mine. If I was you, I'd get that into your thick skull and start behaving appropriately.'

Debbie was stunned as Billy left the flat. She'd done nothing to deserve this treatment, absolutely nothing.

Lifting herself gingerly off the sofa, she staggered over to the record player. 'Alive and Kicking' was playing. After what had just happened to her, it was the last bloody song she needed to hear. At a loss as to what to do next, she climbed into bed. She was too frightened to knock at her neighbours'. If Billy came home and she wasn't there, it would make the whole situation ten times worse.

Pulling the old blue blanket over her head, Debbie started to cry. She was desperately worried about the safety of the child she was carrying, and now knew that her mother and Perfect Peter had been right all along. Who was Billy McDaid? Tonight had proved she didn't know him at all. Devastated, she cried herself to sleep.

Billy was at his mate Andy's flat on the second floor. He'd calmed down by now, the cannabis and Strongbow had seen to that.

'I've had it now, mate, I'm off to bed. You stay as long as you like, Bill,' his friend told him.

As Andy left the room, Billy felt his anger return. It wasn't Debbie who'd caused it this time, but memories of his childhood and the bastard cards he'd been dealt.

Billy McDaid was born in 1955, at home, in a slum in the back streets of Glasgow. Father unknown, Billy had spent his younger years watching a succession of uncles coming to and from the house. His mother barely spoke to him, and most of his time was spent with his brother Charlie, who was seven years older than himself.

Looking back, Billy must have been the only wean in Glasgow who actually looked forward to going to school. The teachers there were nice to him and showed him kindness, something he'd never known at home. When he was seven, his mum bought home a man called Uncle Colin. When he was nine, Uncle Colin came into his room one night, turned him on his front and shoved his penis up his arse.

'This is our wee secret, Billy. One word to your mother and you'll no' see her or your brother again.'

The abuse carried on for years. Every time he was in the house alone with Uncle Colin, he was subjected to the man's sexual depravity. By now his brother had left home and Billy hadn't a soul in the world to talk to about his predicament.

At eleven years old, he could stand it no more. He told his teacher. Mrs McLintock informed the appropriate authorities, who then approached his mum. The social worker stood by and did nothing as his mother then beat him to a pulp.

'You lying little bastard!' she screamed accusingly.

A children's home was the next stop for Billy. Hoping life would be better there, he behaved himself and tried his hardest. He needn't have bothered. He ended up bullied and sexually abused there, too.

At sixteen he made contact with his brother Charlie and went to live with him. It was only then that he found out that Uncle Colin had subjected Charlie to the same abuse as himself.

The next couple of years were the happiest of Billy's so far poxy life. He and his brother lived together, worked together and drank together. Billly felt that he had more or less recovered from his fucked up childhood; unfortunately, his brother felt differently.

Unable to deal with the guilt he felt for knowingly leaving his younger brother in the hands of a paedophile, Charlie began to experiment with heroin. The drug helped him forget what he'd done, but at the same time took a hold of him. He died three months later, of an overdose.

Overcome by grief, Billy went off the rails. He drank himself into oblivion and shagged everything in sight.

Within six months, two girls claimed that they were carrying his children. Unprepared for fatherhood, Billy decided a fresh start was the best thing for him. He headed South and picked up work on a building site in Bow.

Hoping a change of scenery would make him forget the past, Billy worked his arse off and made new friends in the process. Sadly, as the years rolled by and he grew older, the past increasingly returned to haunt him. All his relationships seemed doomed. As soon as he got close to someone, all he could think about was his dead brother, and cuntsmouth Colin. He knew all the problems in his life were his mother's fault. That's why he hated women so much. Slags, they were, all of them. He didn't trust 'em one little bit.

Billy finished his drink and spliff, stood up and brushed the ash off his suit. Debbie, though, was a good girl, different from all the other slags, and he was desperate to make things work with her. He loved her, she'd been the making of him, and he owed it to her to make a go of things, whatever it took.

Shutting Andy's front door behind him, he took the stairs two by two. He was desperate by now to reach the thirteenth floor and put everything right again. Out of breath, he dashed into the bedroom.

'I'm so sorry, Debs, really I am. I promise you, babe, I will never hurt you again. I swear on my life. Please believe me?'

Debbie saw the sincerity in his eyes as he crouched down beside the bed. The baby had been kicking her all night and seemed as strong as ever. The love she felt for her unborn child was worth forgiving its father for.

'Just get into bed, Billy. You were well out of order earlier, but I'll forgive you, just this once. If you ever do anything like that again, me and you are history.'

Later, unable to sleep, she lay wide-eyed as Billy

snored. Tonight had been awful but Debbie wasn't about to give up on him, not just yet. It was obvious now that Peter had been speaking the truth about Billy's past. Well, she'd made her choice and it was up to her to deal with it. Going back to her mother's, cap in hand, wasn't an option. Debbie was stubborn as an ox and the thought of Perfect Peter telling her 'I told you so' was a non-starter.

The only thing she could do now was to think positive: hope and pray that what had happened tonight was a fluke, a one-off. Turning on to her side, Debbie willed herself to go to sleep. Her baby seemed to move about morning, noon and night. She was having a nightmare pregnancy and couldn't wait for it to end.

Debbie wished more than anything that she could ring her mother, talk to her and ask her advice. Angrily, she wiped the tears from her cheeks. She knew she had to be strong. There was no other way.

Peter's last words to her still echoed in her mind.

'Life is full of choices, Deborah. People make their own beds, and if they choose the wrong one, they should bloody well learn to lie in it.'

FOUR

Mickey Dawson pulled up at the top of the cul-de-sac, turned the van around so he wouldn't be seen, parked up and switched off the engine. Positioning the wing mirror so that he could clearly see his mother's front door, he pulled down his baseball cap until it partially covered his eyes. Picking up his copy of the *Sun*, he prepared himself to wait, however long it took.

Ten weeks he'd been out of prison, ten fucking weeks, and he still hadn't seen his mother or sister once, thanks to that jumped-up ponce they happened to be living with. Not wanting to cause them any grief, he'd decided against bowling up to the front door. He'd been itching to knock and give Peter a right-hander, just to wipe the supercilious look off his face, but he knew that in the long run it wasn't the best way forward. Debbie would probably have laughed, but it certainly wouldn't earn him any brownie points with his mother. This was why he'd decided to borrow his mate's plumbing van and was now waiting for the dickhead to fuck off to work before he made his move.

As luck would have it, he didn't have to wait long. Ten minutes later the front door opened, Peter appeared with a briefcase, jumped into his Ford Granada and sped off. Not wanting the nosy neighbours to see him, Mickey grabbed his phone. When he'd gone into nick, mobiles were unheard of and he'd purchased his first one only a couple of weeks ago. It was an absolute godsend, especially in his line of work. His mum's phone was answered on the fifth ring. A lump came into his throat at the sound of her voice.

'Mum, it's me. I'm outside in a Watts's Plumbing van. It's parked on the corner. I really need to see you. Come out for a drive with me and then I'll take you to lunch. Debs can come as well, if you like.'

June very nearly dropped the phone in shock. She didn't receive many calls in the morning and certainly hadn't been expecting this one. Part of her wanted to dash outside and envelop her beloved first-born in her arms, but she was too worried about Peter finding out to go with her instincts.

'Oh, Mickey, what are you doing outside? I'm not even dressed. What if somebody recognises you?'

'Don't start worrying, Mum, I'm in disguise. No one is gonna know who I am. Just put your glad rags on and get your arse out here! I've been sitting here, waiting for the Gestapo to go to work. The least you can do is come out for a drive with me and have a bit of grub. I am your bloody son, after all.'

'Okay, I've already had a bath. I just need to do my make-up and get dressed . . . I'll be about twenty minutes.'

Mickey smiled as he ended the call. It had been nearly three years since he'd last had the chance to talk to his mum properly and he was desperate to rebuild their relationship, even if it had to be done in secret.

Hands shaking as she applied her slap, June finally closed her make-up bag and began to choose her outfit. She settled on a grey jumper dress. She knew she'd gained a bit of weight recently so put a black blazer on top to cover her bulges. Desperate not to look old-fashioned, she added black suede boots and slung on some gold costume jewellery as a finishing touch. Mickey was her only son after all and she was eager to look nice for him.

She was a bundle of nerves as she approached the white van parked on the corner. Walking past it, she gesticulated for Mickey to drive down the road a bit. Her little community was very close-knit and she was determined not to get caught out. Peter would go apeshit.

Conversation was stilted at first – awkward, in fact. Mickey politely asked June how life was treating her. And June tactfully asked him about prison.

'So how's Debs?' he continued. 'Ain't she at home, Mum? I've been dying to see her. Where is she, at work or something?'

June felt guilty as she explained the situation. 'Haven't you heard, son? She's pregnant. She doesn't live at home any more, she's living in Barking somewhere. She won't have no more to do with me and Peter. We tried to help her, really we did, wanted to pay privately for an abortion, but you know how headstrong Debbie is. She stormed out and I haven't seen her since. I think about her all the time, son, I'm so worried about her.'

Spotting a lay by, Mickey pulled over. 'Our Debs, pregnant? Fucking hell! What's her address? I'll go and see her, make sure she's all right. I can't believe she's up the duff. What's his name, the geezer she's with?'

'Oh, Mick, she's picked a real wrong 'un. His name's Billy McDaid. Peter had him checked out. He's got a terrible track record. Been inside for drugs, violence, and Christ knows what else! Years older than her, he is. We tried to tell Debs, make her see sense, but you know what she's like . . . she wouldn't listen to us, thought we were making it all up.'

'I can't believe it, Mum. I'll tell you one thing, though,

our Debs ain't silly. Surely the bloke can't be that bad. Leave it with me. I'll find out who he is and have him checked out my way.'

June patted his arm. 'Thanks, Mick, but don't go round there like a bull in a china shop. I'm desperate to know she's all right, but I don't want you getting in no more trouble.'

'I won't cause no agg, I promise ya. I'll just find out where she's living and then I can keep an eye on the situation, check up on her and that. I'll have a quiet word in the geezer's shell-like, too, make sure he treats her okay. It won't hurt for him to know Debs has got a big brother. If he's cute, he'll know what he's dealing with.'

June smiled. 'You are a good lad, Mickey.'

'I'm always there for you and our Debs if you need me, you know that, Mum. Now, how about that bit of lunch? There's a nice little boozer down the road, does some lovely home-made grub.'

'Sounds great, son.'

The meat pie, potatoes and fresh veg were melt-in-your-mouth material, but neither of them ate a lot. They had too much catching up to do. Finally Mickey paid the bill and cuddled his mum as he led her back towards the car-park. He loved her dearly and was overjoyed at being able to spend some time with her.

'Are you plumbing now, love?' June asked innocently, noticing the writing on the van.

Mickey chuckled. She didn't have a clue, bless her. 'No, I ain't, Mum. I borrowed the van off me mate. I wanted to keep a low profile and my motor would have stood out like a sore thumb.'

'Why's that then, love?'

'Oh, no reason, Mum. Just thought the van was more discreet to pick you up in.'

He daren't tell her that he was swanning about in a

brand new Merc. She'd have given him a Spanish Inquisition about where he'd got the money from.

'So what are you doing for money? Are you working at the moment, love?'

Mickey chose his words carefully 'I'm doing okay. I'm working as a party organiser, setting up functions and stuff.'

June shot him a surprised glance. She had her Mickey down for a lot of things, but planning parties wasn't one of them.

'What do you mean? What sort of parties?'

'You know . . . weddings, birthdays, anniversaries. All sorts of stuff, Mum.'

June knew he was lying, but decided not to pry. The less she knew about his lifestyle, the less she would worry.

'Where do you want dropping, Mum? I take it you don't want me pulling into the turning.'

'Drop me by that little shop, Mickey. I need to get a loaf.'

Bumping the van on to a stretch of kerb, Mickey leaned over and hugged her tightly. 'Does Peter always leave for work at the same time?'

June ruffled her son's dark hair, just as she'd done a million times when he was a little boy. 'I can't get out a lot, Mickey, you know what Peter's like. I can probably manage it about once a month. He's normally gone to work by ten but ring first, just in case. And do me a favour, son – find out how Debbie's doing. As soon as you have any news, ring me and let me know. I've been worried sick about her.'

'I'll ring you when I've seen her, but I have to say a lot of this is your own fault, Mum. You should never have lost contact with her, nor with me. We're your kids, at the end of the day. I know we're not perfect but blood's thicker than water. You shouldn't let that prick dictate to you. You have to learn to stand up to him before it's too late.'

June opened the door of the van and climbed out.

'Let's not spoil a good day, Mickey. I can't deal with this conversation right now. I'll see you soon, love. Ring me as soon as you have any news about Debs. Take care, son. Love ya.'

June had tears in her eyes as she left her beloved boy and began the short walk home. She knew what he'd said to her had been right. She also knew that she was too weak to do anything about it. Peter was so bloody domineering and if she started standing up to him, she was worried her days as his wife would be numbered. In Peter's world women were to be seen and not heard.

Mickey hit the A13 and headed back towards Bow. He'd been living there since he'd come out of the Scrubs. It was only a temporary thing, just till he got back on his feet. He was planning to move out to Essex once he got a few bob behind him, but for now Bow and his one-bedroomed bachelor pad suited him fine. He'd spent a fair few years as a kid there, working on Roman Road Market, and he knew the area and its inhabitants inside out. In fact, most of his contacts came from that neck of the woods.

Life was sweet for Mickey at the moment and had been since the day he'd walked out of nick. The money was rolling in thick and fast. He'd hooked up with an old pal of his, Big Stevie Roberts, and they were currently on to a nice little earner.

Big Steve had told him about his newfound business venture while he'd been on the inside. It wasn't until Mickey was released that he realised just how big it really was. Illegal raves were fucking massive, and he and Steve were currently netting a fortune, organising the little beauties. This was the score. Scour the M25, find a friendly

farmer, smile at him, offer him a big wad of money ...
and Bob's your fucking uncle.

Mickey was now in charge of finding the right venues
and chatting the owners up. He looked the part and had
the spiel. Steve was no good at all at that. A massive
bastard, with a skinhead haircut, he looked like an out
and out thug. He had a heart of gold, but the farmers
weren't to know that.

There was a real biggie organised for a fortnight's time.
It was due to be held at a disused airfield on the outskirts
of Essex, and Mickey had been running around like a
blue-arsed fly, trying to get things sorted. Everything
about these raves had to be kept hush-hush. The old bill
were doing their utmost to put a stop to them, and any
tip-off they received was a tip-off too much.

Because of this, the advertising was mainly done on
the night, via pirate radio stations who would give out a
mobile phone number. Partygoers would ring up from a
phone box to find the exact venue. The M25 would then
fill up like rush hour as thousands of pilled-up punters
headed off for the night of their lives. It was a bit like a
game of cat and mouse with the filth, and so far the boys
in blue were on a losing streak. Mickey and Steve were
absolutely loving the chase, and up to this point hadn't
had one rave cancelled.

Smiling to himself, Mickey thought about his mum. It
had been so good to see her. She'd changed a lot since
he'd seen her last. She had never been a stick insect but
was now quite plump, with a real mumsy look about her.
She looked even shorter than he'd remembered, though
at only five foot she'd never been tall in the first place.
Maybe it was the weight she'd put on. Mickey decided
he liked his mum's new look. Her clothes were top drawer,
her short dark hair cut into a modern style, and he thought
she looked just like a mum should.

Parking the van he'd borrowed outside his mate's, Mickey stuck the keys through the letterbox and jumped into his Merc. He immediately punched Big Steve's number into his mobile. 'What you up to, mate?'

Steve was having a swift half in his local. He'd been hard at it all morning, trying to sort out the security for their latest rave, and was now having a well-earned rest.

'I'm in the Needle Gun, having a beer with Terry. Why, what's up?'

'How do you fancy a trip to Barking? Apparently me sister's got herself knocked up by some wrong 'un and I need to sort it out.'

'Okay, count me in,' Steve said, downing the rest of his lager.

After Mickey had filled Steve in, the lads decided the best way to do their homework was to pay a visit to a few boozers around the Barking area. They struck gold in the very first pub. The spotty kid of a barman was only too willing to spill his guts at the sight of a fifty pound note. Tucking it safely into his shirt pocket, he ushered them over to a quiet corner.

In ten minutes flat the lads knew Billy McDaid's life story. They were told where he lived, where he drank, and where he punted his puff and speed. They also learned that he wasn't exactly fucking popular.

'Wonderful! She's got herself knocked up by a middle-aged, drunken drug dealer *and* he's Scotch an' all,' sighed Mickey as they left the boozer.

Much to his pal's annoyance, Steve burst out laughing.

'Don't wind me up, Steve. It ain't fucking funny. What are we meant to do now?'

Trying to keep a straight face, Steve looked at his mate. 'Sorry, I didn't mean to laugh. It's just, well, the cunt couldn't have sounded any worse, could he?'

Mickey let out a worried sigh. 'No, he fucking well

couldn't. My mother's gonna go apeshit if I tell her the full SP. I'm gonna have to keep schtum and pretend he's not as bad as we first thought. How do you reckon I should handle it, Steve? Should I knock seven colours of shit out of him, or should I go and see Debbie first? Check he's treating her all right?'

'You'll have to go and see your sister first. You can hardly go in with both feet, not if she's carrying his nipper.'

Mickey started the engine and looked at the address on the bit of paper he'd been given. 'Yeah, you're right. But I'll tell you this, Steve – if he ain't been treating her right, he'll pay for it. She's my sister, I love her, and believe me, if it came to it, I would fucking kill for her.'

FIVE

Mickey checked the address on the piece of scrap paper, in case his eyes were deceiving him, and felt his bad mood worsen.

'Look at the state of this fucking dump. What a shit-hole! Christ knows what my little sis has got herself roped up with here.'

Steve looked at the rundown tower block. 'It looks like Nelson Mandela House on *Only Fools and Horses*, don't it?'

Debbie was hanging her washing out on a line over the bath when she heard the tap on the front door. Thinking it was one of the neighbours, she opened it without first checking the spy hole and nearly keeled over at the sight of her brother standing there, with a big skinhead by his side.

'Mickey, what a wonderful surprise,' she managed to stutter.

'This is me mate Steve. Ain't you gonna invite us in then, sis?'

'Nice to meet you, Steve. Of course you can come in. I'm sorry, Mick, it was such a shock seeing you, I forgot me manners. Go and sit down and I'll put the kettle on.'

Debbie was all of a fluster as she poured boiling water over the coffee granules. She was pleased to see her brother. It had been ages and she'd missed him like mad. She just wished she'd known he was coming so she could have spruced herself and the flat up a bit more.

As he sipped his coffee, Mickey nudged his mate and told him to pop downstairs and check on the car. He needed to have a one-to-one with his little sis, a proper chat, family only kind of stuff. As soon as the front door clicked shut, Mickey jumped out of the threadbare armchair that had seen better days, walked over to the window and stared out at the far from appealing view.

He had to tread carefully here; he knew how fiery Debs could be and didn't want to rub her up the wrong way. He'd never be able to keep an eye on her if they had words and she fucked him off. But, guessing what was coming, Debbie decided to make it easier for him.

'Come on then, Mick, cut the crap. What are you really doing here? Has Mum sent you round to check up on me or what?'

Mickey turned to face her. 'Mum never sent me, although she is worried about you. So am I, Debs. What are you doing living in a shit-hole like this? You can't bring a kid up round here. And who's this geezer you're with? Does he work? Is he looking after you okay?'

Picking up her brother's box of cigarettes, Debbie lit one and took a deep drag. She'd given up the stinking habit as soon as she found out she was pregnant, but the way she felt at this moment, she could literally smoke the whole box. She flicked her ash into the chipped ashtray then turned to face her brother, determined to stand her own ground.

'Look, Mick, I'm a big girl now. You don't have to worry about me, honestly, I'm fine. Billy's as good as gold. We have our ups and downs, like anyone else does, but overall he treats me really well. He usually works on building sites, but to be honest even when he's not at work, he's never short of money. Anything I ask him for, or need, he gives to me. As for this flat, I'm not stupid, I know it's not the Ritz, but it's only temporary. Once the baby's born, I'll be eligible for a council house, hopefully in a much better area.'

Mickey looked at his sister and just for a moment blamed himself for her predicament. He'd always looked after her when they were kids, always been there for her, and if he hadn't been locked away in the slammer, she certainly wouldn't be in the position she was in now. Over his dead body would he have let any of this shit happen to her.

'Look, Debs, I don't wanna burst your bubble or fall out with you, babe, but I need to meet this geezer, just to put me own mind at rest. If he's always got money, even when he's not working, he's got to be a bit dodgy, ain't he?'

Debbie could feel her temper bubbling to the surface and was determined to stick up for the father of her unborn child.

'Look, Mick, don't give it Snow White with me. *You* never go to work and *you've* always got money. Maybe he does the same shit as you do. I don't know what he does, but you of all people have no right to get on your fucking high horse! At least my Billy hasn't spent the last couple of years slopping out shit buckets in Wormwood Scrubs, like you bloody well have.

'You make me fucking die, you do. You've always put yourself first, Mick. And as for my caring mother – she's shoved so far up Peter's arse, I'm surprised she can even breathe. Now, all of a sudden, everyone's worried about poor little Debs? Well, bollocks to the pair of ya! I needed you both years ago, not now.

'I'll tell you something else an' all, shall I? When you

left home, my life was absolute shit. You didn't give a toss that I was stuck there with Mum and that arsehole Peter on my own, did ya? I mean it, Mick, my life has got sod all to do with you or Mum now, so you can both keep your fucking trunks *out*.'

Holding up his hands in defeat, Mickey walked towards her, intending to give her a hug.

Debbie was having none of it. 'Don't try and be nice to me, Mick, you've upset me now. I've tried to make a life for meself and all you can do is come round and pick fucking holes.'

'Come on, Debs, I'm your big bruv and I love ya. Sorry if I've been a bit brutal with ya, but I'm bound to be worried. I wouldn't be much of a brother if I wasn't.'

These words moved Debbie in a way nothing else he had said had. The fight went out of her and she suddenly felt tearful.

'Now come on, don't cry,' Mickey said as he held her in his arms.

'Oh, ignore me,' Debbie said, half laughing, half crying. 'It's just me hormones playing up.'

Letting her go, Mickey reached inside his jacket and took out a pen. 'Get us a bit of paper, sis, and I'll give you my mobile number. Are you on the phone here?'

Debbie shook her head. 'We've no phone, but Billy has promised he'll get one put in nearer the birth.'

Taking a wad of notes out of his pocket, Mickey rolled off a bundle. 'No arguments, Debs, take this and make sure you get a phone put on. Do it as soon as possible, and treat yourself to something nice with the rest of the money.'

'Thanks, Mick. I'll pop next door to Sharon's. She's with BT, I'll get her to ring them for me.'

Mickey rubbed her arm. 'Good girl, and don't worry

about the bill. If you get stuck, or you're a bit short, I'll always pay it. Now put my number away safely. You can ring me anytime on that, day or night.'

'I'll put it in me purse. But I'll make a note of it some-where else, just in case I lose it.'

'Right, I'd best be going now, Debs. Me and Steve are gonna have a couple of beers round here, before we shoot home. What pub does your Billy drink in? I'll buy him a pint if I meet him. I'd like to get to know him.'

Debbie felt her heart sink. This was all she bloody well needed.

'He probably won't be in the pub today, Mick. He had to be somewhere earlier.'

'I'll have a look anyway, Debs. Where's he likely to be, if he's about? I mean, if we're gonna be family, I need to introduce meself and that, don't I?'

Debbie knew there was no point in lying. He was a clever bastard, her brother, and he'd find out anyway. If she lied, it would just look like she was hiding something.

'If he's about, he'll be in the Westbury, the Brewery Tap or the Hope and Anchor. Promise you'll be nice to him if you do bump into him, Mick?'

'Of course I will. I just wanna buy him a pint and that. You worry too much, Debs.'

As Debbie kissed him goodbye, she felt as if she had the weight of the world on her shoulders. Ever since the night Billy had laid into her then apologised, things had been going pretty smoothly. Billy had been attentive and caring once more and she didn't need her brother or anyone else upsetting the apple cart.

Feeling shattered, she lay on her bed, imagining her partner and her brother getting on well together. She knew she was kidding herself, though. Deep inside she had a terrible feeling that they'd hate one another on sight.

* * *

37

Billy McDaid nodded to one of his regular punters to follow him out to the toilets. The guv'nor, Fred, was in today, and even though Billy knew he was aware of what went on here, he didn't want to take the piss by serving up right under his nose.

'Want a drink, Fred?' he asked innocently as he returned from the Gents.

'Yeah, go on, I'll have a large Scotch,' the landlord replied, busying himself behind the bar. He couldn't stand McDaid. In fact, he couldn't stand any of his customers. Scumbags and wasters, the whole bloody lot of 'em. He'd lived through a world war. These arseholes round here wouldn't be able to survive a fucking thunderstorm!

Billy chatted away happily to a couple of cronies up at the bar. He'd been much more relaxed in himself over the last couple of months and finally felt that his life was on the up. Serving up in pubs suited Billy down to the ground and was much more appealing to him than freezing his plums off on a building site. He'd first fallen into his new career by accident. He'd been dealing to his mates, word had got around, and it had escalated from there. He didn't sell anything heavy, just a bit of speed and puff, and he worked it from his three locals. He visited each boozer at a set time, on a daily basis, so his punters always knew where to find him.

Billy never took his work home with him. All of his stash was hidden downstairs at his mate Andy's, along with his scales, wraps, clingfilm, and any other evidence that could incriminate him. If it all came on top, the last thing he wanted was to get Debs involved. They'd been getting on so well lately, he would hate anything to jeopardise that.

Noticing that the pub had suddenly fallen silent, Billy swung round on his barstool to find out why. He smelled trouble as soon as he clocked the two heavy geezers walk up to the bar and order a drink. Outsiders weren't welcome in the Hope and Anchor; it was a locals' boozer where everyone knew everyone. They certainly didn't look like old bill, but they didn't look like mugs either. If anything, the pair of them looked pretty handy.

Mickey and Steve sipped their pints and chatted quietly to each other. They knew which one of the punters was supposed to be McDaid because they'd paid a little kid outside a score to look through the window and point him out. Not wanting to make a tit of himself, Mickey decided to watch and wait. He needed to check if his intended target had a Scottish accent, hear him called by name before he made himself known. For all he knew the kid outside might have been pulling a fast one and he was damned if he was gonna mug himself off.

Sensing trouble brewing, Fred decided to call it a day and leave the honours to his barmaid Julie. He hated the pub; they could smash it to smithereens, for all he cared. 'See ya, Bill. Bye, lads,' he shouted as he made a rapid exit.

Hearing the name Bill, Mickey knew that he'd struck gold. Over the next hour or so he watched three or four punters come into the pub, follow Billy into the toilets and immediately leave the premises without even buying a drink.

'Classy,' Mickey said sarcastically to Steve. 'He must use the khazi as his office.'

Steve laughed. 'What we gonna do then, Mick? We can't just stand here all day.'

Telling his friend to stay put, Mickey walked over to where McDaid was sitting.

'You got a minute, Bill?' he asked casually.

Billy was shitting himself. He was sure he didn't know this cunt from Adam, but with all his mates' eyes firmly on him, was determined not to show his fear.

'How do you know my name? Who the fuck are you?'

As Mickey moved closer, he looked the skinny gutted arsehole straight in the eye. 'Don't you notice the family resemblance?' Holding out his hand, he smiled as he clocked the alarm on Billy's face.

'Mickey Dawson, Debbie's brother. Now, shall I ask you again, have you got a minute?'

'Aye, nice to meet yer, Mickey. I've heard lots about yer. What are yer having?'

'I don't want a drink, Billy, I just want a quick word with ya. Let's go outside, eh?'

Unlocking the Merc, Mickey told Billy to get in the passenger seat.

'I dinnae want to go for no drive, ye ken. My pals are all inside the boozer and I cannae leave them.'

Mickey smiled at him. 'You worry too much, Billy. We're not going anywhere.'

Once in the car, Mickey turned to face him. 'Right, I've been to see me sister who informs me that you treat her okay and that she's happy and so on. Me personally, I don't like the sound or the look of you, but you're my sister's choice and not mine. Obviously, being her older brother, I will always be about to protect Debs and keep a watchful eye on her. At the moment, even though you're obviously selling drugs from a khazi, I'm willing to give you the benefit of the doubt. But – and I mean *but* – if you ever get her arrested, lay a finger on her, or treat her badly in any way, then you'll have me to fucking deal with. Do you understand what I'm saying to ya, Bill?'

Lost for words, Billy nodded dumbly. Feeling nervous, he searched for the right words. 'Look, I love your sister, man, I really do. I'd never treat her bad, I swear I wouldnae.'

'Well, that's okay, then. As long as we understand one

another, we won't have a problem. Now let's go back in the pub and I'll buy you a pint.'

Mickey nodded to Steve to join him and Billy as they re-entered the pub. He then spent the next half an hour chatting to his sister's choice of man and trying to be as polite as possible. It was difficult; the geezer was an out-and-out prick. Finishing the last of his drink, Mickey forced himself to shake Billy's hand.

'Well, I'm glad I've met ya. I'm going now, but as I said I'll be popping round again to check on me sis. I left her some money today to get a phone put on, so make sure she does, eh, Bill?'

'Definitely. I'll sort it, nae problem.'

Mickey smiled. 'Good stuff. Oh, and by the way, I'd appreciate it if you didn't tell Debs the ins and outs of our little conversation. Just say that we had a beer together, got on fine, and leave it at that, okay?'

'No probs,' Billy said as he waved them goodbye. As soon as Mickey and Steve walked out the door, though, Billy's temper began to boil. The more cider he drank, the angrier he got. He was extremely annoyed with himself, for being so gutless and not giving Mickey what for. Billy was a face round here in Barking, everyone knew him, and that twat had had the cheek to come and belittle him, make him look a prick in his own local? Ordering a pint of snakebite, he vented his true feelings to his mate.

'Andy, you listen to me – Billy McDaid. You see that prick . . . that mug? I didnae lose it with him 'cause of Debs. But I'm telling yer now, if that cockney cunt ever comes back in here and pulls me out of this pub again, I'm gonnae *do* him, believe me, man. I'll kill him. And if I find out Debs has been slagging me off behind my back, I'll kill her as well. May God be my judge, I swear I'll kill the fucking pair of 'em.'

SIX

Debbie eased herself into a sitting position. For what seemed like the umpteenth time, she hauled her oversized body out of the armchair and stood staring out of the window. She was worried sick about her Billy. He loved his grub. Like clockwork, he popped home about six for his dinner, and if by any chance he couldn't make it, he always sent a pal round to tell her he would be late. It was now eleven o'clock and she hadn't seen hide nor hair of him. She just hoped he was okay. Surely if he had been arrested or involved in an accident of some kind, someone would have informed her.

It seemed too much of a coincidence, today of all days, when her brother had gone to look for him, that this had happened. Maybe they had got on that well they'd embarked on a bender together. Somehow, though, she couldn't imagine that. She was kidding herself. And even if they had gone out on the piss, Billy would still have made time to let her know.

Debating whether to knock next door and borrow Sharon's phone to ring her brother's mobile, Debbie decided against it. It was late now and she didn't want to become a pest. She'd already knocked twice earlier, to ring around Billy's locals.

'He's not in here tonight, love,' had been the answer to her question in all three pubs. Billy didn't normally venture anywhere else. If he wasn't in his usual haunts, she was stumped as to where he was. Defeated, she wandered out into the kitchen and left a note on the top, telling him that his shepherd's pie was in the oven. Then, not knowing what else to do, she got into bed and prayed for his safe return.

Billy McDaid staggered down the dimly lit road and angrily kicked out at a cat that had the cheek to get in his way. Still fuming over the events of earlier, he'd got himself paralytic, hoping to improve his mood. Instead of making him feel better, though, the snakebites he'd sunk had had the opposite affect. Kicking over a dustbin, he reeled into the tower block and repeatedly pressed the lift button. He swayed out of the lift and with difficulty managed to fit his key in the lock at the second attempt. Debbie had barely slept a wink and was relieved when she heard the sound of the front door opening.

'Is that you, Bill? Where have you been?'

Billy let out a loud belch. 'Mind your own fucking business.'

Debbie was shocked by his viciousness. 'What's happened, Bill? Are you okay?

Kicking the door shut, Billy slammed his fist against the wall. 'Am I okay? Do I sound okay? You silly fucking slag!'

The tone of his voice told Debbie not to say any more.

Staggering into the kitchen, Billy clumsily retrieved the shepherd's pie from the oven and dropped a quarter of it on the floor. He scooped it up with his hands, slopped it back on to the plate, picked up a fork and ate the bastard thing. Burping, he opened the fridge door, took out a can of cider and greedily downed it.

43

Debbie felt her whole body start to shake from head to foot as she heard him approach the bedroom. She hadn't a clue what she was meant to have done wrong, but guessed it was something to do with her brother. Feeling the baby kick, she prayed for its safety.

Billy staggered into the bedroom and lunged at her. Dragging her out of bed by her hair, he swung her round to face him. 'You been telling tales on me, you fucking cunt?'

Debbie started to sob. She knew from past experience that there was no reasoning with him when he was like this. 'I haven't said anything bad about you. I love you, Billy, why would I say anything bad?'

Lip curling, like a dog that was about to bite, Billy spat in her face. Then, losing it completely, he head-butted her as hard as he could. As his spittle ran down her chin, Debbie sank to the ground.

'Billy, don't!' she screamed, as he repeatedly kicked her. Lost in a red mist, Billy was unable to control himself. Thoughts of his childhood and his mother overwhelmed him, as he drew back his foot again and again.

'The baby, Billy! You're hurting our baby . . . '

It was the mention of his unborn child that brought Billy to his senses. Sinking down onto his knees, he cuddled Debbie's battered body to him.

'I'm so sorry, hen. Please, don't leave me! I swear to you, I'll get help. I'll go for counselling, I'll do whatever you want me to. I love you, Debs, I really do.'

Debbie had taken such a beating she could barely speak. 'Go next door,' she muttered. 'Use Sharon's phone . . . ring for an ambulance.'

'You can't go to hospital,' he pleaded. 'I'll get nicked. They'll put me away.'

'I have to, Bill, I can't feel the baby moving. Go and

44

ring one, quick! I promise I won't grass you up. I'll tell them I fell down the stairs or something.'

Panicking, he pummelled on the neighbour's door. 'Sharon, for fuck's sake, open up! Debbie's had an accident,' he screamed. He didn't even feel drunk anymore. He just felt sick with fear.

Sharon leaped out of bed and opened her front door. 'What's the matter? What happened to her?'

'Just call a fucking ambulance, will yer?' Billy was agitated now. He was in Shit Street and he knew it.

Sharon dialled 999. 'What are her injuries, Billy? They're asking me what's happened to her.' Receiving no reply, she handed the receiver to him.

'Just fucking hurry up, will yer?' he told the ambulance service. 'She's over eight months pregnant.'

Putting on her dressing gown, Sharon ran next door to help her friend. As soon as she saw Debbie, she put her hand over her mouth in shock. The poor little cow looked like she'd gone ten rounds with Mike Tyson.

'You bastard, how could you do this to her?' Sharon screamed at Billy.

'I didnae do nothing! She was putting the rubbish out . . . she slipped and fell down the stairs.'

'You lying fucking cunt,' Sharon said, through gritted teeth. 'You keep away from her, Billy McDaid, do you hear me? I'll go to the hospital with Debs. She needs you like she needs a hole in the head.'

Billy put his head in his hands then sobbed like a baby. 'I'm so sorry, Debs,' he said, stroking her bloodied hand.

Debbie was in too much shock to speak. Instead, she nodded dumbly.

Sharon carried her sleeping children into Donna's, who lived the other side of Debbie. Donna was only too glad to look after the kids and be of help. She liked Debbie, she really did, and couldn't believe what she was being told.

Sharon ran back into Debs's flat and pressed the release button on the buzzer to let the ambulance men in downstairs.

'Get away from her,' she said vehemently as she noticed Billy stroking her friend's battered face.

Knowing when he was beaten, and not wanting to face the wrath of the ambulance men, Billy took her advice. Still sobbing, he grabbed his fags and lighter and bolted down the stairs to spill his guts to Andy.

The ambulance men took one look at Debbie and glanced knowingly at one another.

'I fell down the stairs,' she managed to mumble.

Yeah, right, they each thought.

Inside the ambulance, Sharon held Debbie's hand and assured her that everything was going to be okay. 'You're going to be just fine, Debs, and so is that little baby of yours.'

Debbie was given some oxygen to help with her breathing. Sharon felt so sorry for her friend as she noticed her tears dripping on to the stretcher.

Once at the hospital, Debbie was classed as an emergency.

'You'll have to wait here,' Sharon was told as her friend was rushed off surrounded by doctors.

As she sat down on an uncomfortable plastic chair, Sharon wished she had asked Debs if there was anyone she could contact for her. She knew Debs had a mum and a brother but didn't have a clue where they lived. Debbie rarely spoke about either of them. Sharon had only known Debs a matter of months but liked her immensely. She was funny, genuine and honest and certainly deserved a lot more from life than the no-good-bastard she had got herself entangled with. She had been looking forward so much to the birth of her baby and had spoken of little else over the past couple of months. Sharon prayed the opportunity of becoming a mother wasn't about to be cruelly taken away from her.

Meanwhile, Doctor Agomonga pulled his colleague to one side and explained that there was something wrong with Debbie's breathing, possibly due to damage to her lungs. The baby was also a major concern as they could only detect a faint heartbeat.

'Miss Dawson is adamant we put the baby first. I think we must perform a caesarean section, deliver the child, and sort the patient's breathing out afterwards.'

Debbie asked to speak to her friend alone for a few seconds, before they wheeled her to theatre.

Sharon put on a gown, washed her hands in some surgical disinfectant and went in to face Debbie. She spoke faintly, her breathing laboured.

'I've told the doctors that I've no next-of-kin, so if they need anything signed, I've given permission for you to do it. If anything happens to me, I want you to contact my brother Mickey. His number's in my purse. You've still got my bag, haven't you?'

Sharon nodded, unable to stop the tears from streaming down her face. 'You'll be fine, Debs. I've gotta go now . . . the doctors are waiting to operate.'

'And,' Debbie whispered, grabbing her arm, 'promise me, Sharon? If I die and my baby survives, look after it for me. Tell my brother and everyone what Billy did to me. Make sure he doesn't get his hands on the baby. If I'm okay, keep quiet, and say nothing to no one, apart from Donna.'

'I promise,' Sharon said.

Debbie's last thoughts, as the anesthetic took hold, were of her own funeral. She could visualise her mother, shoulders hunched, being supported by Peter. She could see her brother Mickey sobbing at the graveside.

Overcome by tiredness, she closed her eyes.

SEVEN

Billy McDaid sat on a wooden bench, trying to muster up the courage to walk through the glass doors ahead of him. It was over forty-eight hours since the birth of his son, and he was desperate to visit both Debbie and the boy.

He'd been constantly ringing the hospital since the morning after Debs had been admitted, but getting any information out of the bastards had been like extracting blood from a stone. Today, however, he'd decided to try a different tactic and, amazingly, it had worked.

Albert, one of the old regulars who drank in the Hope and Anchor, had made the phone call for him, pretending to be Debbie's uncle. Glad to be rid of the suspected abuser with the Glaswegian accent who kept ringing up, the hospital had swallowed old Albert's yarn and told him the facts. Hence Billy's arrival at the hospital, armed with a bunch of flowers and a teddy bear, waiting for the right moment to go in.

Deciding that after what he'd done to Debbie there was never gonna be a right moment, he took a deep breath and marched through the glass doors. Shit or bust, he needed to be with his family.

Debbie took a sip of lukewarm tea and looked lovingly into the cot beside her bed. He was gorgeous, her son, tiny but perfect. She was amazed that she had actually created such a beautiful creature. The nurses had only allowed him to be in the same room as her since this morning. They'd said she wasn't well enough before that. Her injuries were bad, but not as serious as the doctors had first suspected.

A collapsed lung, two fractured ribs and a broken nose were the result of Billy's frenzied attack on her. The staff had been pleased with her progress, though, and Debbie no longer cared about her injuries. She was alive, her baby was okay, and that was all that mattered. The only distressing thing for her now was that she'd been advised not to breast-feed.

Not wanting to dwell on what she couldn't do, Debbie had decided it was time to think positively. At one point in the ambulance, her breathing had been so bad she'd thought she was dying and wouldn't be around to see her precious baby.

Her friends Sharon and Donna had both been fantastic, absolute stars. Sharon had turned up with a bag full of night clothes and underwear, and had also offered her a place to stay when she was discharged.

'I've made room already,' she told Debbie. 'You'll be fine, living with me, until the council sort you somewhere out. I know it's not ideal living next-door to that bastard, but don't worry, I'll look after you, I promise.'

Debbie was especially grateful that Sharon had kept her word and told no one about what had happened.

'Wendy and Jenny asked me round the shops and I just told them you'd gone into labour early. They're like the *News of the* fucking *World* them two. Good job I never slipped up or everyone in Barking would have been told by now,' Sharon had laughed.

Debbie prayed her Mickey didn't turn up again soon. She just hoped that, because she hadn't rung him with the promised landline number, he wouldn't call in at the flat unexpectedly. If he did turn up when she got back, she would just make the excuse that the baby had arrived early and, with a bit of luck, by then her injuries would probably be healed.

In all honesty, though, her brother was the least of her problems. Billy was her main concern and she'd been thinking about him all day. Her head told her that she hated him, despised him, and was well rid. Trouble was, her heart told her differently. She knew he had problems of his own and was worried that, without her in his life, he'd do something stupid. Part of her would always love him, always care for him, and she couldn't just switch off her feelings. She hadn't told Sharon and Donna how she felt, nor would she tell anyone else. People would think she was mental and deserved all she got.

Her thoughts were broken by the sound of her son crying. Debbie buzzed the nurse and waited patiently for her to arrive. She hated having to buzz for help just to attend to her baby, but was under strict orders from the doctor to stay in bed and take things slowly.

'What are you going to call him?' the nurses kept asking her. She and Billy had both agreed on Charlie for a boy. It was Billy's idea really; he'd wanted to name him after his dead brother. Debbie hadn't mentioned this to the nurses, but had just told them she was undecided. This was true. If she wasn't with Billy anymore, she might as well name him after her own brother, or pick a completely different name which suited the baby more.

Debbie took her son from the nurse and fed him his bottle. He looked nothing like her, he was more like Billy. As she studied him, she racked her brains for a name that would suit him. For some strange reason, she couldn't think of one.

*   *   *

Billy ducked out of the way of an oncoming doctor and stood at the entrance to the obstetric ward. He knew that Debs was in a side room, as the nurse had told old Albert so, but he was frightened to ask any of the medical staff for directions. His accent would definitely give him away.

Feeling more and more like a dickhead, with a teddy in one arm and a wilting bouquet in the other, Billy was quite relieved when a young girl pushing a tea trolley stopped and asked him if he was looking for anyone in particular.

'I'm looking for my sister, Debbie Dawson,' he lied, imitating a cockney accent to the best of his ability.

The girl smiled. She liked her new job and wanted to be helpful. 'Debbie's in that room over there,' she pointed, 'last door on the right.'

So far, so good, Billy thought to himself. He'd expected it to be an ordeal just to get to Debs, but it had been an absolute doddle. Feeling nervous as hell, he opened the door and walked in.

'Hiya, Debs. Please don't chuck me out. Can we talk?' he pleaded.

Shocked by his unexpected appearance, Debbie felt nervous and awkward. 'Sit down over there if you want,' she said.

Seeing her lying in bed, bruised, fragile and with his son in her arms, brought a lump to Billy's throat. He hadn't come prepared with a speech and was stumped as to what to say to her next.

'I'm lost for words, Debs,' he finally admitted. 'I cannae explain why I did what I did. All I can say is that I am so, so sorry. I cannae believe how badly I've treated you. I know you must hate me and I'll understand if you never wannae see me again, but I'm begging you, please, give me just one more chance. I'll get help for my temper, I'll do anything you say. I love you, Debs and I want us to be a proper family. I'll do whatever it takes. I'm nae talking shit, I really do love you. Please say you'll give me another chance. I'll make it up to you, I swear I will.'

With tears dropping on to her baby's face, Debbie held the child as close as her sore ribs would allow. Annoyed with herself for getting all emotional, she stopped crying, cleared her throat and spoke the truth.

'I don't know if I can forgive you, Bill. I nearly lost the baby because of you. In fact, I nearly died. At one point the doctors said it was touch and go because my breathing was that bad. How can I give you another chance? I'll be treading on eggshells for the rest of my life in case I say or do something to set you off again. I can't live like that, Billy, I really can't. And, to be honest, I'd be petrified for the baby's safety. When you lose it, Bill, you're like a madman. There's no reasoning with you. What is wrong with you? Why do you do it?'

Billy knew that what she was saying was true. Unable to take his gaze off the little bundle in her arms, he walked towards her. 'Can I hold him for a minute, Debs, so I can have a proper look at him?'

'No, you can't,' she said, clinging on to her son for dear life. 'I've just asked you a question, Billy. Don't change the bloody subject! Why did you beat me up? What is it that triggers you off? Is there something in your past that you haven't told me about?'

Her words and questions struck a nerve. Billy flopped down into his chair, held his head in his hands and began to sob. 'Yes,' he managed to mutter. 'Something really bad happened to me . . . but I've never told anyone, Debs, only my brother. It's so bad, I cannae tell yer.'

Debbie looked deep into his eyes and could see nothing but fear there.

'Move your chair nearer,' she urged him. Then, squeezing his hand comfortingly, she spoke kindly to him.

'You have to tell me, Billy. Whatever it is, I need to know. If you don't, I can't help you.'

Billy held his hands over his face and kept them there. He was too embarrassed to look at her. Feeling thoroughly ashamed, he told her all the horrors of his childhood. As he finished spilling his guts, Debbie was stunned. She'd guessed he had some secret in his past, but never this. Poor Billy. Her heart went out to him.

'Look at me, Billy, please,' she said gently.

Getting up off the chair, he ignored her and walked over to the window. He couldn't look at her in case he saw a look of disgust in her eyes. He was used to seeing it in his own. He saw it every day of every week, and every week of every year, whenever he glanced in the mirror. Opening the dirty window, he gulped in the fresh air. Unlike him, it felt clean and unspoiled.

As Debbie lay there in her hopsital bed she felt completely lost for words. She knew from the past odd comment he'd muttered about his mother, that he'd had a shit childhood. But never in a million years would she have thought him the victim of sexual abuse. The signs just hadn't been there.

Desperate to comfort him but not knowing what to say, she was almost relieved when the baby started to cry.

'Come on, Bill, don't stand over there. What happened to you wasn't your fault. I'll help you get through this, I promise. Now come over here. Our son's crying and he needs his daddy.'

Shoulders slumped, Billy walked towards her, managed a half-smile and took his baby in his arms for the very first time. As he rocked him to and fro, he studied the baby intently and was pleased to see that he had the same colour hair and sharp features as himself. Smiling for the first time in days, he looked at Debs.

'He's a bonny lad, eh? Looks just like his daddy.'

Glad to see his mood had lifted, Debbie smiled back. 'He's your double, Billy, he's a ringer for you. Now we must decide on a name. Do you still want to call him Charlie, after your brother?'

'Can we?' he asked, surprised. After what had happened, he hadn't expected any choice in the matter. 'Can he still have my surname?'

'Of course he can.'

After kissing his son gently on the forehead, Billy handed him back to her.

'Can I stay a bit longer, Debs, or would you rather I go now and pop back tomorrow?'

She took a deep breath. 'I'm a bit tired now, Bill. I could do with some sleep. Why don't you come back then, eh?'

'Okay.' He stood up. 'Are we still an item, Debs, me and you?'

A nurse entering the room then saved Debbie from replying to his question when she didn't know the answer. 'We'll talk tomorrow, Bill,' she said softly as she took her medication.

As she watched the nurse put the giant teddy bear on the chair and take the flowers away, Debbie lay deep in thought. She knew in her heart that she still loved Billy, but she was worried about putting her and her son's safety at risk. She knew Billy needed her and that she couldn't walk away from that. How could she leave him after what he'd told her earlier? She might be stubborn and hard on the outside, but underneath her tough exterior she was kind and gentle and would do her utmost to help him.

Debbie gently guided the bottle into Charlie's mouth. As she watched him feed, she knew she couldn't deny him the chance of having his father around. Boys needed a daddy, and she was damned if she was going to let her son miss out, for the sake of her pride.

Perhaps now that Billy had told her everything, his evil temper would cease to be a problem. He had someone to talk to now, to discuss his problems with. Maybe that would calm him down, stop him losing his rag. Hoping against hope that she was making the right decision, Debbie smiled at her little bundle of joy.

'I don't know if I'm doing the right thing, Charlie, but I think me and you should give Daddy one more chance. If he messes up, son, then it's just me and you against the whole wide world. What do you think, eh, boy?'

Charlie finished his bottle, took one look at his mother and screamed.

EIGHT

Debbie looked at her shiny new phone and knew that the first call she had to make was the one she'd been most dreading.

She had to ring her Mickey and invite him round to see the baby. Her brother was a clever bastard, and would get suspicious if she put him off any longer. She had no excuse now anyway as the tell-tale signs of the hiding she'd endured were long gone.

It was three weeks to the day since Charlie's birth and she'd been back at home in Barking for just under a week. Giving Billy another chance hadn't been easy, but she'd felt it was the right thing to do. She still hadn't totally forgiven him; that would come in time, she hoped. But since she'd been home, Billy had been a different person. He'd been extra-kind and attentive, and when he wasn't out working, had been waiting on her, hand and foot.

Sharon and Donna had been there to offer any advice she needed about motherhood, but the pair of them refused to come into her flat any more.

'We want nothing more to do with that no-good bastard, and neither should you,' they'd told her in no uncertain terms. Sharon, in particular, was furious with Debbie for giving him another chance. 'You gotta be fucking mad,

Debs,' she'd insisted. 'A leopard don't change its spots, mate. He'll do it again, you mark my words.'

Debbie had shrugged her shoulders, knowing that there was every chance her friend was right. There was no way she could explain why she'd taken him back, she couldn't betray Billy's confidence, so she'd just kept quiet and let her best friend think she'd taken leave of her senses.

Taking a deep breath, Debbie took the bit of paper Mickey had given her out of her purse and dialled her brother's number. He already knew that she'd given birth to Charlie because she'd called him from Sharon's phone a few days earlier, and given him a load of cock and bull about a premature labour.

'I reckon they got the dates wrong, Mick,' she'd lied.

Mickey had wanted to rush straight over to meet his little nephew, but Debbie had put him off. She'd told him that she felt like shit and needed to rest up for a few days before she had any visitors. 'As soon as I feel well enough, you can be my first visitor,' she'd promised.

Now, as the phone was answered, Debbie did her best to sound happy and jovial. 'I feel much more like meself now, Mick, and little Charlie can't wait to meet his uncle. When do you wanna come round?'

'Tomorrow lunchtime okay, sis? I've got little Charlie loads of presents, and I've got a surprise for you as well.'

'Great,' Debbie said unenthusiastically. 'See you tomorrow then, Mick. Come after one.'

She replaced the receiver, put her head in her hands and cried. She really didn't feel like playing happy families, but knew she couldn't avoid it.

The last couple of weeks had been hard for her, bloody hard, and since she'd come out of hospital she'd had very little sleep. It wasn't Billy, he'd been fine. It was Charlie who was causing her untold worry. The kid just didn't stop crying, and since she'd brought him home he'd got worse and worse.

She would feed him, rock him, cuddle him, but nothing seemed to work. Now she was at the end of her tether. He'd been fully checked over at the hospital and a health visitor had popped in to see him at home, assuring her that the baby was just fine and things would become easier in time.

Debbie flopped down on the bed, feeling thoroughly exhausted. Billy had gone back to work today and she felt a failure trying at coping alone. The baby seemed to respond better to his father than to her. If Billy picked Charlie up, his tears subsided. When she tried, they worsened. The child hated her, she could sense it. Either that or she was being paranoid and imagining things. Perhaps she had that post-natal depression.

After another night with virtually no sleep, Debbie's mood was no better the following day. Her brother was due in a few hours and she was absolutely dreading it. She still hadn't forgiven him for the day he'd had a beer with Billy and earned her a bloody good hiding.

Debbie wasn't in the mood to do anything, but forced herself to have a bath. The sight of herself in the cracked mirror did nothing to lighten her mood. She looked dreadful, and even though most of the baby weight had disappeared, still had rolls of fat around her middle, which looked disgusting.

She tried on her old Levi jeans, but they wouldn't do up so she chucked on a pair of old black trackie bottoms and a baggy black T-shirt. Feeling frumpy and ugly, she applied some lipstick and eye shadow. The end result was awful. She felt even more hideous. As she was about to get changed once again, Charlie began screaming his head off. Time for his bottle. Feeling physically drained, she shuffled into the kitchen.

Debbie was just about to feed her son when the buzzer went. Unfortunately for her, Mickey had arrived half an hour early. She felt like tearing her hair out as she laid Charlie back in his cot and answered the door. As if things couldn't get any worse, to her horror, not only was her brother standing there, but her mother was as well.

'I told you I had a surprise for you,' Mickey announced, not noticing her anguished expression. Laden with bags of presents for the baby, he dumped them all in the hallway and walked back towards the door. 'I've gotta go down to the car, sis, to get his big present out. Have a chat with Mum for a minute, eh?'

Completely taken by surprise, Debbie went on to autopilot and offered her mother a cup of tea. Picking up screaming Charlie, she took him into the living room and thrust him towards his nan.

'Meet your grandson, his name's Charlie. Oh, and by the way, I must be a shit mother as he doesn't stop fucking crying!'

Debbie stomped out into the kitchen and waited for the kettle to boil. She was gonna have her Mickey for this. Fucking cheek, bringing Mum round here without her say-so!

June Dawson sat down on the battered old sofa and tried to soothe the distressed child. As she studied him, she felt there was something unusual about him. She had expected to melt at the sight of her first born grandchild, but instead felt no maternal stirring whatsoever. Maybe it's because its Billy's child, she thought, noticing that the poor little mite had inherited his father's rat-like features.

Looking around the living room, though, June understood the child's misery. 'Shit-hole' did not even begin to describe this place. The furniture was threadbare, the curtains ill-fitting, and it didn't look as if any housework had been done for weeks.

June smiled as her daughter brought in the tea. 'He's gorgeous, Debbie,' she lied as she offered the child back to her. 'So, apart from him crying, are you coping okay, love?'

Debbie took Charlie from her mother and looked defiantly into her eyes. 'What are you really doing here, Mum? I thought you wanted nothing to do with us. Why the change of heart?'

June took a sip of her drink before answering. 'Mickey asked me to come. I've been so worried about you and was desperate to make sure you were okay. You are my only daughter, Debs, and believe it or not, I love you very much.'

Debbie went straight on the defensive. 'Don't give me that old bollocks,' she said, as she gently laid her son over her shoulder to rub his back. 'I bet you love me so much, you haven't even told Peter you're coming to fucking see me.'

Unable to meet her daughter's stare, June was saved from answering by Mickey returning with the most expensive buggy he'd been able to find.

'What do you think, sis?' he asked casually.

'Thanks, Mick, it's a beauty.'

He smiled. 'Give us the little bruiser 'ere, I'm dying to meet him.'

As Mickey took Charlie into his arms he felt himself shudder. The situation reminded him of the episode of *Only Fools and Horses* when Rodney had first looked at Del boy's kid. Difference was, the guy who played Rodney had been fucking acting! 'He's a belter, Debs,' lied Mickey. Desperate to get rid of the child, he handed him over to June. 'Go see Nana,' he said in a silly voice.

As Debbie watched her son bond with his family, she felt her mood lighten. Both granny and uncle were obviously besotted and she was overjoyed to see it.

*   *   *

Billy McDaid thanked his two punters, sat back on his barstool and sipped at his pint. He had his shitty old workman's clothes on today because he'd told Debs he had a few days' graft on a building site. It wasn't true, he'd just wanted to make a good impression, let her know he was trying hard to change. Selling a bit of gear was easy money for Billy and he was fucked if he was jacking it in. He needed the money now, anyway, what with three mouths to feed. What Debs didn't know wouldn't hurt her, and after a week or so he'd tell her there was no more work and he'd gone back to serving up, just to keep the wolf from the door.

Things had been going really well since she had come home from hospital and he found he was thoroughly enjoying being a father. Obviously with babies you were limited as to what you could do with them, and secretly he couldn't wait until Charlie was that bit older. Billy was gagging to introduce his son round the local pubs, take him to football and do the whole father-and-son routine. He was over the moon that Debbie had decided to give him another chance and was determined not to fuck it up this time. Since telling her about all the shit he'd endured in his childhood, he felt as if he'd unloaded some of his problems, shared the burden. Although his past would never go away, he felt that by offloading himself to Debs he had brought them closer together. At least now she could finally understand him as a person.

She still drove him mad at times and probably always would. She was always moaning and getting on his case about work and shit, but he'd come to the conclusion that all women were the same. If they opened their mouths, they whinged. Simple as that. On the other hand, he knew his Debs was one of the most decent birds he'd ever met and that he'd struggle to find a better one.

'Do ya want another drink, Bill?'

He politely refused. 'Nae thanks, mate, I'm gonna get meself home to Debs and the wean.'

Billy left the pub feeling happy with himself. A bonny wean and a beautiful lassie, what more could a man want? Smiling, he decided to stop at the offie. His woman deserved a treat and he was just the man to buy her one. Browsing the shelves, he bought a bottle of wine, a box of Milk Tray and six cans of Strongbow. He'd had a good day today and had nicked at least a fifty. Deciding to really push the boat out, he headed to the local Chinese, and ordered a tenner's worth of takeaway.

'I'm home, hen,' he called cheerfully as he entered the flat. 'I've brought you loads of goodies, lassie.'

Debbie had had a good afternoon since her mother and brother had left. After the initial awkwardness, it had been really nice to see them and although no arrangement had been made to meet up again, she knew all she had to do was pick up the phone. She hadn't had a go at Mickey after all. Her mother, for all her faults, had seemed genuinely pleased to be with her. Debbie had even put up with June doing her Hyacinth Bucket bit, allowing her to vac, polish and do some ironing.

After her family had left, Debbie had for once managed to get Charlie off to sleep. She now felt miles better after some much-needed shut-eye herself. In fact, she'd only woken an hour ago.

'Surprise!' Billy announced as he stood in the doorway.

'Bill, come and look at all this stuff!' Debbie called to him excitedly. She'd just been going through all the bags her Mickey had left for Charlie and he'd bought some blinding gear. Baby jeans, cord dungarees, little boots, the tiniest Nike trainers you ever did see, a base-ball cap, toys . . . he'd thought of everything.

'Look, Bill,' she said again as she clapped her hands

together in excitement. 'Mickey got all these up Bethnal Green. He reckons there are some fantastic baby shops there. He said he'll take me and I can pick out whatever I want.'

As Billy stood there with the Chinese in one hand and the carrier bag in the other, he felt like a complete and utter prick.

'What you brought me then, Bill?' Debbie asked cheerfully.

'Nothing much,' he said dejectedly. 'Only a Chinese and that.'

She jumped up and slung her arms around his neck. She'd already decided not to mention the fact that her mum had visited, just in case it upset him. 'Oh, you're a darling. Go and dish it up, Bill, I'm starving! Let's get stuck in while Charlie's still asleep.'

Billy walked into the kitchen and threw the Chinese on to the worktop. He took the Milk Tray out of the bag and slung the box straight into the bin. His blood was boiling and he was fucking fuming. He'd thought Debs would be over the moon with his surprise, but no, her cunting brother had had to arrive here first like fucking Santa Claus and make his present look like a burnt offering.

As he chucked the special fried rice on to the plates, he took a few deep breaths. He had to keep his temper in check, couldn't lose it, not now.

'Mickey fucking Big Shot Cunt,' he muttered to himself, as he shovelled prawn balls on the side. He hated being belittled and, for the second time in months, Deb's brother had managed it quite easily.

'What you doing, Bill? Hurry up, I'm starving!' Debbie shouted innocently.

'Coming, dear,' he growled, gritting his teeth with anger. He couldn't be made to feel a loser any more by her brother.

He'd had enough of it. He'd have to put a stop to his visits, cause a row, do something. Mickey fucking Dawson was hardly Reggie Kray. The sooner he got the cunt out of their lives, the better.

NINE

December 1994

'Do you mind waiting behind for a few minutes, Debbie? Only I need to have a word with you in private.'

Debbie sat down on one of the plastic chairs and watched all the other mums and kids straggle out of the building. Feeling her cheeks redden, she braced herself for the worst. She didn't have to wait long. Two minutes later Charlie's teacher sat down next to her, a pitying expression plastered across her face. In her most patronising voice, Mrs Jones listed all the naughty things that Charlie had been caught doing that particular week. These included punching a little girl, spitting at a little boy and showing his willy to her and everybody else in his class.

As her son sat on a nearby chair, rocking in his seat and giggling uncontrollably at the stories of his own antics, Debbie cringed with horror. This wasn't the first time she'd had to deal with this kind of situation, but she still didn't know what to say.

She cleared her throat. 'I'm so sorry, Mrs Jones. I promise I'll have a word with Charlie's father as soon as I get home, and I can assure you he will be punished for his bad behaviour.'

Mrs Jones nodded her head sympathetically. In all her years of teaching children, she had never come across one as intelligent as Charlie. He was approaching genius level developmentally. Streets ahead for his age, he was three going on thirteen. But so far as his behaviour went, he was the worst child she had ever taught. He was rude, constantly swore, had an extremely violent nature and was way too sexually aware for his tender years. Mrs Jones glanced at the child, still gleefully rocking on his chair and pulling faces at her. Turning her attention back to his mother, she felt nothing but relief as she delivered her final blow.

'I'm so sorry, Debbie, but I think it would be best all round if you found another nursery for Charlie to attend. We've been extremely patient with him and given him so many chances, but we simply haven't the staff to deal with him here. He seems to need constant attention and we have to divide our time equally between all of the children.'

'He won't misbehave again, I promise, Mrs Jones. Please, just give him one more chance?' Debbie pleaded.

'No,' said the teacher firmly. 'Charlie has had too many chances as it is. Recently we've had far too many complaints from the other parents. I'm afraid we have no choice other than to ask you to remove him. I'm really sorry, Debbie, but we just can't control him and also feel that he'd benefit from a change of school. As you know, his intelligence is not in question, but unfortunately he needs far more attention than we can offer him here.'

Debbie stood up. 'Okay, well, thank you for your time, Mrs Jones.'

'Old bag, old bag, old bag,' Charlie chanted, and started to laugh hysterically.

Grabbing her child out of his seat, Debbie dragged him towards the door. Telling him off was useless. He'd obey Billy, but with her it went in one ear and out the other. Five minutes from home, she happened to remember that she'd forgotten to collect her Family Allowance. With

Christmas on the horizon, money was much needed so she decided to take a detour towards the Post Office.

'Nooooo, wanna go home!' Charlie screamed, sitting down on the pavement and refusing to budge.

'Please, Charlie, now come on, be a good boy for Mummy. If we don't go to the Post Office, Father Christmas won't bring you any presents next week.'

'Don't care,' he replied, folding his arms. 'Father Christmas not real. I want toys today.'

Debbie wearily reverted to the only tactic she knew would work. 'You be a good boy, Charlie. Come to the Post Office with Mummy and you can pick out any toy you want.'

Smiling, Charlie got up from the pavement. As young as he was, he knew exactly what buttons to press with his silly mummy.

At the Post Office, Debbie was greeted by the sight of a long queue and her heart sank. Charlie and queues didn't really go together. Holding his hand and forcing him to stand next to her, she prayed for him to behave and not make a show of her. Her prayers must have fallen on deaf ears. Five minutes later, he pointed at the woman in the sari standing in front of them and screamed, 'Look, Mum – Paki, Paki, Paki.'

Debbie was mortified. Billy had taught Charlie his foul and racist language, not her. Coon, Paki, cunt, wanker... she'd heard Billy laugh as he'd made his son repeat the words after him. Trouble was, with Charlie being so bloody intelligent, he knew exactly what the words meant and who they were aimed at. As she noticed the horrified expressions on faces around her, Debbie apologised and quickly left the queue. Sod the allowance, she didn't need the money that much.

'I want my toy,' Charlie screamed as they headed home. He refused to walk, chucked himself to the ground, and in the end Debbie had to nigh on carry him over her shoulder.

Reaching the tranquillity of her flat at last, Debbie locked her son in his room and turned the radio on to drown out the sound of his tantrum. Today had been awful, and to say she'd felt embarrassed was putting it mildly. What the hell had she done so bloody wrong as a mother? Stressed beyond belief, she put her head in her hands and sobbed.

When his temper subsided, Charlie sat down on his bed. Tall for his age, his looks were a perfect match for his character. Dark-haired and dark-skinned, he had the smile of an angel and the eyes of a devil. As he thought of Mrs Jones, he smiled. Her face had been a picture when he'd called her an old bag. As for shouting out 'Paki' in the Post Office, that had been really fun. Giggling, he picked up his teddy and bounced up and down on his bed. As his laugher turned into hysterics, he leapt higher and higher.

Debbie opened the fridge door and reached for one of Billy's strong ciders. Her life at the moment was totally shit, an absolute nightmare, she dreaded waking up in the morning.

Looking back now, part of her secretly wished she had listened to her mum and Peter. At the time, Debbie hadn't thought she had much going for her before she'd met Billy when really she had. Now she was stuck here in a rut. A horrible, shitty rut that she'd probably never get out of.

At times she still loved Billy, but deep down knew that he was no good for her. He was one of life's losers: dossing about, selling a bit of gear, drinking his life away. She knew that if she stayed with him, she'd never have the nice car, spacious house and happy lifestyle that she craved. The area they lived in didn't help either. It was a rundown, depressing dump, full of junkies, winos and lowlifes.

Unfortunately for their situation, Billy had years ago managed to wangle a two-bedroomed flat out of the council by telling them he had kids in Scotland who would be coming to stay. Getting out of a one-bed was hard enough, but getting out of a two-bed was nigh on impossible, so they were stuck in the tower block from hell.

Debbie had often wondered how life would be if only they could get a transfer to Dagenham. Surely if they got out of Barking and were given a nice little house with its own garden, Charlie would be better behaved? Maybe that was all her son needed, a backyard where he could play, run about and let off steam.

Charlie's behaviour was a massive cause for concern to Debbie. She knew it wasn't her fault, everyone told her what a good little mum she was, but she had no control at all over him. Charlie did exactly what Charlie wanted, and some of the things he said and did would shock even the most open-minded person. None of her friends' children were as badly behaved. They were normal kids. Mischievous but manageable. Trust her to give birth to a problem child.

The only time her son seemed happy or even behaved to a certain extent was when Billy was about, and that made Debbie feel like an out and out failure. He spent no more than a couple of hours a day with his son, but had a bond and mutual understanding with him that she could only dream of. She was the one who spoiled Charlie, she knew that. Maybe that was why he seemed to have no respect for her, but bargaining with him, buying and giving him things, was the only way she could get him to do as he was told.

Billy certainly hadn't helped matters. She'd scold Charlie for swearing, and then Billy would be ecstatic when the child said the word 'fuck' or 'wanker' in front of him. He'd bounce him up and down on his knee, telling him what a top boy he was. It was no wonder really that Charlie was so badly behaved. He probably didn't even know what was right and what was wrong.

Billy kept on and on lately about having another kid. Debbie couldn't think of anything worse. Still wary of his temper, she'd outwardly gone along with his plan of adding to their brood and agreed to come off the pill. Unbeknown to her partner, though, she was still taking her contraception daily, hiding the evidence in the lining of her handbag. The thought of another child put the fear of God into her. She couldn't control the one she had and dreaded the thought of a second.

What Billy didn't know wouldn't hurt him, she'd decided. She knew he wasn't the type to march up to the fertility clinic to find out why she wasn't falling. He was far too proud for that, and wanking into a jar certainly wouldn't be his idea of a family day out.

If Billy found out that she'd been lying, Debbie knew there would be murder. He still lost his temper on occasions and wasn't averse to giving her the odd clump here and there. He had improved, though, and had never really lost it with her since the time she'd landed up in hospital. The only digs she'd received since then were due to her brother's visits. Billy hated it when Mickey turned up, laden with gifts, and every one of his visits caused untold grief afterwards.

Thankfully, over the last couple of months Mickey had been so busy he'd hardly had time to pop round. He had some new business venture on the go and was spending a lot of time flitting between France and Spain. Debbie never asked him what he was up to, but she'd guessed he was getting hold of cheap booze and fags. Every time he visited, he turned up with bundles of the stuff.

With Mickey in and out of the country, the only contact Debbie had had with her mother recently was via the phone. This suited her down to the ground, as whenever June was due to visit Debbie flew into a flustered panic and would spend hours tidying the flat up before her mother arrived. Problem was, no matter how much she vacced, dusted and tried to make the place look presentable, within five minutes of arriving her mother always found fault with it. Many times she'd heard the words, 'Debs, bring in a dustpan and brush, love, you forgot to do under the sofa,' or, 'Get us a cloth, Debbie love, your skirting needs a good wipe.'

Charlie's behaviour in front of his nan hadn't exactly helped their relationship. Mickey didn't seem to take much notice of her son's naughtiness, but her mum was a different kettle of fish.

'Hello, Charlie, does Nanny get a kiss?' her mum would ask.

'Bollocks, bollocks, bollocks,' Charlie would reply as he galloped around the room.

More than once, June had pulled her aside about this. 'I swear, Debs, that's not normal behaviour. Whether you like it or not, I'm telling you, love, there is something terribly wrong with that child!'

Luckily Mickey always came to her rescue. 'He's all right, Mum. He's just a proper little boy. He's got the Dawson spirit, that's all.'

'Mmm,' replied June, with a disdainful look on her face.

'Mummy!'

Debbie's thoughts of her family were interrupted by her son's frantic scream. Charlie had bounced so high he'd gone head first into his wardrobe and was now lying in a crumpled heap on the floor.

Shit, Debbie thought. She'd just been about to prepare

dinner and do a few jobs. She knew from past experience that once Charlie demanded her attention, she got very little else done. Chucking the chicken and potatoes into the oven, she went into his room, picked him up and carried him into the lounge.

'Are you gonna help Mummy cook Daddy's dinner?'

'Nooooo,' Charlie screamed. 'Wanna play games.'

'Okay,' Debbie said. The veg would have to wait until Billy got home. Luckily, it was no more than fifteen minutes later that she heard his key in the door.

'Daddy!' Charlie yelled as he ran to greet him.

Debbie gave Billy a peck on the cheek, and told him to amuse their son while she sorted out the dinner. Cooking had never been her thing until she'd moved in with Billy and she was still no Delia Smith. Somehow, though, she'd managed to teach herself the basics and now did a mean roast, which was Billy's favourite.

Billy tucked into his grub with a smile on his face. As he listened to the story of his son being excluded from nursery, he almost fell out of his seat with laughter. Hearing about Charlie showing the whole class his willy, Billy roared, put his plate on the carpet, sat his son on his knee and ruffled his hair. He opened a can of cider with one hand as he tickled his pride and joy with the other.

'You're such a top boy, Charlie. At least you went out in style, eh, wee man?' Charlie laughed. 'Do you wannae know a secret? Your daddy used to flash his willy at the teacher too.'

Watching father and son giggling together on the sofa, Debbie was seriously fuming.

'You're meant to be telling him off, Billy, not encouraging him to be naughty. It's not funny, you know, when he behaves like that. It's not you who has to go through the embarrassment of it every day, is it?'

'Willy, willy, willy,' Charlie shouted.

As he looked at Debbie's serious expression, Billy's laughter grew louder. He was well pissed by now. He had been in the boozer since lunchtime and consequently thought Charlie's antics hilarious. In fact, he couldn't wait to tell all the lads in the pub that his boy had flashed his cock at the teacher. How funny was that?

Debbie picked up the dirty plates, stormed out into the kitchen and slammed the door behind her. No wonder her son had behaviour problems with a father who encouraged his every bit of wrongdoing. Why, oh why, hadn't she listened to her mother and Peter and chosen a better partner to have kids with? It was at that precise moment that she knew she was gonna have to do something, and soon. The longer she stayed with Billy, the fewer chances in life her son was going to have.

Going back to her mother's wasn't an option; Perfect Peter would strangle Charlie in five minutes flat. Deciding that her brother was her best bet, Debbie resolved to get Christmas and New Year out the way, then get in touch with Mickey and ask him to help her. Rubbing her tired eyes, she picked up the tea-towel and dried the last of the plates. She was nervous about her future, but convinced that she was making the right decision.

Debbie wasn't a religious girl. As she put the plates away in the cupboard, she had no idea that Him up above had already dealt her hand. Getting away from Billy wasn't destined to be easy. Downright impossible, maybe. But easy . . . no fucking way!

TEN

Debbie was awoken early on Christmas morning by an excited Charlie who'd decided to jump up and down on top of her.

'Presents, Mum, presents!' he screamed. Nudging Billy, so that he wouldn't miss out, Debbie got out of bed, chucked on her old pink dressing gown, and shuffled out into the kitchen to make a coffee.

Three o'clock she'd finally got to bed that morning. It had taken her till that time to wrap all of Charlie's presents. Thirty-two they'd bought him in total and she'd had to hide the bloody things next door in Sharon's. Her son was a nosy little sod and would have found them weeks ago if she hadn't kept them well hidden away.

Billy had brought over half of them home from the many pubs he frequented. Apparently, at this time of year the junkies and lowlifes were out thieving on a daily basis, and toy shops were an easy target for their thieving little hands. They would then go round the local pubs selling their hooky wares for cheap and cheerful prices. The likes of Billy would offer them puff, whizz or cash in exchange.

Hearing a commotion in the front room, Debbie rushed in and was dismayed to see that Charlie had already opened half of his gifts and chucked them to one side.

'Now stop it,' she scolded him as he lobbed a football

across the room, sending the Christmas tree flying. 'I told you to wait for Mummy, you naughty boy. Let Daddy get out of bed before you open the rest.'

Ten minutes later, a bleary-eyed Billy sat on the sofa in his boxer shorts, feeling as rough as old boots. He'd intended on having an early one last night, so he'd be nice and fresh for his fatherly duties today, but he'd ended up doing the exact opposite and hadn't rolled home till four o'clock this morning.

As soon as the final presents were opened, Billy thanked Debbie for the jumper and jeans she'd bought him, slung his clothes on, and announced he was popping down to Andy's to get her presents and another big one he'd brought for Charlie last night.

He returned over an hour later and handed her a fake Cartier watch, a bottle of hooky perfume and a stolen M&S dressing gown and slippers that were both far too big. For Charlie there was a large plastic car. Billy looked as proud as a peacock as he watched his boy pedalling around, knocking into all and sundry on his way.

'That's a bit big for in here, Billy,' Debbie said, horrified by the monstrous-looking thing with which her son was gleefully bashing up the flat.

Billy put his arms around her. 'Lighten up, Debs, it's Christmas and he loves it. Nae matter about the damage, the furniture's old anyway. Oh, and I hope you don't mind, but I felt so sorry for Andy sitting downstairs on his own that I invited him up for dinner. The poor bastard has nae family nearby so I said he could spend the day with us.'

'Whatever,' Debbie said as she marched out into the kitchen to peel the potatoes and veg.

Andy was pleasant enough but permanently stoned and spent most of his days in his own little trance. He wasn't particularly the type of influence she wanted around her precious son. Charlie had enough problems of his own without having any more. Deciding to keep her thoughts to herself rather than start World War Three, Debbie lost herself in daydreams of her brand new life. She would have a nice house with a big garden. Charlie would behave impeccably, at home and at school. Maybe she would get him a dog, a cute little puppy for him to play with and love . . .

Her daydreams were interrupted by a knock at the door. She wasn't expecting any visitors so she guessed it was either Andy arriving or one of the girls from next-door. Looking through the peephole, she could see no one.

'Surprise!' shouted her brother as she opened the door. Debbie's heart turned over. Her Christmas was destined to be shit as it was, without this. Laden with two big sacks full of presents, Mickey followed his sister into the kitchen and accepted her offer of a can of lager.

'Sorry I couldn't get round before, sis, but I've been so busy. You know how it is.'

Debbie was a bundle of nerves as she dragged her brother into the living room. He usually turned up when Billy wasn't about and she knew that there was no love lost between them.

Mickey grinned. 'All right, Billy, how you doing?'

'Yeah, fine,' Billy answered politely. Inside he was seething. He hated Mickey with a passion. Just hearing that cocksure voice wound him up practically to the point of no return.

'What have you brought me, Uncle Mickey?' Charlie yelled, bouncing up and down with excitement as he spotted the two big sacks in the hallway.

Mickey smiled falsely at the child that he'd tried, but was unable, to like. He was however determined to carry on his role as doting uncle, for his sister's sake if no one else's. 'By the looks of it, Father Christmas has brought you enough as it is,' he said, winding the kid up. 'Maybe

I should take my presents home with me and give them to some other poor little boy who hasn't got any?'

'Nooooo!' Charlie screamed at the top of his voice. 'My presents, I want them!'

Billy sat with a fixed smile while he watched his son open the expensive presents his shit-cunt of an uncle had bought him. Charlie leapt up and down with pure delight at his latest haul.

A toy garage full of cars; a robot that walked about at the switch of a button; a cowboy outfit which looked like the real thing; and finally an electronic train set with stations, people, warning signs . . . the whole fucking lot! Unable to watch any more, Billy was saved by a knock at the door and Andy's arrival. He dragged his pal into the kitchen, handed him a can of Strongbow and downed his own in record time. He was furious, really wild, and needed to calm himself down.

Opening the kitchen window, he nodded at Andy to shut the door, requested one of his joints and leaned out of the window for a smoke, hoping to mellow his temper. He felt undermined once again, like he was the weak man in his own fucking house. He'd brought his son so many presents, but nothing could compete with the top-of-the-range stuff that Mickey fucking Big Potatoes had turned up with.

Billy flicked the last of the joint out of the window and took a deep breath before walking back into the living room. Debbie was calling him and he didn't want to mug himself off, that would really give old Mickey boy something to get his teeth into. 'What's up?' he asked.

'Look,' she said, handing him a wrapped up box. 'Mickey's bought you a present.'

'Thanks,' Billy said, ungratefully.

'Well, open it then. Look at what he got me,' Debbie said, her eyes shining.

Billy glanced at the expensive gold cross hanging around her neck from a thick gold chain.

'Aye, that's nice,' he muttered as he tried to get the wrapping off his own present. Billy took one look at the gold hoop earrings inside and quickly shut the box. He knew without a doubt that Mickey was taking the complete and utter piss out of him, and was unable to control himself. 'Earrings? Bird's fucking earrings! Do I look like some kind of shit-stabber or what?'

Mickey gave him a cocky smirk. 'Well, I knew you wore them,' he said with assumed innocence, pointing at the two sleepers in Billy's right ear, one of which had a cross hanging from it.

'Not like these I fucking don't!' Throwing the box on the floor in temper, Billy grabbed Andy by the arm. 'We're off to the pub,' he said as he stormed out the door.

Debbie was really annoyed with her brother. 'Why did you have to buy him them, Mick? He's not stupid, you know. He can see you're taking the piss out of him. You're bang out of order,' she insisted.

'What am I meant to have done wrong?' he said, holding up his hands and still acting the innocent. 'I knew he wore earrings. The ones he had looked old, so I bought him a new pair. I don't understand what his problem is.'

Debbie sat on the sofa with her head in her hands. She didn't need this shit, not today of all days. It was all right for her Mickey, he'd fuck off soon and have a decent Christmas elsewhere. It was her that was stuck here and would have to bear the brunt of Billy's temper.

'Cheer up, sis. What's the matter?' Mickey slung one arm around her shoulders. 'You're not frightened of the cunt, are ya? He ain't ever clumped you, has he? 'Cause I swear, if he ever lays a hand on you, I'll fucking kill him.'

'Stop it, Charlie!' Debbie screamed as her son rammed

his new car into her legs for the second time. She felt ill with worry but had no choice other than to lie. 'Of course he's never hit me. It's just that . . . oh, I dunno, Mick, sometimes I'm not sure if I'm that happy with Billy.'

'Liar, liar, liar.' Charlie leapt out of his car and viciously kicked his mother in the leg. 'Daddy kicks you . . . I saw him. He kicks you like this,' he said proudly.

Debbie grabbed her son, smacked him and put him in his bedroom. She couldn't speak openly in front of Charlie. He had a strong bond with Billy, was a clever little sod, and would probably repeat her conversation word for word. Turning the telly up to drown out her son's screams, she sat down again next to her brother, who looked concerned.

'Tell me about this kicking thing then, sis?'

'I swear, Mick, he doesn't kick me. Take no notice of Charlie. He has an overactive imagination. I am thinking of leaving Billy, though. Charlie's behaviour is going from bad to worse and Billy doesn't support me with disciplining him. He laughs when he swears and encourages him to be naughty. He thought it was hilarious when Charlie got himself excluded from nursery school. I've got to get Charlie away from him or he's gonna grow up into a monster.'

Mickey squeezed his sister's hand. 'Look, Debs, Billy's a mug, a complete wanker, and you can do so much better. You don't wanna be living in a shit-hole flat like this, and the area's diabolical. Leave right now . . . come back to my flat with me. I'll sort a place out for you and Charlie, somewhere decent in a respectable area.'

'Thanks, Mick,' she said gratefully. 'But I can't leave today. I couldn't do that to Billy. Let me get New Year out of the way and then I'll ring you. Billy's got a lot of problems, stuff you don't know about. I need to sit down with him and sort things out properly.'

Mickey glanced at his watch and stood up. 'The choice is yours, sis. I can't make you come with me. I do worry about you living here, though, especially with that cunt. But I'm afraid I'm gonna have to be making tracks now. I've got a new bird on the scene, Danielle, and I've been invited round for Christmas to meet the parents. Between me and you, I don't do families and I'm dreading it!'

Debbie hugged him. 'They'll love you, Mickey. How could they not?'

'Now are you sure you're gonna be all right, Debs? You've got me mobile number. If that tosser comes in and starts, you ring me, okay? Danielle only lives on the Isle of Dogs. I can be here in quarter of an hour if you have any grief.'

'I'm fine, Mick, honestly. You go and enjoy yourself. As soon as I'm ready to leave Billy, I'll give you a ring, okay?'

Mickey winked at her. ''Bye, Charlie,' he shouted as he opened the front door.

'Fuck off, fuck off, fuck off,' was his nephew's reply.

Mickey gave his sister a sympathetic smile. 'That kid has something severely wrong with him. The quicker you get him away from this dump and his scumbag of a father, the better. If you don't, sis, you're gonna have agg . . . major, major agg . . . trust me.'

Debbie nodded and they said goodbye.

Mickey thought he was giving her good advice, but all he'd done was tell her what she already knew. Monster . . . terror . . . horror . . . Debbie knew exactly what the world thought of her son. Family, friends, teachers, strangers – she'd seen their shocked expressions, clocked their sly glances and heard their snide comments. Difference was, Charlie didn't belong to them. He belonged to her. She'd created him, carried him and brought him into the world. He was her responsibility. No matter what became of him, she knew she would always love him unconditionally.

ELEVEN

As she looked at the dried-up turkey and stone cold veg lying on top of the clapped out oven, Debbie knew she was in Shit Street and wished she had taken up her brother's earlier offer.

It was now nine p.m. and she still hadn't heard a dickie bird from Billy. She had guessed he had a strop on when he stormed out earlier, but she'd fully expected him to come back with Andy for his dinner. Debbie knew from past experience that silence from Billy was a bad omen. Worried, she reached for her purse, took out the screwed up bit of paper and dialled her brother's number.

'It has not been possible to connect your call,' a woman's voice announced. Unable to think straight, Debbie headed for the fridge and opened the bottle of Liebfraumilch that was to have accompanied their completely ruined festive dinner. She hadn't touched a drink all day, but now needed one desperately.

Should she stay in the flat or should she get the hell out of here? Debbie repeated the same question over and over to herself.

'Mummy, Mummy, Mummy!' Her child's screams prompted her to make a decision. She picked up the telephone and dialled Sharon's number. With a bit of luck her friend would let her stay there.

'Shal, I'm sorry to bother you, I know you've got company, but I'm petrified. Me brother upset Billy earlier, he stormed out and I haven't seen him since. I've got a really bad feeling. I think he's gonna come in and start on me again. What am I gonna do?'

Sharon sighed. She was sick of the Billy/Debbie saga and, as much as she loved and felt sorry for her friend, wasn't going to have her own Christmas spoilt. Over and over again she'd told Debbie that Billy was an arsehole. She should never have gone back after he'd put her in hospital. Debbie had chosen her own bed, and if it wasn't comfortable enough, it was her own bloody fault!

'Look, Debs, any other time you could come and stay here, you know you could, but not tonight, mate. I've got my mum, my cousin Tracey and my Aunt Ivy here, and there's no room, love. The best thing you can do is put yourself to bed and I'll listen out for Billy coming home. If I hear any shouting or banging or anything untoward, I'll be there like a shot, I promise.'

Debbie thanked her and said goodbye. She had little choice now other than to stay in the flat. Her other neighbour, Donna, was away for the holiday at her mum's house, and with no other close friends in the tower block, Debbie's options were limited.

It was just before midnight when she heard the front door slam shut. She lay shivering nervously under the cheap, thin quilt. She'd been thinking hard all night and had reached the decision that she would contact her brother first thing tomorrow and ask him to come and collect her and Charlie as soon as possible.

As Debbie lay still, she heard grunting and gulping noises coming from the kitchen. She knew her partner's grotesque habits off by heart, and guessed he was shoving his dinner down his throat and washing it down with cider. The loud belch that followed confirmed her suspicions.

Billy aimed a half-eaten turkey leg for the rubbish bag and missed. He had stuffed his face, felt as sick as a pig and could eat no more. Wiping his greasy mouth on the sleeve of his new jumper, he staggered into the living room and fell on to the sofa.

He had left the pub at lunchtime. Twelve until two were the strictly observed opening hours on Christmas morning, and guv'nors shut their bars promptly so they could enjoy the day with their families. With none of their local haunts open, he and Andy had been at a loose end. Not exactly laden with invitations from any of their pals, they had bought a couple of crates from the pub and headed off towards Andy's flat to drown their sorrows. Two minutes from their destination, they'd bumped into Dave the Druggie who'd popped out of his notorious address to buy some fags.

'Fuck Christmas! It's a load of old bollocks. Come back to mine, I've got a right old assortment indoors,' he'd insisted. Dave had no family and was desperate for some company and someone to get high with.

Although he sold bundles of gear, Billy wasn't usually the biggest user in the world. He liked a joint here and there, and a bit of speed to liven him up on a night out, but apart from that, after what had happened to his brother Charlie, he'd steered clear of any heavy shit. Today, though, was different. He was wound up, fucked off and desperate to get out of his nut.

The day had now taken its toll on him. He'd puffed, dropped some acid, and downed numerous snakebites. He'd also dabbled in needles for the first time in his life, injecting himself with speed to put him on a high and then Temazepan to bring him back down. Now he felt fucking rotten – and it was all Mickey Bigshot's fault. If that cunt hadn't turned up this morning, none of this would have happened. Billy would have had a nice

Christmas with his bird and son, and not spent it jacking up round some junkie's flat.

Off his face, he decided it was time to sort out the problem. He would ring Mickey fucking Big Bollocks immediately and bar him from coming anywhere near his family ever again. He staggered into the bedroom, ripped the quilt off Debbie and smacked her round the face.

'Right, bitch, give us your brother's phone number. Now!'

As Debbie looked up into Billy's glazed eyes, she shook like a leaf. 'I don't know where it is offhand,' she lied.

Billy put his hands around her throat. 'You willnae lie to me, you fucking whore!'

'I-It's in the zip compartment of my h-handbag,' Debbie stammered. 'G-give it here and I'll find it for you.'

Billy leapt off the bed, grabbed the black handbag and clumsily tipped it upside down on the floor. As he rummaged through the contents, which included a lipstick, baby wipes and box of Tampax, he could feel himself getting angrier and angrier.

'It's in the zip bit, Billy.' Debbie was by now desperate to be helpful. His mad expression left her with no choice.

As he tugged at the zip, Billy noticed it was stuck. Fuming, he ripped the lining with both hands. He shook the bag upside down and was shocked to see a packet of pills and a diary fall out. Now, Billy was no genius when it came to women's shit, but in seconds he realised the pills were of the birth control kind and had been purposely hidden there away from his prying eyes. Face reddening with anger, he checked the day of the week on the packet before he threw them at Debbie.

'Have you been taking these, you cunt? No wonder you havenae fell pregnant, you lying fucking slag!'

Debbie said nothing. What could she say? Billy had her diary in his hand and she was too nervous to open her mouth. How could she have been so stupid? What had possessed her to keep a written account of all her thoughts, fears and dreams?

As Billy flicked through the pages, he started to laugh hysterically. His eyes bulged as he mimicked Debbie's voice: "'Charlie bad today, played up in supermarket. Billy laughed as usual. Need to get Charlie away from him.'" He frowned and read on. "'Spoke to Sharon today, told her I was seriously thinking of leaving Billy. She said she couldn't believe I was still with him and should have left ages ago.'"

The last extract had been written on Christmas Eve. Billy read it slowly, his voice filled with sarcasm. "'Really pissed off today. Charlie worse than ever, Billy no help getting stuff ready for Xmas. Def. decided am going to get New Year over and leave him.'"

Sobbing with fear, Debbie lay paralysed in bed. The sheet beneath her felt damp and she knew without looking that she'd wet herself.

Billy sat on the edge of the mattress with his head in his hands. His first instinct was to sob like a baby. His second was to stand up and repeatedly punch the wall. Losing it completely, he trashed the bedroom before lunging at Debbie. 'You fucking bitch . . . you whore! You think you're taking my kid and leaving me, do you? Over my dead body, you fucking cunt!'

Dragging her from the bed by her brother's cross and chain, Billy slammed her against the wardrobe. He picked up the alarm clock then and battered her round the face and head with it, over and over again.

'If I cannae have yer, I'll make damn sure no one else will want yer, you fucking slut!' he screamed.

Woken by the commotion, Charlie picked up Mr Teddy and toddled out of his bedroom. As he watched Daddy hitting Mummy with the alarm clock, he began to giggle.

Debbie lay on the floor with two of her teeth on the bare boards beside her. When Billy saw his son, he dropped the alarm clock and froze. As injured as she was, Debbie spat out a mouthful of blood and managed to say, 'Go back to your room, Charlie.'

Unsettled by his son's presence, Billy ran out of the room. 'Fuck, fuck, fuck!' he shouted as he head-butted the fridge.

Charlie picked up his mother's teeth and tried to fit them into Mr Teddy's mouth. 'Mummy ill,' he giggled.

Debbie tried to sit up, but was unable to. Her poor, poor baby. No child should ever have to witness what he had just seen. 'Please, Charlie, be a good boy. Give Mummy the teeth and go to your room.'

'Nooooo,' Charlie screamed. He was enjoying himself far too much to go back to bed. Sitting down next to his mum, he stared at the puddle of blood by her head. Smiling, he picked up Mr Teddy and rubbed his face in it. 'Mummy bleed, Teddy bleed.'

Debbie took one look at her son's gloating expression and finally burst into tears.

Sharon was dancing around the living room with her eldest kid and her Aunt Ivy to Wizard's 'I Wish it Could Be Christmas Every Day', when she heard the bangs and crashes coming from next-door. Guessing that Billy was home and it had kicked off, she picked up her phone and calmly dialled 999. She wouldn't dream of intervening personally. She knew exactly what Billy McDaid was capable of.

Billy paced up and down the kitchen, talking to himself like a madman. Spotting his son, he picked him up, held him in one arm and lit a fag with the other hand.

'Can I watch Mummy die?' Charlie asked.

Billy smiled, 'Okay, wee man.'

Debbie squinted. Her head was banging and she was unable to focus properly. 'Take Charlie into the other room, Billy, don't let him see me like this,' she whispered.

'Fuck off,' he said, aiming a sly kick at her swollen face. 'He's my son and I'll do what I want with him, you stupid bitch.'

Charlie giggled. 'I'm hungry, Daddy.'

'Shall Daddy make us some sandwiches?'

Charlie nodded. Billy aimed one more kick at Debbie and, with his son hugging him tightly around the neck, strolled out into the kitchen to butter the bread.

By now, Debbie was too weak to move. She was sure her leg was broken, and was having trouble keeping her eyes open. 'Please God, help me,' she whispered.

Sharon let the police into the block and gave them the lowdown. 'Look, it might be nothing, but you have to check on her. There was a terrible commotion earlier and now it's gone deathly quiet. He's beaten her to a pulp before. Could you just check to see if she's all right?'

Debbie could feel herself drifting off to sleep. The knock on the door woke her up.

'Open up, it's the police!'

'Help,' Debbie tried to say. Her mouth opened, but her voice failed her.

'Ner, ner, ner, ner, ner, ner, ner, ner,' Charlie screamed, as he jumped up and down excitedly. He had a real thing about blue flashing lights.

'Shhh, be quiet,' whispered Billy.

The old bill smiled when they heard the child's voice. 'Open up, McDaid. We know you're in there.'

DC Longman had had a lot of dealings with Billy in the past and despised the fucking scumbag. To nick him tonight would be the best present he could wish for. Far better than anything Santa had brought him.

'You've got one minute to open this door, McDaid, else I'll break it down.'

Billy stood frozen to the spot. He was fucked now, well and truly, and he knew it.

As the front door began to splinter, he panicked. Grabbing his son, he ran into the living room and opened the main window. 'Nooooo, daddy, nooooo!' Charlie screamed as he was dangled head first out of it.

Out of his head on drugs, Billy smiled as he eyed the plod. 'You move one step nearer and the kid's a goner.'

'Mummy, Mummy, Mummy!'

A semi-conscious Debbie was dimly aware of her son calling for her. The realisation of why he was doing so made her lose consciousness completely.

TWELVE

As she placed the last of the buffet on to the serving trolley, June stood back, admired her handiwork and smiled tenderly at Peter. 'Well, what do you think?'

'It looks absolutely fabulous, darling, I knew you wouldn't let me down.'

June smiled. It was indeed a feast fit for a king. Cooked meats of various kinds, home-made coleslaw, potato salad, vol-au-vents, sausage rolls, quiche, and the biggest selection of gateaux you could imagine. In fact, there was enough food there to feed the whole British Army, let alone the four couples who had been invited over to join them for Boxing Day.

Today was important to Peter and June was determined to make sure everything would be perfect for him. His friends included the Chief Constable of the Essex police, an up-and-coming Tory politician, and the captain of the extremely posh golf club he'd recently joined.

Peter smiled at his wife and kissed her on the forehead. The sound of the doorbell made him straighten up. It was time to greet the first of his guests.

Mickey Dawson thanked the doctor for his time and pondered his next move. His little sis was in Intensive Care and he was absolutely devastated. He'd only just found out the full extent of her injuries. At first the doctors thought that Debbie had a serious head injury. Thankfully, a brain scan had ruled that out. They'd had to shave her hair down one side to check her out properly and Mickey was dreading her reaction to that. Debs weren't a bad-looking girl, but had no confidence in her appearance whatsoever. Sporting half a Grant Mitchell haircut would do nothing to improve her already low self-esteem.

Grabbing a much-needed coffee from the vending machine, Mickey sat on one of the battered plastic chairs and tried to get his thoughts in order. He'd have McDaid for this, fucking kill him with his bare hands if he got the chance. But seeing as he'd just been informed that the Glaswegian piece of shit was currently in custody, there was fat chance he could get anywhere near him, unless the scum got bail. The only hope of getting to him was if he was sent to the Scrubs. Mickey had gained a lot of respect and friends in clink and knew he only had to give the word. A nice bucket of sugary scalding water wouldn't go amiss on good ole Billy boy.

Mickey shook his head at the bastard day he was having. He'd had a well-earned lie in this morning and hadn't got up till after eleven. By the time he'd bothered switching his phone on it was past midday.

Within minutes, he'd received a distraught phone call from Debbie's neighbour, Sharon, who had given him a blow-by-blow account of his sister's savage beating. Billy being violent towards Debbie hadn't surprised Mickey; he'd always known he was capable of it. But dangling his own kid out of the window of a tower block for ten minutes was beyond belief. The police had apparently had a terrible job trying to coax him into putting the boy down safely before they'd finally arrested Billy.

Sharon had been blunt with him. 'Look, Mick, I know

things are awkward for you, but I can't look after Charlie for more than a day or two. He's playing up something chronic, keeps upsetting me own kids, and to be honest, I think he needs to be around his own family. I'm going to stay at me mum's for New Year and there's no way I can take him there with me.'

'Don't worry, Sharon, I understand,' Mickey had said. 'Just keep him for a day or so, till I can sort out somewhere for him to stay. I'm gonna go up the hospital now to see what's happening with Debs. I'll call you later, yeah?'

Now he slung the last of his stone-cold coffee into a nearby bin. He'd do anything for Debs, but there was no way he could look after her son. The kid gave him the fucking willies. He still felt like Rodney Trotter whenever he looked at the little bastard. Sighing, he headed back towards Intensive Care to check on his once bright and bubbly sister.

After another chat with a second doctor, Mickey was informed that Debs's condition was no longer classed as critical and she would probably be moved into a ward of some kind in the next day or two.

'Can I see her?' he asked.

'A couple of minutes at the most,' the doctor told him.

At the distressing sight of seeing his sister out for the count, battered and bruised and with her head swollen to nearly twice its normal size, tears came to Mickey's eyes. Squeezing her limp hand, he gently leaned over her and brushed her forehead with his lips.

'I don't know whether you can hear me or not, sis, but I've gotta go soon as the doctor says you need to rest. You're gonna be okay, you know, and don't worry about Charlie – he's fine, Sharon's looking after him. As for that bastard that's done this to you, Debs . . . he's dead meat. I swear I'll have him for this. He'll get his comeuppance, sweetheart, just you wait and see.'

With a lump in his throat and his heart feeling like it weighed a ton, Mickey left the hospital, jumped into his motor and picked up his phone. He needed to think fast. It was gonna be a long while before Debs was well enough to go home and look after her son. What should he do? The only person he could think of to approach for help was their mum, but she wasn't exactly Mrs Doubtfire. He might as well ring her now, though. He would have to inform her about Debbie at some point. And after all, she'd brought up two kids of her own and was Charlie's gran . . . it was her duty to fucking help.

Pissed off that his mother always put Peter in front of her own family, Mickey angrily punched in her number. If she let him down and refused to muck in, he'd tell her her fucking fortune once and for all.

Peter was topping up his guests' glasses with the festive favourite, brandy and Bailey's, when he heard the shrill ringing of the telephone. 'Can you get that, dear?' he shouted to June, who was out in the kitchen preparing Irish coffees.

At the sound of her son's voice, June's heart flew into her mouth. She quickly shut the door behind her. 'Peter's here. I told you not to call me over the holiday,' she whispered into the receiver.

'Stop worrying about yourself for a moment, Mum, and fucking listen to me!' Mickey shouted. 'Your daughter is in Intensive Care. That bastard McDaid has beaten seven colours of shit out of her and probably broken every bone in her body. There's no one to look after Charlie, Mum, so you're gonna have to have him. Her neighbour's got him at the moment, but she can only look after him until tomorrow. If you don't help out, he'll be taken into care and that will break our Debs's heart.'

Feeling faint, June steadied herself and sat down at the kitchen table. 'Oh, my God. My poor Debbie. Have you seen her, Mickey? What hospital is she in?'

He lit a cigarette and inhaled deeply between sentences. He'd had to exaggerate his sister's injuries just to get his mother's attention. 'She's in Oldchurch. I'm up here now, in the car park. She's still unconscious although the doctor just told me she's no longer classed as critical. She's in a real bad way, though, Mum. Looks terrible. You need to get your arse up here, I'm all on me own and I don't know what to do.'

'It's a bit awkward, Mickey . . . I'm in the middle of a party. What am I meant to tell Peter? He doesn't even know I'm in contact with you or Debbie.'

Mickey felt his temper reach boiling point. 'What are you meant to tell Peter? Are you having a fucking laugh, Mother? Just tell the jumped-up ponce the truth for once – and as for your precious guests, tell them all to fuck off home! You never fail to disappoint me, Mum. You gave birth to me and our Debs. You know, you really need to get your priorities sorted.'

June felt awful. Her Mickey was right. For years she'd put Peter above her own flesh and blood. Well, no more. If her children needed her then, whatever the consequences, she would be there for them. 'I'm so sorry, Mickey. I've been a terrible mum to you and Debs. Can you come over and pick me up now, son?'

He breathed a sigh of relief. Finally, she had seen sense. 'I'll be there in ten minutes. I'll bib outside.'

As June walked into the lounge, Peter noticed that his wife looked a whiter shade of pale. 'Are you okay, darling? What's the matter?'

'I need to talk to you alone for a minute.'

June gesticulated for him to follow her out into the kitchen. She didn't want their guests to overhear this conversation. After repeating what Mickey had just told her, she anxiously awaited his reaction.

'The silly, silly girl! I tried to warn her, June. I told her something like this would happen,' Peter sighed.

'I know you did, love.' Hearing a loud toot outside, June grabbed his arm. 'I have to go to her, Peter. You do understand, don't you?'

Peter looked at his wife in horror. 'You can't go now! What the hell am I meant to tell my friends? You haven't even brought the cheese board out yet. I can hardly entertain them alone.'

With Mickey's words still ringing in her head, answering him back came easier than June had expected. 'My children need me, Peter. I will be there for them, whether you like it or not. And as for your friends . . . tell them what you bloody well like! I'm sick of you ruling my life. From now on I'm putting my foot down. As far as I'm concerned, my kids come first from this day onward.'

With her head held high, June marched out of the front door, leaving her flabbergasted husband practically foaming at the mouth.

'Good for you, Mum,' Mickey said proudly as she relayed what she had said to Peter.

'I know I've done the right thing, but I am worried he'll leave me now, Mickey. How will I manage if he does? I love my little house and our pretty cul-de-sac. What am I gonna do if he asks for a divorce?'

Mickey comfortingly squeezed her hand. 'Here, don't worry about that. The house is half yours, and whatever happens, you'll be able to afford a decent place of your own. But he won't divorce you, Mum, you'll see. Truth be told, it's probably done you the world of good, sticking up for yourself. Once he gets over the initial shock, he'll respect you more for it and see you in a different light.

Mark my words, he won't get anyone better than you and deep down he must know that.'

'Thanks, love,' June replied gratefully.

As Mickey parked the car at the hospital, he turned to face his mother. 'What we gonna do about Charlie? If Debs is awake, that'll be the first question she asks us. Billy dangled him out of the window and nearly killed him, for God's sake. Someone has to help the kid. Will you take care of him for her, Mum?'

June thought before answering. The idea of looking after her monster of a grandson didn't exactly enthral her, but she knew deep down that she had no choice.

'Yeah, I'll look after him. If Peter won't let me bring him home, then I'll have to stay at yours.'

'Thanks, Mum,' Mickey said, relief flooding through him. He couldn't have handled the little bastard himself, that was for sure.

Seeing her daughter lying in Intensive Care, surrounded by wires and tubes, reminded June painfully of every maternal shortcoming she'd ever had. Her poor girl, to come to this . . .

Debbie was still drugged up to the eyeballs, but as her eyes flickered open a couple of times, June was sure that she knew her mother was there. Debs probably wasn't able to hear her clearly, but June spoke to her anyway. 'Now don't worry about Charlie. I'm gonna take real good care of him for you.'

The doctor spoke to June and Mickey and assured them that Debbie was expected to make a full recovery. 'Physically her injuries should heal in months, but mentally they may take longer,' he warned. 'Some form of counselling or therapy will help, once she's back on her feet.'

The enormity of the situation hit June as she left the hospital. Seeing her Debbie like that, lying so lifeless and helpless, filled her with anger and bitterness. She hoped with all her heart that Billy McDaid would meet a painful death and afterwards rot in hell.

Mickey held his sobbing mother in his arms, whispering good old East End words of comfort. 'Don't worry about McDaid. He's a dead man, trust me. He'll never go near our Debs again, I'll make sure of it.'

'You are a good boy, Mickey,' June said proudly. She knew exactly what her son's intentions were.

He swung the Merc into the empty car park of a nearby pub. 'I think we need a drink, and then we can sort out what we're gonna do next.'

June readily agreed. Half an hour and two brandies later, she plucked up the courage to ring Peter. Explaining that she had no choice but to look after her grandson, she waited nervously for his reaction. If he refused to allow her to bring Charlie home, she was going to collect some of her things and move temporarily into Mickey's.

In fact, June was shocked by his helpfulness. 'Our guests have gone now, darling. Collect your grandson and bring him home immediately. In times of need we must help others.'

Mickey laughed as June repeated the conversation to him. 'What a wanker!' he said.

He headed for the bar, ordered himself another pint and his mother another brandy.

Handing his mum her drink, he smiled at her. 'I suppose I'd better go and pick up the devil child in a minute. Have you told Peter, by any chance, that Charlie isn't exactly a normal kid?'

June smirked as she sipped her brandy. 'Of course I bloody well haven't! He doesn't even know I've seen the child.'

Mickey tried to keep a straight face. Sipping his pint,

he thoughtfully rubbed the stubble on his chin. 'Poor Peter. He's in for a shock . . . a very fucking big shock!'

'I won't be a minute, kids,' Sharon shouted, as she popped next-door with Debbie's spare key to sort out Charlie's stuff. She couldn't wait to get rid of him. The kid was driving her insane. Her brood had never been angels, but Charlie was in a league of his own. Sharon could honestly say she had never met such a horrible child in her entire life.

As she rushed back into her own flat with the monster's clothes and toys, Sharon was stunned to hear the manic screams of her own children. 'Whatever's wrong?' she shouted as she kicked the front door shut.

She had only been gone five minutes and had left them playing happily with Tiger, the kitten she'd bought them for Christmas.

Sharon stopped in her tracks at the door to the living room. Standing at the open window, swinging Tiger outside by his tail, was none other than a grinning Charlie.

'Puddy cat, puddy cat, puddy cat,' he chanted.

Tiger's whole body was rigid with fear. He gave a faint squeal and waited for someone to rescue him.

'Meow, meow, meow.'

THIRTEEN

Tiger used up one of his nine lives that day, saved only by a quick-thinking Mickey who had turned up at the flat to collect his nephew.

'Bring the kitten away from the window, Charlie,' he ordered.

Charlie laughed. 'Puddy cat, puddy cat, puddy cat.'

'I mean it, Charlie, don't fuck with me.'

Charlie ignored his uncle. He was enjoyed terrorising the cat far too much to come away from the window.

Mickey decided a change of tactic was needed. 'I've brought you loads of presents, Charlie. Put the kitten on the carpet and you can open them in the car.'

Now Charlie might be evil, but he certainly wasn't stupid. Even at his tender age, he knew that anything his uncle bought him was well worth having.

Obediently, he stepped away from the window and dropped the terrified kitten on to the floor.

'Meeow!' he said, giggling.

Mickey grabbed him by the arm and dragged him into the hallway. 'I'm so sorry, Sharon,' he said apologetically.

Sharon felt sick to her stomach at what she'd just witnessed. Fuming, she gave it to Mickey in no uncertain terms. 'Look at the state of my kids! Don't you ever, ever bring that horrible little bastard near me again. There is something very fucking wrong with that child and if I never see him again, it'll be too soon.'

Mickey actually agreed with her. He felt totally embarrassed. Taking a wad of notes out of his pocket, he rolled off a hundred quid and handed it to her. 'Take your kids out and treat 'em to something nice, eh?'

Snatching the money off him, Sharon breathed a sigh of relief as Charlie walked out of the front door.

Once in the front seat of his uncle's Merc, the boy's beady little eyes scanned the inside of the car. 'Where's my presents?' he demanded.

Mickey started the engine and threw his nephew a look of pure hatred. What he had just witnessed had shocked him to the core. He personally loved animals and had no time for any bastard who hurt them. Deep in thought, he drove towards his mother's house. How she and Peter were gonna cope with Charlie boy was anyone's guess. Luckily for them, they had no pets.

'I want my presents and I want them now!'

The sound of his nephew's cocksure tones made Mickey see red. Deciding to teach the nasty little bastard a lesson, he took a detour. Pulling over in a secluded lay by, he turned to face the child. 'If you ever, ever hurt another little animal like you tried to earlier, I will fucking kill you. Do you understand me, Charlie?'

Head bowed, Charlie looked at his feet. 'Sorry. Can I have my presents now?' he asked meekly.

'No you fucking can't! I'm taking them all back to the shop. And do you wanna know why I'm taking them back?'

A sulky Charlie didn't answer.

'Because you're a nasty little boy who doesn't deserve anything. Now, I'm gonna take you to stay at your nan's house until your mum's better, and I'm warning you . . . if you play her up or misbehave, you'll have me to deal with. And I am not a person to mess with, believe me. If I hear any stories from Nanny about you being naughty, I will give you such a hiding you won't know what's hit you. Do you understand what I've just said to you?'

For once, Charlie was lost for words. Unable to meet his uncle's frightening gaze, he sat in silence and nodded.

'Good,' Mickey said. Restarting the engine, he headed off towards his mother's house.

'Right, that's the last of his stuff, Mum. If you're short of anything, let me know. I've got Debbie's key and I'm gonna go round the flat tomorrow with Big Steve and get all of her and Charlie's stuff out of there. The last thing she needs when she comes out of hospital is to return to that shit-hole with all its bad memories.'

'Where will she live?' June asked, worried.

'I'm gonna rent her a place, Mum, down this way somewhere. If I put a deposit down for her, the Social will cough up the rent. She'll be happy in a nicer area, and it'll be better for him too,' Mickey said, nodding towards Charlie who was sitting at the kitchen table, sipping orange squash and nibbling on a biscuit.

'Oh, you are a good boy, Mickey,' June said, smiling. She was very proud of her strapping, handsome son and was as pleased as punch that he was taking matters into his own hands and sorting his sister out somewhere nice.

'Why don't you stay for a cup of tea, love? I'll make you something to eat, if you like?'

'No, you're all right, Mum. Thanks anyway but I've had a long day and I just wanna get home. I might pop out for a pint with me mate later. Where's Peter, by the way?'

'He had a bad headache. He's upstairs, lying down. It was probably the shock of me answering him back, eh, son?' June giggled.

'Right, I'd best be off now. I'll pick you up early tomorrow afternoon, Mum, and we'll go and visit Debs together.'

June hugged him. 'Thanks, love. I rang the hospital about half an hour ago. She's stable, but still out for the count. They're moving her as soon as she comes round, putting her in a side ward.'

'See ya then, Mum. 'Bye, Charlie,' Mickey said, edging towards the front door.

Charlie sat in silence. He hated his uncle and wished he would die.

'He's ever so quiet, Mickey,' June said, nodding towards her grandson in the kitchen.

'He'll be all right, Mum. He's just had a lot to deal with, and he must be missing our Debs.'

June smiled. He was such a kind boy, her Mickey, so thoughtful. 'Yeah, you're right. I'll make a fuss of him tonight, make him feel at home.'

After waving Mickey goodbye, she went into the kitchen and sat at the table opposite Charlie. 'Your Uncle Mickey brought your toys over from the flat. Do you want to play a game with Nanny?'

Sullenly, Charlie shook his head.

Racking her brains as to how to cheer the child up, June tried to tempt him with food, asked him if he wanted to watch telly, even offered to show him his room and read him a nice bedtime story. Charlie declined every suggestion.

'Why don't you tell Nanny what you want to do then, love?' she said, running out of ideas.

'Don't wanna do nuffink,' came the stroppy reply.

Mickey rang Big Steve on his way home. On learning that Steve was enjoying a quiet beverage in the nearby Needle Gun, he eagerly joined his friend. He'd had the day from hell and was in desperate need of a pick-me-up. Not in the mood to get involved with the little firm Steve was boozing with, Mickey ushered him over to a table in the corner where they could talk undisturbed.

As he listened to his pal's version of the day's events, Steve shook his head in amazement. 'Fucking hell! Is Debbie gonna be all right?' he asked, genuinely concerned. Steve had only met Mickey's sister once, but was worried all the same.

Mickey took a gulp of his much-needed pint. 'Physically, the doc says she'll be okay, but she's been through such an ordeal that mentally it'll take her a lot longer to recover. Hopefully, she'll be fine in the end. She's a strong character, our Debs. If anyone can get over something like this, she can.'

'What you gonna do about McDaid?'

Mickey gave him a knowing look. 'What do you think? I can't do nothing yet though, unless he gets put in the Scrubs. Other than that, I'll have to wait till they let him out . . . and when they do, I'll have the cunt's guts for garters. Make no mistake about that, Stevie boy.'

Steve stood up to get another round. 'I'll be right by your side, Mick. I'd love to give him a dig meself. Anyone who does that to a woman, especially the mother of his kid, deserves everything they've got coming to 'em. As for dangling his own son out the window, that's beyond fucking belief!'

Steve ordered another couple of pints and some chasers then sat back down and listened to the drama of Charlie and the kitten. 'Jesus Christ. Do you reckon he'll be all right at your mum's, Mick?'

Mickey let out a worried sigh. 'It ain't just the cat thing, Steve. The kid ain't normal, mate. He's like that fucking Damien out of that *Omen* film. He's evil – takes after his father. Honestly, I ain't lying, I've seen it all along. I mean, the only reason I used to splash out, buying him loads of presents, was to help our Debs. Inwardly, I've never liked the kid. He's not a child you can take to, there's something not right about him. He's a spiteful little bastard. Nastiness runs through his veins. Honestly, Steve, I feel awful saying bad things about him. He's my own nephew, for fuck's sake, the first nipper in the family, but he's horrible – and I mean *really* horrible.'

Steve nodded sympathetically. He could see his best mate had had a shit time of it, so came out with the only suggestion he could think of. 'Let's get out of here, eh, Mick? Come back to mine. I've gotta bottle of JD sitting at home. Let's crack it open. You'll feel better if you drown your sorrows.'

Mickey didn't need asking twice. 'Let's go.'

Peter opened his eyes gingerly. Relieved that his migraine had now cleared, he headed downstairs to make amends with his wife. It had come as a complete shock when June had shouted and sworn at him. Once he'd got rid of their guests, he'd sat down and thought the whole situation through. He loved his wife immensely and the thought of life without her didn't bear thinking about. That's why, although he'd been fuming at first, he'd decided to swallow his pride and forgive her.

Being lumbered with her grandson was the last thing he needed. He couldn't think of anything worse. Peter hated kids at the best of times. He'd only fathered the one himself and split up from her mother shortly after. He lacked practice and patience with them, but was determined to give it his best shot this time. Hopefully, June's grandson would be a cute little chap, well-behaved and polite. Peter trudged down the stairs and walked into the kitchen to meet his house guest.

June had never been so pleased in her life to see her

husband. The last hour had been awful for her, with Charlie playing up something rotten. He'd chucked the turkey sandwich she'd made him on to the floor, sworn at her and refused to go to bed.

'Fuck Nanny, fuck Nanny, fuck Nanny,' he shouted.

'Oh, thank God you're here. This is your Granddad Peter, Charlie. Be a good boy and say hello to him.'

'Nooooo,' Charlie screamed. 'I want my daddy.'

Peter knelt down next to the distressed child. 'Hello, Charlie. I'm Granddad Peter, and I'm going to be looking after you with your nana.'

Charlie screwed up his little face 'Go away, I hate you! Bastard, bastard, bastard.'

As Peter looked at June, he struggled to contain his horror. 'Charlie seems tired to me. I think it's bedtime for the child, don't you, dear?'

A flustered June explained that for the last hour she'd been trying to coax Charlie to bed. 'He won't budge,' she said.

'Oh, well, we'll see about that, won't we? Come on, Charlie, it's nearly ten o'clock, well past your bedtime.'

Seeing that the child had no intention of moving, Peter leaned over to pick him up. If carrying him up the stairs was the only option, then so be it.

'Nooooo, don't wanna,' Charlie screamed, wriggling like a snake as he was lifted from his chair. Peter had a hell of a job trying to carry the thrashing child up the stairs.

'Cunt, cunt, cunt. Hate you, hate you, hate you.'

Peter was appalled by such language which belonged on the football terraces and not in his home. How did a child of that age even know such words? Disgusted, he put Charlie into bed fully clothed.

'Get some sleep now, child, and we'll talk in the morning. You are a guest in my house and will learn to do as you are told.'

'Bollocks!'

Being a man of some influence locally, Peter was used to being listened to, agreed with, and obeyed. As Charlie's spittle sprayed his face, he realised that tonight was a first for him.

Charlie smiled as he watched his Granddad Peter leave the room. 'Silly Granddad, silly Granddad, silly Granddad,' he chirped. Happy once more, he laughed himself to sleep.

FOURTEEN

Charlie's behaviour went from bad to worse over the next few days and June was at her wits' end. Peter had had a gutful after twenty-four hours, and had taken to working late at the office and popping to the pub afterwards rather than face seeing the child.

'I'll be home at nine from now on, dear,' he told June. 'By the time I return, I expect your grandchild to be tucked up in bed and out of my bloody sight.'

June did her best to charm and entertain the boy, but nothing seemed to please him. He was sullen, ignorant, uncouth and extremely ungrateful. June couldn't wait to offload him and get her life back to normal. With New Year on the horizon, she and Peter had originally arranged to go away with some friends from the golf club, staying at a posh country manor. Obviously, they'd now had to cancel and had invited a couple of Peter's local councillor friends over to the house instead.

'I've told all our guests to arrive at eight o'clock, June. Please make sure your grandson is snuggled up in bed by that time, dear.'

'Of course.' She had been surprised he'd invited friends over at all, with Charlie on the premises, but had decided to keep her thoughts to herself. The child was so unpredictable, you could never judge what he was going to do or say next. She just hoped that the evening would go without a hitch, for Peter's sake.

June spent the morning of New Year's Eve practising her culinary skills. She loved entertaining and always pushed the boat out in the food department, forever trying out mouthwatering new recipes.

Mickey was picking her up this afternoon and they were taking Charlie up to the hospital to see his mum for the first time since she'd been admitted. Debbie had regained consciousness the day after Boxing Day and had been moved into a little side ward. She had been asking to see her son for the last few days, but because she'd been so poorly, June had decided against taking the brat up there before now. However, yesterday Debbie's condition had apparently turned a corner and the nurse had told June that seeing her son would now do her the world of good.

'Come on, Charlie, be a good boy. Put your coat on for Nanny. Your Uncle Mickey will be here in a minute to take us to see Mummy.'

'Don't wanna go,' he said, ignoring the little Puffa jacket held out towards him.

'Now come on, don't be naughty. We need to make Mummy better, and seeing you will make her feel great again.'

Charlie sat on the floor, arms folded. He enjoyed winding his nan up. Silly old cow, he couldn't stand her. 'Don't like Mummy, don't care if she dies,' he said, smirking.

Horrified, June used the only trick she knew would work. 'You are one nasty piece of work, Charlie. Now get this coat on or else your Uncle Mickey'll come in and give you a bloody good hiding!'

Wary of his Uncle Mickey, Charlie did as he was told.

* * *

Debbie was elated to see her son and made as much fuss of him as her injuries would allow. 'Come and sit on Mummy's bed,' she urged.

Charlie shook his head. 'Don't wanna. You look like a man.'

Debbie felt sad. Her injuries must look awful, they were obviously upsetting her son. 'Mummy's missed you so much, Charlie. I hope you've been a good boy for Nanny.'

Finger up his nose, Charlie shook his head. 'Don't like Nanny. Wanna live with Daddy.'

Debbie glanced at June. 'Mum, take Charlie and get him a chocolate bar for me, I want to have a quick word with Mickey. Give us five minutes, eh?'

As soon as they'd left the room, she turned to her brother. 'Any news on Billy yet, Mick?'

'He's still locked up, apparently. Peter rung up a couple of his police pals to find out the SP and he's due up in court on the tenth of January. He'll obviously try and get bail before it goes to Crown Court.'

'You don't reckon he'll come after me if they let him out, do you, Mick?'

Holding his sister's hand, Mickey did his utmost to reassure her. 'I doubt he'll get bail, to be honest, but if the cunt does, I'll be waiting for him. He won't come within a mile of you, trust me, I'll see to that. You just concentrate on getting yourself better. Don't worry about that piece of shit, you leave him to me.'

'How's Charlie been behaving, Mick, and I mean truthfully? He seems ever so subdued. I'll never forgive Billy for what he did to him. Charlie's bound to be scarred mentally by it. What if it screws him up for life?'

Not wanting to worry his sister, Mickey chose his words carefully. 'Mum said he's played up a little bit round there. I don't think he's said much about his dad, but to be honest, once you get out of here, I think it might be a good idea to take him to see someone, maybe a kiddie shrink or something.'

'I'm not taking him to one of them, Mick. He ain't mental, he's just confused. Maybe now that Billy's out the picture, his behaviour will improve of its own accord.'

Seeing Charlie and his mum walk back into the room saved Mickey the awful job of confessing to his sister that he didn't think her kid was quite right in the head. Another time, another place, would be better for that. The serious shit would have to wait until Debs was up to hearing the truth about her offspring. Smiling, he quickly changed the subject.

'I'm going to have a look at a couple of properties in the next few day, Debs, right near Mum. They'd be ideal for you and Charlie.'

Debbie looked at her brother in amazement. She'd been so ill that she hadn't given a thought to where she was going to live. 'It's a lovely idea, Mick, but who's gonna pay for it? I'll have to go back to the flat, else how am I gonna get my stuff back? Everything that me and Charlie own is inside that place.'

Squeezing her hand, Mickey informed her that he and his mate Steve had already collected all of her belongings. He then explained that he had a pal who owed him a couple of favours and dealt in renting out properties.

'Honestly, Debs, all I've gotta do is go and view 'em and pick the one I want. I ain't even gotta give him a deposit because you're my sis. The Housing Benefit mob will pay your rent for ya.'

'Oh, that's brilliant, Mickey. It'll be so much better for Charlie, living in a decent area. He can go to a nice little school and make new friends. It'll be the making of him, I know it will.'

June and Mickey shot each other a knowing glance. They both felt that Charlie's problems were far too deep-rooted for a change of area to make any difference. Neither of them wanted to burst Debbie's bubble, though, so they both agreed with her.

As Debbie waved goodbye to her family, she felt more confident than she had for a while. Thinking positively, she decided that once she was discharged, she would definitely get her life back on track. Obviously, her hair would have to be shaved completely and she would need dentistry work to repair the two teeth she'd lost, but she was determined to bounce back stronger than ever before. She certainly wasn't going to let a no-good piece of shit like Billy McDaid ruin her life.

She was adamant that from now on there would be no more men in her life and she would just concentrate on herself and her son. Tired but determined, she drifted off to sleep.

On the way home, with an unusually quiet Charlie crashed out on the back seat, June and Mickey discussed how much chirpier Debbie had seemed.

'She'll be fine, Mum, I know she will. She's a strong 'un, our Debs, tough as old boots. Once she's in a nice little house, round the corner from you, she'll be as right as ninepence.'

June glanced at the sleeping child, sprawled out on the back seat of the car.

'I know it's a horrible thing to say,' she whispered, 'but it's a shame she's got him, isn't it? Without him she'd have no ties to McDaid, and if anything is going to drag her down, it'll be that little bastard, mark my words. I can't see him changing, acting normally, can you?'

Changing gear, Mickey shook his head. 'There's no way he's gonna change. Unfortunately for Debs, she's given birth to fucking Damien.'

June smiled at her son's humour. She'd loved the *Omen* films and thought that Damien was a perfect name for her grandson. The smile was quickly wiped off her face when Mickey told her the story of how Charlie dangled the kitten out of Debbie's neighbour's window.

'You should have seen the look on his face, Mum. Honestly, I've never seen anything like it, not even in prison. He was totally getting off on the terror of the poor animal, I could see it in his evil little eyes.'

Charlie smiled to himself. He often pretended to be asleep, and loved it when he was the topic of conversation. Remembering the look on Tiger the kitten's face, it was a struggle to stop himself from giggling. Then overcome by the wonderful memories, he did burst out laughing.

'Shhh, he's awake,' June said as she quickly changed the subject. 'So, where you going to see the New Year in, Mick?'

'Club up town, Mum. A pal of mine runs it.'

Pulling up outside his mum's house, Mickey jumped out of the car and opened her door for her. 'The one good thing that's come out of this, Mum, is at least we're all close again, like a proper family. It's just a shame that Debbie had to take a beating for that to happen.'

'You're so right, Mick. I'm to blame for that, though. I should never have put Peter ahead of you and Debbie. I'm really ashamed of meself.'

'Oh, forget it now, Mum. You came up trumps when we really needed ya, and that's all that matters.'

'I love you, son.'

Mickey blew her a kiss and drove off.

At 7.30 p.m. exactly June added a diamante necklace and earrings to her expensive new dress and checked herself out in the full-length mirror. Pleased with the results, she made her way downstairs for Peter's approval.

'You look beautiful, darling. Perfect, in fact,' he said as he admired the jade green number she'd spent hours choosing.

Charlie, clad in his pyjamas and watching cartoons on his nan's video, turned around to see what the commotion was all about.

'Nanny fat, Nanny fat, Nanny fat,' he chanted.

Taking no notice of him, June turned off the video. 'Come on, bed-time for you, young man.'

'Not going, not tired.'

'Now come on Charlie, don't mess me about,' June said sternly.

'Noooooo, not going.'

As he lay on the floor, having one of his famous temper tantrums, Charlie remembered what his nan had said about him earlier. She had said it was a shame that he'd ever been born. Smiling, he decided it was payback time. Taking the lid off his beaker of Ribena, he giggled as he chucked the contents all over Nanny's new dress.

June was in shock as she looked at the state of her outfit. 'You evil little bastard!' she screamed. Crying with anger, she ran up the stairs, leaving Peter to deal with the child from hell.

'You are a nasty, naughty, horrible little boy. You will go to bed this very minute,' Peter said as he dragged the hysterical child up the stairs.

'Bastard, bastard, bastard,' Charlie screamed.

Peter opened the bedroom door. 'Get in that bed and go to sleep *now*, child.'

Charlie hated his granddad. Screwing his face up, he spat at him and missed.

Overcome by anger, Peter lifted the brat off the bed by his left arm and repeatedly smacked his bottom.

Though still extremely flustered, June and Peter managed to pull themselves together in time to greet their guests. As host and hostess they had a reputation second to none, and were determined to keep it that way.

At five to midnight, Peter tuned into a local radio station. 'Ten, nine, eight, seven . . . '

June cracked open the vintage champagne. ' . . . six, five, four, three, two, one. Happy New Year!' As *Auld Lang Syne* blared out from the speakers, the three couples stood in a circle, arms crossed.

Charlie sat bolt upright in bed. The music, screams and guffaws had woken him. Deep in thought, he sucked his thumb. He hated living in this horrible house. He'd been happy before, living in the flat with his daddy. Why hadn't his daddy come to get him? He hadn't seen him since they'd played the scary window game. His dad had been upset that night. He was crying when he'd gone off with the nasty policemen.

Charlie grabbed hold of his new toy and hugged him. His nan had taken Mr Teddy away from him because he was covered in blood. She'd said that Mr Teddy was ill and needed to go into hospital, like Mummy. She'd given him Deputy Dawg to play with instead. Apparently, the dog had belonged to his mum when she was a little girl. No longer tired, Charlie toddled down-stairs to see what all the commotion was about. Peter was horrified to see him appear, and quickly scooped the child into his arms.

Hilary Forsyth-Smith and her husband Duncan had never been lucky enough to conceive a child themselves. 'Oh, look, bless him! Please let him stay for a while, Peter,' Hilary pleaded.

'Goodness, no, it's way past his bedtime,' Peter said firmly.

'Pleeease.' Hilary was extremely drunk and wasn't taking no for an answer. 'Aren't you a little cutie?' she said, tickling Charlie under his chin. 'And look at your

114

little Superman pyjamas . . . aren't they adorable? Please, Peter, let me hold him.'

Seeing Hilary's outstretched arms and noticing the mad 'I'm desperate for a baby' glint in her eye, he didn't have the heart to say no. He had to put on an act. He'd spent ages earlier telling his guests how he and June had taken the boy in and were caring for him like he was their own. He hadn't mentioned what a little bastard the child was, naturally, but had made the situation sound idyllic, Granny, Grandpa and cute little Charlie. He knew without a doubt that he had scored political brownie points with Duncan with that act, just as he'd intended. He could hardly banish the child now.

Peter stood watching Hilary dote on the child, feeling very on edge. 'Come on then, Charlie,' he said finally, feeling that these past ten minutes spent without incident were more than he could have hoped for. Better not push his luck.

'Show me how your little doggy walks,' Hilary said, still all gooey and starry-eyed.

'Don't wanna,' Charlie said, hugging the toy close to his chest.

'Oh, pleeease, come on. Auntie Hilary wants to see Doggy Woggie.'

Wriggling out of the madwoman's arms, Charlie turned to look at her. She reminded him of a horse with her great big teeth. Knowing he was about to be whisked back off to bed by his surrogate grandfather, Charlie decided to go out in style. Giggling, he pulled down his pyjama bottoms, grabbed his dinkle and thrust it towards Hilary.

'Suck my cock, suck my cock, suck my cock,' he shouted, laughing gleefully.

Hilary put her hand over her mouth in horror. She had never sucked Duncan's dinkle in all the years they'd been married, the mere thought had always appalled her.

115

June and Peter glanced at one another. Their party was well and truly over along with their reputation for respectability.

Ordering June to take the child to bed at once, a shell-shocked Peter lit up one of his Hamlets and apologised profusely. He needn't have bothered, the evening was already ruined.

Hilary grabbed Duncan's arm. 'Could you take me home, dear? I am feeling rather faint and insist we leave immediately.'

Duncan looked at Peter, raised his eyebrows and walked out.

Peter said goodbye to the last of his guests and slammed the door. What a bloody show-up. He had never felt so embarrassed in the whole of his life. Charlie's behaviour had just spelt the end of his political career, that was for sure. Word of tonight's events would spread like wildfire amongst his colleagues, and where would that leave him? A bloody laughing stock, that's where! He most certainly would not allow that to happen. Tomorrow he would do the decent thing and walk away with his head held high. His resignation from the Council would be handed in with immediate effect.

FIFTEEN

Debbie was finally discharged from hospital, three weeks to the day after she was first admitted. The weather was dull, rainy and miserable, and it matched her mood completely. Yesterday was the first time she'd looked into a mirror since the beating and she'd been surprised she hadn't cracked the bastard thing.

Obviously, she had known all along that she'd lost a couple of her teeth and that her hair was now cropped. Her mum had brought Peter's razor in and evened it up to match the side that had already been shaved. The nurses had forbidden her to look into a mirror until the bruises and swelling had lessened so she'd had no idea just how bloody repulsive she looked, until now. Hence her mood today as she hobbled out of the hospital on crutches along-side Mickey.

Glancing at his watch, he realised it had taken them ten minutes to reach the end of the corridor. 'Why don't you let me get you a wheelchair? The nurses said you could borrow one.'

Debbie paused and pulled the Nike baseball cap he'd lent her over her eyes. She could see all the passers-by staring at her, pitying expressions on their faces.

'I am not being pushed about in one of them bloody things. What do you think I am, some kind of an invalid?'

117

Mickey smiled to himself. Every day this week he'd seen more and more of the old Debbie return. She'd been entirely different with that bastard McDaid, a shadow of her former self.

Glancing round at her, he clocked that she'd barely moved an inch in the last five minutes. Now Mickey might have a lot of virtues, but patience wasn't one of them. 'For fuck's sake, Debs, we'll be here all night at this rate! Sit on that fucking seat over there while I go and find you a wheelchair.'

Watching her brother storm off in the direction from which they'd just come, Debbie allowed herself a wry smile. They weren't even out of the hospital door and already they were arguing like cat and dog. They'd had a massive row yesterday when she'd first looked into the mirror.

'Look at the fucking state of me, Mick. I look like a freak,' she'd wailed, expecting some sympathy.

Not that great with women's hang-ups and insecurities, Mickey said what he thought she'd want to hear.

'I think you look proper, Debs. I really like your hair cropped. I prefer it to when it was long. It suits you . . . makes you look pretty, like.'

If Debbie had been sitting near enough, she'd have smacked him straight in the teeth. She had never looked pretty in the first place, let alone now.

'Pretty! Are you having a laugh, Mick? I've got no fucking teeth and me hair looks like I'm suffering from terminal cancer. Pretty? I look like something out of bloody *Cell Block H*. Now fuck off and leave me alone.'

Mickey had slunk from the room like a naughty puppy that had just had its first scolding. 'Fucking women, I'll never understand 'em,' he'd mumbled to himself.

Hearing the rumble of the clapped out wheelchair

approaching, Debbie's thoughts snapped back to the present.

Originally, it had been decided that for the first couple of weeks, she would stay with her mum and Peter, to help her out with Charlie and give her some time to recover. This idea, however, had gone out of the window last week. At the end of his tether, Peter could take no more and finally tackled June. 'I'll say this once and once only, my dear. I cannot spend another day around your grandson. That child is Lucifer himself. Either he goes or I do.'

June had no choice but to pack up some stuff and move with Charlie into the pretty little two-bedroomed house that Mickey had rented for Debbie. She didn't blame Peter. Secretly, she thought he'd been marvellous to suffer the child as long as he had. If the boot had been on the other foot, she couldn't have put up with it.

As Debbie arrived at her new home, which was literally five minutes from her mother's, she felt her mood lift.

'Oh, Mickey, it's beautiful, I love it,' she crowed as she hobbled excitedly from one room to another. It was spacious, modern, had a pretty garden and a massive kitchen. The house Mickey had found was absolutely ideal for her. Situated on the outskirts of Rainham and Elm Park, it formed part of a little close with nine other houses. It was a far cry from Junkie Town and Nelson Mandela House.

'Mick, I'll be so happy here! You're the best brother in the whole wide world.'

He smirked as she clung around his neck. He'd obviously done something right for once. Only yesterday she was calling him every cunt under the sun. Fuck getting married, he thought, as he hugged her back. Women were too unpredictable for his liking, he'd never understand their way of thinking.

June watched her two children laughing and bantering and was secretly as proud as a peacock. Damien, as she still privately called Charlie, was upstairs asleep and it was nice to have a bit of quality time, just the three of them. She'd guessed by now that her Mickey was no party organiser. She didn't care. He was her son, she loved him dearly, and what she didn't know couldn't hurt her.

Leaving her kids chatting away happily in the lounge, June headed to the kitchen to make a brew. She was parched and guessed they must be as well.

'Right, girls. I've got a bit of an announcement to make meself,' Mickey said on her return.

June put the mugs on to coasters and felt her heart leap with excitement. Maybe he was getting married? she thought as she fleetingly pictured her own outfit. She sat waiting with bated breath.

Mickey smiled. 'I've bought a little house down this way meself. I've wanted out of the East End for a while now. It's changed so much up there, far too multicultural for my liking, so I decided Essex was to be me next move. A nice three-bedroomed gaff I bought. Got it on the cheap an' all, I did. It needs a bit of work done, but me mate Steve's gonna move down here with me, rent a room off me, like. He's pretty handy and we can do any work that needs doing in our spare time.'

'That's fantastic son,' June said, nearly choking on her biscuit. She wished he'd settle down properly, though, move in with a girl. She'd been hoping he would shack up with a Susie or a Sandra, not a bloody Steve. Surely he wasn't gay, she thought. You never knew these days . . . Worried about him, she gave a half-smile.

Mickey knew exactly which way his mother ticked and guessed what she was thinking. Deciding a wind-up was on the cards, he winked at Debbie and cleared his throat.

'Look, Mum, Debs, there's something I need to tell you and I don't know how you're gonna take it.'

Trying not to laugh, he put on his most sincere expression and stared at his mother.

'Oh, this is so awkward, I dunno where to start. I've known what I was from an early age, but was frightened to tell ya. So I rang that gay helpline and they told me I had to be honest. Me and Steve, Mum, we're lovers and we're hoping to get married this summer. A gay vicar has offered to do the service and, well, I was wondering if you could ask Peter to be my best man.'

Debbie roared, unable to contain herself.

June dropped her mug and its contents all over Debbie's new carpet. Her handsome, macho son a shit-stabber . . . surely not? What would she say to Peter?

Laughing hysterically, Mickey and Debbie held their stomachs. The look on their mother's face was a picture, an absolute classic. 'He's winding you up,' Debbie screamed.

Relieved it had all been a big joke, June rushed out to the kitchen. Returning with a cloth, she got down on her hands and knees and mopped up the mess.

It had been a long time since Debbie had had a laugh like this. Enjoying herself, she carried it on.

'Can you imagine Mrs Bucket having to tell Peter and her friends that her son's a raving iron!'

Seeing the funny side herself now, June went into a fit of giggles and was unable to get up off her hands and knees. 'Christ, don't bend over with your arse up like that, Mum. Steve'll be round in a minute and he always gives me a good seeing to when I'm in that position!' Mickey shouted.

The raucous laughter and crude humour went on for a good ten minutes and only came to a halt when a miserable-looking Charlie entered the room.

'Mummy's home, Charlie. Do you like our new house? Come and give me a cuddle,' Debbie said happily.

'I hate it. It's 'orrible,' Charlie replied tactlessly.

The change in the atmosphere was like someone turning a switch off. Mickey glanced at his mother, threw his nephew a look of pure hatred, and feeling like Rodney Trotter once again, stood up.

'Right, girls, I'll let yous two get sorted now, I'm gonna shoot. I've gotta bit of business to sort out later.'

Mickey kissed them both and, for Debbie's sake, forced himself to say goodbye to Damien. When he got no reply from the ignorant little shit, he slammed the front door, jumped into his motor and shot up the A13.

Mickey had really enjoyed the day with his mum and sis, but as usual that horrible fucking kid had spoiled things. Normally he loved children. Some of his mates had little 'uns and Mickey had all the time in the world for them, but Charlie was the devil in disguise. In fact, he was a ringer for his no-good cunt of an old man.

Flicking through the radio channels, Mickey opted for Kiss FM. He liked rave music, it had made him wealthy. As he cranked the sound up as loud as it would go, he tried to banish to the back of his mind any thoughts of what he'd like to do to his nephew and bloody Billy McDaid.

June and Debbie fell into a nice little routine over the next few days and Debbie was glad of her mother's company.

As usual the only fly in the ointment was Charlie, who continued to be rude, sullen and surly, showing neither his mum nor his nan any respect or affection at all.

'I'm really at the end of my tether, Mum. I honestly don't know what to do with him any more. I've tried everything. I've smacked him, taken his toys away, locked him in his room . . . but nothing seems to work. I just can't seem to connect with him. Billy could, he had him eating out the palm of his hand, but me . . . I just feel like he hates me. And I'm his mother, for Christ's sake.'

Not knowing what to say to Debbie in case she said the wrong thing, June suggested that they open the bottle of wine Peter had given her earlier. 'To help you cope,' he'd said sarcastically. He was bloody spot on, June thought as she poured it.

'What am I gonna do, Mum?'

'I don't know, Debs, I really don't. You and Mickey were angels compared to Charlie, and I thought you were both naughty at the time. You've just got to hope that he'll change when he starts proper school in September.'

'Please God he does, Mum, but I can't see him changing. I've never told you before but he got excluded from nursery school for being a little bastard. He walloped a couple of kids there and flashed his willy at the teacher.'

June sighed and decided now was as good a time as any to tell Debbie about the New Year's Eve débâcle.

'Oh, Mum, I'm so sorry. I feel terrible. You must have been horrified.'

'Well, it was a night to remember, Debbie, especially when the little sod started shouting "suck my cock" at Hilary. You know how posh Peter's political friends are? As for Peter, he was that mortified, he handed in his resignation the following day.'

Debbie didn't know whether to laugh or cry. June made the decision for her. The two glasses of wine she'd drunk had gone straight to her head and she erupted into a fit of giggles.

'I know we shouldn't be laughing, Debbie, but if you'd have been there and seen this Hilary's face! It was a picture, love.'

'Oh, Mum. The Tory Party was Peter's life. Fancy him having to leave because of Charlie.'

'Well I ain't gotta put up with his boring friends no more. I never liked 'em much anyway. And a least now he's got more time to do my fucking garden!' Screaming with laughter, June topped up their glasses.

Mickey was sitting in the Needle Gun, having a quiet pint with Big Steve, when he received an unexpected phone call from an old pal of his, Tommy the Fence.

'What's occurring? Long time no hear from. How you been, Tom?'

Never a man for exchanging pleasantries, Tommy came straight to the point.

'Just to let you know, Bobby Turner was up in court today and that McDaid that did your sister walked . . . he got bail. Just thought you should know, son.'

The line went dead. Downing his pint in one, Mickey nodded to Steve to hurry up and finish his. 'What's the rush?' he asked, innocently.

'McDaid. They've let him go. Now it's our turn to prosecute the cunt, Stevie boy.'

SIXTEEN

Billy McDaid wasn't as easy to find as they'd first thought, and spending day in, day out, scouring around the piss-hole pubs in Barking wasn't Mickey's idea of fun. By day five he'd had a gutful of it and needed a break.

'I dunno about you, Steve, but I think we should call it a night. My stomach thinks me throat's been cut. Let's go and have a bit of Chinese or something. We'll have a sit down, eh?'

Never one to refuse a meal, Steve agreed and the pair of them left the depressing streets of Barking and headed off to Chinatown in Ilford. As they tucked into a selection of dishes, they discussed what they should do next. Shovelling a succession of spare ribs into his mouth, Mickey spoke between mouthfuls.

'I think we should give up the search, just for a couple of days. He's obviously laying low somewhere. And the more he hears we've been hunting for him, the further away we're gonna push him. I think we should concentrate on moving our stuff down to the house in the next couple of days. Adam Prior said we can borrow his transit van. Let's get all our shit sorted and then we'll worry about McDaid after.'

Steve had some ideas of his own. 'Look, we know from when we was looking for McDaid before that he's not the most popular of geezers. Why don't we pop back to a couple of his locals and ask a couple of junkies to help us find him? These people are lowlifes, Mick, they'll bite your hand off for a tenner. If we offer 'em, say, hundred quid for the right information, we'll have 'em queuing up to help us.'

Sipping his beer while he mulled over the suggestion, Mickey decided that they had nothing to lose. 'That ain't a bad idea, you know, big man. Why should we do all the fucking hard work?' he said, chucking some money on to the table.

Ten minutes later the pair of them were back in Barking, searching for suitable candidates.

Billy McDaid heard a noise coming from the landing outside and felt his heart-rate quicken. 'Go and have a look through the spy hole, Andy, see if anyone's out there,' he whispered.

A stoned Andy informed him that it was the kid next door, playing football with an empty beer can.

Breathing a sigh of relief, Billy took out a Benson and Hedges and carried on chain-smoking.

It was six days now since he'd been given bail and he'd been stuck in Andy's flat ever since. Not once had he set foot outside the door, nor even seen the light of day. He'd fully expected Mr Mickey fucking Bigshot to have come knocking on the door by now and had made preparations just in case.

Andy had a big broom cupboard in his one-bedroomed flat which had a decent-sized loft above it. Billy had already moved the hatch aside and put the ladders in place, in case he needed to make a quick escape. Staying at Andy's was fine on a temporary basis, but he was at a dead loss as to what he was going to do in the long run.

For obvious reasons, he couldn't go back to his own flat and, apart from Andy, he had no other real friends who would risk their neck for him. Going back to Glasgow was a definite no go. Cuntsmouth Colin, his slut of a mother, and memories of his brother's death were more than enough to stop him from returning there. One day he'd like to go back, but not now.

'We're out of cider, Bill, and I'm running low on fags. I'm gonna go down to the offie and get some. I'll pop to the chippy as well. You hungry?'

Billy shook his head. He hadn't eaten in days and, the way he felt at the moment, didn't think he'd ever have an appetite again. Ordering his mate to be as quick as poss, Billy cracked open the last can of cider and stared list-lessly out of the window.

He'd hated being banged up, it hadn't suited him at all, and the thought of doing a long stretch, filled him with dread. Sitting in a cell on his own had given Billy far too much time to think. He'd thought a lot about the past during his time at Andy's too, and all the shit he'd been through, but most of all he'd thought of Debbie and little Charlie boy.

Over and over again, he wished he could turn the clock back to Christmas morning. Why the fuck hadn't he handled things differently? Billy felt terrible about the hiding he'd given Debbie, but that was nothing in compari-son to the guilt he felt over what he'd done to his son.

Dangling his own flesh and blood out of a thirteenth-floor window was the action of the lowest of the low, and the memory of it would haunt him until the day he died. The only thing he could blame it on was the drugs, but even that was no excuse.

'Nooooo, Daddy, nooooo!' His son's screams would live with him forever. All he could hope for was that in time Charlie would forget that his father had threatened to kill him, just to save his own sorry arse. Disgusted with himself, Billy sat on the floor, held his head in his hands and sobbed.

Mickey and Steve were lugging a sofa into their new abode when Mickey's phone started to ring.

'All right. Is that Mickey?' said a drugged up voice.

'Yeah, speaking. Who's that?'

'It's Scott. You gave me your number yesterday and told me to ring you if I found out where Billy McDaid was. Well, I've found out where he's staying but I want me money first.'

Nodding to Big Steve to chuck the sofa inside, Mickey made a meet with the kid and the pair of them shot off straight away.

They made Barking in eight minutes flat.

'You Scott?' Mickey asked the spotty-looking teenager.

'Nah, I'm his brother Ricky. Scott's waiting round the corner. He don't want anyone to see him meeting ya. Follow me.'

Hoping they weren't being arsed about, Mickey and Steve reluctantly followed the kid round to a row of disused garages. 'You ain't fucking leading us up the garden path 'ere, are you, son?' Mickey enquired menacingly.

'I'm not, honest,' Ricky said nervously. As he let out a loud whistle, his brother appeared like magic. After a brief conversation, Mickey handed the kid a score.

'We said hundred, where's the other eighty?' Scott asked in dismay. He was going to a rave later and was relying on this money to keep him in Ecstasy tablets for the evening.

Mickey smiled. 'For all I know you might be lying. You'll get the rest of your dough after I've found McDaid. Wait down the bottom of the flats and if your story rings true, I'll slip it to you on the way out.'

Scott wasn't easy with this arrangement. 'What if someone sees me wiv ya? Grasses ain't popular round here, yer know. My name'll be shit if anyone finds out.'

Noticing an empty McDonald's bag drifting across the pavement, Mickey picked it up and shoved eighty quid in it.

'If all goes to plan, I'll make sure I drop this on the floor as I come down the stairs, right?'

'Okay,' Scott said dubiously. He'd only ever dealt with druggies and thieves, and lived in a world where it was the norm to pull a fast one.

As he walked away from the garages, Mickey turned back towards the boys. 'By the way, I forgot to ask ya. How do you know the cunt is definitely staying at this flat? You seen him with your own eyes?'

'No,' Scott replied truthfully. 'My dad bumped into his mate, Andy, in the chip shop last night. He told him Billy was staying there and was gonna climb into the loft if anyone came looking for him.'

'Good lad,' Mickey said, as he broke into a run.

'Slow down, for Christ's sake,' Steve said, falling behind his pal.

'You need to lose weight, you fat bastard,' Mickey informed him.

The pair of them entered the tower block like Batman and Robin. The lifts were working and it didn't take them long to track down their destination. Tiptoeing up to the door, they listened in silence for a good couple of minutes.

'I can definitely hear talking and music or something,' Steve whispered.

Mickey knocked on the door, but got no joy.

'Look, if they ain't answering, it must mean the cunt's in there. We'll have to take a chance, Steve, kick the door down. If we've got it wrong, we'll buy the poor bastard that lives there a new one and bung him some dosh for his inconvenience.'

Stevie boy was a big old lump and an expert at hurtling through locked doors. Within seconds they were in.

As Andy sat shivering on the sofa, Mickey stood over him. 'All right, lad, where's your mate?'

'I d-don't know what you're t-talking about,' stammered Andy.

'Oh, I think you do.'

Picking Andy up by his dirty Led Zeppelin T-shirt, Mickey shoved him against the nicotine-stained wall.

'Where's your loft, you junkie cunt?'

Petrified, Andy nodded towards the cupboard in the hallway and was relieved when Mickey dropped him on to the floor like a piece of old rubbish. Mickey nudged Steve and pointed at the ladder. Climbing up a few rungs, he pushed the hatch open.

'Oh, Billy boy, Uncle Mickey's here to see you. You do remember me, dontcha? I was once your friendly brother-in-law. Now, be a good boy and come and say hello to me.'

Billy sat huddled in a corner of the loft, knees pressed to his chest. He was scared beyond belief and felt like a rabbit caught in the headlights.

Mickey climbed up higher. He could see fuck all, it was pitch black up there.

'Pass us your lighter, Steve.'

He handed over his Ronson and held the ladder firmly. Igniting the flame, Mickey smiled as he found what he'd been looking for.

'Right, I can see you, McDaid, and you've got two choices here. Either you come down now or I'm gonna come up there and drag you down head first. The choice is yours.'

Billy felt as if he was having a flashback to his childhood. It was a reminder of being paralysed with fear every night as he'd listened to Colin's footsteps getting closer and closer.

'Right, you cunt, you've had your fucking chance! Now I'm coming to get ya.'

Pushing Billy out of the hatch, kicking him into the lift and slinging him into the boot of the Merc made Mickey feel on top of the world. Now he knows how my Debs must have felt, he thought as he smelled the cunt's fear.

As he remembered the money that was due to Scott, he told Steve to start the car while he delivered it. There was no one about as he dropped the bag but he was sure the kids were somewhere close by, awaiting their payout.

Billy McDaid gasped for air as he lay squashed into the boot of the car. His life to date had been fucking shit. He prayed to God to take him now as that would still be better than what he had coming.

The last thing he remembered was the smell of his own diarrhoea and the feeling of it running down his legs before, overcome by panic, he lost consciousness.

SEVENTEEN

Steve lit up two fags, passed one to Mickey and took a deep drag on the other.

'What happens now then, Mick? Where we taking him?' he asked.

'Epping Forest, where no one will fucking well find him.'

Feeling a bit nervous, Steve fished for more information. 'What we gonna do to him when we get there? We can't do him in, Mick.'

Mickey threw him a look. 'Well, what do you suggest we do then, Steve, take the cunt for lunch?'

Choosing his words carefully, Steve spoke slowly but thoughtfully. He might not be the sharpest tool in the box, but when it came to shit like this he knew the score. He was damned if he was gonna end up at the sharp end of some murder charge for a scumbag like McDaid.

'Look, Mick, the whole of Barking knows we've been chasing around looking for this piece of shit, and if he's found brown bread it ain't gonna take one of them junkie scumbags five minutes to open their mouth. We only offered 'em a hundred quid and *we* got a result. I'm telling ya, Mick, *you* might wanna spend the next twenty years inside but *I* fucking well don't.'

'Stop worrying, will ya?' Mickey said as he swerved

the car into a lay by. 'Get out and check the cunt's okay in that boot. Make sure he's breathing and that.'

Steve opened the boot and was greeted by the unadulterated smell of shit. Holding his nose, he prodded and poked a semi-conscious Billy.

'Wake up! Oh, for fuck's sake, are you all right?' he shouted.

McDaid felt desperately weak, but managed to answer. 'Not enough air,' he gasped. Walking round to the driver's side of the car, Steve told Mickey the score.

'Pull the back seats down so he can breathe and you sit in the back. Make sure he don't fucking move.'

Seconds after the seats were released, the stench of shit hit Mickey's nostrils.

'Dirty cunt,' he muttered to himself as he weaved his way through more country lanes.

Finally satisfied he'd found a secluded spot safe from prying eyes, Mickey stopped the engine and nodded at Steve. 'This'll do. Bring that shovel and rope and I'll bring him.'

Billy's legs turned to jelly as he was dragged from the boot. Overcome by panic, he collapsed in a crumpled heap on the floor.

'Please don't kill me,' he pleaded. 'I swear, I'll do anything you ask, but please don't kill me.'

'Get up, you cunt,' Mickey shouted as he grabbed him by the elbow.

He dragged his prisoner along until he felt happy with their surroundings. Positive that they were now deep enough in the forest not be disturbed, he roughly shoved McDaid to the ground.

'I'm so sorry,' Billy sobbed. 'I didn't mean to hurt Debbie, I loved her so much . . . '

'Loved her? *Loved her*, you fucking mug?'

Mickey lifted his right foot and kicked Billy in the

mouth as hard as he could. He smiled as he saw two teeth fly out and land amongst the twigs. Pleased with his precision, he booted him again, this time in the bollocks. Then, asking Steve to hand him the rope, he winked at his pal.

'Right, I want you to start digging Billy's grave for me, Steve.'

McDaid sobbed like a newborn. 'Mickey, please, no . . . you can't bury me. Help me . . . help!' he shouted.

Mickey looked at him and laughed. 'Shut up, you prick. You're in the middle of a forest. Who the fuck's gonna hear you out here, you thick bastard?'

'I'm sorry, Mickey. I'll move back to Scotland, never go near Debbie or Charlie again, I swear. I'll do anything you ask, I promise. But please don't bury me – not alive.'

Mickey was by now enjoying himself immensely, and was even more pleased when he saw that McDaid had pissed himself with fright. Pointing to the wet patch on Billy's jeans, he chuckled loudly. 'Ah, you done wee-wees, have ya? You should have said if you wanted a piss, Billy.'

Steve, who was busy digging the grave, took a break to join in with the banter.

'Yeah, we'd have found you a toilet, Bill. Anyway, who said we were gonna bury you alive? You'll be lucky. We'll probably have to kill you first, won't we, Mick?'

Roaring with laughter, Mickey took a packet of Benson's out of his pocket and handed one to Steve.

'Do you want a final fag before I wipe your life out, Billy?' he asked, grinning at his victim.

Billy's hand shook as he took the cigarette that was offered to him. Watching his tormentors puffing away happily, he plucked up the courage to ask for a light.

Mickey blew smoke into his face. 'A light? You've got the cheek to ask me for a light? You might get your last wish on Death Row but not in Epping Forest, you cunt.

The only light you'd get off me was if I decided to pour petrol over ya and set ya on fire.'

Fag break over, Mickey stood up. 'Right, carry on digging, Steve, while I sort out our Scottish friend here.'

Pulling Billy up from the ground by his hair, Mickey marched him over to a nearby tree.

'Take your clothes off,' he ordered as he took a Stanley knife out of his jacket.

'What you g-gonna d-do to me?' Billy stammered, his eyes bulging like organ stops.

'Just do it,' Mickey replied viciously.

Standing there in just his boxer shorts, Billy shivered.

'Take your shorts off,' Mickey said, noticing he hadn't removed them.

'I-I can't,' Billy screamed, collapsing on to his knees.

Mickey crouched down beside him. 'You either take them off yourself or I'm gonna cut them off with this.'

Scrambling around amongst the leaves, Billy managed to get his boxers off. Mickey laughed, picked him up and chucked him against a tree trunk.

'Well, well, well. 'Ere, Steve, come and 'ave a look at this.'

Steve stuck the shovel in the ground, glad of some respite.

'What's occurring?'

'Not a lot, I just wanted your opinion. Have you ever seen a cock as small as our Billy's?'

Steve walked over to the shivering wreck standing pinned against a tree trunk and glanced down at his John Thomas.

'Christ, you'd never have made a male stripper, would you, Billy boy?'

As Mickey noticed that the slight drizzle of rain had suddenly become heavier, he ordered Steve to bring the rope over to him. Still holding the knife, he looked Billy straight in his beady little eyes and spoke clearly and confidently.

'Right, you Scotch cunt. If I do you the favour of sparing you a burial, will you promise me you'll go back to Scotland and never, ever return?'

'I p-promise,' Billy stuttered.

Mickey smiled at his obvious distress. 'And will you also promise never, ever to contact my sister or her son again?'

'I'll d-do whatever you say, Mickey.'

'Well, I'm gonna give you a reprieve then. Not 'cause I like ya. I'm doing it because you're so fucking worthless, you're not worth doing bird for. But I'm telling you now, Billy, if you ever break your word, I personally am gonna kill ya, do you understand me?'

'Y-yes Mickey. Thank you.'

Gesturing to Steve to hold one end of the rope, Mickey walked round and round the tree, securing Billy to the trunk.

'Right, Billy boy, I've tied you up. If someone finds you, you'll live. If they don't, you'll starve or freeze to death, and be munched on by foxes.'

Billy McDaid felt weak, very weak, and knew that if he was left tied to this tree, he wouldn't live to tell the tale.

'Please untie me! I promise I'll do everything you say. You'll never see me again.'

'I wanna word,' Steve said, pulling Mickey aside. 'Look,' he continued, 'we've taught him a lesson, but we can't leave him here like this. We might as well have just fucking shot him. No one will find him in time, Mick, and what with the hole I've just dug, we'll have the old bill all over us.'

Mickey smiled. 'Do you think I don't know that, Steve? Do you think I'm stupid or something? I've no intention

136

of leaving him tied up. I'm just teaching the cunt a lesson that he'll never forget.'

A look of relief spread over Big Steve's face. 'Thank fuck for that. Come on, Mick, let's get out of here now. I'm soaking wet and starving.'

Walking back over to McDaid, Mickey smiled in satisfaction.

'My mate Steve reckons I should untie you. Now, I'm not giving you your clothes back, 'cause you look better naked. When you find your way out of this jungle, Billy, and your little cock goes on display to the general public, I want you to tell whoever finds you that you've been out on a stag night and got stripped off as a prank. As for your teeth and the bruises, tell 'em you were pissed and fell over.'

Billy nodded. He felt so ill now, he was almost unable to speak.

Pulling a wad of notes out of his pocket, Mickey counted out fifty quid and handed it to him. 'That's your train fare. I want you to take the first train back to Glasgow. And if I find out you haven't, I'm gonna cut your little cock off and shove it down your throat. Got it?'

'Got it,' Billy said faintly.

Mickey cut the rope and laughed loudly as Billy fell to the ground in a crumpled heap. Unable to resist one last kick, he aimed it deep into Billy's stomach.

'That's from Debbie,' he said, as he picked up the rope and any other evidence they may have left.

Noticing just how weak and ill Billy looked, Steve was still worried. 'I'm telling ya, Mick, he ain't gonna make it out of this forest if we leave him here. Let's get him dressed, help him back to the car and drop him off at the nearest station.'

As much as Mickey would have liked to see McDaid lost forever in the forest, dying a slow painful death and eventually eaten by anything hungry, he knew that what Steve was saying made sense. Mickey had big plans for his own future and doing bird for a piece of shit wasn't part of them.

'Get dressed,' he growled at Billy, as he chucked his shit-stained jeans at him.

The walk back to the car took ages. As Mickey finally started the engine, Steve bundled McDaid into the back seat.

'He ain't looking too good, is he?' Mickey said, stating the obvious. Part of him was still buzzing with adrenaline. The other part of him was worried that he had gone a bit over the top. He could certainly do without Billy croaking it. He and Steve would be in Shit Street if that were to happen.

Steve felt anxious as he glanced at their prisoner. 'I think we should stop at a McDonalds on the way, Mick. Let's get some grub down him and some fluids. Hopefully, that'll liven him up a bit.'

Mickey smiled. Only Steve could come out with that idea. Food was his answer to everything.

After a short food stop, where they tried to shovel a Big Mac, chips and milkshake into Billy's mouth, Mickey headed for the nearest tube station.

'Right,' he said, as he noticed the Central Line sign. 'Time for you to return to your native Glasgow, Billy boy. Chop-chop, out ya get, son.'

Thankful to be alive, Billy stumbled from the car.

As Mickey and Steve drove away that day, both of them were absolutely sure that they'd seen the last of Billy McDaid.

Unfortunately for them, they were wrong.

EIGHTEEN

Eight Months Later

'Now come on, Charlie, put your blazer on for Mummy, there's a good boy.'

'Don't wanna wear it,' came the sulky reply.

'Don't start, Charlie. You know you have to wear it.'

'Don't, don't, don't.'

Exasperated, Debbie picked up his school bag, grabbed him by the hand, and with the blazer slung over her arm, dragged him out of the door and towards the infants' school he'd just started attending.

As she waved goodbye to him at the school gates, she couldn't help but notice all of the other children playing happily amongst themselves. Instead of joining them, Charlie stood alone against a wall, a sullen expression plastered across his face.

'That child will be the death of me,' she mumbled as she headed back home to begin her day's chores.

After she'd done the washing and ironing, Debbie sat in the garden for a fag and a coffee break. With the sun shining brightly, she tilted her head to face the warmth of its rays and lapsed into one of her daydreams.

It was just over eight months since she had hobbled out of the hospital door on crutches. Her life had changed so much since then. Her physical injuries had virtually disappeared, and apart from a slight limp, there was no evidence of the brutal attack she'd endured. Mentally, she was still suffering, though. The slightest noise or sudden movement would make her jump out of her skin. An unexpected knock at the door, especially at night-time, would send her into a paranoid frenzy. But worst of all were the nightmares, which came every time she shut her eyes. Many a night she would wake up drenched in sweat and shaking uncontrollably.

Although the nights were a problem, by day Debbie was the happiest she'd been in ages. She absolutely adored the little house that Mickey had found her and had made good friends with a neighbour, Susan, who had a teenage daughter. The relationship between her and her mum had never been better either. Debbie's ordeal seemed to have bridged the gap between them and brought back the closeness they'd shared years ago.

Peter's pomposity still grated on her, but Debbie could tell that he really loved her mum, and if June was happy, that was good enough for her.

Debbie was closer than ever to her brother Mickey. He was her hero, her saviour. She'd been overjoyed the day he'd come round to tell her that she wouldn't be hearing from Billy any more.

'I've sorted McDaid out, sis. He won't bother you or Charlie ever again.'

'Thanks, Mick,' she'd said, relief flooding through her. 'What about the court case? Will I still have to give evidence?'

'You can forget about that now. I doubt he'd have attended anyway, and me sorting it out saves you from going through all that shit.'

Mickey had rarely mentioned Billy since that day and neither had she. Sometimes she wondered what had happened to him. She didn't think her brother was capable of murder but would've loved to have known if Billy had suffered, just like she had. She'd asked Mickey once but he'd given nothing away.

'Look, Debs, let's not talk about that cunt, eh? Believe me, it's sorted and that's all you need to know.'

Just lately, Mickey had been spending more and more time abroad on business, so he'd asked his mate Steve to look after his interests, which included her.

'When I ain't about, Debs, Big Steve'll be popping round to see if you're OK.'

Debbie was a bit put out at first when the giant skinhead kept appearing on her doorstep, but as the months passed, she got used to his visits and looked forward to them more and more. Underneath his thuggish appearance Big Steve was a gentleman, and Debbie felt safe and secure, knowing he was only a phone call and five minutes away. He was a funny bastard as well and, once the ice was broken between them, regularly had her in hysterics with his deadpan sense of humour.

Charlie hated Big Steve coming round. 'Horrible man, Mummy, don't let him in.'

'Don't be so silly, Charlie, he's your Uncle Mickey's best friend,' Debbie said each time he complained.

With Billy out of her life, Charlie was Debbie's only real headache. Her son's behaviour seemed to go from bad to worse. Driven mad with him under her feet all day, she was relieved when he'd finally started school. It was guilt that made her succumb to his every whim when he was home. After what he'd been through with his father, she couldn't help but spoil him. A few months ago she'd taken some unwanted advice from her brother. Mickey had paid her a flying visit and Charlie had been acting up as usual, refusing to eat his dinner and chucking it all over the floor.

Pulling her to one side, Mickey had handed her the

business card of a child psychiatrist. 'Look, please don't think I'm interfering but this geezer's meant to be good, sis. If you don't get Charlie sorted now, you're gonna regret it. You've got to do it, for his sake. Book an appointment. I'll pay for it, Debs.'

Not overjoyed with the idea of her son needing a shrink, Debbie stuck the card and the money in her purse and forgot about it. It was Charlie kicking and spitting at an old lady on a bus ride home from Romford that jogged her memory.

The appointment was booked for a week later. 'Nooooo, nooooo, nooooo!' Charlie screamed as he was dragged, kicking and screaming, into the waiting room of the clinic in Hornchurch. But, to Debbie's amazement, as soon as he entered the premises, her son turned from monster to cherub.

'Hello, Charlie. My name's Dr Foster.'

'Hello, Dr Foster,' Charlie replied angelically.

The doc let him play with some toys and gently asked him a few questions. Charlie answered every single one, intelligently and politely. Trying a different tactic, the psychiatrist handed Charlie a crayon and some paper and asked him to draw pictures. Charlie liked drawing and was happy to oblige. Dr Foster then told Debbie to pay at reception and to book a follow-up appointment with his secretary.

Four appointments and a hundred and sixty quid later, Debbie realised that she was wasting Mickey's money and her time. Every time Charlie entered Dr Foster's clinic he changed from little bastard to little cherub. At the end of the fourth visit, the doc pulled Debbie aside.

'To be honest, Miss Dawson, I don't think Charlie needs our help. He's a very bright, stable, cheerful little boy, and although I'm quite happy to keep on taking your money, I can assure you, with my thirty years of experience, I consider that there is nothing wrong with your son what-soever.'

'Thank you, Doctor,' Debbie said, taking Charlie by the hand.

Five minutes down the road, the cherub was gone and in its place was the bastard.

'I want McDonald's,' Charlie demanded.

'No, not today, Charlie. Mummy's cooking you a nice roast dinner. You can have McDonald's at the weekend.'

'Nooooo,' he screamed, pulling away from her hand and sitting firmly on the ground.

'Get up off that pavement now,' Debbie said.. Charlie had as usual attracted the attention of passers-by.

'You're not being a naughty boy for your mummy, are you?' asked a little old lady.

'Cunt, cunt, cunt,' Charlie said, smiling at her.

'I am so sorry,' Debbie said apologetically.

Wondering if her hearing aid had been deceiving her, the little old lady walked away in shock.

'Get up now!' Debbie screamed at her son.

'No. If you don't get me McDonald's, I'm gonna run in the road,' he said, still smiling. Debbie knew that she was making a rod for her own back by giving in to him all the time. Her mother, Peter, her brother . . . they'd all said the same thing. Deciding it was high time she made a stand, she lifted up the kicking and screaming child and half dragged him to the nearest bus stop.

Now, Charlie was not a child to appreciate being thwarted. Deciding to pay his mother back in the worst way that he could, he flashed her his angelic smile.

'Sorry, Mummy. Put me down now?'

Debbie was as pleased as punch that, for once, she'd stood her ground and won.

'Will you promise to be a good boy?' she asked gently as she put him on his feet.

'Yes, Mummy.'

Charlie stood next to her, waiting to seize his opportunity. He wasn't stupid, he had no intention of killing himself, but he needed to teach silly Mummy a lesson. He watched the cars trundle past and waited for the appropriate moment to make his move. Then, quick as a ferret, he darted into the road.

'No, Charlie, no!' Debbie screamed as she chased after him.

Ten minutes later she was sitting in McDonald's, watching the little fucker munch happily away on a cheeseburger and fries.

'Want a chip, Mummy?' he asked innocently.

Debbie shook her head. She was still shaking from shock. Deciding that she couldn't face going back to the bus stop, she called one of the staff over. 'Excuse me, I'm sorry to bother you but my little boy just nearly got run over. It's made me feel ill. Would you be able to call me a cab, please?'

After putting Charlie to bed that evening, Debbie reached for the bottle of wine that had lain unopened in her refrigerator for the past week. She felt a complete and utter mental wreck.

Meanwhile, upstairs, Charlie lay in bed so hyped up that he was having difficulty sleeping. He smiled to himself. His mum, nan, uncle, the doc – they all thought they could work him out, but they had no chance. Only he knew how his mind ticked and he intended to keep it that way. Today had been a great day. He liked his visits to the silly doctor. As for his mum, her face had been a picture when he'd run into the road. Giggling, he stood on his bed. Laughing hysterically, he bounced up and down.

Debbie topped up her glass and stared at the bottle. She'd had the day from bloody hell. The trips to the psychiatrist had been a complete and utter waste of time. She was no nearer to understanding her son than she ever had been.

Debbie sat up thinking into the early hours that night, more worried about Charlie than before. Momentarily she had felt such relief when Dr Foster had said there was nothing wrong with him, but deep down she had known she was only kidding herself.

'How can a five-year-old child con a professional, with over thirty years' experience?' she muttered as she tried to fathom the impossible.

Even as she said it, she realised that it was because her child was cleverer than the psychiatrist. Unlikely, but true. And despite her annoyance with him, she felt suddenly proud of her son. Giving birth to her Charlie had been the best day of her life, Debbie told herself firmly. She would rather die than give up on him now.

NINETEEN

Mickey Dawson walked back from the bar with a pint in each hand and two packets of peanuts dangling from his mouth. Sitting down opposite his pal, he opened his jaws and let the nuts fall gracefully on to the table.

'Right, come on, Steve me old mucker, let's have it. What's bothering ya?'

Steve shifted uncomfortably in his seat, unable to look Mickey in the eye.

'What you on about? I'm fine,' he mumbled unconvincingly.

'Come on, it's me you're talking to, you soppy bastard. You can tell me anything, you know that, Steve.'

Wiping the beads of sweat off his forehead with his arm, Steve knew it was now or never to bring up the subject that had been plaguing him for the last few weeks.

'Well, it's a bit awkward, Mickey. I don't really know where to start . . . '

Mickey smiled at his pal's embarassment and decided to wind him up a bit more. Pointing at Steve's groin area, he tried to keep the humour from his voice.

'You ain't got trouble with the old meat and two veg, have you, son?'

'No, I fucking well ain't,' Steve said angrily.

Enjoying himself immensely, Mickey carried on. 'Only,

if you've caught a dose or your old pecker's packed up, I know a good cock doctor. I'll book an appointment for you if you want. I'll even go with you, if you can't face going alone.'

'Fuck off, Mick, there's nothing wrong with me cock,' Steve replied, agitated.

'Well, what is it then?' Mickey asked, laughing out loud.

Steve took a deep breath. 'You know me and your Debs have been seeing quite a bit of each other? We get on well, and to be honest, Mick, I really like her. Well, I was thinking of asking her out on a proper date, but I didn't know if you'd approve. What with all the shit she's been through and her being your sister, I dunno if it's the done thing. I don't wanna make things awkward between me and you.'

Mickey sipped his beer and smiled. 'After watching Debs waste her life with McDaid, I'd be pleased if she told me she was going out with Adolf Hitler, let alone you, you tosser. Go ahead and ask her, Steve. I'd be more than happy if you and our Debs got it together.'

'Cheers, mate,' Steve said, relieved that his big secret was now out in the open. 'Do you think she'll go on a date with me, Mick? She's always inviting me round for dinner and that, but a date's different, innit?'

Mickey handed him a fag. 'Look, if she didn't like you, she wouldn't be asking you round there all the time. Whenever I go round there, she's always "Steve this" and "Steve that". In this life, you've gotta take your chances, mate. If you don't ask, you don't get. Now get your arse in gear and get me another drink. I've gotta mouth like a nun's crotch.'

As he looked at his pal's lumbering physique, Mickey smiled to himself. Steve would be a great bloke for Debbie. He was a big old lump with a heart of gold and Mickey just hoped that Debs didn't knock him back. Steve was great with blokes, a typical man's man, but around women he seemed to lack confidence. He and Debs would be a match made in heaven.

Debbie carefully put the mashed potato on top of the mince and popped the shepherd's pie into the preheated oven. Hearing a racket coming from the living room, she stopped in her tracks.

'What are you doing in there, Charlie?'

'Just watching telly, Mummy.'

Knowing he was doing no such thing, Debbie went to inspect. 'You naughty boy, why have you done that?' she asked, noticing that he'd ruined her carefully laid arrangement on the dining table.

Charlie giggled.

'Right, bath and bedtime for you, I think.'

'Nooooo,' Charlie screamed, as he lay on the floor and refused to budge.

As Debbie tried to repair the damage, she was furious to see that he'd also drawn in crayon over her fresh white tablecloth. That was the final straw. Grabbing him by the arm, she dragged him kicking and screaming up the stairs, then locked him in his bedroom.

'I want my daddy. I hate you!' he shouted through the door.

Determined not to let Charlie spoil her night, Debbie went into her bedroom to get changed. She'd bathed and washed her hair earlier, and all she needed was a bit of slap and a change of clothes. As she looked in the mirror, she smiled. She looked passable now. She'd tanned up well, the garden had seen to that. The recent dentistry work which had repaired her two front teeth, kindly paid for by Mickey, had added to her confidence no end. The only hang-up she still had was about her wonky nose, but she could live with that, if the rest of her features looked okay. Even her hair had grown back and been trimmed in a trendy layered cut.

Realising that the shouting and swearing in Charlie's room had stopped, she quietly opened the door and was relieved to find him sleeping peacefully. Curled up on top of the quilt in his Batman pyjamas, he looked almost angelic. It was hard to believe that this was the same child who spewed out vulgar words, morning, noon and night. Where he got them from was a mystery. He swore more now than when Billy had been around.

Tiptoeing down the stairs, Debbie went to check on the shepherd's pie.

Steven Arthur Roberts tried on his third and final shirt. Realising he'd put on weight and couldn't do up the buttons, he took it off and put on the first one again. It was almost three years since Steve had last worn a shirt and that had been for a funeral. Noticing he was running late, he grabbed the keys to his pick-up truck and steamed out of the door.

Debbie re-laid the table and sat twiddling her fingers. Nerves getting the better of her, she headed to the fridge to pour herself a glass of wine. She didn't really know why she felt the way she did. Big Steve had been a good mate for a few months now. At first she would never have believed that she could feel anything other than friendship for the hulking, muscular, shaven-headed sort who happened to be her brother's best friend. But lately her feelings had changed. The more time she spent in Steve's company, the more she liked him. For some reason or other, he made her feel safe, secure and womanly, and all of a sudden she couldn't stop thinking about him.

'All right, Debs?' Steve greeted her gruffly when he

arrived on her doorstep. He handed her a cold bottle of Chardonnay.

'You look nice, Steve. I've never seen you in a shirt before.'

Embarrassed but quick witted, he replied, 'I thought I'd make the effort. Anyway, you can talk . . . you've got a skirt on. I didn't know you had legs!'

Thrusting a beer at him, Debbie burst out laughing. 'Get your arse in there and sit at the table, you tosser.'

The rest of the evening passed pleasantly. Steve wolfed down his own dinner and finished off Debbie's. The pair of them drank plenty and didn't stop bantering and laughing, throughout the meal and afterwards.

Charlie woke up just the once, but Debbie managed to settle him down again quickly.

She then stuck on the video of *An Officer and a Gentleman* and Steve took the piss all the way through it. As the credits rolled he glanced at his watch. It was one in the morning and he knew he had to say something. It was now or never.

'Better make a move, Debs,' he said, picking up his keys.

'All right. Thanks for coming round, I really enjoyed it,' she replied, meaning every word.

Steve hovered awkwardly by the door. He was sweating like a pig. He stuttered and stammered as he tried to find the right words. 'Debs, can we go out? You know, on a proper date, like? I'll take you somewhere really nice. If you don't wanna go, I'll understand and still be your mate.'

Debbie looked at the gentle giant standing three feet away from her and felt nothing but admiration for him. 'Of course I'll come. I thought you'd never ask me, you silly sod.'

Overjoyed by her response, but not used to being in

this situation, he gave her a quick peck on the cheek. It was the type of kiss you'd give to an aunt you didn't like. He promised to ring her the next morning, then shot out of the door like a greyhound leaving the traps at Romford.

Giggling at his shyness, Debbie poured herself the last drop of wine left in the bottle. She'd had a wonderful night and being asked out was the icing on the cake. Steve was such a nice guy and looked out for her like her brother always had. Billy she had found physically attractive, but with Steve it was different. Over the months he'd been coming round she'd fallen for him as a person. He was kind, generous and extremely funny. Debbie finished her drink and went happily to bed.

Steve opened the front door and was relieved to see that Mickey wasn't there. He wanted to think over all that had happened tonight and didn't need his best pal winding him up.

Unable to stop smiling, he cracked open a can of Foster's and flicked through the TV channels. He was ecstatic that Debs had agreed to go on a date with him. He couldn't wait to take her out properly and decided he would treat her like a queen; she deserved it, and he would never let her down.

Steven Arthur Roberts, aka Big Steve, had been born in a tiny flat above a hardware shop along the Bethnal Green Road. The eldest of two boys, Steve had been extremely close to his mum, Maureen. Big Mo, as she was known, had brought up him and his brother on her own and he was devastated when she was diagnosed with breast cancer and cruelly taken from them. At sixteen years old, determined that his younger brother Lee would not fall into the hands of Social Services, Steve took up the reins. With the help of his Auntie Doll, he brought up his brother himself and did a bloody good job of it.

Apart from his mum and Auntie Doll, Steve had had very little to do with women, though. At school he'd ignored the girls. He was more interested in making a few bob and boxing than in messing about with birds. After leaving school, he met a girl called Sandra in a pub one night. Forward, and as rough as old boots, Sandra seduced him and he lost his virginity to her. He was gutted when he found out she was the local bike and had only shagged him for a bet.

Put off women for a long, long time after that, he was twenty-two when he met Julie. She was a lively one, a bit of a party girl with bleached blonde hair and a thing for Spandau Ballet. Steve treated her really well and spent all his hard-earned money on her. He worked hard, running a shoe stall for a geezer in Roman Road Market.

Julie spent all her spare time on the stall with him. Steve thought it was because of her love for shoes as well as him, but unfortunately it turned out she was shagging the geezer opposite who had a stall selling discount handbags. Once he had found out the truth, Steve went to work the following Saturday morning and beat the object of her affections into next week. The market inspector and the police were called, and so was Steve's guv'nor who had no choice but to sack him on the spot.

Jobless and loveless, Steve decided women were nothing but fucking trouble. He started ducking and diving for a living, someone had to put food on the table for his little brother. It was around this time that he met Mickey, only a kid then himself and also working on the market. A couple of dodgy deals later, Mickey jacked in the Roman and the pair of them set up in business. With Steve's brawn and Mickey's brain, they worked well together and had never looked back since, apart from Mickey's short spell inside. Steve was not involved in that. He hadn't liked the set-up and had opted out, urging his pal to do the same, but Mickey being Mickey had learned the hard way.

Finishing his beer, Steve turned the telly off and happily climbed the stairs. He was in love and it felt great. Being older and wiser now, he knew this time was different. Debbie was nothing like the Sandras and Julies of this world and he was determined, given a chance, to make her the happiest girl alive.

Grinning, he jumped into his pit. Third time lucky, as the old saying goes. She was the one, he knew it. He could feel it in his bones.

TWENTY

Steve rang, as promised, the next day and the big date was arranged for the following Saturday evening. June was overjoyed and booked herself in to baby-sit.

That morning, Debbie jumped on a 103 bus and dragged her whingeing son to Romford where she intended to purchase a new outfit for her big night out. She hadn't bought anything new for ages, partly because of money worries, and partly because she rarely went out and didn't see the point in wasting what little spare cash she had on herself when she could spend it on Charlie instead.

Her mum was living and breathing Debbie's news, though, and slipped fifty quid into her bag, telling her to treat herself to something nice to wear for the big occasion.

Shopping with Charlie was an ordeal, however. By the time she hit the third shop, Jane Norman, Debbie had had a gutful and wanted to get home.

As she picked up a top, she heard a commotion behind her, turned around and found Charlie lying on the floor amongst a pile of clothes. Unfortunately, he'd swung on a rail and toppled the bloody thing over. Embarrassed, Debbie picked up the only thing she even remotely liked, an army-green safari dress. She apologised profusely to the young shop assistant, hurriedly paid for the item and left the shop red-faced, hoping against hope that the bloody thing fitted.

Later on that evening, she was pleasantly surprised with the results. The dress clung to her and the style suited her to a tee. She'd already made her mind up that if it looked like shit, she'd wear her old faithful black dress and take the new one back on Monday morning. Thankfully, now she wouldn't have to.

To finish her outfit off, she chose thick black tights, long black boots, a black handbag and a cute little bolero. Debbie wasn't used to wearing frocks, but this one was a bit of her. The accessories she'd chosen added femininity to it and she was more than happy with the result.

Debbie headed downstairs to seek her mother's approval. 'Well, how do I look?'

Tears of pride welled up in June's eyes. 'Oh, Debs, you look beautiful. I can't believe we've finally got you in a bleeding dress.'

Charlie turned away from the cartoon he was engrossed in and stared at his mother. He knew she was going out with that horrible man who kept coming round and was determined to put his little boot in. He chose his nasty voice and spoke extra loudly. 'You look fat, Mummy. Pig, pig, pig,' he chanted.

Seeing the hurt expression in her daughter's eyes, June took matters into her own hands. 'Right, bath-time for you and then bed,' she shouted to her grandson, wishing she could leave him alone in the bathroom and that the little bastard would drown.

'Nooooo,' screamed Charlie, lying face down on the floor while he punched and kicked the carpet.

'Well, behave yourself then. One more word out that vulgar little mouth of yours and I'll put you to bed for the night, understand?'

Charlie might have been a lot of things but stupid

wasn't one of them. He knew by the stern sound of his nan's voice that she meant business.

'Sorry, Nanny. Sorry, Mummy,' he said with false remorse.

Ignoring him, June turned to her daughter. 'Let's go into the kitchen. We'll have a nice glass of wine and you can tell me all about you know who.'

Charlie watched them both leave the room. 'You know who' meant 'Big Fat Bastard'. Did they really suppose he was so dumb he didn't know who they were talking about? He could read, write, understand and spell like a good 'un, and they'd have to be a damn' sight cuter to get one up on him. Annoyed, he turned his attention back to *Wacky Races*. His mum had introduced him to the programme. It had been a favourite of hers when she was a little girl and she'd bought him all the videos. Charlie loved Dastardly and Muttley. They were his favourites, and always cheered him up when he felt angry with life.

Steve sprayed himself with Kouros aftershave and glanced at his reflection in the mirror. He'd shot up the Bethnal Green Road this morning and invested in a new suit and shirt. Pleased with his smarter image, he headed downstairs to the anticipated piss-taking from Mickey.

'Well, well, well. If it ain't Weight Watchers' answer to Johnny Cash. You look like you're going to a funeral, you cunt. What did ya buy black for?'

'Fuck off, Mick,' Steve said, half-laughing but annoyed at the same time.

'Where you taking her then, the fucking Ritz?' Mickey was surprised by the effort his pal had gone to, but secretly chuffed all the same.

'I'm taking her up West. I've booked a nice little Italian and then I'll take her to a couple of clubs I used to do the door on. We might even end up in Stringfellows –

just go with the flow, like. What you doing? You going out yourself, Mick?'

Mickey took a sip from his can of Foster's. 'By the looks of it, I might as well sit here and prepare me best man's speech! No, seriously, I've having a night in. I feel absolutely shattered. I'm gonna order a Chinese later . . . takeaway that is, not a bird . . . and have a few cans, stuff me face and watch *Match of the Day*.'

'Right, I'm off then,' said Steve, picking up the keys to Mickey's Merc.

'You can't take our Debs out in that monster of a truck. You'll look like something out of the *Dukes of* fucking *Hazzard*,' Mickey had pointed out earlier, before offering his friend the use of his car for the evening.

Driving towards Debbie's, Steve was as nervous as hell. His heart was beating ten to the dozen. He felt like a schoolboy about to have his first wank.

'He's here, Debs,' June shouted excitedly when she heard the doorbell go.

Debbie answered the door and was presented with the biggest bouquet she'd ever seen, let alone received. 'Oh, Steve, they're beautiful! You shouldn't have. Come in a minute, so I can put them in water.'

Steve shuffled into the hallway and stood awkwardly by the staircase.

'Where you gone?' Debbie shouted. 'Don't be shy, come and say hello to me mum.'

After shaking June's hand and giving her a polite kiss on the cheek, he chatted to her for about ten minutes, mainly about Mickey.

Determined not to be forgotten, Charlie wandered into the kitchen.

Steve ruffled his hair. 'All right, son?'

'You're not my dad. Go away. I hate you,' came the charming reply.

June shoved him back into the lounge and smacked him before returning to apologise. 'I'm so sorry, Steve. He's a little shit, honestly.' She lowered her voice and shut the kitchen door. 'Between me and you, he's got a lot of problems. Been through a bit too much, what with his father and all that.'

'It's fine, don't worry. Mickey's told me the score,' Steve replied.

Debbie opened the kitchen door. 'Ready to make tracks?'

'Don't she look lovely, Steve? Beautiful, ain't she?' June said.

'Mum, shut up, will you!'

Squirming, Debbie shoved Steve out of the door before her mother started with her baby photos.

'Sorry about that, Steve. She's a bloody nightmare.'

Starting up the engine, Steve smiled at her. 'She's right, though, you do look beautiful.'

'Not you an' all. Just shut up and drive, will ya?' Debbie said, punching him playfully on the arm.

The Italian restaurant that Steve had chosen was top drawer and the food was exquisite. With neither of them used to too much class, they had a right old laugh trying to work out what the dishes on the menu were. Eventually they included the waiter in their banter with Debbie joking, 'We're only used to pie, mash and liquor. Give us a hand to order, mate, eh?'

After three bottles of wine and some of the best pasta he'd ever tasted, Steve's nerves had gone and he was his normal, entertaining, piss-taking self.

'Where we going next then?' Debbie asked, as he shouted for the bill.

'I used to do a lot of door work in this neck of the woods. I'll take you to a couple of the clubs I used to work at. We'll drop the motor off first, though. There's a

158

pal of mine who lives five minutes round the corner. I'll leave the car there, we'll get a cab, and me and Mickey'll pick the car up tomorrow.'

Having never been for a night out in the West End before in her life, the clubs Steve took her to were a proper eye-opener for Debbie and she loved every minute of it. They met rich people, wacky people, tourists . . . it was a world she had only heard about before.

When Steve left her for a few minutes to visit the Gents, Debbie sipped her cocktail and thought what a loser Billy had been. What she'd seen in him, she would never know if it turned round and smacked her in the face. Steve was different, a proper geezer. The way he'd been greeted in the three clubs they'd visited so far showed her just how respected and popular he was.

'What you thinking about?' Steve asked, rubbing his wet, freshly washed hands on her cheeks.

'Just thinking about you and how different you are from Billy. He was such a wanker, Steve. What was I thinking, eh?'

Planting a soft kiss on her forehead, Steve smiled at her. 'Forget Billy boy. We all make mistakes, girl. Your past is your past. Me and you, we're the future. Now, how do ya fancy Stringfellow's?'

'Yes, please!' she cried, clapping her hands excitedly.

As she stood in Stringfellow's later, drinking yet another cocktail, Debbie thought she'd died and gone to heaven. Recognising two soap stars, a footballer and spotting a TV presenter, whom she couldn't quite place, she couldn't believe that she, Debbie Dawson, was standing here amongst these famous people. With Billy she'd never gone further than the Hope and Anchor in Barking. She couldn't believe the change in her luck.

When Peter Stringfellow headed their way, shook Steve's hand and ordered them a drink on the house, she stood rooted to the spot, eyes like organ stops. As he walked away, she frantically nudged Steve. 'How do you know Peter Stringfellow?'

Taking a sip of his drink, Steve casually said, 'Just through the doors and stuff. He knows Mickey as well. We've been here a few times over the years.'

Astonished by her date's popularity, Debbie had the most exciting evening of her life, but sadly the cab journey home was too much for her. The numerous cocktails proved fatal and unfortunately she slung her guts up in the back of the black cab.

'I'm really sorry, mate,' Steve said, bunging the driver fifty quid, plus the fare, as he chucked them out in the middle of nowhere.

'Oh, God, Steve. I'm not used to drinking such large amounts,' Debbie managed to say, retching at the same time.

'Shhh, you're okay, babe. Just bring it all up and you'll feel better. Stick your fingers down your throat if you have to,' he replied, rubbing her back as if she were a newborn baby.

Twenty minutes later, Debbie felt more with it and a lot more sober. After gratefully taking some chewing gum from Steve, she apologised over and over again.

'I don't know what you must think of me. I haven't been out for ages . . . I'm so sorry if I've spoiled the evening.'

'Shut up, you dopey cow,' he said, and took her in his arms.

Holding her close to him, Steve kissed her gently on the forehead. He'd had a great night, probably the best night out with a bird he'd ever had, and he certainly wasn't gonna be put off by a bit of vomit. Deciding she looked well enough to travel again, he hailed another cab.

Outside Debs's house, he asked the driver to wait a minute while he made sure she got in all right.

'Do you fancy a coffee, Steve? My mum will be in bed by now and you're more than welcome to come in,' Debbie offered.

Looking at his watch, Steve decided against the idea. 'It's nearly four o'clock, Debs. I'd better shoot. Mickey'll have me up at the crack of dawn once he sees his car never made the journey home. I've gotta fuck about picking that up.'

Debbie felt a slight pang of disappointment. She was dead tired herself, but would have liked a kiss and a cuddle. Praying she hadn't put him off by making a show of herself, she took the initiative. 'What you doing tomorrow night then? I could cook you a nice dinner, if you like, to say thank you for a wonderful night out.'

He smiled and dropped a kiss on her nose. 'That'd be nice, Debs, really nice.'

Debbie breathed a sigh of relief as they arranged to meet at eight o'clock that evening. Jumping back into the cab, Steve gave the driver directions for the short journey home.

'That your girlfriend, mate?' the driver asked nosily.

Feeling like the King of England, Steve slung his arm across the top of the seat. 'Yeah, mate, that's my girl,' he said confidently.

The driver looked at his fare in the mirror. He was tired and chatting kept him awake after a long shift. 'I hope you don't mind me saying, but you look really well suited. I see all sorts in this job, but I rarely see anybody as happy as you two seem to be.'

Steve smiled. 'Well suited ain't the word, mate. I love that girl and very soon I'm gonna make her my wife!'

TWENTY-ONE

June buttered two slices of wholemeal toast, put the eggs into dainty little cups, stirred the coffee and took the laden tray upstairs to Debbie.

'Wakey, wakey. Well, how did it go? I've been like a cat on a hot tin roof all morning – you know what a nosey cow I am. Where did he take you? Do you really like him?'

Sitting up in bed made Debbie realise just how severe her headache was. The sight of her breakfast was the final straw. She ran, gagging, towards the bathroom.

A disappointed June headed back downstairs to keep an eye on her naughty grandson. Glancing at the clock on the kitchen wall, she noticed it was midday. 'Shit,' she mumbled as she remembered she'd promised Peter she'd be home by lunchtime for the surprise he had in store for her. Not knowing what to do for the best, she decided to use Debbie's phone to let him know she was going to be late.

Ever since she'd stood up to Peter over his attitude to her kids, he'd treated her with more respect and given her more leeway. On a personal level he had virtually nothing to do with Debbie or Mickey, but he always enquired after them and seemed happy to listen to whatever stories June told him about her children. Charlie was a different story, though. Understandably, he hated her grandson with a passion. Resigning from his council position had affected Peter deeply. He kept himself to himself now. He avoided Masonic parties, scarcely ever played golf any more, and rarely went out without her.

Having him under her feet all the time secretly drove June round the bend. He was the old-fashioned type who insisted the man should wear the trousers in the home and, to keep the peace, she found it easier to let him do so, no matter how much it grated. The only thing that had changed was that she now put her own kids first, as she should have done in the first bloody place.

June dialled her home number and waited patiently while it rang. Peter was going to have the right hump, she knew that, but what else could she do? Debbie was upstairs spewing her guts up, and she could hardly leave Charlie downstairs on his own to wreck the joint. Taking the child home with her was a definite no go. Peter had banned him from the house for life.

Finally there was an answer. 'Hello, Peter speaking.'

June braced herself. 'Oh hello, love, it's only me. I've got a bit of a problem. Debbie's got gastroenteritis . . . she can't stop being sick. I'm going to have to stay here and look after Charlie, there's no one else to have him.'

Peter was annoyed, very annoyed. He had been looking forward to this afternoon for weeks and had planned it with his usual precision.

'June my dear, today of all days you must not do this to me. I've made a lovely picnic for us and I'm taking you somewhere very special. If you let me down, my love, I won't be a happy man, especially after all the trouble I've gone to to arrange this.'

June held the receiver away from her ear. He was so bloody patronising sometimes. No wonder he'd always got on her kids' nerves. Deciding to stand her ground, she spoke calmly but firmly.

'My daughter needs me, Peter. Where were you meant to be taking me anyway? Can't we do it another day?'

Not liking his surprises to be spoiled, but realising he had no other option but to let her know what she would be missing, Peter said proudly: 'Today, my dear, I am taking you to see the home of the one and only Winston Churchill. I have organised a tour around the house and grounds, and we will enjoy our picnic sitting romantic-ally in his garden.'

June could feel her blood boiling. A surprise for *her*? She didn't bloody think so! She'd been dragged up in the East End of London and had never taken any interest whatsoever in politics. She listened politely whenever her husabnd spoke about them, and had always shown a proper interest in his one-time political career, but secretly it bored her shitless. To her, politics was a complete and utter load of old bollocks. They were all lying bastards, and once they got into government ended up breaking every promise they'd bloody well made in the first place.

Fuming to hear about her so-called surprise, June let him have it. 'If you think for one minute that I'm going to put a trip to a dead politician's house in front of helping out my own daughter, my flesh and blood, you've got another think coming! As for the actual surprise . . . I couldn't think of anything worse. It's all about you, isn't it, Peter? You're the one who's into politics, not me. So why is it *my* fucking surprise?'

Shocked by her outburst and atrocious language, Peter spoke calmly but with a hint of sarcasm. 'Do you have to swear, my dear? You sound like a fishwife. Is it really so terrible that I made us a lovely picnic and arranged a pleasant day out? You can be very ungrateful at times, June. As for young Deborah, are you sure she's not suffering from alcohol poisoning rather than gastroenteritis? It was only last night she was out partying. Bit of a coincidence, don't you think?'

Lying through her teeth, June hit back at him. 'How dare you! That poor little cow never goes out, and when she does she hardly drinks. I know my own daughter, and I know when she's ill . . . and I certainly don't need *you* calling me a liar. I may not be a perfect parent, Peter, and I'm the first to admit that my kids have their faults, but at least we're a family. We care about each other. You've been a terrible father, you have. I've never known a man have less contact with his child, except for my ex . . . and *he* was an arsehole. You don't speak to your Dolores from one year to the next, so you're certainly not in any pos-ition to be judging other people's family values.'

Annoyed that she'd brought up his strained relationship with his own daughter, Peter became even more sarcastic.

'*Your* family is like something off that bloody soap opera, *EastEnders* or whatever it's called. Prison sentences, unwanted pregnancies, domestic violence – there's always a bloody drama! And as for that evil little grandson of yours . . . he'll prove to be the biggest drama yet. I may not speak to my Dolores as much as I should, but that's because she's extremely busy. Unlike your brood, she's made something of her life. The girl is a top-class lawyer and has done fantastically well for herself, thank you very much. Which is more than I can say for the Dawson tribe.'

Insulting her was one thing, June could take that with a pinch of salt, insulting her kids was a different story.

'Well, if me and my kids aren't good enough for you, Peter, you know what you can do. Divorce me, you wanker, see if I fucking care!'

165

June slammed the phone down and flopped on to Debbie's sofa. They'd rowed before, but never like this. Shaking with temper, she headed out to the kitchen in search of alcohol. She found half a bottle of wine in Debbie's fridge and poured herself a glass. She needed to calm down. Annoyed with herself for letting her guard slip and showing her common side, she took a long sip from the glass.

Dressed up in his cowboy outfit, Charlie had been playing in the garden, shooting imaginary Indians. Hearing raised voices, he'd sneaked into the kitchen and heard the whole row. Seeing his nan sitting at the table looking sad, he decided to try and cheer her up.

'I don't like Granddad. I hope he dies, Nanny.'

Not quite believing her ears, June couldn't help but scream at the child. 'Get out of my fucking sight! I'm not in the mood for you, Charlie. Believe me, I'm not.'

By the look on her face, he knew she meant business. Giggling to himself, he headed outdoors to shoot more Indians and, hopefully, next-door's cat.

Debbie had heard the commotion downstairs and decided it was time she got up and pulled herself together. Feeling slightly better, she chucked on her dressing gown and went to face the music.

June cried as she relayed the whole story.

'I'm so sorry, Mum. This is all my fault. I feel okay now, you get home to Peter and sort things out.'

'Are you sure, love?' June asked, already picking up her handbag.

'Positive, Mum.'

Cursing herself for losing her temper, June waved to her daughter and started the short walk home. Peter annoyed her, wound her up no end, but in her heart she loved him and would be devastated if they were to split up. Now she'd calmed down, she felt terrible about the nasty things she'd said to him. She didn't lose her temper often but, when she did, she lost control completely and swore like a washerwoman. As the old saying goes: You can take the girl out of the East End, but you can't take the East End out of the girl. Furious with her own big gob, she headed home to try and put things right.

Walking around Tesco with the hangover from hell *and* Charlie was no mean feat, but somehow Debbie managed it. As she unpacked her shopping she smiled to herself and began to look forward to the night ahead. Sirloin steak, sautéed potatoes, mushrooms and beef-flavoured rice was her chosen menu, followed by a shop-bought apple pie and cream. She hated bloody cooking, but Steve was well worth the effort.

'Mummy, I'm hungry.'

As she sat down next to Charlie, she watched him greedily devour his chicken nuggets, chips and beans. Smiling at his appetite, Debbie gently ruffled his hair and decided that now was as good a time as any to have a quiet word with him.

'Mummy's friend Steve is coming over later, Charlie, and I was thinking . . . if you're a good boy, Mummy will let you stay up for a bit. Maybe we can all play some games, or watch a cartoon together. What do you think?'

Charlie's previously happy expression instantly changed to a dark one. 'Don't want him here. Don't wanna play games. Don't wanna do nuffink.'

Debbie handed him his vanilla ice-cream and tried to bargain with him. 'Please, Charlie. Be a good boy for Mummy. Steve's a nice man when you get to know him and Mummy's got to have friends, hasn't she?'

With his bottom lip pouting spectacularly, Charlie threw his spoon on to the floor. Looking at his mother out of the corner of his eye, he decided to be naughty. He knew she hated him saying bad words, so he thought of the worst thing he could say.

'Are you sucking his cock, Mummy?'

Horrified, Debbie grabbed him by the arm. 'You naughty boy! Get up them stairs and into that bedroom – now.'

'Nooooo,' Charlie screamed, knocking the ice-cream bowl on to the floor and smashing it.

Debbie locked him in his bedroom, cleared up the mess in the kitchen, sat down at the table and poured herself a much-needed hair of the dog. Her child was enough to make a saint scream and she was at a complete loss as to what to do with him.

To seek professional help was totally out of the question. He'd already made a mug out of one psychiatrist and, at forty quid a shot, it was a rather expensive hobby. Racking her brains, she tried to think of the answer. Suddenly it came to her. What Charlie really needed was a man around the house. Someone who would take no shit off him, and really take him in hand. The boy needed to be taught manners and respect. She knew he would never listen to her. Mickey wasn't around a lot, but when he was Charlie played up a lot less, which only proved her point.

What her son needed was rules and discipline, and it was too late in the day for her to enforce them. With a man's backing she could do it, but not on her own. Sipping her wine, she decided that Steve was the ideal candidate to sort Charlie out. He was a no-nonsense sort, just what her son needed. Whenever Steve had come round for dinner in the past, she'd made sure Charlie was safely tucked up in bed. He'd only had contact with the child when he'd popped round in the daytime. Hopefully, now, things could be different.

Daydreaming of her happy family life-to-be, Debbie

went upstairs to get ready. Pleased with her efforts, she went downstairs to make a start on dishing the dinner up. Steve would be here soon. A typical bloke, he was always starving and wanted feeding on the spot. Happily stirring the rice, she turned the radio on.

'You Are the Sunshine of My Life' was playing. Singing along with the soulful voice of Stevie Wonder, Debbie thought how appropriate the song was. Maybe it was a sign of good things to come, her turning on the radio at that particular moment.

As the doorbell rang, Debbie stopped singing. Smiling, she put the wooden spoon on the table and went to greet the man she hoped would bring some much-needed sunshine into her own life.

TWENTY-TWO

Billy McDaid lay back on the uncomfortable wooden bench and stared at the graffiti on the scuffed paintwork of the walls.

His game was up, he had no doubt about that. He also knew that very shortly the police at the Glasgow cop shop where he was being held would see through the false name he'd given them and then the fun would really start. He'd been pulled in for a drunken brawl and could kick himself for being so bloody stupid.

From the moment Billy had stepped off the train, battered and bruised from the hiding he'd taken from Mickey, he'd kept his head down and his nose clean. Hating Glasgow more than life itself, due to the memories that it held, he had returned only reluctantly, not knowing where to go or what to do. After sleeping rough for a couple of nights, he had decided to pay his Auntie Mary a visit, to see if she could put him up until he sorted himself out.

Mary was his mum's older sister. Complete opposites, his mother and aunt had never got along. Because of this, Billy had never had a great deal to do with his aunt, but on the odd occasion he had bumped into her she'd always been warm and kind to him. The day of his brother's funeral stood out in his mind particularly. His mother didn't even show up. It was his aunt who had held him, soothed him and wiped away his tears.

'If you need anything, laddie, anything at all, you come and see me. You know where I live and my door is always open to you,' Mary had told him. He could tell, by the look in her eyes, that it was a genuine offer. He could also tell that she felt sorry for him as she was well aware what kind of an upbringing he and his brother had had.

When he knocked on her door that day, he felt and looked like a tramp. Praying that she hadn't recently moved house, he was overcome by relief when she opened the door, made a fuss of him and welcomed him in with open arms. Things had looked up for Billy from that day onwards. After a lazy few weeks where he had done nothing but sleep, let his injuries heal and enjoy his aunt's wonderful cooking, he picked himself up and found a job, working locally on a building site. Normally work-shy, he was reasonably content with his new life. He liked the lads he was working with, they were a good laugh, and having a break from the drugs and drink had more or less cleared his head.

The main problem he had was himself. For Billy good things never lasted. His short attention span meant he got bored very easily. Unfortunately for him, boredom equalled trouble. Living with his aunt was good at first, she made him feel safe and secure, but gradually, as the weeks turned into months, he'd become more and more restless and had craved a part of his old life back. He wasn't being ungrateful; his aunt had been wonderful to him, and he would never bite the hand that had fed him so kindly. But, yearning to be the old Billy again, he made the fatal mistake of moving out of his Auntie Mary's and into a bed-sit with a guy he'd palled up with at work.

Johnny Archibald was a pisshead, a puffhead, and one of life's losers. In fact, he was the ideal person to help

171

Billy return to his old ways. Within weeks of moving in together, they had both been fired from their job for throwing sickies and turning up late. Billy then decided to go back to what he knew best: selling drugs. He and Johnny pooled their money together and started punting their trade around the roughest pubs in their local area.

Everything had been hunky-dory until last night when they'd accidentally trodden on somebody else's stamping ground and all hell had broken loose. Hence the reason why Billy was now locked up in a cell in Glasgow town centre, nervously awaiting his fate.

Because of his near-death experience at Mickey's hands, he had had no choice other than to jump bail for the assault on Debbie. It would all come out now, and he wouldn't see the light of day for a while, that was for sure. He was bound to be stuck here on remand until his case came to court. He'd given a false name last night, but the old bill were having none of it. Deciding to be a man and get it over with, he shouted for one of the officers. Within forty-eight hours of revealing his true identity, Billy McDaid was back in Pentonville, slopping out buckets of piss and shit.

The relationship between Debbie and Steve progressed rapidly after their first couple of dates. The pair of them had both been nervous about making love for the first time, and had ended up fumbling around like inexperienced teenagers. After losing their initial awkwardness, however, they were now thoroughly enjoying themselves. Steve was so much gentler with Debbie than Billy had ever been. He handled her like a priceless piece of china, whereas Billy had just shoved it in and pumped away. There had been no foreplay of any kind with him, just a quick wham, bam, thank you, mam, generally when he was inebriated or stoned out of his brain. Steve was kind and considerate, in bed and out, and had shown Debbie what true love could really be like.

The only downside to their relationship was Charlie's attitude to it. Debbie knew that her son hated her new man. Steve had tried with Charlie, he really had. He'd taken them on as a package, and apart from their lone nights out, when her mum baby-sat, tried to include Charlie in everything they did. At first Debbie had hoped that having a man with Steve's qualities around would bring her son out of himself, but it had turned out to have the opposite effect. Charlie was now a forlorn figure, lost in his own little world, and as hard as she tried, Debbie wasn't able to reach him at all. He still played up something chronic when she was alone with him, but when Steve was around he retreated to his bedroom and refused to come out. He talked constantly to an imaginary friend named Timmy, which Debbie found quite alarming. Many a time she'd listened outside his bedroom door and heard snippets of the conversations he was having with his make-believe pal. They included talk of death, torturing animals, and references to sex which were way too disturbing and advanced for a child of his age.

Charlie's schooling was another problem. Three times she'd been called in to have a word with his headmistress about her son's unusual and disruptive behaviour. Now he'd been issued with a final warning.

'We'll give Charlie one more chance, but after that, you'll have to find him a different school. Academically he's very promising, but his behaviour is appalling and he refuses to abide by our rules. His sexual awareness has also become a problem. His bad language and constant innuendos have begun to affect the other children. Thanks to your son, "suck my cock" has become a catchphrase in his class. This kind of conduct is not acceptable, Miss

Dawson, and I would advise you to have a very serious talk with Charlie.'

Not for the first time in her life, Debbie shuffled out of her son's school, red-faced and truly ashamed.

Sitting in a rough and ready café along the A13, Steve tucked into his fried breakfast, enjoying every mouthful. As he dunked bread into a yolk, he asked Mickey the question that had been uppermost in his mind.

'Mick, you know I'm taking Debs away this weekend for her birthday . . . well, I need your opinion on something. I'm thinking of getting a ring and proposing to her. Do you think she'd be up for it or do you think I'm jumping the gun?'

Mickey gulped down his tea to stop himself from choking. 'Fuck me! You don't hang about, do you, mate?'

Steve laid his knife and fork on the plate and stared intently at his friend. 'I love her so much, Mick, and things have moved really fast. We get on so well, why waste time? She's the one for me, I know that and I don't even care if we have a long engagement. I just wanna put a ring on her finger so I can say that she's mine, if you know what I mean.'

Mickey lit up a cigarette and thought seriously about the situation. He wasn't much of a one for relationships himself. He always had a bird in tow, but he chopped and changed 'em like the weather. Birds were aggro, and business came first with Mickey. That was why he was still single. He had the looks and the charm to pull any girl he wanted, but the dolly birds he tended to go for soon got the pox of him when they realised he was too busy to spend much time with them.

'I dunno what to say to you, Steve. You know what I'm like . . . relationships just come and go with me and I don't give a shit about any of 'em. You and Debbie are different, you've got something special. I mean, you're not stupid. If you feel the time's right, then go for it. I'd love to have you as a brother-in-law, you know that, and I couldn't pick a better geezer for our Debs.'

Shaking his best pal's hand, Steve sat at the table as proud as a peacock. He'd got the okay from Mickey and that meant the world to him. Now it was all down to Debs accepting his proposal. Deciding there was no time like the present, he asked Mickey for one more favour.

'I ain't got a clue about rings and stuff. Come with us, Mick, and help me choose a nice one.'

The weekend away to celebrate Debbie's birthday was a surprise for her and Steve didn't tell her where they were going until they'd reached the airport. She'd thought they were going somewhere in England, but he'd got hold of her passport on the quiet and sorted out a nice trip to Marbella. A pal of his and Mickey's owned a villa on the outskirts of Puerto Banus, and because he owed them more than a few favours had lent it to Steve in the hope of wiping the slate clean.

Steve had played his cards right by inviting Charlie along. He'd even had June sort out a passport for the child, but Charlie had flatly refused the offer of a holiday.

'Nooooo, nooooo, nooooo,' he'd screamed. 'Wanna stay here with Timmy. Hate you, hate you, hate you.'

Thankful that June had agreed to baby-sit, Debbie decided to forget about her troublesome son, even if it was only for one weekend, and enjoy a carefree birthday trip.

As they arrived at the airport she was full of excitement. She'd only ever been abroad once before, for a week in Menorca with her mum and Peter. Running around in the duty free section, she was like a kid in a sweet shop. 'Look, Steve. This is well cheap, clock this!'

175

'You pick out whatever you want,' he insisted.

Not used to such kindness but not wanting to take advantage of his good nature, Debbie chose her purchases sparingly, picking only a bottle of perfume, a lipstick and a book.

'It that all you want?' he asked, surprised.

'I don't need anything else,' she said honestly.

The flight was on time and Debbie loved every moment of being on the plane. She spent the first hour gabbling away to Steve and, when he dozed off, read the Jackie Collins novel she'd purchased at the airport.

On arrival, Debbie drank in everything. The midday humidity. The happy faces of holidaymakers. The nice Spanish man at Customs. Being with Steve made Debbie feel alive. Without having to worry about Charlie, she guiltily enjoyed the freedom she hadn't felt for a long time. Steve led her to a taxi and spent the entire journey giving her a history lesson.

'Look to your right, Debs. See that massive place over there? That belonged to Charlie Wilson. He was one of the Great Train Robbers.'

Buzzing with excitement, she craned her neck.

'And see that big white gaff on that hill . . . that's Freddie's. He was into gold bullion. He's a mate of your brother's. In fact, I think Mickey's been out here and stayed with him once or twice.'

Debbie was astounded. The properties were amazing and she couldn't believe that her brother and Steve knew all these people. It was a different world from her previous life with Billy. 'Wow, this is fantastic!' she said as she stepped into their villa.

'Ain't bad, is it, girl?' Steve grunted. Inwardly he was as pleased as punch that the place had turned out to be the nuts, but he wasn't one to show it.

'You are the best boyfriend I could ever wish for,'

Debbie screamed, as she dragged him towards their own private swimming pool.

Smiling to himself, Steve patted the ring that was hidden in his trouser pocket. Monday was her birthday. He planned to present her with it late on Sunday evening.

The weekend passed in a bubble of happiness. They ate, drank, made love, and barely left the villa.

On the Sunday morning, Steve told Debbie that he was popping out for a stroll, to see a man about a dog.

'I'll come with ya,' Debbie said, chucking a sarong over her bikini bottoms.

'You can't, Birthday Girl. I need to sort out your present.'

The evening that followed was one that Debbie would never forget as long as she lived. Steve walked into the living area that night wearing grey slacks and a crisp white shirt. He then presented her with a beautiful white gold and diamond bracelet. After telling her to put her glad rags on, he admired her new black dress, took her hand and escorted her to the most exquisite little restaurant she'd ever seen in the whole of her life.

The bistro specialised in seafood and was set within yards of the beach. Debbie felt like she'd died and gone to heaven as she sipped her fruity wine and watched the waves lap against the shore.

'You order for me, Steve,' she said, passing the menu back to him. She didn't have a clue about seafood and didn't want to make herself look an idiot. Taking the initiative, he opted for the lobster. He knew Debbie wasn't used to places like this and to be honest neither was he, but he'd had a damn' sight more experience of them than she had.

Debbie polished off the last of the sautéed potatoes. After wiping her mouth with a serviette, she smiled at Steve. 'Christ, that was lovely. It was the best fish and chips I've ever had.'

Steve laughed at her uneducated comment. She was a girl after his own heart. A night at the dogs and a curry was all she was used to, and he bloody well loved her for it.

'What are you laughing at?' Debbie asked, annoyed.

He was saved from answering by the singer starting his session. '"Teardrops keep falling fwom my Spanish eyes . . ."' he crooned.

Steve took Debbie's hand and dragged her on to the tiny, dimly lit dance floor. 'I don't arf love you, girl,' he mumbled as he wrapped her in his strong arms.

The rest of the evening passed in a romantic blur as the pair of them danced, drank and sang. At five to twelve, Steve nodded to the waiter to bring out the surprise birthday cake.

'Ladies and gentlemen, can I have your attention, pleeze?'

Picking up his guitar, Fernando the singer walked towards Debbie and Steve.

Juan the headwaiter walked out of the kitchen followed by the rest of the staff.

'"Happy Birthday to you, Happy Birthday to you, Happy Birthday, dear Debbie, Happy Birthday to you,"' they all sang in broken English.

As the cake came towards the table, Steve got off his chair and awkwardly dropped down on one knee.

'What you lost?' Debbie asked innocently, thinking he'd dropped something under the table.

Then her eyes fell on the white iced cake.

The words, 'Debbie will you marry me?' leaped out at her in bright green icing. She was speechless. This was totally unexpected and felt almost surreal.

Luckily Fernando, who loved nothing more than the sound of his own voice, was only too happy to take control of matters.

'Now ve have a special wequest for Debbie. Her boyfwiend Steph vant to ask her vewwy special question.'

Even though he'd had a skinful, Steve was as nervous as a kitten coming face to face with a Rottweiler. Shaking, he took the mike with one hand while pulling the velvet box out of his pocket with the other. He glanced around. Everyone in the restaurant was staring at him, customers, staff, there was even a stray dog outside that seemed to be looking his way . . . Suddenly the enormity of the situation hit him and he wished he had done things more privately. Talk about make yourself look a prick, he thought, as he reached for his wine and downed it in one. At last, he found his voice.

'Debs, I'm not the best with words so I'll keep this short and sweet. Since I've met you, girl, you've made me the happiest man alive and I love you so much. I know we ain't been together long, but I also know, without a doubt, that I wanna spend the rest of my life with you. Will ya marry me, babe?'

Thrusting the diamond ring towards her, he stared intently into her eyes. The staff, the customers, the singer, even the stray dog, sat rooted to the spot. Would she? Wouldn't she? The whole restaurant waited in silence.

TWENTY-THREE

Debbie wasn't used to being the centre of attention, and wished the ground would promptly open up and swallow her. For an unconfident person, she couldn't think of a worse way to be proposed to.

But as she looked into Steve's pleading eyes, she forgot about the gawping audience and smiled. She couldn't be angry with him, not after all the effort he'd gone to.

'The answer is yes, you silly sod. Of course I'll marry ya.'

Her reply seemed to take forever to come, and then the whole restaurant erupted into a mixture of cheers and clapping.

'Champagne on ze house,' shouted an excited Juan.

Pleased to have his mike back in his hand, Fernando dedicated the first song to Debbie and Steph. 'Love is in ze air, everyvere I look awound,' he sang, absolutely murdering the John Paul Young classic.

Steve wasn't happy. Twice now the Spanish cunt had said his name wrong.

'I'm gonna fucking kill you when I get you back to the villa,' Debbie said through gritted teeth as she dragged him onto the dance floor.

'What have I done?' Steve shrugged his shoulders, a picture of innocence.

Waving at an elderly couple who were mouthing 'Congratulations' in her direction, Debbie answered him like a ventriloquist.

'I've never felt such a prat in my whole life. We're surrounded by people we don't know from Adam, yet because of you, ya tosser, we're the evening's entertainment!'

Knowing that she wasn't really annoyed with him, Steve planted a smacker on her lips and carried on the banter.

'I had to do something special. I wanted to give you a night to remember.'

'Oh, you've certainly done that, dear. I'll never forget it till the day I die, you wanker!'

As the last verse of 'Love is in ze air' faded out, Debbie grabbed Steve by the hand and pulled him back to their table, thankful that the showcase was finally over.

The rest of the evening passed in a happy blur before the pair of them finally left the restaurant about three. Both of them were very drunk and Steve had major trouble opening the door to the villa.

'Fucking wonderful, Steph,' Debbie joked, plonking herself down on the steps to wait. 'As if it ain't bad enough you've made a complete show out of me tonight, I'm now gonna sit here freezing me tits off.'

On about the ninth attempt, the door opened and Steve fell arse up over the threshold. Debbie nearly wet herself, she was laughing so much. Steve picked himself up, picked her up, carried her into the bedroom and flung her down on the luxurious bed. The pair of them were out for the count within minutes, sleeping fully clothed in one another's arms.

The next morning Debbie woke up to the hangover from hell. 'I'm never mixing my drinks again,' she mumbled as she retched into the toilet.

'You said that after our first date, you fucking lush,' Steve told her, jokingly.

After showering and changing Debbie felt slightly better and agreed to go to breakfast with her fiancé. As she watched him tuck into a full English, though, she immediately felt queasy again.

'I hope I'm gonna be all right on the flight. What time we gotta leave?' she asked, turning her chair around slightly. The grease swimming around on his plate was doing her no favours at all.

'The flight's at three, I've called the cab for twelve,' Steve replied, squeezing her hand. He wasn't surprised she felt rough, considering the mixture they'd consumed the previous night. Wine, champagne, shots, Bailey's . . . they'd gone through the card. Even he had felt like shit this morning.

The flight home was slightly delayed, and when they finally got on the plane Debbie slept for the whole journey with her head on Steve's shoulder. Mickey had taken them to the airport and was waiting patiently for them now in the Arrivals hall.

'Well, how did it go?' he asked.

On hearing their good news, he hugged the pair of them. He was just as excited about it as they were.

By the time they hit the M25, Debbie felt a lot better and had livened up. 'Honestly Mick, I was so embarrassed at the time, but it turned out to be an hilarious night. The singer in there was such a wanker. "To ze happy couple," he kept saying. He couldn't say Steve's name properly, kept calling him Steph, and then he wouldn't stop singing songs for us. Steve kept taking glasses of champagne up to the stage for him, then about two o'clock I heard him singing "My Way" and all of a sudden he fell off the stage and had to be helped up by one of the waiters. Oh, Mick, it was so funny, honestly. I wish you'd been there, you'd have slaughtered him.'

Mickey nearly pissed himself laughing. Taking his eyes off the road, he glanced round at Steve. 'All right, Steph. That's them man boobs, ya cunt. I told you to lose some fucking weight.'

Not finding the joke at all funny, Steve nudged Debs. 'Thanks a lot, babe. I'll never hear the last of that now.'

Debbie smiled at his annoyance and quickly changed the subject. 'You staying tonight, Steve, or going home?' she asked.

'I dunno, babe, it's up to you.'

Mickey was still in hysterics. 'Why don't I stop at an offie and get some champagne? Mum'll definitely wanna join in the celebrations. I mean, it ain't every day a mother learns that her daughter's marrying a geezer called Steph!'

If Steve had been sitting in the front he would have clumped him. 'Just stop and get the drink, Mick, you wanker.'

'What's all this then?' June asked, as Mickey walked in carrying a case of champagne followed by Steve and Debbie.

'Shhh, where's Charlie?' Debbie asked softly. She knew how much her son would hate her good news and wanted to break it to him gently.

'I put him to bed about an hour ago, love. He's played me up rotten all day. Now don't keep me in suspense, what's going on?' June asked.

Ordering Mickey to go and get some glasses, Debbie ushered her family into the living room and shut the door. 'Guess what, Mum? Me and Steve are getting married,' she said happily, flashing her ring.

'Oh, Debs, that's fantastic news. I am so pleased for you, darling.' June's eyes filled with tears as she fell into her daughter's arms. Turning her attention to Steve, she hugged him too.

'Steve, welcome to the family, son.'

June studied Debbie's ring. 'Oh, Debs, you are such a lucky girl . . . it's beautiful.'

'I know,' Debbie said, truly meaning it.

June looked at her children with pleading eyes as she sipped her champagne. 'I promised Peter I'd be home soon, but I'd rather stay here and celebrate. Do you mind if I ring him, tell him the good news and invite him round?'

Debbie glanced at Mickey who shrugged his shoulders and answered for her.

'We don't mind, Mum, but I doubt he'll wanna come. He don't usually.'

June picked up the phone. 'He's been a lot better since I told him his fortune and has promised to make an effort to be more of a family man. With a wedding to arrange, we have to build some bridges.'

She took the phone into the kitchen so she could speak to her husband in private. Somehow she managed to persuade Peter to come round within the hour. 'Your wish is my command, my dear,' he told her sarcastically.

Debbie fiddled with the tuner on her stack system and found Capital Gold. In her eyes you couldn't have a celebration without a bit of music, and it was her mother's favourite station.

With June out in the kitchen, rustling up sandwiches, Debbie left Steve and Mickey talking business and tiptoed upstairs to check on Charlie. Opening his bedroom door, she crept into the room and sat on the edge of his little bed. He was fast asleep, bless him, with his arms firmly around Deputy Dawg. She studied him, taking in his handsome face with the slight smile that always made him look so happy as he slept. For some reason his features completely changed on awakening. Once his eyes were open, Charlie's lack of contentment altered his face and stole his beauty.

After kissing his forehead, Debbie sat down at the top of the stairs, deep in thought. She'd been so swept up in her trip to Marbella and surprise engagement that she'd barely had time to consider her son or his feelings. He hadn't taken to Steve, that was obvious. All she could do was hope and pray that he would begin to accept having him around the house and, as he grew older, build a relationship with him. Maybe, in time, Steve could take him to football or fishing. And in the future perhaps Charlie would have a brother or sister to play with. Maybe both. She was saved from worrying any more by the sound of the doorbell and the arrival of Peter.

The rest of the evening passed pleasantly and the champagne went down very nicely. Debbie was full of the proposal and the memorable evening they'd had. June asked questions galore. Peter, who still unfortunately suffered from a personality bypass, smiled politely and said nothing.

The sandwiches were eaten in minutes and June, forever the hostess, rushed into Debbie's kitchen with the empty plates and came back with mounds of cheese on toast.

'So, any idea when you'll set the date for?' she asked excitedly.

'We haven't had time to speak about it yet,' Debbie replied, smiling at Steve.

He turned to June. 'I'll leave it all to Debbie to decide. I love her to bits and would marry her tomorrow, she knows that.'

'Ahhh, it's so romantic! Do you remember our wedding, Peter? We had a wonderful day, didn't we, love?' June said.

'Yes, dear, it was very nice.' Peter loved his wife to death, but wasn't one for showing his feelings, especially not in front of other people.

Hearing 'Love is in the Air' come on the radio, Debbie cranked the volume up and danced around the room, doing funny impressions of Fernando.

Charlie woke up and rubbed his beady little eyes. Hearing voices, laugher and loud music, he decided to investigate. 'Come on,Timmy,' he said, inviting his imaginary friend to join him. Realising his Uncle Mickey and Granddad Peter were downstairs, he decided to sit at the top of the stairs and earwig. He hated the pair of them and wished them both dead.

'One day, when we're big and strong, Timmy, we'll beat up Uncle Mickey and Granddad Peter and chop their heads off,' he said.

'Yes, Charlie,' he replied in the squeaky voice he always used for Timmy.

Sucking his thumb and sitting still for what seemed like ages, Charlie caught snippets of conversation, but because the music was loud he couldn't hear anything clearly. As the lounge door opened, he shifted himself out of sight.

'Thanks, Mum, for looking after Charlie for me,' he heard his own mum saying.

'Any time, love. It was worth it to see you so happy,' replied his silly gran.

About to say something funny to Timmy, the next sentence made Charlie bite back his words as his blood ran cold.

'Thank you for coming as well, Peter. I know we've had our differences over the years, but now that I'm getting married, I'm really glad we've buried the hatchet,' his mother was saying.

'Me too, dear,' Peter replied.

Charlie turned to his imaginary friend, his little face contorted in anger. 'Come back to the bedroom *now*, Timmy.'

'Okay,' Charlie said, his assumed voice filled with rage too.

'Sit there,' he demanded once back in his room. 'My mum is *not* gonna marry that fat man, Timmy. We have to stop her. We hate him. He's a bastard, bastard, bastard.'

Timmy stayed silent. Overcome by anger, Charlie flew at him. 'Talk to me. Please talk to me, Timmy,' he pleaded, as he kicked and punched his friend.

Timmy stayed schtum.

Charlie got into bed and sobbed, 'I'm sorry, Timmy. Please talk to me. I didn't mean to hurt you. Please, can we still be friends?'

'I love you, Charlie. You will always be my friend,' said a badly shaken Timmy.

Relieved by his friend's forgiveness, Charlie pulled the Batman quilt over his head. Worn out by his eventful evening, he fell asleep within seconds.

TWENTY-FOUR

Debbie took the tinsel out of the box and wound it round the Christmas tree. She added some baubles, smiled, and turned to Charlie.

'Why don't you come and help Mummy decorate the tree?'

Charlie ignored her.

Kneeling down in front of him, Debbie did her best to entice him. 'I've brought you some special chocolate decorations. Help Mummy hang them on the tree and you can have one now.'

'Don't want one. Go away. I hate you.' Kicking her in the shin, Charlie ran out of the room.

Exasperated, Debbie put her head in her hands and cried. Recently, the relationship between her son and her had deteriorated to the point of no return. The situation was slowly but surely breaking her heart. Ever since Charlie had found out about the wedding, he'd made her life a complete misery. At first he'd begged her not to go through with it.

'Nooooo, Mummy, nooooo. I promise I'll be a good boy and never be naughty again. I don't wanna new daddy. Please, Mummy, don't marry that man,' he'd screamed.

Debbie had been really upset by his behaviour. Some

days she even toyed with the idea of postponing the event until her son was old enough to deal with it.

'You will do no such bloody thing. You can't let your life be ruled by a five-year-old child, Debbie. And what about poor Steve? He'd be devastated,' her mother had said in no uncertain terms.

Debbie reluctantly agreed with her and carried on planning the big day, but guilt was eating away at her. She was due to get married in seven days' time and, instead of being excited and full of beans, she was worrying constantly about her son. Charlie rarely left his room except for school. He lived in a little make-believe world he'd created for himself. Apart from the invisible Timmy, he'd talked to no one. Now, hearing the front door open, Debbie frantically tried to wipe away the evidence of her tears.

'What's up, babe?' Steve asked as soon as he saw her.

Sobbing, then, Debbie let it all pour out. 'It's Charlie . . . he still won't talk to me. What am I gonna do, Steve? I love him so much, but I just can't get through to him.'

'Shhh, come on, everything will be okay,' Steve said, hugging her tightly.

'I dunno what to do, Steve. This is my big day and I should be so excited, but Charlie's ruining everything for me. He's refused to come to the wedding and we've no-one to baby-sit him. We can't leave him with a stranger, he'd terrorise 'em. How are we gonna manage?'

Stroking her hair, Steve spoke to her, quietly but firmly. 'You're way too soft with him, Debs, you let him get away with murder. I know you feel guilty 'cause of what happened with Billy, but you've gotta try and put that to the back of your mind now. If he ignores you, give him a taste of his own medicine and ignore him. I bet he soon talks to you then. And as for the wedding, we'll just drag him there, kicking and screaming, if we have to.

Look, Debs, I don't like to get too involved in the

situation between you and him, but why don't you let me have a chat to him, man to man, like? He's wary of Mickey, you know. Won't play up in front of him. He needs a firm hand, Debs, trust me.'

Unable to think of a better idea herself, she agreed. 'Don't be too hard on him, though, will you, Steve?'

He gave a little tap and opened Charlie's bedroom door. Charlie was furious to see who the intruder was. 'Go away,' he said as he put his head under the covers.

Steve ignored his command and sat down on the edge of his bed. 'I think me and you need to have a little chat, don't you, Charlie?'

'Nooooo,' the boy screamed.

Steve grabbed the cover from his face and moved nearer to him. 'Now shut the fuck up and listen to me. Me and your mum are getting married next week, whether you like it or not. Now, I don't like you and you don't like me, but we're gonna make an effort for your mother's sake. You will come to the wedding. And while you're there, you'll behave yourself and be a good boy. Do you understand me, Charlie?'

'Won't. Can't make me,' he said obstinately.

Furious, Steve lifted the child off the bed by the neck of his pyjamas and put his own face right next to Charlie's. 'You will do as I say, you fucking little shit!'

Charlie wriggled like an eel. Unnerved, he nodded his head.

'Good. Now, in a minute, you're gonna walk downstairs and tell your mum you're sorry. And if I find out you've played her up at all in the future, it'll be me you'll be dealing with, not her. Do we understand one another?'

Shocked into silence, Charlie nodded dumbly and was relieved to see Steve finally leave his room.

'How did it go?' Debbie asked, her voice filled with dread.

'Yeah, fine, he was as good as gold. He's coming down in a minute to see you.'

Not quite believing what she was hearing, Debbie was even more amazed when she heard footsteps on the stairs. Standing in front of her, clutching his beloved toy dog, was Charlie and he was actually apologising.

'I'm sorry, Mum, if I was naughty, and I promise to be a good boy from now on.'

'Oh, bless ya,' Debbie said, hugging him.

Charlie pulled himself away from her. 'Can I go back to my bedroom now?'

'Of course you can,' Debbie said, stunned by her son's change of heart. 'Whatever did you say to him?' she asked Steve as soon as Charlie was out of earshot.

'Just had a little chat. As I said before, Debs, he needs a man's touch,' Steve replied, unable to look her in the eye.

Over the next few days, because of Charlie's turnaround, Debbie was able to concentrate on the wedding. Her mum was a great help and the pair of them spent hours organising the last minute bits and bobs. Debbie had refused to get married in church and opted for a quick ceremony in a Register Office, together with a handful of family and close friends.

'I don't want loads of fuss and there's no way I'm floating up the aisle in a wedding dress, being stared at by all and sundry,' she'd told Steve.

'As long as me and you get married, I don't care if you wear a boiler suit and we say our vows in the middle of Romford fucking Market. We'll do whatever you wanna do, babe. Just tell me the date and the time and I'll be there.'

June had been a bit put out at first that her daughter hadn't opted for the works. 'Peter and I will pay for it, Debbie. You must have a church wedding, love. It's the biggest day of your life.'

But Debbie was adamant. 'Mum, I'm ugly. I've got a wonky nose, me hair's too short and makes me look like a lesbian, I ain't even got me own fucking front teeth . . . If you think I'm parading meself about in a church, looking like I do, you can think again.'

June got ever so upset when Debbie put herself down. She was attractive, everybody said so. If only her daughter could look into the mirror and see what everybody else did. Knowing when she was beaten, though, June decided to keep her trap shut from that day onwards and abide by Debbie's wishes. It was her big day, after all.

The hen night and stag nights were two small affairs because neither Debbie nor Steve particularly wanted them.

Steve held his in a boozer up in Bow and could have throttled Mickey and the lads when some Roly Poly stripogram turned up. Bendy Wendy, she called herself. He nearly died when she got out her massive pair of jugs and rubbed them in his face.

Debbie opted for a sit-down meal in a local Chinese and was joined by a few old school friends, two distant cousins and Susan, her friend from across the street. Her mum was unable to attend as she was the only person on earth capable of baby-sitting Charlie.

The night before the wedding, Debbie sent Steve back home and had her mum stay with her. Steve hadn't formally moved in with her yet, though he stayed at least five or six nights a week.

On 23 December, the morning of the wedding, Debbie was overcome by nerves and couldn't get off the toilet. 'Drink that, darling, it'll calm you down,' June said, thrusting a glass of champagne at her.

Debbie's old classmate, Alison, arrived at ten. A qualified beautician, she'd promised to do her friend's make-up, hair and nails.

'Oh, Debbie. I'm so proud of you! You look absolutely

fantastic, darling,' June crowed as she admired the finished results.

Instead of a wedding dress, Debbie had opted for a beige pinstripe skirt and jacket. She accompanied this with a white, wide-collared blouse, high tan suede boots, a small beige hat and a bouquet of cream-coloured flowers. Looking in the mirror, she was surprised to see how nice she looked. Temporarily, her confidence soared.

'Are you ready to see how cute your little boy looks?' June asked excitedly, pulling a sullen-looking Charlie into the bedroom by his clammy hand.

As Debbie looked at him in his little grey suit, white shirt and pink tie, she felt as if she was about to burst with pride. He looked so grown up, bless him.

Peter turned up at twelve o'clock and told them that the car was waiting outside. Much to June's delight, Debbie had agreed that he should give her away. With her brother already snapped up as best man and her real dad six feet under, she hadn't really had a lot of choice in the matter.

Insisting that Charlie should sit next to her in the car, Debbie squeezed his hand. 'Are you all right, darling?'

He nodded without answering. His behaviour had been a little odd all this last week, she mused. He'd been polite, but only ever spoke when spoken to and answered with a complete lack of expression. He'd stopped playing up so much, which was one good thing, but spent even more time in his bedroom, talking to his make-believe friend. Concerned for him but not wanting to spoil her own big day, Debbie resolutely turned her thoughts back to her husband-to-be.

As the music played and the ceremony began, Steve glanced around and caught sight of his bride walking towards him. The love he felt for her choked him. Debbie looked so beautiful that he was unable to stop his tears.

Seeing his friend's emotion, Mickey patted him on the back reassuringly.

Peter felt quite honoured to be giving Debbie away. The man he was handing her over to wouldn't have been his first choice of chap, but he could tell that Steve genuinely loved his step-daughter and that was good enough for him. Peter's own emotions were running riot. He'd found out only yesterday, by email, that his own daughter Dolores had just got married on a secluded beach in Thailand. Apparently she'd been given away by a complete stranger. He hadn't told June the news yet. She would be so upset for him and he didn't want to spoil her big day.

The ceremony was short and sweet. As the happy couple made their vows, there was hardly a dry eye in the house. June, Mickey, Peter . . . they all shed a tear. Only Charlie showed no emotion. Head bowed, he stared at the floor.

A short photographic session in the pretty adjoining gardens was followed by a slap-up meal at a restaurant in Hornchurch town centre.

Steve gave a short but moving speech in which he thanked Debbie for making him the happiest man alive. Peter got up next and said a few polite words on behalf of June and himself. Not surprisingly, it was Mickey's acid tongue which completely stole the show, as usual. The whole restaurant was in hysterics as he delivered his hilarious best man's speech.

'As you know, Marbella is full of famous people. Many a villain has left these shores to live it up there. Ronnie Biggs once lived there . . . Mickey Green . . . Freddie Foreman . . . the list is endless. I happened to be over there recently, conducting a bit of business, and was very surprised to find that this man here,' Mickey paused to pat Steve on the back, 'is as well known as anyone. No matter what bar or restaurant I went in, the name on everyone's lips was Stephanie Arthur Roberts.'

Steve felt himself go beetroot red as the whole place erupted into laughter. Mickey carried on: 'Now let me tell ya a little story. I hadn't known Steph that long when he decided to take me over West Ham. Anyway, we're queuing up at the ground and we finally gets to the turnstile. So, I've gone through, looked round and I can't see Steph anywhere. I couldn't work it out. I knew he was right behind me. Anyway, I wanders back towards the entrance to see if I can spot him, and you'll never guess where he was . . . '

Steve put his head in his hands as all the guests urged Mickey to tell them. He was such a piss-taking bastard, Steve would kill him for this.

Mickey smiled as triumphantly he finished his story. 'Poor old Steph was that fat, he'd got stuck in the fucking turnstile! The stewards were pulling on his oversized arms, but they couldn't dislodge him. And the funniest part of it was, the crowd who were queuing up behind, clocked what was going on and broke into song. All I could hear was half of Upton Park singing, "Who ate all the pies, who ate all the pies? You fat bastard, you fat bastard, you ate all the pies!"'

'I'll fucking kill you for that, you cunt,' Steve joked as Mickey sat back down.

The evening reception had been arranged and paid for by the best man and was held at a pub in Rainham village. Another hundred or so guests joined in the celebrations there and put the finishing touch to a completely successful day.

As Debbie sat at a table next to her mum, she noticed her son staring into space. 'You all right, Charlie? Are you gonna come and have a dance with Mummy?'

He shook his head and stared down at the floor.

'Shall I get you something to eat from the buffet? They've got chicken nuggets – your favourite. Mummy ordered them especially for you.'

'Not hungry,' he replied, still staring at the floor.

Debbie ruffled his hair and dragged June to the Ladies. 'I'm really worried about him, Mum. He hardly touched his food in the restaurant and he's barely said a word all day. You don't think he's ill, do you?'

'Not on your nelly,' replied June. 'There's sod all wrong with him. He's just playing up, trying different tactics. I'll keep me eye on him. You go and find your husband and have a bloody good time, love.'

Taking her mother's advice, Debbie let her hair down and spent the rest of the evening singing, drinking and laughing. She sat with Steve's friends and family, and was overjoyed, but not surprised, to find out just how popular and highly thought of he was.

'Honestly, Debbie, you've got yourself a good 'un there. If it weren't for Steve, I'd have been shoved in a home as a kid. He fed me, clothed me, put me on the right track in life. If he hadn't guided me, I'd probably be inside now, like most of me old mates are,' insisted Steve's little brother Lee, who'd been granted special leave by the army for his brother's big day.

The latter part of the evening passed in one big happy blur. The DJ called Debbie and Steve on to the dance floor and played Cliff Richard's 'Congratulations'. Everyone stood in a circle and surrounded the happy couple. Debbie and Steve then smooched to Elton John's 'Your Song', which had been a favourite of Steve's mum. Completely oblivious to anyone else, they gazed lovingly into one another's eyes.

'Do you think we'll always be this happy, Steve?' Debbie asked him.

'Of course we will, babe. Nothing and no one can spoil what we've got,' he insisted.

*

196

At the very moment that Debbie and Steve were enjoying their last dance, Billy McDaid lay wide awake in his cell, unable to sleep. He had no idea that Debbie was even with Steve, let alone that they'd got married that day. He'd been sentenced the previous week and had received five years for his crime. He no longer loved Debbie; in fact, he hated her and blamed her for everything bad that had ever happened to him. Closing his eyes, he pictured his son, his precious little Charlie boy.

'I love you, son,' he said softly as he kissed a photo of the child. Talking to Charlie kept him sane in this place. 'One day me and you will be together, boy.'

'Shut up, bloodclot,' came the dulcet tones of his cell-mate Clinton.

Billy was frightened of the big, black six-footer he was sharing with, so quickly shut up. Smiling to himself, he pictured the day he and his son were finally together again.

Billy had heard that he'd also fathered a couple of kids up in Scotland. Obviously, he'd never met them. He had no wish to. In his mind, Charlie was the only child who truly belonged to him. One day, when he got out of this shit-hole, he'd make things right with his son. Billy had always regarded himself as a bit of a face. Surely his wean would turn out to be a chip off the old block. The child bore his surname, after all.

Once a McDaid, always a McDaid.

Like Billy himself, the kid was destined to become a legend.

TWENTY-FIVE

December 2005 – Ten Years Later

Realising that the girls were due to be picked up in less than half an hour, Debbie gobbled the last of her sandwich, picked up the keys to her latest birthday present, a BMW X5, and headed off for the drama school to collect her daughters.

As she sat in heavy traffic, she thought briefly back over her past. The Billy saga was virtually forgotten now, little more than a distant memory to her. She had a wonderful life and, truth be told, it was all thanks to Steve. Marrying him was the best decision Debbie had ever made, and she loved him more as each day passed.

Over the past ten years her life had turned around completely. When she looked into the mirror these days she could barely make out the shy, wonky-nosed individual she had once been. She was now the mother of two beautiful little girls, Gracie aged eight and Rosie who had just turned six.

Steve was a wonderful father, strict but fair, and the girls were a credit to their parents. Polite and intelligent, they excelled at dance and drama and were loved by anyone and everyone who came into contact with them. On the birth of his first daughter, Gracie, Steve had made the life-changing decision to give up crime and go legit.

'I ain't missing out on seeing my daughter grow up so

I'm going straight,' he'd announced. True to his word, he'd managed to badger Mickey into going halves with him to buy a pub. Debbie's brother had been dubious at first but had stuck up half the cash, opting to be a silent partner. He was more surprised than anyone when the venture turned out to be a huge success. A bit put out that Steve had cracked it without his help, Mickey soon got involved in the running of it himself.

Mickey and Steve were still very well known and respected in certain criminal circles and it wasn't long before the pub was packed out with their own kind. The customers who drank there felt safe. They knew Mickey and Steve were two of their own and consequently all kinds of business could be discussed freely and openly, without their having to worry. Within a year of its opening, the pub had made enough money for the boys to expand their thriving business. They were now the proud owners of four boozers in total and had just added a gentlemen's club to their rapidly growing empire.

Neither Mickey nor Steve was involved in running the premises now. They'd hired managers for each establishment to do the actual work. Their own job was to keep an eye on the overall running of the businesses and flit from one to the other of them, turning up at unannounced times on a daily basis to make spot checks. Mickey had taken Steve's lead and four years ago decided to go straight himself. There were two reasons for his change of heart. First, he'd had a tip off from a bent copper he knew, telling him the old bill were on to him, and the second reason was Karen.

As fate would have it, he'd met her in one of this own pubs. Even though he hated to admit it, she'd been the absolute making of him and had brought him more personal happiness than he could ever have believed possible.

Enchanted by her long dark hair, delicate features, hearty laugh and wicked sense of humour, he'd fallen head over heels for her within weeks. A feisty, fiercely independent single mum of one, Karen had been a hard nut to crack. Mickey was used to women falling at his feet, and the challenge she'd presented only made him love her more.

Determined to win her over, Mickey upped the charm stakes. It must have worked as a year later they were married and had since produced a son, Alfie, now eighteen months old. Mickey had also legally adopted Karen's fifteen-year-old daughter Lois. As the proud father of two children, he was the happiest he'd ever been. He idolised Karen and vice versa. They were soul-mates and very, very happy together.

Debbie's thoughts were jolted back to the present by the sound of her mobile ringing. Seeing her son's name flashing on the screen, she mounted a kerb to take the call.

'Hello, love, you all right?'

Charlie did not bother to answer his mother's question but came straight to the point. 'Where are you, Mum? I need some money. How long you gonna be?'

Debbie sighed, exasperated. The only time her son ever rang her was when he wanted something. 'I gave you twenty quid last night, love. You have more pocket money than any other kid I know. I'm not a bank, Charlie.'

Hearing an ominous silence at the other end of the phone, Debbie did what she always did when it came to her son – she gave in. 'There's fifty quid in an envelope in the top right-hand drawer, take twenty out of that.'

'Can't I take thirty?'

'No, you can't.' Debbie was annoyed as she ended the call. Her son was such an ungrateful little sod.

She arrived ten minutes early at the school and sat

in the car thinking. Overall her life was pretty good. She was even content with her looks and figure now since Steve had treated her to a nose job and she'd joined the local gym. Charlie was the only downside to her otherwise happy existence, and she was beyond knowing what to do about him. Steve didn't have a clue how much money her son wheedled out of her every week; he'd have gone apeshit if he knew the exact amount the boy demanded. What Charlie did with that money was anyone's guess. Debbie knew that because she felt guilty for spending most of her time with her two adorable daughters, she tried to compensate her son with constant hand-outs. Charlie was bright at school, disruptive but clever, the teachers said. The main concern Debbie had was that he had no real friends and the vibes she always got on open evenings told her he was extremely unpopular.

Her son went out sometimes of an evening, but she didn't know where, and when she inquired, he told her precisely nothing. During the time he was at home, he was always holed up in his bedroom. He was obsessed with computer games and spent most of his time playing them. His only other interest was surfing chat rooms on the internet. He never joined in with anything they did as a family. Debbie always tried to include him, but Charlie flatly refused to comply.

His relationship with his sisters was awful. The only time he spoke to them was to torment them. The girls had loved him when they were little and had looked up to him, but he'd rejected them from day one. As they'd got older, they'd learned that keeping out of his way was the best option.

Steve hated the sight of Charlie and suffered him only for his wife's sake. Debbie knew the score, and to be honest couldn't blame him. If the boot had been on the other foot, she'd have struggled herself. Her son was still wary of Steve and oozed politeness on the odd occasions he was forced to spend in his company. When Steve wasn't around, he'd talk to her and his sisters like they were pieces of shit. Debbie never told Steve about this. Keeping her trap shut equalled a quiet life, and that was the way she liked it.

Seeing her daughters running happily towards her, Debbie forgot her worries. She hugged them tight and asked them about their class.

'We did tap dancing and sang songs,' they answered excitedly.

Debbie smiled to herself as she drove home. The girls were in the back, gabbling away ten to the dozen, and some of the things they came out with were just hilarious.

Considering neither she nor Steve was an oil painting, it was a mystery how they'd been blessed with two such pretty girls. With their long dark hair and dark eyes, they were both stunning kids. Charlie wasn't so fortunate. Now a plain, tall boy, he was slightly overweight, with beady eyes and an untrustworthy look. In fact, he looked like a younger, fatter version of his father.

'How many days to Christmas now, Mummy? What time does Santa bring the presents?' Rosie asked excitedly.

'There is no Santa,' Gracie replied, giggling.

'Yes, there is. Don't spoil things for her, Gracie. This time next week is Christmas Day, and Santa waits until you're asleep and delivers his presents the night before,' Debbie told her youngest.

This would be the first Christmas in their new house and Debbie couldn't wait. It was her turn to have all the family over. They'd only moved in six months ago. A five-bedroomed house in a rural part of Brentwood with a couple of acres attached, it had turned out to be the home of Debbie's dreams. It had cost a little more than they'd intended paying but, on realising his wife had fallen in love with the property, Steve had stuck a bid in. After a bit of bargaining, the deal was done and Debbie was overjoyed.

They'd previously lived in a three-bedroomed semi in Upminster and Debbie had been keen to move while the girls were young. The schools were far better in Brentwood and she wanted the best for her daughters. Charlie only had a year and a half left at his school in Upminster and opted to stay there. This wasn't a problem as it was only a bus ride away.

'Mum, Dad's on the phone!' Gracie shouted.

Debbie was putting salt on the drive, which had begun to freeze over. Dropping the shovel, she ran indoors.

'You took your fucking time. Where were you – Calcutta?' Steve joked.

'I was just chucking some salt down outside, you cheeky sod.'

'I'll be home in about half-hour, babe. I know you don't like cooking, so I wondered if you wanted me to bring a Chinese in?'

Debbie laughed. The relationship between them had not changed since the day they'd first got together. They still loved nothing more than taking the piss out of one another.

'Go on then, you've twisted me arm. Get a mixture of dishes, Steve. You know what the girls have, don't ya?'

'Don't worry, Debs. The woman in the Chinese gets the order ready without even asking what the fuck I want. "Hello Mr Steve," she says when I walk through the door. I bet she thinks I'm one of these poor single dads. I'm gonna tell her one day, I've got a lazy fucking old woman.'

Laughing, Debbie cut him off.

Charlie sat in his mate's bedroom in a council house in Harold Hill. His heart was pumping with excitement as he took the DVD out of its case and handed it to his friend.

Kevin was the only mate he had. They had the same interests and the same things in common, which included smoking joints, watching porn, listening to heavy rock music and playing violent computer games. Kevin Newley was an oddball through and through. Unwanted by his mother, he'd been raised by his psychotic grandmother Doreen who had done him no favours whatsoever. A fat boy with glasses, Kevin was unkempt and rarely came into contact with soap or water. He was an almost complete loner and totally in awe of his one and only friend. If Charlie said jump, Kevin would do it. That's why their friendship worked.

Being unpopular too, Charlie was glad of his only pal. Kevin was fat and minging, but his house came in handy to doss round. His nan was senile so they could puff, watch films, drink beer . . . in fact, they could do whatever they bloody well wanted here. The situation suited Charlie. He was a bully, liked getting his own way, and Kevin was well and truly under his thumb.

Seeing the DVD flicker into life, Charlie's excitement grew, along with his hard on. He had his own DVD dealer, a little Chinese bloke called Lee, who got hold of all the real hardcore stuff, and had managed to get *Animal Farm* for him. Charlie had built up quite a collection which was kept safely hidden under Kevin's bed. Sometimes he'd sneak a couple home and watch them when the house was empty, but he was always careful not to leave them lying about. His mum would have a fit. As for Steve, he'd rip his stepson's head off if he got wind of Charlie's little hobby.

Charlie was clever and had learned how to play his

mother and Steve over the years. He was never talkative, but always tried to be polite. Sometimes he'd give his mum a bit of stick if Steve wasn't about. He knew she wouldn't say anything, she was too soft. He hated his sisters, especially Rosie who was a trappy little cow, and on more than one occasion had fantasised about throttling her and watching her gasp for her last breath. That thought made him giggle. Gracie had been the same once upon a time, but he'd taught her who was boss and managed to shut her up. Shame he'd never done the same to Rosie.

Turning his attention back to the film, he cheered with delight at the sheer filth of it. He'd heard about this film on a porn chat room and had been told it was an all-time classic.

'Er, that's disgusting . . . look what's she's doing with that horse,' Kevin chortled.

The boys enjoyed the film immensely and at the end of it discussed the juiciest bits over a joint.

'Birds are slags. That film proves it. I mean, what sort of person would shag animals for money?' said Charlie.

Kevin thought about this. 'I dunno. Weren't that how AIDS was started – by shagging sheep? I'm sure I saw that on the internet.'

Charlie ignored his pal's question and slapped him on the back.

'What me and you need, mate, is some real pussy. Watching it on films is all right, but we need to get ourselves some of the real thing.'

'You're right,' Kevin agreed.

Finishing the spliff, Charlie put on his Puffa jacket. 'Leave the pussy to me, I'll sort us out. Look, I'd better go now, I've gotta get my bus. I'll ring you tomorrow.'

As he walked towards the bus stop, Charlie saw a young blonde girl on the other side of the road. Slag, he thought, as he clocked her short skirt and white stilettos.

The fucking whore was asking for trouble, walking about like that.

Feeling his cock rising, he imagined grabbing her and shoving himself right up that short skirt of hers. It'd serve her right.

Aware that she was being stared at, the girl glanced in his direction. Charlie put his hands over his cock, made a thrusting movement with his hips and waved his tongue at her. Frightened, the girl quickened her step and ran towards the safety of her home.

TWENTY-SIX

Debbie and Steve were awoken early on Christmas morning by two excited little girls, impatient to open their presents.

'Charlie,' Debbie said, knocking on his door. 'we're going downstairs to open the presents. You coming, love?'

'Later,' was the gruff reply.

The girls squealed with delight as they ripped the paper off the abundance of gifts supposedly delivered by Santa. Nudging Steve, Debbie urged him to show them their big surprise.

'Mummy and Daddy have got something special out the back for you, girls. Shall we go and see what it is?'

Gracie and Rosie screamed excitedly as they followed their parents to the field at the back of the house.

Their little faces were a picture when they saw the two ponies in the newly built stables. 'Are they really ours, Daddy?' Rosie asked.

'Can we keep them forever, Mummy?' Gracie pleaded.

'Yep, they're all yours.' Steve squeezed Debbie's hand. He loved his girls more than anything on earth, and making them and Debbie happy meant the world to him.

'I'm gonna call mine Britney,' Rosie piped up.

Laughing, Debbie tried to usher them indoors.

'You can go back out and see them later, after dinner.

Louise who lives down the road is going to look after them for you. She'll teach you all you need to know. She already works as a stablegirl and me and Daddy have asked her to help you with your ponies. She's promised to pop in later to feed them, and tomorrow she'll start to teach you how to ride.'

Charlie scratched his genitals, let out a fart, and ventured over to the window. He could hear the commotion outside. It had woken him up. Clocking the ponies, he immediately guessed that they were Christmas presents for the two spoiled brats. He hated animals, always had done. They were a waste of space; all they ever did was piss, shit and eat.

Slinging on a pair of tracksuit bottoms and a T-shirt, he smiled to himself as he walked down the stairs. He could use his sisters' Christmas presents to blackmail them. 'Do this for me, Rosie.' 'Get this for me, Gracie . . . ' And when they said no, he would threaten to dismember the bastard creatures.

'Morning, love. What you laughing at?' Debbie asked, surprised to see her son looking cheerful for once.

'Nothing. Do us some breakfast, Mum.'

It was an order, not a request. Rustling him up a couple of sausage sandwiches, Debbie put the sauce on for him, just the way he liked it.

'When you've eaten that, love, come into the lounge and open your presents.'

Wiping his plate clean with the last bit of bread, Charlie sauntered into the front room and was relieved to find there was no sign of his stepdad or sisters.

'Where is everyone?'

Debbie handed him his gifts and waited for him to open them. 'Steve's gone to pick Nanny and Granddad up. The girls have gone with him.'

'Thanks, Mum,' Charlie said, after he'd unwrapped the last present.

'I didn't really know what to get you this year, love. That's why I gave you mainly money. I thought you'd appreciate buying your own stuff now.'

Glad he had his mum to himself, even if only for a little while, Charlie experienced one of his rare sentimental moments. These didn't happen very often. Throughout the entire course of his life, he could count them all on one hand. Smiling, he walked towards Debbie and awkwardly gave her a hug.

'Happy Christmas, Mum.'

Unable to remember the last time he'd voluntarily put his arms around her, Debbie had tears in her eyes as she watched him walk away up the stairs, carrying his gifts. He wasn't a bad lad, bless him. He was just a typical teenager, all mixed up and confused.

Steve arrived home with the girls, June and Peter, and they were followed in by Mickey, Karen and the kids, who had turned up nigh on the same time.

'Oh, Debs, I love that handbag,' Karen said, spotting the Prada that Steve had bought her.

Debbie adored her sister-in-law. They were like best friends and often shopped and lunched together.

June grabbed Peter's arm to give him a grand tour of the new house. He'd seen it before, but not since it had been redecorated.

'Very nice, dear,' he said, showing little real enthusiasm. He'd have liked to have reminded his wife that the property had probably been paid for with ill-gotten gains.

'Don't she look stunning, Karen?' Debbie said, looking enviously at Lois.

Karen put her arm around her daughter's shoulders and replied quietly, 'Don't tell Mickey but she's been spotted by some model agency. They approached her in Romford and want her to go up town for a photo-shoot. She's so shy, though, Debs – she's not sure if she wants to do it. I won't broach the subject with Mickey until she's decided if she's going. He's so protective of Lois, it ain't worth causing World War Three until we know if she wants this or not.'

June, playing the hostess as usual, got everyone a drink. Debbie, being a lazy cow, was only too happy to let her mother do the honours. But spotting June sneaking a duster out of the cupboard, Debbie politely asked her what planet she was on.

'But I've just spotted some dust on the rungs of the dining chairs, dear.'

'Mum, you don't have to do your Mrs Bucket bit now, you know. I have a cleaner who comes in twice a week,' Debbie said indignantly.

'You should sack her then, dear. She's obviously not doing her job properly.' Debbie and Karen roared with laughter at this. June would find fault with Buckingham Palace if she was allowed in there for the day.

Steve and Mickey sat at the kitchen table, having a brief discussion about the new club's takings. Opening a bottle of bourbon, Steve handed his brother-in-law a tumbler.

'To us,' they said, clinking their glasses together. Their businesses were raking it in. Both money-oriented, they couldn't have been happier with the way things were going.

'Mum, quick, look at Alfie! He's dancing.'

Debbie turned around to see her nephew swinging his hips to a Justin Timberlake tune. 'Oh, ain't he cute, Karen? I love his little boots, where did you get them?'

'Mickey got them in a shop up Roman Road. He idolises his boy. There's not a week goes by when he doesn't come home with an armful of presents for Alfie.'

Debbie took a sip of wine. 'He used to be like that with Charlie when he was little. He was forever buying him stuff.'

'Where is Charlie?' Lois asked, desperate for someone of her own age to talk to.

'He's up in his room, love. He's probably on his computer, or playing a game of some sort. Go up and see him.'

'He might not want me to,' Lois replied, her shyness getting the better of her.

''Course he will,' Debbie said, desperate for her son to have some company. 'Last room on the right,' she shouted as the girl walked up the stairs.

Karen felt a bit apprehensive as she watched her daughter leave the room. She didn't like Charlie, never had done. Mickey had filled her in on his past and had always portrayed him as an evil little bastard.

'Shouldn't we give your mum a hand with the dinner?' Karen asked, desperate to tell Mickey that Lois had gone up to Charlie's room.

'No, leave her. She's happy as Larry while she's cooking. We'll only get in her way,' Debbie said.

'Who is it?' Charlie asked, as he heard the gentle tap on his door.

'It's Lois.'

What the fuck does she want? he thought, logging off his chat room. Unwanted visitors were a fucking nuisance. Feeling pissed off, he yanked open the bedroom door. The sight of what stood behind it cheered him up in no time.

'Christ, you look different,' he stammered, lost for words at the change in her. It had been a year to the day since he'd last set eyes on Mickey's stepdaughter, and she'd altered so much that had he walked past her in the street, he wouldn't have recognised her. Gone was the plump girl with the dodgy braces on her teeth and fried eggs for tits. In her place was a slim absolute stunner with massive knockers.

'Come in. Sorry about the state of me room,' he said, frantically trying to tidy up.

Politeness and good manners oozed from Charlie as he did his utmost to impress. He wasn't good around girls as a rule. He attended an all boys school so had very little dealings with them. He'd only ever had one girlfriend. She was called Lucy and he'd met her at a fairground when he was thirteen. The relationship had lasted all of two weeks. She'd dumped him, calling him a pervert for trying to shove his hand up her skirt.

'So, what do you like doing? Where do you hang out?' Charlie pried.

'I don't really go out a lot, not of a night. My mum and Mickey are quite strict. I'm allowed to go over to a friend's house or they come round to me, but I'm not allowed out on the streets.'

'What about weekends in the daytime and that?' he persisted.

'I normally go to Romford. Me and my friends love shopping and sometimes we go to the pictures or for a pizza,' Lois replied, confused by his show of interest.

'I'm in Romford a lot at weekends,' Charlie lied. 'Maybe we could meet up. Give me your phone number?'

Sitting opposite him, Lois felt embarrassed. She'd always looked upon him as a cousin, but could tell by the way he was staring down her top that he looked upon her as nothing of the sort. Not wanting to hurt his feelings, she gave him her number. Her phone was in her hand, so she could hardly lie and say she didn't own one.

Charlie eagerly rang her number and demanded she store his. Making a mental note never to answer his calls, Lois was relieved to hear her mum's voice calling her.

'Lois, your dinner's ready!'

As Charlie grabbed hold of her arm, Lois felt the hairs stand up on the back of her neck. 'What are you doing?' she asked.

'Nothing,' he replied. 'I just wanted to say to you, don't tell Mickey or your mum that we've swapped numbers. Keep it as our little secret.'

'Okay,' Lois said, relieved to be walking out of his room and down the stairs. Charlie had given her the creeps. She was determined never to be alone with him again.

The change in Charlie's behaviour during the rest of the day was a shock to everyone. Charming and amiable, his manners were impeccable. He offered to help his nan wash up, assembled Rosie's new toy, happily trotted outside to meet the new ponies and even joined in with some party games.

'What's got into him?' June asked Debbie, on the quiet.

'Oh, he's a good lad really, Mum. He's a typical teenager but a good boy deep down,' she replied defensively.

Good boy, my arse, June thought. Conniving little bastard more like. Always had been and always would be.

Steve eyed his stepson suspiciously. He knew what game the boy was playing because he'd clocked him making eyes at Lois all day. Mickey was pissed, thank God, and hadn't noticed. Steve was positive Karen had, though.

Not wanting to cause havoc for Debbie, Steve decided to keep schtum. Mickey would go apeshit if he clued him up and then there'd be a massive row. Ever-protective of her son, Debbie would stick up for him, and Steve would be bang in the middle of it. He'd have a word with Mickey on the quiet instead, when he was sober. He could tell by

213

Lois's behaviour that the feelings weren't reciprocated. The poor little mare had spent the best part of the day averting her eyes from her admirer.

'Let's have a bit of Chas and Dave, Debs,' June demanded, the drink as always bringing out the cockney in her.

As 'Rabbit' filled the speakers, Peter excused himself and went outside for a cigar. His wife's behaviour was flawless in front of their own circle of friends, but as soon as she got with her family she behaved like a navvy. As for Chas and Dave . . . they should have been shot at birth, he thought. Peter was extremely cultured himself and loved nothing more than a bit of classical music. How anyone could listen to that cockney apples and pears rubbish when they could be listening to Beethoven was beyond his understanding.

'Mum, Alfie's fallen asleep on the kitchen floor,' Gracie said, tugging at Debbie's arm to stop her dancing.

Debbie was enjoying leaping about too much to stop. 'Karen, Alfie's crashed out. Take him upstairs and let him sleep in one of the bedrooms,' she shouted at the top of her voice.

Karen went to tend to her son. 'I don't need your help, I can manage, Lois,' she said as she noticed her daughter still glued to her side.

'But I want to put Alfie to bed with you, Mum.'

Tucking her son in, Karen turned to face her daughter. 'What's the matter, love? You've been ever so quiet. Are you feeling okay?'

'I'm fine, Mum,' Lois lied. Part of her wanted to confide in her mother, tell her that Charlie had given her the heebie-jeebies, but considering he hadn't actually done anything, she didn't want to make herself look stupid. She daren't tell her mum she'd given him her phone number. She'd already had her mobile confiscated once this year for giving her number to a weirdo on the internet.

Knowing her daughter better than she knew herself, Karen guessed what might be bothering her. 'Is it Charlie? Did he say or do something to upset you when you were upstairs with him?'

Lois forced a smile. 'Of course not, we were just talking about school and stuff.'

Relieved, Karen smiled and took her daughter by the hand.

What Lois didn't know as she ventured downstairs to rejoin the festive celebrations was that if only she'd put her trust in her mother then, she would have saved herself a whole load of heartache to come.

TWENTY-SEVEN

With both dinner and supper out of the way, Charlie was desperate to get Lois on her own for five minutes. 'Do you wanna come upstairs and play some computer games?' he asked hopefully.

'No, thank you,' she replied, looking at the floor to avoid any eye contact with him. He'd been leering at her all day, freaking her out, and the last thing she wanted was to be alone with him.

> Knees up, Mother Brown,
> Knees Up, Mother Brown,
> Under the table you must go,
> E-eye E-eye E-eye O.

Mickey and Debbie roared as they saw their mother cocking her big old legs in the air. They rarely saw her inebriated, and when they did she was pure entertainment.

Glancing at his watch, Peter decided enough was enough. 'Could you call us a cab, Debbie? I think it's time I got your mother home.'

'Oh, she's all right, she's just enjoying herself,' Debbie replied indignantly, thinking what a boring bastard her step-dad was.

But Peter wasn't taking no for an answer. He'd had

enough of his wife acting like a Pearly Queen, and as for showing her knickers – that was the final straw.

'I'm not arguing with you, Deborah. Just call me a cab, dear, will you? If your mother wants to stay here, she's more than welcome. I personally wish to go home.'

Debbie decided to do as he asked rather than cause a row. It was the season of goodwill, after all.

'What time are we going, Mum? Can we go soon?' Lois whispered to Karen.

'Are you tired, love?' her mother asked, concerned by her daughter's question.

'Yes, and I've got a really bad headache.'

Gesticulating to Debbie to call a cab, Karen told Mickey that she was taking the children home, but said he was welcome to stay on and have a drink with Steve. Not trusting anyone who drove a mini-cab as far as he could throw them, however, Mickey wouldn't hear of it.

'I'm ready to go meself, babe. Why don't we invite Steve, Debbie and the kids over to us tomorrow?'

Karen loved Debbie and Steve's company and told her husband she'd be only too pleased to lay on a bash for them. Peter's cab arrived first. June, feeling tipsy, decided she'd now had enough and decided to go home with him.

'Thanks for the lovely day. 'Bye, everybody,' she shouted, before falling arse over tit on the driveway.

Debbie went into a fit of giggles as an embarrassed Peter tried to heave her mother off the ground and haul her into the cab. Karen and Mickey's cab arrived ten minutes later.

'I'll see you tomorrow then, sis, about four o'clock,' Mickey said, stroking the head of a comatose Alfie who lay snoring gently in his arms.

Charlie stood in the hallway listening to the following day's arrangements with interest.

217

As Steve tidied up, Debbie washed the remaining plates, cups and glasses. Gracie and Rosie had gone to bed and Charlie was rather surprisingly in the shower. Pleased to have his wife to himself for five minutes, Steve hugged her tightly and kissed her gently on the lips. 'It went well today, didn't it?'

Responding to the warmth of his hug, Debbie rubbed his cropped head, and smiled lovingly at him. 'I had a great day. Really enjoyed myself. Did you see Peter going into one when Mother was doing "Knees Up, Mother Brown"? His face was a picture.'

Steve shook his head and laughed. 'I was probably too busy rabbiting to Mickey.'

'I was really proud of Charlie today, Steve. He was so polite and well-mannered. Maybe he's coming through that stroppy teenage stage now. What do you think?'

Not wanting to burst her bubble, Steve was honest but tactful. 'He's got the hots for Lois, that's why he bleeding well behaved himself.'

'Has he?' Debbie asked, surprised.

'He couldn't take his eyes off her all day. Good job Mickey never clocked it, there'd have been murders.'

Steve's comment angered Debbie. 'What's it got to do with Mickey? Charlie and Lois aren't blood-related. So what if he likes her? He's a normal lad, he's gonna take an interest in girls. There'd be something wrong with the boy if he didn't.'

'I don't think Mickey would see it that way somehow, do you?' Steve laughed, trying to make a joke out of it, but hoping she'd see sense at the same time.

'Nothing he can do,' Debbie replied, annoyed that everyone and anyone seemed to have it in for her son.

Turning the shower off, Charlie put a towel round himself, went into his bedroom and rummaged around in his wardrobe until he found what he was looking for. As he opened the bedroom door, he was pleased to hear voices coming from downstairs, which meant his mother and Steve weren't lurking nearby.

Excited, he put on a DVD and turned the sound down in case he woke his sisters. He loved the film *Pussy Galore*, it was his favourite. Dropping the towel, he lay on his bed, clenched his right hand around his rather large penis and thought of Lois as he shot his load.

Debbie was making breakfast the following morning when Charlie appeared, looking full of the joys of spring and reeking of Steve's expensive new aftershave.

'You're up early, love. To what do we owe this pleasure?' she asked, shocked that he'd risen from his pit so soon.

'You going over Uncle Mickey's later, Mum?'

'Yes,' Debbie replied, thinking he wanted the house to himself.

'I think I'll come too,' Charlie said awkwardly.

Debbie looked at him in amazement. Maybe Steve was right and he did have the hots for young Lois. He usually avoided family outings like the plague and she couldn't remember the last time he'd invited himself out with them.

Swiping Rosie's bacon sandwich off her plate, Charlie shoved it in his mouth, grinned at her annoyance and sauntered back to his room.

Feeling hyper, he rang Kevin and told him all about Lois. Kevin had never even got as far as kissing a girl and was in awe of his friend's expertise with women. 'What does she look like? Has she got big tits?'

'Massive,' Charlie bragged. 'She's well fit.'

'So are you definitely going out with her then?' Kevin asked, hoping that she had a mate for him.

'Yep,' Charlie replied confidently.

He then went into detail about how she'd come to

his bedroom and made a play for him. 'Honestly, Kev, she's well up for it. She couldn't take her eyes off me all day.'

'Find out if she's got a mate for me,' his mate asked optimistically.

'I'll ask her,' Charlie lied. He intended to do no such thing. Kevin was an embarrassment. He certainly wasn't about to introduce him to Lois.

Debbie and Steve stood freezing their bits off as they watched Louise giving the girls their first proper riding lesson.

'Look at me, Mummy,' Rosie squealed excitedly as she held the reins for the very first time.

'Look at me, Daddy,' Gracie piped up, not wanting to be outdone by her younger sister who was looking much more of a natural than she was.

'I'm fucking frozen. Maybe buying poxy ponies wasn't such a good idea after all,' Steve complained under his breath to his wife.

'Cheer up, you miserable sod,' Debbie said, as she aimed a playful punch his way. Frozen herself, she looked at her watch and signalled to Louise to call it a day.

'But, Mum, we've only been out here a few minutes,' Rosie whined.

'I wanna stay with Britney,' Gracie insisted.

'You can see her again and have another ride tomorrow. We've got to be at your Uncle Mickey's by four and you're not even ready yet,' Debbie said sternly.

After ordering the girls to go upstairs and change into the pretty matching dresses she'd bought them for Christmas, Debbie sat down at the kitchen table and eagerly accepted a glass of wine from Steve. 'Did I tell you, Charlie wants to come with us this afternoon?'

Steve was pouring himself a beer and had his back

turned to his wife. Now, normally he trod carefully when it came to Charlie, but since Mickey's stepdaughter was involved he was determined to say his piece.

He swung around. 'I don't think that's a very good idea, Debs. Poor little Lois didn't know where to look yesterday when Charlie was gawping at her and I don't think it's fair to put the poor little cow through that again, especially in her own home.'

Furious, Debbie jumped straight down his throat. 'What the fuck you on about? I was here all day yesterday and I didn't notice anything untoward. You make my Charlie sound like some kind of a weirdo. What if Lois likes him, has that thought even occurred to you?'

Steve gulped at his drink. He and Debbie rarely argued and he absolutely hated it when they did. Normally he just let things sail over his head, but not this time. Not when it involved Mickey and his kids.

'Look, Debs, I don't wanna argue with you but you were pissed yesterday. I wasn't. I saw what was going on and it wasn't pleasant. Lois has got her whole life in front of her, she looks like a model, that girl, and she certainly ain't gonna be interested in someone like Charlie. Anyway, with Mickey being your brother you shouldn't be fucking encouraging it. It ain't on, Debs.'

Debbie was shaking with temper now. How dare he insult her beloved son?

'What exactly are you implying, Steve? That my boy ain't good enough. That what you're trying to say, is it?'

Getting angrier by the minute, he was determined to make his wife see sense.

'Don't put words in me fucking mouth, Debs. All I'm trying to say is, the girl is your brother's daughter. He adopted her. She's Charlie's cousin, for fuck's sake. I ain't into incest and I ain't having it in my house.'

'They're not fucking related!' Debbie screamed back.

'And I'll tell you something now, Steve – if Charlie ain't welcome then I don't go. Got it?'

Throwing his empty can into the rubbish bin, Steve stood up. 'That's fine by me. None of us will go. I'll ring Mickey and tell him why, shall I?'

'Do what you fucking like,' Debbie shouted, storming out of the kitchen.

Hearing his mum coming up the stairs, Charlie crept into his bedroom and shut the door. He'd heard the whole argument, every single fucking word of it, and he was furious. How dare Steve say that he wasn't good enough for Lois? Well, he'd show him. He'd show them all. Anyone who had ever doubted him would have a shock coming to them. Lois wanted him, he could sense it, and he was determined to prove all his doubters wrong. The girl was gagging for it.

Annoyed that his plans had been spoiled and he wasn't going to be seeing her today, Charlie scrolled through his phone to find her number. Deciding to text rather than ring, in case his uncle got wind of their romance, he punched in the letters.

Hi sexy. Mum n Steve have had big row, so wont b cmin over 2day. Mum is ok bout us goin out, but Steve went mad (fat bastard). Wot u doin next wkend? Do u fancy meetin up?

Smiling, Charlie pressed Send, got under his quilt and rubbed himself in anticipation.

Steve picked up his car keys and slammed the front door shut as hard as he could. He was fucking seething and drove down the road like a lunatic. One-handed, he picked up his phone and rang Mickey. 'Me and Debs won't be coming over, we've had a massive fucking fall out.'

'Whatever's the matter?' Mickey asked, surprised.

When he'd left them yesterday they'd been happy as pigs in shit.

Steve asked his pal to meet him for a pint and told him he desperately needed a chat.

Karen gave Mickey the green light. 'I'm knackered anyway, Mick. I still feel hungover from yesterday. You go out and have a drink with Steve. Honest, I don't mind.'

Steve arranged to pick his friend up and forty minutes later they were sitting in one of their old haunts, just off the Mile End Road. Mickey had never seen Steve so angry and wondered what the fuck had happened. He and Debs had been fine all day yesterday. Knowing his pal like he did, Mickey knew something pretty serious must have happened.

Steve was glad that none of their old cronies were in the pub. He shouted up some beers, urged his pal to sit down and, start to finish, told him the story. Mickey's temper was close to exploding point as he heard that his evil cunt of a nephew had a thing for his stepdaughter.

'If he goes within a hundred yards of her, I swear I'll fucking kill him! I'm telling you, Steve, he'll go the same way as his scumbag of a father did, if he tries it on with Lois. I'll beat the cunt out of him, my life I will,' he declared, slamming his bottle down on the table.

Steve tried to reassure him that it was a one-way thing and nothing to do with Lois. 'Honestly, Mick, the girl couldn't wait to leave the house last night. Poor little cow, I felt sorry for her all day. She's clued-up is Lois, and she knows Charlie's a fucking loser.'

Mickey downed his drink. Chucking some money at Steve, he asked him to go back up to the bar again. He had to calm himself down and needed a couple of minutes on his own to do so. He wasn't worried about his daughter being interested in Charlie, as there was no way in this world she would be. Lois was beautiful, with everything

223

going for her, while Charlie was a freak with nothing in his favour. That part was simple. The part that worried him was the fact that he didn't trust his nephew. The kid was a monster. Mickey had never forgotten the kitten episode. Charlie was a ringer for his evil fucking father. A piece of shit, in other words. But the thing that had annoyed Mickey most was Debbie's reaction to this. How could she even think of encouraging that notright of a son of hers to pursue his Lois? Mickey was wild, fucking wild, and he'd have it out with Debbie, if it was the last thing he did. Snatching the drink that Steve handed to him, he assured his pal that he had calmed down and was now okay.

'It all falls into place now, Steve. Karen told me this morning that Lois had been reserved all day yesterday. That's why, innit? She had that fucking piece of shit on her case. And as for my Debbie . . . I'm disgusted with her.'

Steve sipped his drink, trying to find the right words with which to get his wife off the hook. 'She'll soon realise she's wrong, Mick. I think deep down she knows Charlie's not normal and is probably just desperate for him to become the son she really wants. If he had a girl-friend and that, Debs would be over the moon. He's never shown much interest in girls before, so I suppose Debs is just happy he's got a love interest, even if it is Lois.'

'Well, best she fucking thinks again,' Mickey replied angrily.

Meanwhile, back in Brentwood, Debbie was just as angry as her brother. Desperate for somebody to confide in, she toyed with the idea of ringing her mum but quickly decided against it. June and Charlie had never been that close, and if her mum sided with Steve it would only cause ructions.

224

Debbie poured another drink and searched through the contacts on her phone. Normally Karen was the only person she would ring in a crisis, but she could hardly do that this time. Remembering Bev, from the girls' school, she decided to give her a call. Her daughter Ruby was in the same class as Rosie. Single and bitter, Bev had just been through a messy divorce. A self-confessed man-hater, she was a good listener and would be sure to offer a sympathetic shoulder to cry on.

'Oh, Debs. What a fucking bastard!' Bev said vehemently. 'Look, we can't discuss this on the phone. Come round here and we'll have a drink. Ruby's staying over at the arsehole's tonight, so I'm on my lonesome. Surely you can leave the girls with Charlie? I'm only bloody five minutes away. If they need you, they can ring your mobile.'

'I'm not sure I should leave them,' Debbie said awkwardly. She didn't know what to do for the best. Steve hated the girls being left alone with Charlie. 'He's only a kid himself and not capable of looking after them,' he'd always insisted.

Hating all men with a passion after her divorce, Bev loved nothing more than putting her jaundiced views across. 'Look, Debs, your Steve has sodded off out. As we speak, he's probably surrounded by a table full of women, pissed out of his head somewhere. Why should you sit indoors like silly-girl-got-none? I did that and look where it got me. The no-good cunt ran off with his twenty-year-old secretary.'

Debbie laughed at her friend's choice of words. Judgement clouded by the amount of drink she'd consumed, she decided to be a devil. 'Oh, sod it. Give us twenty minutes and I'll be round.'

Rosie and Gracie were sitting in the living room, watching the musical *Oliver* on DVD. 'Girls, I'm gonna pop out for an hour. I'll only be round at Bev's. Charlie's upstairs if you need anything.'

'Okay,' Rosie said.

'Don't leave us, Mummy. We don't want to stay here on our own. Can't we come with you?' Gracie pleaded.

Debbie sighed as her eldest daughter burst into tears. She was always so clingy. Rosie was the opposite, much more independent. Debbie sat down next to Gracie and cuddled her. 'You're a big girl now, Gracie. Don't cry. Look at your sister, she can't wait to get rid of me. You *are* silly sometimes. I tell you what, shall I ask Charlie to come downstairs and sit with you?'

'No,' Gracie insisted.

'I promise I won't be long,' Debbie said as she stood up.

'Oom Pa Pa' had little attraction any more for Gracie as her mother left the room. She was far too upset to concentrate on Nancy.

Feeling guilty, Debbie knocked on her son's bedroom door. 'All right to come in, love?'

Charlie was in a foul mood. He was still waiting to hear back from Lois and wanted to be left alone. 'Go away,' he shouted.

Debbie ignored him and let herself in. 'Charlie, I need a favour from you. I'm popping out for an hour. Your sisters are watching a DVD in the living room. Be a good boy and go downstairs, will you? Keep an eye on them and make sure they're okay for me.'

He smiled. 'No problem, Mum.'

As soon as he heard the front door close, Charlie wandered downstairs. Rarely did he get a chance to torment his sisters, but if and when he did, he grabbed it with both hands. 'Well, well, well, this is cosy,' he said, as he sauntered into the living room.

Rosie smiled. She didn't particularly like her brother

but was far too young to realise just how nasty he could be. Gracie could feel herself shaking. She knew differently.

Charlie sat down opposite Gracie and stared at her. He knew she was scared of him, and her fear made him happy. Leaning towards her, he watched her flinch. He laughed, picked up the remote and switched off the film.

'No, Charlie. We're doing *Oliver* at drama school. Put it back on,' Rosie demanded.

Still laughing, he took the remote into the kitchen with him. He opened the fridge and grabbed a beer. Sitting down at the table, he checked his phone. Still no text from Lois. What the fuck was she playing at? He knew her phone was switched on. He had delivery reports on his, so she'd definitely got his messages. Surely even if her mum and Mickey were about she could have sneaked out of the room? Pissed off, he downed his drink and lobbed the empty can into the bin. He was bored and needed to cheer himself up. Scanning the kitchen, he spotted the bread knife on the work top. He smiled, picked it up and strolled back into the living room.

'Wanna play sword-fighting?' he shouted, as he brandished it towards his sisters.

'Stop it, Charlie!' Rosie screamed, covering her face.

Gracie stayed silent. She wanted to protect her little sister, but was mute and unable to move.

'I know what we'll do.' Charlie was enjoying himself now. 'Let's go and see what the ponies think of the knife . . . I bet they like a bit of sword fighting.'

Gracie and Rosie screamed as he ran off towards the stables.

'Please don't hurt Britney,' Rosie sobbed. 'No, Charlie, no!'

Gracie sat rooted to the sofa as her sister chased after

him. Sobbing, she prayed for her mum to return. Why did she have to go out? Why? Why?

Aware that Gracie hadn't followed them out, Charlie concentrated on Rosie's pony.

'We've got no carrots today, Britney, but you can have this instead,' he said as he pointed the knife at the terrified creature.

Rosie was frantic and her continuous screams did nothing but egg Charlie on. He opened the stable door. 'I think Britney's tail is too long. Shall we give it a little trim for her, Rosie?'

Unable to ignore her sister's screams any longer, Gracie found some inner strength. Taking a deep breath, she stood up and ran after them.

'Leave Rosie and the ponies alone, Charlie,' she called to him. 'I swear if you don't, I'm gonna tell Mum and Dad. And if I tell them about this, I'll tell them everything else as well.'

Charlie smiled at Gracie's threat. He'd terrorised her as a kid. Now, she'd become far too grown-up for his liking. If this, or any of his other pranks, got back to that fat cunt Steve, there'd be murders. Charlie leaned lazily against the stable door. He still had the knife in his hand. 'I'll do a deal with you. I promise I'll never go near either of your ponies again on one condition: you keep your trap shut.'

Gracie nodded. 'Okay.'

Rosie disagreed with this. She clung on to her sister. 'We should tell Mum, Gracie. Charlie would get told off then, like we do when we're naughty.'

Charlie stared long and hard at his youngest sister. 'You say one word, Rosie, and I swear, I'll chop Britney up in little pieces.'

Gracie hugged the by now hysterical Rosie. 'She won't say a word, I won't let her.'

Charlie looked at Gracie and laughed. Still clutching the knife, he walked back inside.

Gracie waited until he was out of sight, then she kneeled down and held her sister's hands. 'Listen to me, Rosie, you mustn't say anything about this. Charlie's evil . . . you don't know what he's like. He will kill our ponies if we tell on him, I know he will. Promise me you won't tell Mum or Dad?'

Rosie nodded. She couldn't risk Britney being hurt, plus her sister was older and wiser than she was. Surely she knew best?

Debbie stood at the front door, unable to find her keys. She was an hour later than she'd intended. She'd got very drunk with Bev and lost track of time. Thank God Steve's car wasn't home. He'd have killed her for leaving the girls. Finally locating the door key, she unsteadily let herself in.

'How's my big soldier and my two little princesses?' she slurred.

Charlie shot out into the kitchen. Huddled together under a quilt on the sofa, Rosie and Gracie glanced at one another. 'Remember what I said? Don't tell,' Gracie whispered.

Debbie staggered into the room and smothered the girls in kisses. 'What have you two been doing? You're not still watching *Oliver*, are you?'

Before they could answer, Charlie walked into the room carrying a large tray. 'I've been taking good care of them, Mum. They've driven me mad with that film, though. 'Ere you go, girls,' he said, smiling at them for Debbie's benefit.

Gracie and Rosie looked at their brother in disbelief as he handed them a plate of turkey sandwiches. 'Are you hungry, Mum? Shall I make you something?' he asked politely.

229

'No, I'm fine, love.' Debbie was smiling as she left the room. Steve was so wrong about him. He was such a good boy, and more than old enough to baby-sit the girls.

'I'm off to bed now, Mum. Night, girls.' Charlie grinned as he walked up the stairs. He'd noted the terror in his sisters' eyes. There was no way they'd be grassing him up. He opened the door and flopped down on his bed. If he turned down the volume, he could watch one of his special films and text Lois again at the same time.

Lois sat on the edge of her bed and switched her phone off. She debated whether to tell her mother about the disturbing messages she'd been receiving all day, but decided against it. Her mum was best friends with her Auntie Debbie and she was determined not to cause any trouble between them. She'd tell her friend Gemma instead. That way she wouldn't cause ructions between their two families.

Lying back on her pretty pink quilt, Lois was filled with worry. The first few texts she'd received had been pretty strange, with Charlie referring to them as a couple and asking to meet her for a date. The last three had been far worse. Disgusting, in fact. She hadn't answered any of them and had no intention of doing so. How dare he text her asking to suck her titties? She was utterly revolted by the whole situation.

Determined not to spoil what was left of Boxing Night, though, she brushed her long hair and put it back into a ponytail. She'd only ever been in Charlie's company on Christmas Day in recent years so hopefully had another year before she must face him again. Trying to erase her worries from her mind, Lois wandered downstairs to watch telly with her mum.

In life people never know what's just around the corner

for them. As hard as poor Lois sat there that night, trying to convince herself that everything was going to be okay, her fate had already been sealed.

TWENTY-EIGHT

'That's my son you're slagging off, Mickey. Who the fuck do you think you are?'

'A father who's protecting his kids, that's who I am. And I'm telling you, Debs, I don't want that boy of yours anywhere near my Lois, you got that?'

'You'd better not be threatening me, Mickey. Your little fucking hangers-on might be shit-scared of you, but I'm not one of 'em. Now do me a favour, will ya? Don't ever fucking contact me again. I don't wanna see or hear from you until the day I die – and that includes turning up at me funeral.'

Debbie shook with anger as she replaced the receiver. How dare he say all those terrible things about her son? The names he'd called Charlie were unforgivable, and as for saying her boy had been born evil . . . that had been really below the belt.

Noticing her son standing in the doorway, Debbie wondered how much of the ten-minute slanging match he'd heard.

'You all right, love?' she asked guiltily.

Charlie nodded. 'At least I know now why Lois hasn't answered any of my calls or returned my texts. Why does Uncle Mickey hate me so much, Mum?'

Looking at her son's forlorn expression, Debbie felt

that her heart was about to break. She pulled him to her and hugged him tight.

'He doesn't hate you, love,' she lied. 'But he thinks of you and Lois as cousins, that's why he's so against the idea of you going out together.'

Not one for cuddles, Charlie loosened his mother's grip. 'But we're not even related, Mum,' he said, moving out of arm's reach.

As she lit up a cigarette, Debbie searched for the right thing to say.

'It wouldn't have bothered me, love, if you and Lois had got together, but Mickey's old-fashioned and dead against the idea. Just forget about her, Charlie. There's plenty more fish in the sea, and a good-looking boy like you can get any girl he wants.'

Charlie left the room without answering. Walking up the stairs, he allowed himself a wry smile. He'd pretended to his mother that he'd been really upset when secretly he'd been pleased. His Uncle Mickey had hated him for as long as Charlie could remember. The feeling was mutual, and he couldn't give a shit what his mug of an uncle said about him. The thing that pleased him most was that he now knew the reason why Lois had not responded to his calls and texts. It wasn't because she wasn't interested in him. Obviously she'd either had her phone confiscated or had been forbidden to talk to him.

Charlie had convinced himself, from the moment Lois had tapped on his door on Christmas Day, that she wanted him badly. Today's argument only confirmed he was right. Lois must have told her mum and Mickey that they were going out together.

Snuggling up under his quilt, he decided to drag Kevin down to Romford on Saturday. With luck, he might bump into Lois there. He daren't ring her any more in case Mickey had her phone.

Thinking of her fit body and pert tits, Charlie put his hand down his tracksuit bottoms and pleasured himself. He imagined he was fucking her and had one of his best wanks ever.

Steve arrived home at teatime to find Debbie furious again. Fortunately, they'd made up a couple of days ago and he was determined to be careful what he said in future. He hated arguing and didn't want another slanging match with his beloved wife.

'I'm telling ya, Steve, Mickey's a fucking cunt! Me and him are finished this time, and I really mean that.'

'Don't fall out with him, Debs. He's your brother and he loves you dearly. Give him a call in the week, when he's calmed down. Sort things out, like.'

'Over my dead body,' she screamed. 'I mean it, Steve. I don't ever want to see him again, not after what he said about my son. I mean, how would he like it if I spoke about Alfie that way?'

Shrugging his shoulders, Steve decided to keep his trap shut. She was a fiery one, his Debs, and if agreeing with her kept her happy, then he'd nod at all the appropriate times.

New Year was quiet and came and went without incident. Debbie and Steve had originally planned to go away with Mickey, Karen and the kids, but for obvious reasons the mini-break had been cancelled and their New Year's Eve was spent at home with Gracie, Rosie, and a Chinese takeaway. Charlie decided not to join in with the celebrations and stayed in his bedroom.

Steve was glad when the holiday was over. It had been a poxy Christmas and New Year, and he couldn't wait to get back to normal. The row between Mickey and Debs showed no signs of repairing itself and Steve was pissed off with the whole situation. 'Awkward' was the only way he could describe how he felt. He seemed to get it in the ear from all angles, when all he really wanted was a quiet life.

Doing things as a family was what he missed the most. He, Debs and the kids used to spend almost every weekend doing stuff with Mickey and his family, and it just wasn't the same without them. It was also unfair on Rosie and Gracie who missed their cousins dreadfully, especially little Alfie, and were continually asking when they could see them again.

Steve had tried to make Debbie see sense and sort things out, but she was having none of it. 'It ain't fair on the girls, Debs. They love Alfie and Lois, they're heart-broken.'

'Tough shit,' Debbie said, her obstinate nature preventing her heartstrings from being tugged.

It was only when the kids went back to school the following week that the enormity of the situation hit home to Debbie. Usually when the boys were at work and the kids at school, she'd spend her days with Karen, either lunching, shopping or going to the gym. Since the argument, they hadn't spoken. All of a sudden, Debbie realised there was now a major gap in her life. Determined not to mug herself off by phoning her sister-in-law, she headed off to the gym at their usual time, hoping Karen would do the same.

Charlie hated being back at school. As the bell signalled lunchtime, he quickly gathered his belongings and dashed off to meet Kevin.

'Oi, watch it, Weirdo!' he heard a voice say as he barged his way through the corridors. Opening his mouth to answer back, Charlie quickly shut it when he came face to face with Dean Summers.

'Sorry,' he muttered, eager to get away.

'So you should be,' Dean replied cockily, giving him a shove for good measure.

Charlie hated Dean Summers more than life itself and, as much as he refused to admit it, jealousy was the main cause of his hatred. A blond, good-looking, popular pupil, Dean was the leader of the pack and Charlie despised him for being everything he himself wasn't. Girls hung around at the gates and fell at Dean's feet. Everything he touched turned to gold, and apparently he had a promising future as a boxer to look forward to. Normally, Charlie wouldn't take shit off anyone and had personally bullied many of the weaker lads in his class, but Dean Summers was a different kettle of fish. Charlie was extremely wary of him and kept out of his way as much as he possibly could.

'Shall we go to the chip shop?' Kevin asked when he'd met up with his pal.

'Might as well,' Charlie replied unenthusiastically. He was still inwardly seething that Summers had made a mug of him in front of everyone.

'I wish I could order a murder weapon off the internet and do away with him,' he confided to Kevin.

Stuffing a handful of chips into his oversized mouth, Kevin nodded. He loved talking about doing away with people. He and Charlie had spent many hours flicking through websites about murderers and fantasising about carrying out the perfect crime themselves.

As they walked down the street, Charlie chucked his chip wrapping into the kerb. He was totally oblivious of the man sitting inside the tatty blue Escort, watching his every move. The man in the car waited until Charlie was out of sight then started the engine and drove off.

Debbie was on the treadmill when she noticed Karen come into the gym. Turning the speed down, she glanced around and waved. Her sister-in-law smiled, she wasn't the type to hold grudges. This argument had nothing to do with her. As long as Charlie kept away from Lois, she couldn't be angry with Debbie.

'All right?' she said as she got on the treadmill next to Debbie's.

'Yeah, I'm fine. You?'

The conversation between them was slightly stilted at first with neither of them wanting to mention the fall-out. An hour later, workout finished, Debbie decided to take the initiative. 'I dunno about you but I could kill for a glass of wine.'

Karen smiled and linked arms with her sister-in-law as they headed to the bar. Three glasses of wine later, Karen decided to bring up the inevitable.

'I'm sure Mickey didn't mean what he said about Charlie, Debs. He only said what he did in temper. He's so protective of Lois. She's really shy and naive in a lot of ways and definitely not ready for the dating scene.'

'He said some terrible things, Karen. Unforgivable, in fact. Charlie's my flesh and blood at the end of the day, that's what hurts me.'

'Honestly, he didn't mean it,' Karen repeated, squeezing Debbie's hand. 'His temper got the better of him. Mickey's such a hot head when he loses it.'

Debbie sighed. 'Don't I bleeding know it? Then again, I'm no different. Me and Mickey both have a temper on us. As kids we'd fight like cat and dog.'

Karen smiled. 'Look, let me have a word with him. I dunno about you, but I really miss meeting up as a family. Weekends aren't the same any more without you and Steve.'

'I miss it too,' Debbie admitted. 'And the girls are pining dreadfully for Alfie.'

'Leave it with me and I'll have a chat with him. I've

237

got to go now, Debs, I've got a nail appointment at two. I'll meet you here same time on Monday.'

'I'll see you then,' Debbie said happily.

Charlie picked up his pen and doodled on the inside of his exercise book. Mr Brooks was rambling on about fractions and Charlie couldn't be bothered to listen. Maths was his least favourite subject and bored him rigid. Glancing around the classroom, he momentarily locked eyes with Dean Summers.

'What you looking at?' Summers mouthed at him.

Charlie quickly looked away. Hearing the bell go, he waited till Summers had left the classroom before he made his way to meet Kevin.

The driver of the tatty blue Ecort looked into his mirror to check his appearance. He'd been told many a time that he was the spitting image of the actor Robert Carlyle. He loved being compared with the popular actor, and had recently had his hair cut exactly the same way, to enhance the likeness.

'What shall we do now then?' Kevin asked, willing to do whatever his friend suggested.

'Look what I've got,' Charlie said, taking a lump of cannabis out of his school bag. Laughing, he waved it in his friend's face.

'Cor, that's a big bit, where did ya get it from?'

'I've got loads of contacts,' Charlie said cockily. 'I've been playing me mum, ain't I? She felt sorry for me, 'cause she thought me Uncle Mickey had upset me, so I milked it and managed to get fifty quid out of her.'

'You're so cool, Charlie,' Kevin said, his eyes gleaming with admiration.

'I'm the bollocks, ain't I?' Charlie agreed. He loved nothing more than blowing his own trumpet.

The man in the blue Escort stared in his wing mirror

and watched Charlie approach. He downed the can of Strongbow he was holding, took a deep breath and opened the driver's door. It was now or never. He had to do what he had to do, before his bottle went. 'Charlie!' he shouted. 'Can I talk to you for a minute?'

Charlie turned around.

'Who's that, Charlie? Do you know him?' Kevin asked, nudging him.

'I don't fucking know who it is,' he replied, agitated.

Charlie was glad he had Kevin by his side. Even though his mate was grossly overweight and couldn't fight his way out of a paper bag, he was still a bit of back up.

'You are Charlie, aren't you?' the strange man asked, in an odd kind of accent.

'I might be,' he replied, trying to sound calm even though he felt unnerved. 'Who wants to know? Who are you?'

The strange man's eyes filled up with tears. Trembling, he held on to the door of the car for physical support. 'I'm your dad, Charlie. I'm your dad.'

TWENTY-NINE

Charlie remained quite still and showed little emotion as he stared into the eyes of his creator. He could feel his heart starting to race, but was determined not to show the way he felt inside.

He had no memories of his father, none whatsoever, and over the years he had invented a picture in his head of what his dad would look like. The stranger standing in front of him looked nothing like the handsome, strapping man he'd spent hours visualising and dreaming about.

The time father and son stood sizing one another up seemed like an eternity. Billy was the first to break the ice. 'It's wonderful to see you, Charlie. I've waited for this moment for years, son.'

Charlie glanced at Kevin, standing silently next to him, agog. Suddenly he felt angry, very angry. He'd needed his dad when he was younger, not now when the worst was over and he was starting to make his own way in life. 'What took you so long to fucking find me then?' he asked aggressively.

Billy shrugged his shoulders. 'I'm sorry, son, but a lot happened. Things were awkward.'

Charlie could feel the hatred bubbling through his veins. 'Awkward? fucking awkward! My *whole life's* been awkward, thanks to you.'

Billy averted his eyes. 'Look, we need to talk and we cannae do it here. Get in the car, son, and we'll drive somewhere, have a wee chat, try to sort things out.'

Charlie stared at his father defiantly. 'I ain't getting in that shit heap. I don't even fucking recognise you. You could be anyone, for all I know. You can't just turn up out the blue and expect me to come running into your arms. Anyway, I'm busy, I've gotta be somewhere.'

Realising that things weren't going to plan, Billy rummaged around inside the car for a pen. He scribbled his mobile number on to an old cigarette packet and handed it to his son.

'Look, Charlie, I know this has been a shock for you, but please call me. I really wannae get to know you, and I'm sure you must have a lot of questions for me. You can ring me, day or night, but you must promise me one thing.'

'What?' Charlie asked stroppily.

'You cannae tell your mother that I came to see you, nor your Uncle Mickey. Can you promise me that?'

'I suppose so.'

Smiling, Billy stepped forward to shake his son's hand. 'I'll look forward to hearing from you then, Charlie.'

Seconds later the tatty blue Escort had disappeared from sight.

Charlie rang his mum to ask her if it was okay for him to stay at a mate's. Not wanting him staying at a stranger's house, but overjoyed that he'd finally found a friend, Debbie reluctantly agreed. 'Okay, love, but only because it's a Friday and you don't have to get up for school. What time will you be home tomorrow?'

'Dunno.' He desperately needed some time alone, to think, and couldn't face being around his mum, Steve and the two spoilt brats. A small part of him felt he should tell his mum that his dad had turned up, but intuition told him there was bad blood between his parents and he'd be wiser to keep his trap shut. His mum had blatantly refused to discuss his dad over the years, insisting that Charlie forget he existed.

'You're better off not knowing him, love. Unfortunately he's not a very nice person,' she'd drummed into him.

Throughout his childhood Charlie had suffered recurring nightmares that his dad was trying to kill him. He would often wake up, sweating and shaking, but could never picture his dad's face during these dreams. The man attacking him was faceless, with a large hood over his head. His night-time experiences had got so bad at one point that he'd cried to his mum about them.

'All kids have nightmares. It doesn't mean anything, Charlie, it's all part of growing up.' Debbie had lied, determined to protect her son from the awful truth. The night frights finally stopped when he was about ten years old and had never returned since.

Billy McDaid sat on a barstool in one of his old haunts in Barking, quietly supping a pint. He'd been back in the area just over a week now and was feeling braver by the second. He'd been wary about coming back at first, but after a discreet bout of snooping had been pleased to learn that Debbie and all her old cronies were long gone from the area.

He'd heard through the grapevine that she had got married years ago, but no one seemed to know who she'd ended up with. Some poor, desperate bastard, Billy mused, chuckling at his own wit.

The years hadn't been kind to Billy. Prison had seen to that. His face was gaunt and lined, and he looked old for his years. His stint in Pentonville had been the hardest one to endure. There'd been a lot of blacks in there. For some unknown reason, they'd hated his guts and made his life a complete and utter misery. On being released from the 'Ville, he'd moved back to the North, this time to Manchester, and made a new life for himself there.

Drugs was the only game Billy knew and he soon found a pub to deal from profitably in the heart of Moss Side. With business doing well, he made the fatal mistake of falling in love once again. This time with a seventeen-year-old wild child called Angela.

Things went pear-shaped within six months of them moving in together. They began to row constantly because Angela could not deal with Billy's possessiveness and his violent, jealous tantrums. Billy was distraught when she finally kicked him out. Refusing to believe their relationship was over, he pestered her constantly and stalked her every time she went out. Finding out that she was dating a twenty-one-year-old musician was the final straw for him. High on drugs one night, he'd lain in wait and stabbed her new beau seven times in a frenzied attack. Once again, his temper had got the better of him. Unfortunately for Billy, the drummer survived and he was arrested.

Billy was made to pay by spending the next seven years in Strangeways. Being back in prison was tough for him, but he kept his head down and did his bird with pride. Being in prison in the North was much better than down South. The lads were friendly and the banter between inmates was good. There were a lot of lads in there from Scotland and having some of his countrymen around him made him feel much more at home than he ever had in the 'Ville.

Billy had too much time to think while on the inside and his son had been at the forefront of his mind for years. Towards the end of his stretch, he heard via his aunt that his mother had died. Instead of feeling sad, he felt only relief and a new determination to make something of his life finally. It was his mother's death that helped him decide to make amends with his own boy. He had to find him, get to know him, build some kind of a relationship before it was too late.

Two days after he was released, Billy bought a train ticket and ventured to London to track down his flesh and blood. Walking towards the Gascoigne Estate was like taking a trip down Memory Lane. As Billy approached the tower block, he felt a mixture of excitement and trepidation. Finding Andy was still living there was a relief to him as without his old pal he'd have been at a loose end for somewhere to stay.

'Billy! Fucking hell. Come in, mate, it's great to see ya,' Andy yelled, pleased to have someone to get stoned with. Billy had spent the rest of that first day puffing, downing cider and listening to Pink Floyd's *Dark Side of the Moon*.

After spending two days drunk, stoned and catching up on old times, he got his arse into gear and started the hunt for his son. Thankfully, tracking Charlie down had been a lot easier than he had envisaged. After a tip off that the boy attended a school in Upminster, Billy struck gold on the second one he visited.

'Do you know Charlie McDaid?' he'd asked a gang of cocky-looking lads who were having a cheeky fag outside the gates.

'Nah,' they'd replied, barely looking at him.

'What about Charlie Dawson?' Billy asked. He guessed Debbie might have changed the kid's name to hers, considering what had happened.

'What's it worth?' one little squirt asked.

Fishing in the pocket of his trousers, Billy pulled out a scrunched up five-pound note.

'Point him out and I'll give you this fiver.'

The squirt scanned the playground and pointed out a

lad, exclaiming, 'That's him. The weirdo over there in the woolly hat.'

Billy wanted to beat up the little squirt. How dare he call his son a weirdo? Chucking the money at him, he decided not to kick off. Seeing his son was more important to him.

Ordering another pint, Billy smiled to himself as he remembered today's encounter with his offspring. He was definitely a chip off the old block. A cocky little sod who didn't take shit off anyone. Charlie didn't look as Billy had imagined he would. 'Lumpy and gawky' was the best way to describe him, and he seemed a lot older than his fourteen years. Facially he looked more like his dad than Debbie, which pleased Billy no end. He was positive that the boy's natural curiosity would get the better of him and he'd call. Billy was also sure Charlie wouldn't break his promise and tell his mother or uncle that he had seen his dad.

Glancing at his mobile to make sure it was switched on and that service was good, Billy moved away from the bar and sat at one of the little tables, feeling pleased with himself. He put his feet up on a chair and made himself comfortable. He'd done all the hard work. Now it was just a case of waiting for that all-important call.

Charlie woke up the following morning with a bee in his bonnet. 'Come on, Kev. Get up, mate. I wanna go down to Romford, see if I can bump into Lois.'

Unwashed, the boys left the house within minutes. Four hours later, after searching all the places she'd said she usually went to, Charlie was about to give up.

'This is bollocks, Kev. It's so packed down here, we'll never find her amongst these crowds.'

Kevin, who was not usually one for bright ideas, came out with a beauty. 'I know Lois ain't allowed to take calls from your phone, Charlie, but why don't you ring her from mine? If her mum or dad answer, you can pretend it's a wrong number. If she answers, then bingo. Tell her you're down in Romford and wanna meet her. And ask her if she's got a mate for me.'

Charlie patted his mate on the back. 'Kev, that's a blinding idea. Why didn't I think of that?' he said, snatching the phone.

Charlie's heart leaped as the call was answered immediately. 'Hello, Lois. Guess who this is?' he said, putting his thumbs up at Kevin.

'I've no idea. Who is it?' she replied truthfully. She didn't recognise the voice at all. The next sentence made her blood run cold.

'It's me, babe, Charlie. I'm in Romford, standing by the cinema. I've been here hours searching high and low for you. Do you fancy meeting up? Are you in Romford?'

'I can't, Charlie,' Lois replied, unable to think of anything else to say. Undeterred, he carried on talking.

'I've been dying to get together with you, you know. Why didn't you take my calls? Was it because your mum and Mickey found out about us?'

Lois felt like screaming 'There is no us', but instead tried to be diplomatic. 'Look, Charlie, I really like you but we're cousins and I'd rather you didn't ring me again. I've got a boyfriend now, so it's a bit awkward if I get calls from other lads. I don't want to fall out with you but it's best this way.'

He could feel his face redden with anger. 'A boyfriend! Whaddya mean you've got a boyfriend? How can you do this to me? You two-timing fucking slag!'

Lois couldn't believe what she was hearing and was determined to get him off her case once and for all. 'You've got to leave me alone, Charlie. There never was a me and you, it was all in your mind. I just look upon you as family, nothing else, and you have to accept that. If you contact me again, I'm going to tell my mum and dad. And I mean that.'

'You fucking whore!' he shouted, before ending the call. He was fuming. How dare she make a mug out of him? Especially in front of Kevin.

'What's the matter? What did she say?' his friend asked innocently.

'Fuck off, you fat cunt! I don't wanna talk about it,' Charlie shouted, before running off and leaving his astonished mate standing in the middle of Romford.

Debbie was dishing up spaghetti bolognese for the girls when she heard Charlie come in.

'Hello, love. Did you have a nice time? There's plenty of spag bol here if you want some.'

'Leave me alone,' Charlie shouted as he ran up to the tranquillity of his bedroom.

Gracie and Rosie shot one another knowing glances. They'd avoided their brother like the plague since the night they'd been left alone with him. Thankful that he wasn't about to join them, they shared a secret smile and tucked into their meal.

Charlie lay on his bed. Thinking of Lois, obscenities spewed from his mouth.

'Slut. Whore. Cunt. Slag,' he muttered viciously.

Putting on one of his special films, he stood a chair against the door handle so that he couldn't be disturbed. As he watched the three men take the girl by force, he fondled himself and came within seconds. All women were slags and they all deserved to be fucking raped.

Turning off the film, he put on his Slipknot CD. His jacket was hanging on the wardrobe and he stared at it for ages before taking the empty cigarette packet out of the pocket. Three times he punched the number into his phone, and three times he erased it. On the fourth attempt, he plucked up the courage to let it ring. It was answered immediately.

'All right. It's me, Charlie,' he mumbled.

Billy McDaid ended the ten-minute call smiling to himself. He was meeting his boy tomorrow and taking him out for the very first time. He was so excited, he could hardly wait.

Charlie lay awake for hours that night, thinking about his dad. Their conversation had gone well and he was now looking forward to the meeting. Desperate not to be tired for his big day, he tried to force himself to sleep. Other people counted sheep to nod off, but not Charlie. He counted rape scenes that he'd watched in his special films. It never failed.

Tonight was different, though. Nervous, apprehensive and incredibly excited, Charlie tossed and turned all night.

Billy McDaid left the pub early and staggered towards Andy's. Charlie was half of him, they shared the same blood, and together they would set the world alight.

'Who's the Daddy?' Billy shouted happily. '*I'm* the fucking Daddy!'

THIRTY

'You're up early, love. Where you off to? Anywhere nice?'

Lying came easy to Charlie; in fact, he was an expert at it. 'Romford, Mum. I'm meeting me mate Kevin and we're going to watch a film.'

'That's nice, love.' Debbie was as pleased as punch that Charlie had finally found a friend. Being a protective mum, she wondered what the lad was like. 'Why don't you bring Kevin round one night for tea, Charlie, so I can meet him?'

Snatching a bit of toast off Rosie's plate, he looked at his mum in horror. 'Why would I wanna do that? It's better where he lives, there's more to do there. It's boring round here.'

'Okay, love, it was only a suggestion,' Debbie said, deciding to shut up quick.

After cadging a lift off his mum to Brentwood station, Charlie sat on the platform, feeling nervous but excited at the same time. He was meeting his dad at eleven at Romford station. After originally feeling dubious, he was now looking forward to the rendezvous.

Billy leaned against the car door and lit up a fag. Dressed in light denim jeans, a black leather jacket, white Reebok trainers and a black baseball cap, he felt good but in reality looked completely ordinary. 'All right, son?' he said as Charlie walked towards him.

Charlie smiled and got into the passenger seat of the Escort. His heart was beating like a drum, but he was determined not to show his nervousness. He wanted to impress his father, not make a prick of himself.

'What do yer fancy doing then, Charlie?' Billy asked, flicking the ignition into life.

Deciding to speak the truth, but not knowing if he was doing the right thing, he decided to chance his luck.

'I wouldn't mind going for a beer.'

Billy looked at this son and smiled. Apart from the kid's attitude, his first impression of Charlie had been neither here nor there. His son's answer had just washed away any fears he may have harboured about the lad.

'We'll go over my way, Charlie. No one will ask questions about your age there.'

Billy flicked through the radio channels, found an illegal rave station and turned the sound up full blast. 'Do you like this type of music, son?' he asked, banging his hands against the steering wheel.

Charlie nodded. It wasn't the kind of music that usually floated his boat, but he pretended to like it. The more he and his father had in common the better.

Billy drove as fast as he could to Barking. He wanted to impress the boy, show him he was with it rather than past it. Screeching to a halt in a side road, he turned the engine off and led his son into a rundown-looking alehouse.

Charlie felt all grown up as he sauntered in behind his father. He'd been drinking for ages, but only when alone indoors or in the privacy of Kevin's bedroom. Pleased that this father was treating him like an adult rather than a child, as his mother did, he was now more than willing to give Billy a chance.

As father and son sat face to face for the very first time, conversation was awkward to say the least. They knew nothing whatsoever about each other and managed only to talk about music, films and football for the first half an hour. Billy was a big Glasgow Rangers fan and was quite disappointed that Charlie had little knowledge of the beautiful game. He shouldn't blame the kid, mind, he'd had no dad there to teach him the basics. Things would've been very different if only he'd stayed around.

Three pints later both of them started to open up.

'How's your mum, son?' Billy asked cautiously.

'Okay, I suppose. I don't have that much to do with her, really. I can't stand Steve. He's the bloke she married. They're both too wrapped up with me little sisters to worry about me, so I spend most of me time in me bedroom.'

Billy looked intently into Charlie's eyes. He could tell by the way he spoke that the boy really wasn't close to Debbie and that pleased him immensely. Fucking bitch! It was her fault he'd missed his son growing up in the first place.

'Who's the dude that your ma married?'

Ramming cheese and onion crisps into his gob, Charlie spoke between mouthfuls. 'He's a wanker. He hates me. He was Uncle Mickey's best mate, apparently, and that's how she met him.'

Billy's blood ran cold as memories of Uncle Mickey's best mate came back to haunt him. Surely not? It couldn't be the same geezer who had nearly killed him, could it? Trying to keep his voice calm, Billy asked the all-important question. 'Is this Steve a fat bastard, by any chance? I remember some of Mickey's mates. The one I'm picturing was a big bloke. He used to have cropped hair.'

251

'That's him,' Charlie replied instantly. 'He's still got cropped hair now. I hate him, and I hate my sisters. I don't like my nan much either, or Granddad Peter. In fact, I hate them all.'

Making the excuse that he needed to use the loo, Billy dashed off. He needed five minutes alone to recover from the shock he'd just had. Memories of the day he'd nearly died often come back to plague him. He couldn't believe that Debbie had ended up marrying the same brutal bastard who had helped to terrorise him that fateful day. After dousing his flushed face in cold water, he stared into the filthy, cracked mirror.

He couldn't tell Charlie the whole story, that was for sure. He would only make himself look like some weak cunt, and he couldn't risk Charlie blurting something out to Steve or his Uncle Mickey either. Billy would be dead meat if that were to happen, that was a dead cert.

By the time he'd pulled himself together and headed back to the table, his son had thought of some questions of his own.

'I've got some things I wanna ask you now. Like, why did you walk out on me when I was little?'

Billy could barely answer, such was his guilt. Not for the way he'd treated Debbie – that bitch had deserved everything she got – but because of the way he'd treated his son.

'Me and your ma never got on, Charlie. We used to fight a lot. I loved you more than words can say, but her . . . she was no good. I wouldnae have abandoned you, you know, but after I split up with your ma, I got arrested and then put in prison. By the time I was released, your ma had moved on. I tried to track you down, but I was skint at the time. When my money ran out, I had no option but to move back up North to sort myself out.

252

'You have to believe me, Charlie, when I say this. There wasnae a day went by that I didnae think of you. In fact, when I was in prison, the only thing that kept me going half the time was the thought of meeting up with you again one day. To be honest, son, I cannae believe that day has finally come. I wanted to contact you before, but I had to wait till you were old enough. I couldnae have got you on your own when you were younger. I had to wait till you were at an age where you'd understand.

'I swear, Charlie, if your mother, Uncle Mickey or Steve got wind of me meeting up with you, there'd be murders. You must promise me, whatever happens, you never breathe a word to them that you've seen me. Can you promise me that?'

'I promise,' Charlie said, liking this man sitting in front of him more and more. He was well impressed that his dad had done a bit of bird. He couldn't wait to tell Kevin. 'What did you go in prison for?' he asked excitedly.

'Violence, son, fighting. I did someone over real badly. Two stretches I did for the same thing.'

Charlie looked at his dad in awe. Obviously, he had no idea that one of this father's victims was his own mother. Feeling that they had more in common than he could ever have dreamed, he confessed to his dad about his own love of violence. 'I've beaten up loads of lads at school and I've got a stash of really brutal films and computer games.'

Billy smiled.

Desperate to impress, Charlie carried on. 'And I love a good porno, I've got loads of them. I'll lend 'em to you, if you like.'

'Good lad,' Billy chuckled, amused to find that his son had plenty of the old McDaid spirit. 'One thing you must remember, Charlie . . . women are slags. They fuck you

253

and then they fuck you up. Do yourself a favour, son. Pull 'em, shag 'em, then get rid.'

'I totally agree with you,' Charlie said excitedly. 'There's this girl, Lois, and she's a prick tease. One minute she's all over me, and the next she don't wanna know. She's Uncle Mickey's stepdaughter, but me and her ain't properly related. I know she's gagging for it. What should I do about it?'

Billy thought long and hard. Uncle Mickey's step-daughter? What a result. What an opportunity for revenge. 'How close is Mickey to this Lois?'

Charlie swigged his pint. 'He proper idolises her. He's adopted her and everything. Apparently her real father was an arsehole – that's what I heard me mum say anyway.'

'Really?' Billy said with interest. 'You leave it to me, son. I'm blinding with birds and can get my wicked way with anyone I want. I'll give you some tips, show you how to reel her in.'

'Cheers, Dad,' Charlie replied, holding his pint aloft.

Realising that this was the first time he'd said the D word, Billy smiled with happiness. Acceptance was a wonderful thing and he'd waited a long time for it.

'Do you like to have a puff, Charlie?'

'Yeah. Why, you got some, Dad?'

Patting his son on the shoulder, Billy picked up his car keys from the table. 'Come on, I'll take you round my mate Andy's. I'm staying there at the moment. We'll go round there for a smoke, eh?'

Charlie was in his element as he followed Billy out of the pub. His dad was well cool. He was almost bursting to tell Kevin what a dude he was. He'd never felt like he belonged at home, felt almost alien somehow to his mother, sisters and big wanker Steve. Well, now he belonged. Not only that, he had the coolest dad in the whole wide world and was loving every single minute of being with him.

Andy was as stoned as stoned could be, but still managed to welcome the boy with open arms. Charlie thought he was pretty cool as well. Andy reminded him of Ozzy Osbourne, and he'd always been a big fan of him and Black Sabbath. The way he'd bitten the head off live bats made Ozzy a hero in Charlie's eyes.

The rest of the evening passed in a drunken, drug-induced blur. Having run out of lager, Charlie started on his father's cider and by ten o'clock was knocked for six.

'You cannae go home like that, son. Your mother'll go mental. Ring her and say you're staying at a friend's. You can stop here and I'll drop you home tomorrow.'

'I can say I'm staying at Kev's, she don't know where he lives,' Charlie slurred.

'Do it now before you crash out then,' Billy urged, noticing his son was fading fast.

Incapable of stringing a text together, Charlie handed the phone to his father and told him what to put. The message read: *Staying at Kev's. I'll be home early to get ready for school.*

A return text came back in seconds. *I want you home 2nite, Charlie. You know you're not allowed to stay out when you've got school the next day.*

Billy laughed as he read Debbie's text. 'Your mother hasnae changed, son. Still a fucking moaner, after all these years.'

Charlie propped himself up against Andy's threadbare sofa. Eyes rolling in his head, he tried to focus on his father. 'What shall I do, Dad? She really gets on my nerves. Shall we wind her up for a laugh?'

'Let me do it, son. It'll give me great pleasure to wind your fucking mother up.'

All three of them giggled as Billy typed in a reply. *Mum, I'm busy shagging a bird. I'll be home tomorrow, OK?*

Debbie was sitting on the sofa with Gracie and Rosie as the second text came through.

'Who's that, Mummy? Can I read it out for you?' Gracie asked.

Debbie quickly shoved the phone into her handbag, away from prying eyes. Steve was in the kitchen, dishing up the Indian takeaway that had just been delivered.

'Just popping upstairs, love,' she shouted, as she ran upstairs with her bag. Hiding in the bedroom, she rang Charlie's number. No answer. She tried again. After the fifth go, she gave up and decided to text him instead.

Billy snatched at the phone as Debbie's text bleeped through. He was in hysterics as he read it out loud. '*OK, love. Don't be late in the morning as you have to go to school. And please be careful, you don't want to catch a disease or get anyone pregnant. Don't forget to use a condom. Love you.*'

Debbie ventured downstairs to eat her Indian takeaway. She felt worried, but was also very happy. Her son was underage, but so what? At least now she knew that her Charlie was growing up into a normal, hormonal teenager. Many a night she'd worried about him being abnormal, but it must just have been a teenage phase he was going through. He had mates now, and girls were on the scene, so surely the worst was over. Tucking into her chicken korma, Debbie felt more content than she had in ages.

Billy helped Charlie into Andy's bedroom. 'Goodnight, son,' he said as he chucked the filthy, drink-stained quilt on top of him.

'Night, Dad. Love you.'

Billy smiled as he left the room. The words he'd just heard were music to his ears. Not only had he acquired a son, he'd also acquired an ally. Between them they could hatch a perfect plan. Get their revenge on every bastard who had ever upset or come between them. The thought made him laugh. An evil, nasty, vindictive laugh. For the first time in ages, Billy's cold, cold heart was filled with excitement and passion at what was to come.

THIRTY-ONE

The newly decorated changing rooms reeked of a mixture of paint, sweat and feet, and Charlie felt nauseous as he changed into the ill-fitting shorts which his teacher had demanded he wear. Charlie hated PE and rarely participated, but due to the excitement of meeting his father the previous day he'd forgotten to ask his mum for the usual letter saying he couldn't take part.

His PE teacher, Mr Marshall, was having none of his lame excuses and had found him some kit to wear from the lost property box. 'Come on, lads, chop-chop. I want you to sprint three times around the football pitch. Whoever's last can stay behind and clean the showers.'

The first to finish was Dean Summers, who broke into song as Mr Marshall patted him on the back. 'Championee, Championee, o-lay, o-lay, o-lay.'

Charlie felt sick as he tried to keep up with the rest of the lads. He was only slightly overweight, but terribly unfit. By lap two, he had given up the ghost and decided to jog instead.

'Come on, Dawson. I've seen hippos move faster than that,' Mr Marshall shouted at him, much to the amusement of the other lads.

Finishing last, Charlie flopped on to the grass, holding

his sides. 'I don't feel well sir. I feel really sick,' he told his teacher.

'That's because you're a lummox, Dawson,' came the sarcastic reply. Charlie was then forced to join in with one of the five-a-side football matches that were in progress. After showering and dressing, he sat on the wooden bench in the changing rooms, waiting for the bell to go. Pretending to be engrossed in a magazine he was flicking through, he couldn't help but listen to Dean Summers going on about his latest conquest.

'Honestly, she's well fit and she's a really nice girl. She looks a bit like a younger version of Jordan,' he bragged.

'Where did you meet her? What's her name?' asked one of the lads.

Charlie's ears pricked up.

'I met her at a party. Her name's Lois. She's a right sort and she's well into me. I've seen her every night since I met her.'

Desperate to hear more, Charlie was annoyed when the bell rang to signal home time. Picking up his school bag, he fell into step behind Summers.

'Where do you think you're going, Dawson?' Mr Marshall shouted. 'You're on shower duty for finishing last, son.'

Chucking his bag to the floor in exasperation, Charlie removed his socks and shoes, rolled up his trousers, and for once did as he was told. Mr Marshall was a well-known ogre and Charlie knew if he refused the task he'd been given, he'd be on detention for weeks on end. He set to work silently, one thought going over and over in his mind. Surely Summers hadn't been referring to his Lois? It couldn't be, could it? It had to be a coincidence. His Lois wouldn't be going to parties. His Uncle Mickey wouldn't allow it.

'I've finished, sir,' he shouted.

After a brief inspection, Mr Marshall gave his grudging approval. 'It's passable. Off you go, Dawson.'

As if Charlie's day hadn't been bad enough, he was in for more unwelcome news on his arrival home.

'Granddad Peter's organising a surprise anniversary party for Nanny and I insist you come,' his mother informed him.

'Why do I have to go, Mum? I hate family parties, you know I do. Can't you just take the girls with you?'

But Debbie wasn't taking no for an answer and, for once, stood her ground with her son. 'Look, Charlie. If it wasn't in honour of your nan, I wouldn't make you go. But she's been good to you over the years, the only one apart from me who has stuck by you through thick and thin. Please, love, don't argue with me. Come, if only for my sake.'

'When is it?' Charlie asked unwillingly.

'It's this Saturday, love. Peter's booked a hall in Upminster, not far from your school. I'm sure you'll enjoy it when you get there, and I think Lois is coming.'

The last sentence swung it, as Debbie had known it would.

'Okay, I'll go, but just for your sake,' Charlie lied.

Debbie smiled. She knew she shouldn't encourage the Lois situation, but her son had a girlfriend now and she would take great pleasure in informing Mickey of this fact if he kicked off on Saturday night.

'So, who's this girl you spent the night with? What's her name?' Debbie asked her son excitedly.

'Samantha,' Charlie said, thinking of the first name that came into his head. He'd watched a porno recently and the bird on that had been called Samantha. Right dirty bitch she was, as well.

'And where did you meet her?' Debbie asked. She

was ever so happy for him and couldn't wait to meet the girl.

'Romford.' Lying came easy to Charlie.

'Why don't you bring her with you to Nanny's party?' Debbie suggested.

Charlie looked at her in horror. 'Nah. I've only just met her, Mum. It's way too early for introductions and all that.'

Desperate to avoid further interrogation, Charlie escaped to the quietness of his bedroom. He was dying to ring his dad, to tell him how much he'd enjoyed yesterday and find out when they were meeting again.

The rest of the week passed quickly and pleasantly for Charlie, who spent three out of the next four evenings in the company of his father. His mum had become a complete pushover since he'd lied to her about having a girlfriend, and gave him far more leeway than before.

'I know you're courting now, love, so I'm gonna let you stay out until midnight on school nights. And if you want to stay over your girlfriend's house at weekends, as long as her parents don't mind, then I don't either.'

'Thanks, Mum,' Charlie said, smirking to himself.

He'd have told her he had a bird ages ago if he'd had known it'd turn her into a total sucker. He used to have to be indoors by ten on school nights and had rarely been allowed to stay out all night before. Now she thought he was indulging in tits and fanny, she was a different person, and Charlie and his dad succumbed to many a laugh at his mother's expense.

Billy loved it because it was his jokey text that had set the ball rolling in the first place. Charlie loved his newfound freedom and exercised it to his own advantage. 'I'm staying round me girlfriend's on Friday, Mum. I'm taking her out for a meal.'

'Take that, love, and treat her,' Debbie said, chucking fifty quid his way.

Charlie had spent the night pub crawling with his father and then dossing round Andy's flat, puffing until the early hours.

'Did you have a nice time, son?' Debbie asked him when he arrived home, looking rather dishevelled, on Saturday afternoon.

'I had a lovely time, Mum, and Samantha really enjoyed it,' he replied, escaping upstairs before she could clock the state of his drug-induced hangover.

The Silver Wedding anniversary party was a complete surprise to June and her face was an absolute picture as she was led into the packed hall, to be greeted by all her friends and family. Peter had pretended to his wife that they were attending a friend's fiftieth and June was more shocked than anyone to find out that she was the real guest of honour.

'Oh, Peter. This is the nicest thing that anyone's ever done for me. Thank you so much,' she said, as her eyes filled up with tears.

'You're worth it, my darling,' he replied truthfully.

Debbie sat down at a table with Gracie and Rosie. Spotting Karen, holding Alfie by the edge of the dance floor, she gesticulated for her to come and join them. Mickey headed towards the bar to help Steve carry the drinks.

'Where's Lois?' Debbie asked her sister-in-law.

'She's coming later. She's gone to a friend's sixteenth birthday party.'

'Charlie's gone out. He's got a girlfriend now. He'll be here later as well,' Debbie said proudly.

'They grow up so quick, don't they? Lois has recently fallen in love for the very first time. She's bringing him with her later. He's such a lovely lad, even Mickey approves. Is Charlie bringing his girlfriend with him?'

'No. He's only been with her a couple of weeks. I told him to bring her, but you know what lads are like, he got all embarrassed.'

Karen smiled knowingly and agreed.

Taking the glass of wine that Steve handed her, Debbie took a large gulp as she saw her brother approaching the table. The argument they'd had had never been sorted and tonight would be the first time they'd come face to face in weeks. Karen nudged Mickey as he sat down. She'd had words with him before they left home and had no intention of letting him forget.

'All right, Debs?' he muttered, unable to look his sister straight in the eye.

'Fine, thanks. You?'

The Mexican stand-off looked set to continue until June intervened. 'Excuse me a minute,' she said to Steve and Karen. 'Right, outside you two. Now,' she demanded, scowling at Mickey and Debbie. Once they were in private, she let rip at them.

'I have never seen such childishness in the whole of my life. You're brother and sister, for goodness' sake. So you had an argument – so what? For fuck's sake, be adult about it and make it up. You've got lovely partners, the pair of you, beautiful children. It's not just you this affects, you know, it's your families as well. We're an East End family and East Enders stick together. The pair of you both need to get down off your high horse and sort things out, once and for all, because I'm sick of it.'

Before she walked back inside the hall, June fired a parting shot. 'If you can't sort things out between you, do me a favour and both go home. This is my party and I'm not having it spoilt by anyone.'

Mickey and Debbie stood looking at one another in shock. Bursting into laughter as her mother stomped off, Debbie was the first to break the ice. 'I'm sorry, Mick.

263

Things ain't been the same without you about. Can we put all the shit behind us?'

Pulling his little sister into his arms, Mickey hugged her tightly. 'I'm sorry, too. I should never have said them things about Charlie. I didn't mean 'em, sis. I just lost me temper.'

'Shall we let bygones by bygones?'

'Definitely,' Mickey replied. Linking arms with his sister he led her back into the packed hall.

Steve nudged Karen as he watched their respective spouses walk towards them. 'Well, thank fuck for that. Yous pair want your bleeding heads smacked together,' he chuckled as they reached the table.

'It's her fault, innit? Obstinate little cow, she is,' Mickey said playfully, cuddling Debbie at the same time.

'Don't you blame me, it's your fault, you tosser,' Debbie replied, enjoying the banter.

June smiled to herself as she spied on her children from the other side of the hall.

'You look happy, my dear. Are you enjoying yourself?' Peter enquired.

'I'm having the best evening ever,' June replied, squeezing his hand.

'All right, Mum?'

Debbie had been that busy mucking about with Steve and Mickey, she hadn't noticed her son approach the table. 'Sit down next to me, love,' she ordered, patting the seat next to her.

Gracie and Rosie exchanged glances as their brother plonked himself next to them. They hadn't known Charlie was coming tonight. He'd kept well out of their way since Gracie had threatened to tell on him, and his absence from their lives had brought them both happiness and relief.

'How's your girlfriend? Did you have a nice evening?' Debbie asked loudly, hoping everybody could hear.

'She's fine thanks, Mum,' Charlie lied, scanning the hall for a glimpse of Lois.

'Mummy, I need to go to the toilet, will you come with me?' whined a tired Rosie.

Not wanting to sit there alone with her brother, Gracie followed her mum and sister.

Karen smiled at Charlie. 'Your mum tells me you've got a girlfriend now?'

'Yeah, Samantha.'

'Lois has got a boyfriend, too. You'll meet him later. She's gone to a birthday party with him first and they're coming here after.'

'That's nice,' Charlie managed to mutter before excusing himself from the table. Needing some fresh air, he left the hall and wandered into the nearby playing fields. After checking no one was watching, he sparked up a ready-rolled joint. His dad had made him a couple of extra-strong ones, to get him through the evening.

'Fucking slag. Slut. Whore,' Charlie spat. The thought of seeing Lois parade her new bloke was enough to do his head in.

Wandering into the hall, he plonked himself back at the table, his face like thunder.

'You all right, love?' Debbie asked, noting his dark expression.

'I'm fine,' he replied abruptly, wishing he could think of some feasible excuse to leave and go home.

'Get Charlie a lager,' Debbie urged Steve as he headed for the bar once more. She was desperate to cheer her son up. Maybe treating him like an adult would help.

Charlie noticed Lois with her long flowing hair, as soon as she entered the hall. She was wearing a figure-hugging green satin dress, silver sandals, and had a squashy silver handbag slung over her shoulder. Noticing she was alone, he breathed a sigh of relief, stood up in a gentlemanly way and offered her his seat.

'No, thank you. I'd rather stand,' she replied, barely glancing at him.

'Where's my future son-in-law?' Mickey asked, tormenting her.

'Talking to someone. Oh, here he is,' Lois gushed proudly.

Charlie hadn't heard Mickey and Lois's conversation due to the loudness of the disco. The first realisation of what was happening hit him like a ton of bricks. Standing next to Lois, with his arm slung casually around her shoulders, was none other than Dean Summers.

Determined not to mug himself off, Charlie plastered a false smile on his face. He had to pretend to enjoy the rest of the evening, there was no other way.

'All right, Weirdo?' Summers asked him at one point, when everyone else was out of earshot.

Charlie bit his lip and kept up the façade. Inwardly, he was seething. He'd never felt so angry or been so humiliated in the whole of his life. He excused himself politely and headed outside for another joint. As he lay flat on the damp grass, his thoughts were all over the place. How dare that slag Lois bring the fucking school bully with her to ruin his nan's party for him? Flicking the last of his joint into a nearby bush, Charlie summed up his options. He could either disappear early, and let them win, or stay the distance and front it out. Deciding on the latter, he headed back into the hall with only one thought on his mind: revenge, no matter what it fucking took.

THIRTY-TWO

As the next few months flew by, Charlie was either on a real high or a complete bloody low. The highs came in the company of his father with whom he now spent more and more time.

Charlie now knew what it felt like to care about somebody other than himself. His mum, nan, even Kevin, he'd sort of liked, but hand on heart, he probably wouldn't have shed so much as a tear if any of them had been wiped out overnight. With his dad, things were different.

He adored Billy, respected him and would be devastated if anything bad were to happen to him. He could sense that the feeling was mutual and, for the first time in his life, Charlie had met someone he truly loved and couldn't live without.

His low moods were a different kettle of fish. He seemed to suffer from them as soon as he walked through the school gates. Listening to Dean Summers going on about Lois was bad enough, but he also had to listen to him brag about the other girls he was getting it on with behind her back.

Charlie was furious that Dean was cheating on Lois. If she'd been his girl, he'd never have done that. He'd have been faithful to her. If it was his cock she was sucking, he certainly wouldn't have felt the need to look elsewhere.

The personal abuse he suffered from Summers had become far worse since his nan's party. Lois had clearly told Dean about Charlie's crush on her and the texts he'd sent her. His love rival had now informed the whole school that he was a sex-case who had hit on his own cousin. He was now commonly referred to as 'the nonce' or 'the pervert'.

Charlie was used to being called a weirdo, he'd had it his whole life, but he hated his new names, and things had got so bad that he dreaded going to school. Now that the Easter holidays were coming, he couldn't wait to take a rain check from the building and the pupils he'd grown to despise.

His dad had promised to take him up to Scotland for the first time and Charlie was well excited at the thought of going away. The only problem was his mother who seemed determined to stick a spanner in the works. He'd told his mum that he was going to a caravan site in Clacton with Kevin and his nan.

'I'm happy for you to go away, love, but I want to meet your friend and his nan before you go.'

'Don't embarrass me, Mum,' an agitated Charlie pleaded with her.

'I'm not trying to embarrass you, Charlie, but I'm not letting you toddle off with people I've never even seen. That's not what good mothers do, love.'

Charlie reluctantly agreed to introduce her to them and clued Kevin and his nutty old bat of a nan up on what to say.

Now deep in thought about his impending holiday, Charlie failed to hear his English teacher shouting his name.

'Are you with us, Dawson, or on a different planet?' the teacher asked sarcastically.

'Sorry, Sir. I was miles away.'

'Probably dreaming about shagging his own cousin,' Dean Summers muttered, making sure he'd said it loud enough for the rest of his classmates to hear.

A few of the lads sniggered.

Putting his head down, Charlie pretended not to notice. He took a deep breath to quell his temper and carried on writing his essay about serial killers.

The rest of the week was purgatory for him. As the bell went on Friday afternoon to signal the start of the Easter holidays, he breathed a sigh of relief that he had a couple of weeks away from the hellhole formally known as school.

Lagging behind the other lads, so that he couldn't get picked on further, he dawdled his way to meet Kevin at their usual rendezvous.

'Is your mum here yet?' his friend asked, excited to be meeting Debbie for the very first time.

'Dunno, I suppose so. Now you know what you've gotta say, don't ya?'

''Course,' Kevin replied confidently.

Spotting his mum's motor, Charlie led Kevin towards the vehicle. He didn't need all this shit, but his mum had been adamant about picking them up so that she could meet Kevin and have a quick word with his nan when she dropped him off.

'Mum, this is Kevin,' Charlie mumbled, shoving his fat friend into the back of his Mum's X5.

Debbie smelt the BO long before she saw the lad it belonged to. 'Hello, Kevin,' she said politely, opening her window to get some fresh air.

'Nice car, ma'am,' Kevin replied, desperate to make a good impression.

Kicking his friend in the leg, Charlie took over the conversation. 'Tell Mum about the caravan holiday, Kevin.'

Debbie listened intently as the boy rambled on about Clacton and his nan.

'So when you meet her she might not come across as normal. Some people can't understand her properly because she's a bit senile,' he explained, in a clumsy attempt to reassure Charlie's mum.

Pulling up outside a rundown house that had a jungle instead of a garden, Debbie switched her car's engine off and followed the boys up the path. As she glanced at the filthy-looking bit of net that was hanging at the window, Debbie noticed a little doll-like figure of what seemed to be a plastic witch hanging behind it.

'Would you like a cup of tea?' Kevin asked, his fat body glistening with sweat at the excitement of having being driven home in a brand new BMW.

'No thank you, love. Just get your nan so I can have a quick word and I'll be on me way.'

Glancing around, Debbie noticed a gang of street urchins looking at her from the other side of the street. Good job she'd refused the cup of tea, she thought. She'd have come out to no wheels on her car, by the look of it.

'Hello, my name's Doreen,' said the wizened-looking old woman who appeared at the front door then.

'I'm Charlie's mum – Debbie.'

Doreen rebuffed the hand that was offered to her. 'I don't shake hands, it's unlucky,' she cackled. 'Now, what do you want?'

'Oh. I'm just checking that it's okay for Charlie to go away with you and Kevin for the weekend? He keeps talking about this Clacton trip and I know boys can be a handful.'

Doreen smiled a gappy smile at her visitor, while trying to remember what her grandson had told her to say. She couldn't remember jack shit so kept her reply short. 'That's fine. Now is there anything else you want?'

'No, that's all,' Debbie replied, rather taken aback by the obvious madness of the old woman. A heavy rain had started to fall, so Debbie said goodbye and nudged Charlie towards the car.

'"I'm singing in the rain, ha ha ha, singing in the rain, he he he,"' Doreen sang after them as they walked down the path.

Putting her foot on the accelerator, Debbie waited till she'd pulled out of the turning before glancing at her son. 'I'm not happy about you going away with them, Charlie. They're notrights, the pair of 'em.'

'Oh, please, Mum.'

'Haven't you got any normal friends, with normal parents, who you can go away with?'

Charlie could feel his trip to Scotland slipping out of his grasp and decided to play his trump card. He rarely ever cried and knew how much his mum hated to see him upset. 'Please let me go, Mum. I know Kevin's a bit odd, but he's the only friend I've got at school.'

Noticing his mum's pained expression, he forced the tears to roll freely as he carried on. 'Honestly, Mum, you don't know what it's like for me. All the boys there hate me. Lois's boyfriend told them that I used to text her. Now they call me a nonce and a pervert. No one will talk to me apart from Kevin. Please, Mum, I really need a holiday. Please say I can go.'

Kerbing the car, Debbie pulled a tissue from her handbag and handed it to Charlie. 'Look, son, it's not Kevin I'm worried about, it's the old girl. She's not the full shilling, love. How are you and Kevin gonna take care of her?'

'Oh, she's no trouble. Just a bit barmy, that's all. Please, Mum, say you'll let me go. I'll be on my best behaviour and I promise I'll ring you every day.'

Looking at her first-born and seeing him so upset, Debbie didn't have the heart to say no. 'All right, you can go. On one condition, though. I want you to leave your mobile switched on all the time and ring me morning, noon and night.'

'Okay, Mum,' Charlie said, relieved that his crocodile tears had worked.

As he looked out of the window, he covered his face with the tissue and smiled.

Scotland here I come, he thought happily.

The trip to Scotland turned out to be everything Charlie had wished for and more. He loved it up there, and felt more at home in Glasgow than he ever had in London. His dad's Auntie Mary, with whom they stayed, was a lovely woman. Within the first couple of days of meeting her, Charlie felt as if he'd known her all his life. She was a very funny lady, and her stories about his dad when he was a young boy entertained Charlie no end.

'What about my nan and granddad?' Charlie asked her one night. He'd asked his father the same question once. Billy had told him they were dead, and never to mention them again.

'Your granddad was unknown. Your nan was a nasty woman, pure evil. Do yourself a favour and forget they ever existed, Charlie,' his aunt insisted.

The rest of the holiday was one almighty piss-up and Charlie loved going from pub to pub, meeting friends and acquaintances from his dad's past. Being introduced to all and sundry as Billy's son made him feel extremely proud. He even enjoyed going to footie, watching Glasgow Rangers play, much to Billy's delight.

'My door is open to yous boys anytime you want,' Auntie Mary said as she waved goodbye to father and son.

The train journey home was a long one and Billy and Charlie amused themselves by drinking cider and tucking into Auntie Mary's packed lunch. As more and more alcohol went down, their conversation turned into a heart-to-heart.

'What really happened between you and Mum? Why did you actually split up, Dad?' Charlie was desperate to know the truth.

'It's a long story, son. Let's not go into it, eh?'

'Please, Dad, tell me. I know there was a fight and you hit Mum and got put in prison, because I overheard someone talking about it in one of the pubs we went in.'

Unable to look at his son, Billy kept his head bowed as he told him the whole sorry story of the time he'd spent with his mother. The only part he left out was the fact that he'd dangled Charlie out of the window to save his own skin. He couldn't tell his boy that, it was too despicable. 'I was out of order, Charlie. I was taking so many drugs at the time, I was out of my head, wee man. I didnae know what I was doing.'

'I understand, Dad. I don't think badly of you.'

'I'm so pleased to hear that, Charlie. I love you, son, and I never, ever want you to think badly of me.'

With his guts already spilt, Billy decided it was the right time to tell his boy about the ordeal he'd suffered at the hands of Mickey and Steve.

'I never wanted to leave you, son, but they ran me out of town. I nearly died that day. The injuries took months to heal.'

Charlie couldn't quite believe what he was hearing. He'd always hated Steve and Mickey and now he hated them even more. How dare they try and kill his dad and leave him for dead?

'You shouldnae really blame Steve,' Billy said, determined to put his son straight. 'It was your Uncle Mickey's idea. He was the one who beat me to a pulp and wanted

273

to leave me tied up to the tree, to die slowly. It was Steve who stopped him from leaving me there.'

'I hate Uncle Mickey! I wish we could get our own back on him, Dad. He threatened me when I was a kid . . . he's always hated me, you know.'

Cracking open two more cans of cider, Billy handed one to Charlie. 'It's probably not personal. He just hates you 'cause you're my boy. That's why I told you I didnae want no one to know you were seeing me. Mickey said if I ever came back to the area, he'd kill me. I only came back because of you, Charlie. I'll hang about now till you're sixteen, and old enough to leave home and live with me.'

'I wish we could move to Scotland, Dad. I hate it at home and I hate school. That boy I told you about, the one who's going out with Mickey's daughter, is making my life a misery.'

Billy slammed his can down on the table between them. 'What's this kid been saying then? What's he been doing to yer?' he asked in a raised voice.

'Just taking the piss out of me all the time. He's told the whole school I'm into incest. That bitch Lois must have told him I asked her out and obviously all the lads at school believe she's my real cousin. They don't know we're not even fucking related.'

'Why didnae yer give him a good hiding, son? Show him who's boss.'

Charlie smiled. 'I would, normally. If it was anyone else I'd have thumped 'em by now, but this Dean's a shit hot fighter. He's been boxing since he was ten and he's never lost a fight.'

Billy sat silently for a few minutes, deep in thought. 'Look, son, you're sixteen next year. Why don't me and you fuck off up to Scotland then? It'll be a new start for the both of us. In the meantime, just put on a brave face at home and at school. And if you want me to come down and have a word with this Dean, I will. He willnae fuck with me.'

'Nah, it's not worth it, Dad. It'll make me look like I can't stick up for meself. Are you really serious about us moving to Scotland?'

'Of course I am,' Billy said, smiling broadly. 'But first we've got to think of a plan to get your Uncle Mickey back. What do you say?'

Charlie grinned at his dad. 'Definitely. I'm up for it. What we gonna do?'

Laughing at his son's eagerness, Billy handed him the last of the sandwiches. 'You leave it with me. I'll think of something that your Uncle Mickey won't fucking forget till the day he bastard well dies. We'll have the last laugh, Charlie boy, you'll see. No one fucks with Billy McDaid and gets away with it. No one.'

THIRTY-THREE

Summer 2006

Happy birthday to you,
Happy birthday to you,
Happy birthday, dear Charlie
Happy birthday to you.

Charlie sat at the dining table, feeling embarrassed. He hated birthdays, especially his own. As his mother presented him with a cake, he obeyed her orders and made a wish as he blew out the candles. Shutting his eyes, he wished for Dean Summers to get knocked out in his next bout and never regain consciousness.

'Time for your presents now, love. You give him ours, Steve,' Debbie said.

'Happy birthday, Charlie,' Steve muttered through gritted teeth.

'Thanks,' Charlie said, as he snatched the gift bags off of the stepfather he hated.

After politely thanking his mum and Steve for the iPod, new mobile phone and J.D. Sports vouchers, he took the bag that Gracie had been forced to hand to him.

'Thanks, girls,' he said falsely, smiling at her and Rosie as he pocketed the HMV voucher.

'Can I go out now, Mum?' he asked, following her into

the kitchen. He was desperate to get drunk, stoned or both.

He was fifteen today and too old for all this birthday bollocks his mum was forcing upon him. It wouldn't surprise him if she handed him a bowl of jelly and fucking ice cream or demanded he participate in a game of Pass the Parcel.

Debbie was disappointed that he was going out so early but forced a smile. ''Course you can, love. Oh, and while I remember, we're going away next weekend with Mickey and Karen. Nanny and Peter are coming as well. I thought it might be nice if you came with us.'

Charlie looked at his mum in horror. He couldn't think of anything worse. 'I'm a bit old for going away with me family now, Mum. Can't I stay here?'

'Well, I suppose so. Will you be all right here on your own?'

'No, Mum, someone might break into the house and murder me,' he replied sarcastically.

'I'm sorry, Charlie. I know you're a big boy now. I'll have a word with Steve, see what he says. I am your mum, I can't help worrying about you, love.'

'Well, don't,' Charlie insisted. Stupid cow, he thought, as he slammed the front door and marched down the road. He was meant to have met his dad at seven and now he was going to be late.

'Happy birthday, son,' Billy said as Charlie finally made it to the pub. Handing him a carrier bag, he smiled at his boy's delight as he pulled out a Glasgow Rangers shirt.

'Thanks, Dad. I love it. I can't take it home, though. Mum will be well suspicious where I got it from.'

'I'd already thought of that. Just wear it when you're with me and you can leave it at Andy's. Right, come on, birthday boy, let's get langered!'

Charlie enjoyed that birthday more than any he had

had before. He'd told his mum that he was staying round at his imaginary girlfriend's house. Being able to spend the whole night with his dad made it extra-special to him.

At school the following day, Charlie got an even bigger treat when he heard Dean Summers telling a couple of the lads that Lois had dumped him.

'She scrolled through my phone and found them texts and pictures that Gemma bird sent me.'

Summers stopped talking as soon as he noticed Charlie standing nearby. 'Fuck off, Nonce Case,' he shouted.

Charlie smiled to himself as he slouched away. Lois had always been too good for an arsehole like Dean Summers. Briefly, Charlie wondered if she had fucked Dean. He hoped not. If she had, then she was nothing but a fucking slag.

The rest of the week dragged by for Charlie. He'd never been left in an empty house before and by the time Friday morning arrived, he was doing buttons to have the place to himself.

When he'd waved his mum, the brats and Fat Bollocks off, Charlie slipped out of his school uniform and changed into a pair of Nike shorts and a T-shirt. He'd pleaded with his mum to let him have the Friday off school but she'd refused, so he was going to forge a letter himself, saying he had a hospital appointment. There was no way he was sitting in a boring classroom when he had this gaff to himself.

He fished under his bed and pulled out the crates of lager he'd hidden. Armed with his most obscene porno, skunk and Rizlas, he wandered downstairs to watch one of his special films on the large plasma screen.

Six lagers, five joints and three pornos later, Charlie was bored shitless. His cock was sore from wanking and he'd also come all over his mum's Persian rug and stained the bastard thing. Fed up, he decided to go for a beer with his dad. He scrolled through his phone and rang Billy.

'I'm sorry, son,' he said sheepishly. 'I've gotta date tonight. I'm taking that little barmaid out . . . you know, the one who works behind the ramp in the Spotted Dog.'

Charlie was fuming as he ended the call. He always spent Friday nights with his old man and now he was being blown out, because of some silly tart. Rolling another joint, he lay back on his luxurious sofa, wondering what to do with himself.

Lois Dawson sat at a secluded table in a corner of Nando's and pushed her plate of food towards her friend Marie.

'Come on, Lois. You've got to eat something. You've barely touched your chicken and no boy is worth wasting a Nando's for.'

Lois forced a faint smile. 'I don't feel hungry, Marie. I feel like shit and I just want to go home. I really loved Dean, you know. I'm so upset. How could he cheat on me? How could he do that?'

Leaning across the table, Marie squeezed her best friend's hand. 'Look, Lois, it could be worse. Thank God you never slept with him. Imagine if you'd lost your virginity to him, you'd have felt far worse than you do now.'

Lois fiercely wiped the tears away from her eyes. 'I know you're right, but part of me wishes I *had* slept with him. I think that's the reason he wandered, because I wouldn't give him what he wanted.'

Marie shook her head. 'Don't blame yourself. You're looking at him through rose-tinted glasses. He's a boy, at the end of the day, and they all think through their willies.'

Unable to take any more of the truth, Lois put her jacket on. 'Marie, do you mind if you don't come round mine tonight? Don't take it personally, I love you to death, but I just want to be on my own.'

'Are you sure you're gonna be all right?'

'I'll be fine,' Lois replied. 'I'll ring you tomorrow.'

After leaving the restaurant, she headed towards the nearest cab firm. All her mates had hated Dean, said he was a flash bastard. Well, it was her choice and she was determined to sort things out with him, maybe even give him another chance. Deciding to ring him as soon as she got home, she broke into a run.

As he watched the next porno flicker into life, Charlie switched it off. He was bored with pussy now, especially with watching it. What he needed was a bit of the real thing. Ringing his dad again, he was disappointed when the call went on to answer phone. He'd wanted his old man to change his mind, blow out the bird and take him clubbing.

He debated whether to ring Kevin, but decided against it. Since he'd been reunited with his father, Kevin had begun to bore the arse off him, and although he was an ally at school, Charlie felt as though he didn't really need him in his life any more. Picking up his phone once again, he scrolled through the dozen or so numbers he had, and stopped at Lois's. Now, should he text her or should he not? He knew she was home alone because he had over-heard his mum talking to Karen on the phone. Now she'd split up with Dean, maybe she could do with a bit of company. With the skunk and lager clouding his judgement, Charlie planned his text with precision.

'Thank you, driver,' Lois said, as she paid the nice Asian man his fare.

Scurrying up the driveway, she let herself indoors and headed to her mum and dad's drinks cabinet. Lois was a good girl and rarely touched alcohol, but the thought of contacting Dean filled her with dread and she needed a bit of Dutch courage. What if he was no longer interested in her or had another proper girlfriend? She poured herself a vodka and she held her nose as she swallowed it.

Charlie opened another can of lager and rolled yet another joint. He was out of his nut now, but felt lively and bois-terous with it. In fact, he felt on top of the world. Three times he'd printed a text, but three times he'd erased it. Now he had come up with one he was ready to send. Putting his lager down, his big stubby fingers went like the clappers as he tapped it out.

The vodka made Lois feel calm, but also woozy. Hoping she was doing the right thing, she checked her text.

Dean, I hav a 3 house n realy need 2 c u. I'm sori 4 us splitin up, plz txt bk x

Feeling brave, she pressed Send.

Dean Summers was at a pal's boxing presentation. He was two sheets to the wind, happy as Larry and, unfor-tunately for Lois, had left his phone at home.

Her heart jumped when she heard her phone bleep.

I realy wana fuk u. We both on r own, so how bout I come round?

Dean's name never came up. How strange, Lois thought, as she typed in her answer.

Hury up, I'm w8in 4 u. p.s. Bring sum johnnies.

Heading back to her mother's drinks cabinet, Lois poured herself another vodka. She was as nervous as hell, but even though he'd been a sod to her, she knew Dean Summers was the one she wanted to do it with.

All her friends who had already done it told her that you knew when the time was right, and Lois knew that her time had come. She was also desperate not to lose

281

Dean and that was a major part in her decision. Her mum and dad would go apeshit if they knew, but this was her choice and hers alone. She quickly ran upstairs to get changed. She was unsure what to wear, but finally chose a denim mini-skirt and pink basque. Tonight was special and she was desperate to look sexy for Dean.

Charlie saw the text come through and couldn't believe his luck. Bring some johnnies? What a result! Searching through his mum's address book, he scanned the pages for Mickey and Karen's address. He knew they lived in Parkstone Avenue, but wasn't sure of the number.

Spraying some Lynx under his arms, he rushed to the bathroom to wash his sweaty cock. Not one for cleanliness, he rubbed a bit of Dove soap around it, dried it with a towel and raced down the stairs to ring a cab.

The cab seemed to take forever to arrive and the journey even longer. 'Can you stop in a garage for me on the way?' he asked the driver.

When they pulled up at an Esso garage, Charlie leapt out and stood in the queue.

'Condoms, please, mate,' he whispered.

'Vot? I cannot hear you,' said the Indian assistant.

'You know . . . johnnies,' Charlie said quietly, embarrassed and all too aware of the posh-looking woman who happened to be standing behind him.

Ranjit smiled. Finally he understood. 'Johnny no vork here,' he said, smiling.

Charlie couldn't get out of the garage quick enough. Fuck the condoms, his dad had always told him it felt far better bareback anyway.

Lois put on her Busted CD and lit one of her mother's scented candles. Nervously, she poured another drink.

* * *

'Pull over here, mate,' Charlie said, recognising the enormous black wrought-iron gates. Chucking the driver a score, he leaped from the car and rang the buzzer. Lois released the intercom and checked herself in the mirror one last time, adding a bit more lip gloss. Then she unlocked the front door, left it ajar and made her way into the lounge. Flustered, she picked up her glass and lay down on the sofa. She was desperate to come across as cool as possible even though her heart was telling her different.

Charlie thought that all his Christmasses had come at once as he closed the front door behind him.

'I'm in here, babe,' he heard Lois say as he made his way towards the lounge.

What a result, he thought, taking a deep breath to quell his growing excitement.

Glancing up from the magazine she was pretending to read, Lois's smile froze in shock.

The glazed expression on Charlie's face told Lois all she needed to know. Her very worst nightmare was about to become reality.

THIRTY-FOUR

'Now come on, girls, don't mess me about. Bedtime . . . pronto.'

'Oh, Mum,' Gracie and Rosie answered in unison with sulky looks on their faces.

'Now,' Debbie said in her no-nonsense tone.

Gracie grabbed Rosie's hand and the pair of them stomped towards their temporary bedrooms.

'Little mares they've been on this holiday,' Debbie said, looking at her mum and Karen for some sort of sympathy vote. Little did Debbie know that the reason for her daughters' outlandish behaviour was their relief at being miles away from their brother. Without Charlie present, the girls could be themselves and let off steam.

June couldn't help laughing. 'They're like clones of you and Mickey at that age, Debs. Both of them have inherited the Dawson stubbornness.'

'Thanks, Mum. Blame me, won't ya?' Debbie replied, laughing in spite of herself.

'It's good they've got a bit of spirit,' Karen piped up. 'I wish my Lois was more like them. At least they stand up for themselves. My Lois is so quiet and shy. Alfie's not so reserved, but Lois worries me sometimes. She came out of her shell when she met Dean, but I think he's cooled it a bit and she's hardly been out of her bedroom since.'

Debbie put her empty glass on to the table. 'Young love, eh? Listen, I'd rather your Lois any day than them two little fuckers. Now, who's for another glass of wine?'

'Yes, please,' June and Karen answered together.

The holiday was proving to be a great success. The kids loved Centerparcs, there was so much to do there, and the adults were loving it just as much. Even Peter, who normally walked around with a face like a smacked arse, was joining in with things and being jovial. Debbie felt she'd made a great choice in hiring the villa for a mini-break. It had been her idea to go there in the first place.

'Wey-hey!' Mickey shouted, amused to see Steve wobbling about, struggling to stay on the bike he'd hired.

'Fuck this for a game of soldiers,' Steve cursed, desperately trying to keep his balance. He hadn't ridden a bike for years. Trust him to lump up at a poxy place where cars were banned.

Hearing a commotion behind him, Mickey looked around, fully expecting to see that Steve had taken a tumble. Noticing it wasn't his friend but Peter who had ridden head first into a tree, Mickey couldn't control his laughter.

'You all right, mate?' he asked, trying not to giggle.

'No, I'm bloody not,' Peter replied, clutching his left ankle.

Wobbling over to where Peter lay and Mickey stood, Steve took one look at his brother-in-law's expression and pissed himself laughing.

'It's not funny, you know. I think I may have broken something,' Peter complained.

'You have, you've broken the fucking bike,' Steve chortled, as he clocked the buckled front wheel.

Unable to control their laughter, he and Mickey fell to the ground in hysterics.

Peter sighed. He should have known better than to

spend the evening drinking with his stepson and friend. They both drank like fish and he'd spent the entire night forcing himself to keep up with them. As soon as he'd hit the fresh air he'd felt drunk, and now this had happened. It was all June's fault. She'd made him go out, was adamant that some male bonding would do him good. 'You go out with the boys, Peter. I'm having a girlie night in with Debbie and Karen,' she'd told him.

Looking disdainfully at the two laughing fools rolling about on the floor, Peter picked himself up and dusted himself down. This was going to be one hell of a weekend and he needed it about as much as he needed Tony Blair in power.

Lois sat on the sofa and felt sick with fear. It had been almost an hour now since Charlie had entered the house, and it had been the longest hour of her entire life. Feeling virtually naked, thanks to her stupid choice of outfit, she grabbed a big cushion and hugged it to her.

'Don't do that, you've got nice legs,' Charlie said indignantly.

Not wanting to upset him, Lois moved the cushion away.

'Let's have another drink, eh? We're in no rush. We've got all night, ain't we?' he said, picking up a bottle of Scotch.

Lois nodded. She was on autopilot now and knew that, whatever she did, she must not upset him. He had gone mad earlier when she'd tried to explain that the text messages she'd sent were meant for Dean, and not for him.

'Slag, whore, prick tease!' he'd screamed while pacing the room, eyes blazing with anger.

As frightened as she was, Lois found a strength within herself that she hadn't known existed. Instinct told her that Charlie was far more dangerous than she could ever have imagined, and she guessed from his glassy expression that he'd been experimenting with drugs of some kind. Deciding that her best, and probably only, way out would be to be nice to him and play him along, she held her glass aloft.

'I'm ready for a top-up now, Charlie. I was just thinking . . . maybe next week me and you can go on a proper date, if you like? Do you fancy the pictures or something?'

Charlie knocked back a large gulp of his Scotch and smiled. What did she think he was, fucking stupid? She was trying to play him, give him false hope by being nice. He could see her true opinion sketched across her face. She hated him. He repelled her. Eaten up with anger, he stood up and walked towards her.

'Do you think I'm silly or something? Do I look like some fucking div?'

'Charlie, you've got me all wrong. I really like you. I want . . . '

He lunged at her and covered her mouth with his hand. 'Shut the fuck up, you silly slag.'

Realising her plan hadn't worked, Lois lashed out with her fists. As she struggled and fought with him, Charlie's excitement grew along with his hard-on. 'I'm all turned on now. Look what you've done to me, you horny bitch.'

As Charlie grabbed both of her hands and held them against his penis, he let out a sigh of pleasure. Overcome by hysteria, Lois let out a piercing scream.

With the exception of Peter, who had hobbled off to bed in one of his moods, the party at Centerparcs was still in full swing.

'I was a good tap dancer in my younger days,' June informed her son- and daughter-in-law.

'She's off,' Mickey laughed, nudging Debbie. They'd had years of listening to their mother droning on about her years in pantomime. Now it was Karen and Steve's turn.

Winking at her brother, Debbie decided to get her mother at it. 'Don't just tell 'em Mum, show 'em your moves.'

June didn't need asking twice. 'Wooh!' she screamed as she broke into both dance and chorus. '"Any time you're Lambeth way, any evening any day . . . "'

'Go on, girl, get stuck in,' Steve shouted above the laughter and applause that her act was receiving.

'" . . . Everything's free and easy, do as you darn' well pleasey . . . "'

'Go on, Mum,' Debbie screamed.

'"You'll find yourself, doing the Lambeth Walk – oi!"'

Finishing off her party piece with a handstand against the door, June fell into a drunken heap on the floor. The ensuing laughter was so noisy and raucous that unluckily for Lois her mother did not hear the phone ringing in her handbag.

'Give us that fucking thing here,' Charlie snarled, snatching her mobile out of Lois's shaking hand.

'Please don't hurt me, Charlie,' she whimpered as he pinned her down once again on the sofa.

The fear in her voice and eyes only added to Charlie's ecstasy. Unable to contain himself, he released his rock-hard cock from his tracksuit bottoms. His sloppy kisses and the feeling of his tongue exploring her mouth made Lois feel physically sick. Gagging, she started to pummel him again with her fists.

'Get off me, you bastard!' she screamed hysterically.

'Wanna play rough, do you, bitch?' Charlie asked. He was too far gone now even to think of the consequences of what he was doing. This was like every porno he'd ever watched, but ten times better. He'd always got off on watching men forcing women, but the reality of doing it for real was the best feeling he'd ever experienced in his life.

He tried to enter her, but had no joy. Lois was wriggling away like an eel beneath him and, being inexperienced and reasonably well-endowed, he couldn't fit himself inside her. Desperate to relieve himself, he opted for a different tactic. Moving up her body he pinned her shoulders down with his knees, opened her mouth with his hands and shoved his throbbing cock inside.

'Suck it, you fucking whore,' he said, over and over again.

Trying to ring her daughter for the third time and getting no reply, Karen temporarily gave up and put the phone back into her handbag.

'What's the matter?' Mickey asked, clocking his wife's worried expression.

'I can't get hold of Lois. I got a missed call earlier from her, but I've tried her mobile and the landline and there's no reply.'

'Have you spoken to her at all today?' Mickey asked, concerned.

'Yeah, this morning and this afternoon. She was going out for a meal with one of her friends.'

'Well, there you are then,' he replied, panic subsiding. 'She's probably having a whale of a time.'

'Yeah, you're right,' Karen said, sipping her drink. 'I'll try her again later.'

Feeling himself about to ejaculate, Charlie was furious when Lois bit the end of his penis with such force, it left him doubled up in pain with his eyes streaming with tears.

'You bitch! You cunt!' he screamed, as she struggled to get away from him.

Hyperventilating, Lois tried to make a dash for the front door. She was trembling from head to foot and running wasn't easy. Panic seemed to have paralysed her. All her movements felt too slow. She grabbed the door handle, safety only seconds away.

Unfortunately for her, Charlie had locked the door on his arrival.

As soon as he arrived home from his boxing presentation, Dean Summers galloped towards his bedroom to locate his mobile. He'd been surrounded by females all night, as per usual, but none of them had interested him. He really liked Lois and was determined to put things right with her. Seeing the text message she'd sent him earlier, he cursed himself for forgetting the bastard thing. He tried to ring her, and slung the phone down in temper when he realised he'd used up all his credit. Slipping his shoes off, he bunged his trainers on. He was a fast runner. If he sprinted, he could be at hers in ten minutes flat.

After failing to unlock the front door, Lois managed to run upstairs and grab the landline phone from her mum's bedroom. She didn't know her mum's or dad's mobile numbers off by heart, so 999 was her only option.

Despite the pain he was in, Charlie forced himself up the stairs after her. Just as she was about to dial, he yanked the wire from the wall, ending her call before it had begun. He grabbed Lois's hair and shoved her on to her mother's bed. His penis was limp by now. Desperate to revive it, he ripped off her knickers and shoved his grubby fingers inside her.

Unable to defend herself any longer, Lois just let him do it. All the fight had gone out of her now. She wished he'd just kill her and get it over with. If he raped her, she wouldn't want to live. She knew without a doubt that her life would never be the same again after tonight.

With Lois no longer able to struggle, Charlie failed to get an erection. Feeling embarrassed by his own failure, he made a suggestion. 'Let's go downstairs and have another drink, eh?'

Lois felt too weak and disgusted even to answer.

Dean put his hands on his knees and caught his breath after his mad sprint. Luckily he knew the security number to open the gates off by heart, so punched it in and jogged up to the house.

Charlie was pouring himself a Scotch when he heard Dean Summers's booming voice.

'Lois, open the door, babe! I'm sorry I never called you earlier, but I've only just got your text.'

'Help! Help! The doors are locked. I've been attacked, Dean . . . please help me!'

A strong lad, he easily snapped a big branch off a nearby tree. With all his might he smacked it against a front window, over and over again, until the glass finally cracked.

Charlie knew then the game was up. He was no match for Dean Summers, that was for sure. Deciding escape was his only option, he ran to the front door, unlocked it, and as he heard Summers climb in through the living-room window, ran for his goddamn' life.

Dean could not have been more shocked when a partially naked Lois threw herself sobbing into his arms.

'You're safe now, Lois, I'm here to protect you,' he soothed, trying to comfort her. 'What happened? Who did this to you?'

'It w-w-was Ch-Ch-Charlie.' Deep in shock, she was unable to get her words out properly.

Dean held her close. 'How did he get in here? Did he break in?'

Lois sobbed. 'I opened the d-door. I thought it was y-you.'

'I'll fucking kill him! Where is he? We've gotta ring the police.'

'Nooooo!' Lois cried. 'No police. I can't handle it. Just ring my mum and dad, they'll know what to do.'

'Where's your phone?'

'I don't know,' she sobbed hysterically. 'He took it off me.'

Dean led her into the lounge and sat her down on the sofa. He'd have liked to chase after Charlie fucking Dawson and give the freak the beating of his life, but he couldn't leave Lois. She was way too distressed.

'Did he . . . you know?'

Shaking her head, Lois looked at the floor. 'Nearly. He tried to,' she managed to say.

Spotting her phone under the chair, she pointed it out to Dean. 'I want my mum,' she sobbed.

Karen had been asleep for almost an hour before the shrill sound of her ring-tone awoke her. Reaching into her handbag, she fished for her mobile.

'Hello,' she said, still half-asleep.

As the realisation at what had happened to her beautiful daughter hit her, Karen pinched herself to check she wasn't dreaming. When she realised she wasn't, she opened her mouth. Her screams could be heard the length and breadth of Centerparcs.

THIRTY-FIVE

'For fuck's sake, Karen, stop screaming.'

Slapping his wife's face seemed to bring her to her senses. They were in bed, he wasn't even sure what was going on.

'Lois has been attacked,' she mumbled, between sobs.

'Attacked? What do you mean? Has she been in a fight or something?' Mickey asked.

Karen shook her head.

He stood up decisively. 'Look, get dressed, babe, and we'll be home in a couple of hours. Come on, that's my girl.'

He was annoyed but calm. Karen was probably over-reacting, but if anyone had hurt Lois, his pride and joy, Mickey would fucking well kill 'em. But surely it was nothing like that. She'd probably had an altercation with a gang of girls around Romford or something, maybe ended up with a cut lip or a black eye for her trouble.

'What exactly did she say, love?' he asked as he slung his jeans on.

Karen was still on the bed, rocking backwards and forwards. 'I should never have left her,' she said over and over again. The shock seemed to have thrown her into a trance.

Mickey knelt down beside his wife and squeezed her

hands. When angry, patience wasn't one of his virtues. He was getting wilder by the minute at Karen's total lack of communication. 'I need to know what she said.'

'She said it was Charlie,' Karen whispered, knowing the words she'd just uttered would rip their wonderful family apart forever.

The fury and hatred that Mickey felt at that moment would live with him forever. The thought of his evil, perverted scumbag of a nephew laying one finger on his beautiful, kind daughter made him want to commit first-degree murder. Eyes blazing, he snatched the phone off Karen and frantically dialled their home number. His blood ran cold when Dean explained what had happened to her.

Steve, June and Peter had all been woken up by the shouting and screaming and, along with the kids, were now wide awake. Knocked for six by all the wine she had consumed that evening, Debbie was still out for the count and hadn't heard a thing.

Throwing on a hooded sweatshirt and shorts, Steve ushered the wide-eyed kids back into their bedroom and tapped on Mickey and Karen's door. 'Are you two all right in there?'

Mickey yanked the door open with such force it nearly flew off its hinges. 'No, we're not. That evil fucking stepson of yours has just attacked our baby . . . our Lois. I swear to you, Steve, nephew or no nephew, when I get my hands on that little cunt, I'm gonna kill him!'

Steve was still half asleep and had no idea as yet of the enormity of the situation. 'Calm down, Mick. Don't do anything rash. You don't know exactly what's happened yet.'

'Don't do anything rash? You cunt! Are you fucking serious? That perverted little piece of scum has just tried to rape my fucking daughter and I will deal with it exactly how I like. Now move out of my fucking way so I can go and get the motor.'

June, standing behind Steve, burst into tears and went into the bedroom to comfort Karen. She'd always known that one day Charlie would show his true colours, but this was just too awful for words.

Not knowing what to do with himself, Peter put the kettle on. Sometimes he wondered what type of family he'd got himself involved with. Thank God he'd stood down from the Council. He could just see the headlines now: 'Councillor's Grandson Rapes and Attacks Cousin'. That would have done his political career the world of good.

Shutting the door of the villa, a shocked Steve followed Mickey outside. 'I just want you to know, mate, that I'm on your side. Whatever you decide to do with Charlie, I'm with you all the way. I've always known deep down that the little shit was an accident waiting to happen, and I've only ever suffered him because I love Debbie so much.'

Looking into the eyes of his best pal, Mickey knew he was telling the truth. 'The kid's a goner, Steve. There's no other way. I ain't letting this one go.'

'I understand. I'd do the same if it were Rosie or Gracie.'

Throwing his big arm around his pal, Steve led him back into the villa.

Debbie was still dead to the world. It took five minutes of Steve shaking her to rouse her from the drunken coma into which she'd fallen. Sitting up, she rubbed her tired eyes. 'What's happening? What's the time?'

Steve was a big softie at heart. His eyes filled up as he struggled to break the dreadful news to his beloved wife.

'I don't know the exact story, Debs, but apparently he attacked Lois and . . . I dunno . . . tried to rape her by all accounts.'

'Never in a million years,' Debbie cried, leaping from her bed. 'I know my Charlie's no angel, but he wouldn't do that. He's just a kid, for Christ's sake.'

Steve looked at her in despair. She just didn't have a fucking clue when it came to her beloved baby boy.

'I shouldn't think Lois made it up. He's obviously done something, Debs, ain't he?'

Grabbing her phone, Debbie frantically dialled her landline and then Charlie's mobile. With no reply from either she grabbed her suitcase and started packing. Her son needed her. She had to get home to him, fast.

By the time Debbie had finished packing, Mickey and Karen were long gone. Alfie was still fast asleep and June had kindly offered to take care of him while they tended to Lois. 'Don't worry, son,' she told Mickey. 'He can stay with me and Peter. I've got loads of clean clothes for him at home, he'll be fine with us.'

Mickey had nodded, led his distraught wife outside and left immediately.

The stony silence in Steve's people carrier on the journey home was broken only occasionally by the sound of June's muffled sobbing. Peter clasped his beloved wife's hand tightly and, for the first time ever, had no words of comfort for her.

Rosie and Gracie sat huddled together in the back. They'd heard the adults talking and knew that something awful had happened, involving their brother. Rosie was innocent and far too naive to understand the actual gist of the conversation. Gracie was more streetwise. She understood completely.

Noticing her big sister start to sob and shiver, Rosie did her best to comfort her. 'Please don't cry, Gracie. It's not us in trouble – we've been good girls. It's Charlie who's been naughty. He's been a bad boy to Lois and now he's upset her.'

The mention of her brother's name made Gracie feel nauseous. Unable to reach the window in time, she vomited into her lap.

It was Steve who stopped the car, cleaned his daughter up and tried to soothe her.

Debbie spent the whole journey with a blank expression on her face, staring lifelessly out of the window. She wanted to hear her son's side of the story before she had him hung, drawn and quartered like everybody else planned to do.

Karen was shaking like a leaf when Mickey screeched to a halt on their driveway. Dean opened the door and briefly summarised all he knew before ushering them into the lounge.

'Oh Lois, my baby! It's okay, Mummy's here now.'

Karen sobbed as she pulled her fragile daughter into her arms.

Lois was trembling so much she could barely speak. The sight of her adoring parents made her feel dirty, embarrassed, and incredibly stupid for having got herself into such a terrible situation in the first place.

'Did you ring the police?' Mickey asked Dean.

'No. I wanted to, but Lois wouldn't let me. She was adamant she didn't want them involved, and I didn't want to upset her any more. I thought I'd best leave that to you.'

The mention of the word 'police' made Lois howl like a wounded animal.

'Please don't call the police! I won't talk to them. I swear, if they turn up, I won't tell them anything. I feel so embarrassed and I can't talk to strangers. Please don't call them . . . please. Tell them, Mummy, I *can't* tell the police, I just can't!'

Karen looked at her husband in despair. They couldn't

let an evil little bastard like Charlie get away with this, surely. Walking over to his daughter, Mickey crouched down and took her quivering hands in his. 'Shhh, stop crying now. Everything's gonna be okay. We won't call the police. They're useless bastards anyway. Daddy will deal with this for you. You have my guarantee, as God's my judge, that Charlie will get his comeuppance.'

'Thank you, Daddy,' Lois said, filled with relief.

She had been absolutely dreading her parents and the police finding out about the drunken text message she'd mistakenly sent to Charlie instead of Dean. 'Bring some johnnies' would make her look just awful, and she couldn't face seeing the disappointment of her parents or the 'she asked for it' looks from the police. She had managed to erase the message sent from her own phone, but was as sure as hell that Charlie would have kept his and would use it as evidence against her, if needed.

Noticing he'd picked up his car keys, Karen asked Mickey what he was doing.

'I'm going to find that evil little bastard, that's what I'm fucking well doing.'

'Not tonight, please, Mick. We need you here with us,' Karen pleaded.

With a face like thunder, he slung the keys back on the table, sat down and put his head in his hands. 'I won't rest until I find him, Karen. He's finished, when I get my hands on him. I'm telling ya, that boy's fucking dead meat.'

'I know, love,' Karen said soothingly. 'But, please, look for him tomorrow. Lois needs you here tonight, and so do I.'

Looking at his two lovely girls sitting opposite him, Mickey could have cried with the unfairness of it all.

Lois was still in no fit state to tell them exactly what she'd been through. But just the thought of that perverted little bastard going anywhere near his beautiful daughter made Mickey feel sick to the stomach; he didn't want to hear the sordid details. Couldn't deal with that side of it. That would have to be Karen's job. Feeling a tear roll down his cheek, Mickey fiercely wiped it away. He never cried and hated men who did. It was a sign of weakness, and weak was the one thing Mickey Dawson wasn't. Determined to pull himself together, he stood up, picked up his mobile and left the room.

He needed to talk to Steve. His mate would under-stand how he felt and together they would sort out Charlie's demise. Pressing the Call button, he listened to the ringing tone and willed his pal to answer.

Steve saw Mickey's name flash up on his phone and rejected the call. He'd just dropped June and Peter off with little Alfie, and could hardly have a proper chat with his best pal in front of Debbie and the girls.

'Why didn't you answer it?' Debbie asked angrily. She guessed the caller had been her brother.

'I'll ring him later,' Steve replied, annoyed by his wife's stroppy attitude.

He would rather she had been in floods of tears than sitting there, with a face like a smacked arse, in complete denial. This was all *her* fucking fault. He'd told her that Charlie shouldn't stay in the house alone. She'd argued and insisted, and now this had happened.

'Look, Debs, you must start facing facts,' he told her. 'I know he's your boy and you love him and that, but the kid's a complete wrong 'un. What he's done to Lois is despicable. Surely, even you can't condone such behaviour.'

'I'm not condoning it, but there are two sides to every story. I mean, we don't even know what did happen yet. For all we know, Lois may have led him on.'

Feeling his temper rising, Steve couldn't help but shout

at her then. 'So what you trying to fucking say, Debs? That Lois is a lying cunt or something? Is that what you're trying to say? Well, is it?'

'Don't put words in my mouth, Steve. I ain't said she's a liar. I'm just saying that, until we know the full story, we shouldn't judge. I mean, come on, Mickey's got security gates like Belmarsh fucking Prison. Lois must have let Charlie in else how the fuck would he have got in there? You know what teenagers are like, Steve. I bet she invited him round. They probably got on the drink, and things got out of hand.'

Slamming his foot down on the brakes, Steve mounted the kerb with such force that Rosie and Gracie both screamed. Eyes blazing with anger, he ignore his by now hysterical daughters and turned on his wife.

'I've had enough of this, Debs, and I ain't putting up with no more of it. That son of yours is the black sheep of the family. He's evil. Slowly but surely he's managed to rip this family apart. Well, I'm putting my foot down from this moment on, so best you listen carefully. If what he's been accused of is true . . . and I personally would bet a pound to a piece of shit that it is . . . I am *not* having him in our house around our little girls.'

Debbie couldn't quite believe what she was hearing. Desperate to stand her ground, she yelled at him, 'So what you trying to say then, Steve? That Charlie's a nonce case and liable to fiddle with his own sisters. Is that what you're trying to say?'

Smacking his hand against the steering wheel to stop himself losing it with her completely, Steve shouted back. 'What I'm trying to get into your thick fucking skull is that them little girls in the back are my babies, my flesh and blood, and I will do whatever it takes to fucking protect 'em.'

Furious, Debbie pummelled him with her fists. 'You

fucking bastard! As if I'd ever let anything happen to our girls.'

'Please, Mummy . . . please, Daddy, stop it! Stop fighting,' Rosie screamed. She was desperately trying to comfort her big sister by putting her hands over her ears to drown out the sound of their parents arguing, but Gracie was hysterical.

The sound of his eldest daughter's panic-stricken screams jolted Steve back to reality. 'It's okay, girls. Mummy and Daddy are fine now,' he said as he turned the engine back on.

Outwardly, Steve chatted happily to his daughters on the rest of the journey home. Inwardly he was seething. Mickey was right, Charlie had to be got rid of, and if killing the little bastard and disposing of his remains was the only way, then so fucking be it.

THIRTY-SIX

Mickey opened his eyes and glanced at his watch. He'd lain awake most of the night but must have dozed off for the last hour or so. Sitting up, he rubbed his tired eyes. Last night seemed like a bad dream. If only it fucking was, he thought to himself as he crept out of bed.

'Did you get any sleep, love?' he heard Karen whisper.

'Not much. How about you?'

'Hardly any,' she replied, her eyes filling with tears.

'Come here,' Mickey said as he leaned across the bed and hugged her tight. 'We'll get through this, babe, I know we will.'

Karen smiled weakly. He was her rock, was Mickey, and was usually right about most things. Her instincts told her, however, that this wasn't one of them. Deep down, she knew that their lives would never be the same again.

'What's the matter, Gracie? Why are you still crying?' asked Rosie, her face full of concern.

Usually they slept separately, but such was Gracie's distress the previous evening, they had huddled up together like two newborn puppies.

Gracie was saved from answering by her dad appearing then. 'Are you all right, Princesses?' he asked, as he

302

crouched down beside his daughters. 'Shall Daddy make you some breakfast?'

'Not hungry,' Rosie said, sucking her thumb.

'Are you and Mummy going to split up?' Gracie asked him, tears clouding her eyes.

'Of course not,' Steve replied, hoping he was speaking the truth.

'Have you stopped fighting now?' Rosie enquired.

Feeling himself getting emotional, Steve stood up and walked towards the door.

'Be downstairs in ten minutes, girls, and Daddy'll have your favourite ready for you – spaghetti hoops and waffles! You up for that?'

'Okay,' the girls replied half-heartedly. Neither of them were hungry, but they didn't want to upset their father by not eating.

Hearing Steve bashing about in the kitchen, Debbie leaped out of bed and headed for the shower. She'd slept in the spare room last night and hadn't spoken a word to her husband since the row in the car. Unable to sleep, she'd had a lot of time to think about things and knew she had to get to Charlie before Mickey did. With a plan already in mind, she quickly got dressed. Her son needed her and she was determined to be there for him.

Steve had just served the girls their breakfast when he heard the front door slam. Looking out of the window, he saw the back end of Debbie's X5 disappearing off the drive.

'Bollocks,' he muttered, realising she'd sodded off and left him with the kids.

'Where's Mummy gone?' Rosie asked innocently.

He was saved from answering by the shrill tone of his mobile.

'I'm ready to go looking for the cunt. Are you with me?' Mickey asked bluntly.

'Debbie's just fucked off out. I'll ring June and get her to have the girls. I'll be round within the hour.'

'See you then.'

Hearing a noise, Mickey turned round to see Karen helping Lois down the stairs. She looked dreadful, just a shadow of the pretty, carefree teenager she'd been a couple of days ago.

'Are you okay, sweetheart?' he asked, realising full well she wasn't, but not knowing what else to say.

Lois nodded and forced a brave smile. 'Is Dean still here?'

'He's in there,' Mickey said, nodding towards the lounge. 'Do you want him to stay here all day with you, or shall I drop him home as I go out?'

'I think I just want to be with Mum today,' Lois said weakly.

'He'll understand. Go and say goodbye to him, though, Lois.'

Mickey watched, heartbroken, as his damaged daughter did exactly as he'd asked. Seeing her the way she was made him want to break every bone in Charlie's evil fucking body.

Debbie drove slowly along Kevin's street, searching for the right house. Seeing the plastic witch dangling at a window, she got out of the car and ran up the path.

'Is Charlie here? Have you seen him?' she asked the boy when he opened the door.

'No, I haven't heard from him for a couple of days,' Kevin replied truthfully.

'Look, love, Charlie is in a lot of trouble and I desperately need to find him. You know him better than anyone – where else is he liable to be? Don't worry about getting him into trouble. I swear, you'll be doing him a favour if you tell me. Now, I know he's got a girlfriend. Do you know where she lives?'

Kevin looked at the floor, debating what to do for the best. He didn't want to grass his mate up, but he could tell that something serious had happened. He'd never been a good liar, especially when it came to adults. Shuffling his feet, he stayed silent.

'Kevin, you must tell me where he is. His Uncle Mickey's looking for him, and if I don't get to him first, you'll probably never see Charlie again.'

Kevin's eyes bulged. Charlie was the only friend he'd ever had and the prospect of losing him didn't bear thinking about. 'He hasn't really got a girlfriend,' he mumbled. 'He lied to you because he's been spending time with his dad.'

Debbie felt a wave of shock go through her as the words hit home.

'His dad! No, it can't be. Are you sure, Kevin?'

'I've seen him with me own eyes, so I know it's true. He turned up one day at school. Charlie didn't want to know him at first, but then he started seeing him. That's why he said he had a girlfriend, so he could get out and meet Billy.'

'Where does his dad live? Has he told you? You *must* tell me.'

'I don't know the address, he's never invited me round there. I know it's in Barking, in a tower block, but that's all I know. I swear that's the truth.'

Andy's! Debbie thought. He has to be at bloody Andy's. Thanking Kevin for his help, she ran back down the path, leapt in her motor and headed towards the Gascoigne Estate.

Charlie opened another beer and paced up and down in the living room of Andy's flat. His dad hadn't come home all night and had his mobile switched off. Charlie was a bundle of nerves as he had no idea how else to contact him.

'Sit down, son. I'll put some music on. Chill out with your Uncle Andy.'

Charlie declined the offer of a puff. He was paranoid enough as it was, and being stoned would only make him feel ten times worse.

'Try me dad again, Andy,' he demanded, unable to relax. The call went straight on to voicemail.

Mickey kissed both Karen and Lois goodbye. Neither of them asked where he was going as neither of them had to. 'Now, remember what I said, don't let anybody in,' he told them. 'Don't go out at all, and if you're worried about anything in the slightest, just ring me. I've patched the window up and me mate Tony's gonna fix it properly tomorrow.'

'We'll be fine,' Karen said, pushing him towards the front door. She was desperate to have some time on her own with her daughter and, until now, this hadn't been possible.

''Bye, Lois, I'll call you later,' Dean said as he bowled out behind Mickey.

Dean's house was less than a five-minute drive away. Mickey thought now was the best time to have a quiet word with the boy.

'Thanks for everything you've done, son, you've been a star, but you've gotta promise me one thing. I don't want one word of what happened yesterday getting out to no one. You mustn't say jack shit – not at school, your boxing club, not even to your parents. Do you understand where I'm coming from, Dean?'

The boy shifted uncomfortably in his seat. Mickey might be putting things in a nice way but there was no mistaking the threat behind what he was saying.

'I promise you faithfully, I won't say a word.'

'Good lad,' Mickey said, ruffling his hair before he got

out of the car. 'You look after me, Deano, and I'll look after you.'

''Bye, Mr Dawson,' Dean shouted as he legged it up the path.

'Where to now?' Steve asked as Mickey got back into the car.

'Go to the lock-up first, I've got some rope there and tools, then head to the club and we'll get the gun out the safe.'

Steve put his foot down and they sped along in eerie silence.

Debbie turned the engine off and sat facing the tower block. She felt weird and her heart-rate was rising by the second. She hadn't thought about Billy or what he'd done to her for years. She'd believed she was completely over her past experiences. But hearing his name earlier, and sitting here now, somehow told her differently. She would never forget what the bastard had done to her, and the thought of walking into the flats and coming face-to-face with him again filled her with absolute terror.

Billy McDaid lit up a fag, lay back on the bed and stretched out like a starfish. Cindy the barmaid had turned out to be a cute little sort. Twenty-five, funny and tarty, she was Billy's type of bird. When she dragged him home and treated him to the bunk-up of a lifetime, he thought he'd died and gone to heaven. The gaff she lived in was a palace compared to Andy's dive. The only downside was that she lived with her three little nippers whom she'd just shot out to collect from her mum.

Finishing his snout, Billy jumped up and decided to have a snoop around before she returned.

* * *

After picking up the tools and gun, Mickey and Steve were at a loose end as to where to start looking.

'Charlie's got one mate called Kevin who I've never even fucking seen but apparently he lives in Harold Hill. Debbie reckons he's also got a girlfriend, but I don't believe that in a million years.'

'What's the bird's name?'

'No idea,' Steve replied, shrugging his shoulders. 'She's invisible, no cunt's ever seen her. Listen, forget the bird, there is no bird. Concentrate on the mate.'

Mickey nodded. 'Harold Hill it is then.'

Billy's hopes and dreams of getting his feet under the table in a new abode were blown up in smoke as soon as the kids arrived home. Monsters, they were, in every sense of the word. They were that bad, they made Charlie as a child look like a choir boy.

Switching his phone on, he prayed that someone had contacted him. The bleep of a message would allow him to make a quick escape. As luck would have it, his phone bleeped numerous times. Twenty-one, in fact. Something's fucking happened, he thought. No bastard ever rang him, only Charlie here and there, his aunt once a month, and a few druggies wanting gear. The first couple of messages gave nothing away.

'Dad, where are you? Ring me, it's urgent.'

The next few followed suit. Although the panic had heightened in his son's voice, he revealed little more. It was message number ten that made Billy pay proper attention.

'Dad, please help me. I'm at Andy's. I've done some-thing really bad . . . I've attacked Lois and sort of . . . raped her.'

'Where's the nearest cab firm?' Billy screamed at Cindy.

'Top of the road. Do a right and then first right again.

You're not going yet, are you, Bill? When am I going to see you again?'

Without answering, Billy bolted out of the door. As he got to the end of the road, he stopped running and started walking. He needed to plan things and running stopped him from thinking straight. Getting Charlie out of the area had to be his first priority. Billy had had first-hand experience of Mickey's fury and was damned if he was letting the same happen to his boy. Problem was, money was tight. He'd been surviving by selling a bit of smoke in a couple of the local pubs, but he'd been working it on a very small basis, earning just about enough to get by on.

Billy sat in the cab and rang Charlie. Guessing by the answer-phone message that the kid had switched his phone off, he rang Andy and asked to speak to his son.

'Look, Charlie, keep calm and don't panic,' he told the boy. 'You'll be fine, trust me. I'll be home in ten minutes and then we'll put our heads together and work out what to do next.'

'Okay, Dad,' said his relieved son.

Billy tucked his mobile into his jacket pocket, threw his arms across the back seat and allowed himself a wry smile. Things just couldn't have worked out better. His boy, his own flesh and blood, had come up trumps for him. In fact, the kid had played an absolute blinder. Billy let out a nasty, evil laugh. Revenge was sweet and he was determined to enjoy every second of his. After years of waiting, thanks to Charlie he was finally going to have the last say.

THIRTY-SEVEN

'All right, Missus? Nice motor. What you after? We can get you whatever you want. Just name it and we'll sort it.'

Debbie opened her window and stared at the four little lads standing nearby. 'I'm not after anything, lads. I'm just here to visit someone and you wanna be careful who you try and sell stuff to. I could be anyone, for all you know.'

'You're not old bill, are you?' the dirty-faced boy asked. He was the mouthpiece, the ringleader.

'No, I'm not. Far from it, in fact,' she replied, smiling at his cockiness.

Chatting with the lads was a welcome distraction. She became so engrossed in the bit of banter that she failed to notice Billy McDaid get out of a cab and stroll into the tower block.

Mickey and Steve's search was proving fruitless. They had no success at all as they scoured the streets of Harold Hill, asking everybody and anybody if they knew of Charlie or a lad called Kevin.

'This is fucking bollocks,' Mickey said, looking at his watch.

Steve shrugged his shoulders. 'What else do you

suggest we do? The cunt's got no mates, no hobbies . . . finding him was never gonna be easy, Mick.'

'I know it weren't, but driving round here like a pair of prize pricks ain't exactly helping, is it? What about his bedroom, Steve? Can't you have a snoop round, see if you can find any clues as to where the cunt goes?'

'I could try. It all depends if Debs is in.'

Sparking up a fag, Mickey stared at the big splashes of rain, pounding against the windscreen. The weather was dismal. It matched his mood perfectly.

'Drop me off at the nearest pub. You go home, search for clues, and pick me up when you're done.'

'Come with us, if you want. I doubt Debs is in, and even if she is we'll make some excuse,' Steve said, doing a U-turn.

'You're having a fucking laugh, ain't you? I can't be near her at the moment,' Mickey said honestly. 'Things are never gonna be the same between me and Debs. And once that perverted son of hers disappears into thin air, she'll be gunning for me anyway.'

Feeling as if he was torn between the devil and the deep blue sea, Steve made the rest of the journey in silence.

'Oh, Dad, I'm so pleased to see you,' Charlie exclaimed as his wanderer of a father returned.

'We got any cans?' Billy asked Andy.

'Nah, we've drunk the last of 'em.'

'Do us a favour, mate. Go down to the offie and get us some.'

Billy handed Andy a score, glad to be rid of him so he could talk to his boy alone.

'What exactly happened, son?' he asked solemnly, not wanting to show the glee he was feeling inside.

'I'm sorry, Dad, but it weren't my fault. She asked me round and told me to bring some johnnies. I'd had a beer and a puff and that. I just thought me luck was in, and I suppose I got a bit heavy-handed with her. She reckoned the text was meant for someone else, not for me. I was so angry with her, I just lost it, Dad!'

'It's nae your bloody fault! She's a prick teaser and deserves all she got. Don't blame yourself, laddie.'

'Do you reckon they've called the police? 'Cause if they have, I've got the text message she sent me on my phone. That'll prove me innocent, won't it, Dad?'

'Mickey willnae want the police involved,' Billy said. 'He's always been a dodgy bastard and he wouldnae want the filth sniffing round. What was the outcome? Did you actually rape her, Charlie?'

'Sort of. I forced her to do things and stuff.'

Ruffling his boy's hair, Billy smiled at him. 'Serves her fucking right. And Mickey as well. Look, Charlie, you've told me Mickey's always despised you, and remember what he did to me. He nearly killed me, the cunt. Dinnae feel bad about what you did, I'm proud of you. You've paid him back for the both of us, in the best way possible.'

Charlie locked eyes with his creator and smiled. He and his dad were two of a kind, and he was glad now he'd done what he had. 'What do you think will happen, Dad? I can't go to Mum's. Mickey and Steve'll kill me if I go back there.'

Handing his son a fag, Billy lit one himself and took a deep drag. 'You willnae have to go back to your mother's. Look, no one knows we're here at Andy's. We'll just doss here while I get some money together, and then fuck off, as far away as possible.'

'I love you, Dad, and I'm so glad you found me.'

'I love you too, son,' Billy replied, his voice filled with emotion.

*   *   *

Debbie sat in a pub along the A13 and ordered her third large glass of wine. After chatting to the four scallywags, her bottle had gone and she'd decided she needed a drink if she were to risk coming face-to-face with Billy McDaid. Sitting outside the tower block, knowing that her ex was back on the scene, had filled Debbie with emotions and memories she'd buried long ago. The thought of raking up the past filled her with dread.

Gesticulating to the barman to bring her a fourth, she decided to make this the last. The drink had started to make her feel calm, courageous in fact, and she knew she had to go to that flat, whether she liked it or not. Fuck Billy McDaid, she thought. Charlie was her son, and she'd be the one to decide what happened to him now. It'd been she who had fed him, clothed him, soothed him through his illnesses, comforted him through his nightmares, and stuck by him through thick and thin. Charlie was her responsibility, always had been and always would be, and she wasn't going to let his arsehole of a father, who had turned up like a bad penny, stop her from performing her parental duty.

Chucking the last of her wine down her neck, she stood up, grabbed her handbag and strolled confidently out of the pub.

'Please let me make you something, Lois. I know you're upset but you must eat, love. You'll be ill if you don't.'

'I can't eat, Mum,' Lois whispered. Unable to keep her experience to herself any longer, she burst into tears. 'He made me suck his thingy! Oh, Mum, it was awful.'

Karen hugged her daughter tight and cried with her. It had been a terrible day for the pair of them. She'd tried to encourage Lois to talk about what had happened, but until now her daughter had just clammed up and trembled from head to foot. Karen felt indescribably angry to see the state Lois was in and for the first time in her life, she wished the worst for Charlie. Hopefully, her Mickey would be able to oblige and make that wish come true.

Debbie patiently waited for the lift doors to open. Stepping inside, she breathed in the familiar smell of urine and filth. The journey to Andy's floor was short but seemed to take forever. Reaching her destination, Debbie took a deep breath before rapping on the door.

'Shhh, keep quiet. Dinnae answer it,' Billy said immediately.

'Charlie, I know you're in there . . . Kevin told me. Open the door, love. I know you're with your dad and I'm not angry, but I really need to talk to you. I'm here to help you, nothing else. Please, son, let me in.'

'Fucking hell,' Billy grunted angrily.

Walking into the hallway, he peeped through the spy hole to check that Debbie was alone.

'Open it, Dad,' Charlie whispered. 'There's no way she'd bring Steve or Mickey here with her, and we might get some money out of her.'

Forever the coward, Billy urged Andy to do the honours. 'All right, Debs,' he said awkwardly.

Coming face to face with Billy was something Debbie had always feared. One look at him now told her differently. She realised that the hold he'd had over her was long gone. She felt zilch. No dread, no emotion, nothing. It was almost as though he'd never been a part of her life.

'Long time, no see,' she said boldly.

'You look really well,' Billy replied, unable to make direct eye contact with her.

Glancing at her surreptiously, he was taken aback by how good she looked. Her new, improved image was a far cry from the way she had been when she'd lived with him. Unnerved by her presence, Billy made a quick exit to the kitchen, dragging Andy with him.

'We'll leave you to it,' he said, shutting the door.

'What happened, love?' Debbie asked, turning her attention to Charlie.

'She invited me round there, Mum, honest she did. "Get some johnnies" she put on her text, and then when I got there she bottled it, pretended the text was for someone else. We were both quite drunk. She was drinking her dad's vodka and I was drinking his Scotch.'

'And I suppose things just got a bit out of hand, love, didn't they?' Debbie urged, holding the boy's hands and finishing his story for him.

'Yes, Mum, but I'm telling the truth, I swear. If you don't believe me, you can look at my phone. I kept her text message on there.'

Debbie glanced at it. 'I never doubted you anyway, Charlie,' she said without hesitation. 'I knew there'd be a simple explanation. The thing is, what are we gonna do next? It's Mickey I'm worried about. He's a lunatic when he loses it and I'm scared of what he might do to you, son.'

'I don't wanna come home, Mum. Please don't make me. Can't I live with my dad for a bit?'

Unable to think straight, Debbie stayed silent. Her precious baby living with Billy was the last thing she wanted, but what other option did she have? He couldn't stay at home now, not after this. For a start Steve wouldn't allow him to be around the girls, and Mickey would never forgive or forget.

Finally she spoke. 'I'm not happy about you living with him, Charlie. And where would you go? You can't stay here, love.'

'I wanna move to Glasgow with him, Mum. He has a nice aunt up there and she said we can stay with her. I hate it round here. I'm bullied at school, Steve hates me, and now Mickey's gonna kill me. Please, Mum, say I can go?'

'Go and get your dad, I need to speak to him alone for a minute.'

Doing exactly as he was told, Charlie smiled as he left the room. Ever since he was a baby, he'd sensed he could wind his mother around his little finger and today was no different. Telling Billy to go and speak to his mum, he opened up a can of cider and chatted to Andy.

Billy felt awkward as he walked back into the lounge and faced his ex.

'You look lovely, Debs. Your nose looks different. Have you had it done?'

She looked at the piece of shit standing opposite her and felt nothing but contempt for him. She would never know, till the day she died, what she'd ever seen in Billy McDaid. Determined to get the better of him now, she looked him straight in the eye.

'Yes, I had to have it done, Billy, as the last time you beat me up you smashed it to smithereens. Oh, and by the way, have you ever told your son that you dangled him out the window and threatened to kill him?'

Billy shook his head and looked down at the thread-bare, drink-stained carpet.

Knowing she had him by the short and curlies, Debbie carried on.

'Let's cut the shit, Billy. Charlie said he wants to move to Glasgow with you, and as much as I hate that thought, I don't see I have any real choice. It's either that or Mickey's gonna kill him. Now the punchline is, can you look after him?'

Billy answered her as truthfully as he could. 'I'm nae perfect, Debs, but I love the wee man. I'll do the very best I can.'

'Where will you live?'

316

'I'll take him to my auntie's. She's got plenty of room in her house and she'll spoil him rotten.'

'What about money, Billy? Have you got any?'

He felt a complete loser as he answered, 'No, I'm skint. I've spent all my money while I've been living here.'

Debbie enjoyed watching him squirm. 'Look, I'll sort some money out for you, but you have to promise me you'll take good care of him.'

'I will,' Billy agreed.

Calling Charlie back into the room, Debbie explained what had been decided. 'Now, I'm gonna give you and your dad some money and I want you to promise me that you'll buy a new mobile out of that and text me the number. I'll take your old phone with me and keep it as evidence, just in case the police get involved.'

'Okay, Mum,' Charlie said. He was ecstatic. He had a new life with his dad to look forward to and couldn't wait to start it.

'You need to get away from here as soon as possible,' Debbie urged. 'The bank will be shut today but I'll go there first thing tomorrow and draw out some money. In the meantime, I'll pack some of your stuff from indoors and bring it to you when I pick you up tomorrow. I'll be here by half-ten.'

'Thanks, Mum,' Charlie said.

Debbie didn't answer, she couldn't. She could never remember feeling so sad in the whole of her life. Her only son, her baby, and she was having to say goodbye to him for the sake of his own safety.

The situation was soul-destroying, totally horrendous, and all she could do now was hope and bloody pray that she'd made the right decision. Sobbing her heart out as she left the flat, she clambered back into her car and headed home.

*   *   *

Charlie and Billy couldn't stop laughing. 'I cannae believe she's gonnae bung us the money,' Billy said excitedly.

'I told you, Dad, she adores me. I can get anything out of her I want.'

Billy broke into song, holding his son's hands and swinging him around the room. '"I belong to Glasgow, dear old Glasgow town."'

'Sing some more, Dad,' Charlie pleaded.

'"But what's the matter with Glasgow, for it's going round and round. I'm only a common old working chap as anyone here can see. But when I get a couple of drinks on a Saturday, Glasgow belongs to me!"'

THIRTY-EIGHT

Mickey had sunk half a dozen drinks by the time Steve arrived back at the pub.

'Well?' he asked expectantly.

'No good,' Steve replied, shrugging his shoulders. 'I looked everywhere, Mick, but there's nothing. I found some dodgy-looking films, Rizlas, that type of stuff, but nothing that's liable to help us find the little shit.'

While Steve went to get himself a beer, Mickey pondered over what to do next. In usual circumstances, he'd have had no trouble hunting someone down. Charlie, though, was a different ball game. He was a creep, a waste of fucking space, so unpopular he had no regular haunts to visit or mates to threaten. Mickey didn't have the first clue how to find the evil little bastard.

'What's plan B, then?' Steve asked, as he rejoined his ally.

'I'm fucked if I know,' Mickey replied, taking a sip from his bottle of Bud. 'The only lead we've got so far is this Kevin kid and if he's Charlie's mate, then he's bound to be a weirdo. Therefore no cunt we stop and ask in Harold Hill is gonna know him. It's a shame it's the school holidays, or we could suss him out there. At least get an address for him.'

'Why don't we break into the school?' Steve suggested.

'No point,' Mickey replied. 'Not without a surname. Knowing our luck, we'll only set the fucking alarms off, and besides there'll be about fifty Kevins at the poxy place.'

'What about Lois's boyfriend, wouldn't he know where this lad lives?'

Mickey shook his head. 'I already thought of that one. I tapped Dean this morning but he ain't got a clue. He said the kid's a complete freak. I left him my number, told him to ring round everyone he knows, see if he has any joy.'

Mickey slammed his bottle down on the wooden table. 'Debbie would know where the cunt lives, but she ain't gonna tell us, is she?'

Steve shrugged. 'I'll have a word with her later. She may tell me, you never know.'

'Don't waste your fucking time,' Mickey said sarcastically.

'Listen, I'm gonna ring Dean back and tell him I'm offering five hundred quid for this fucking Kevin's address. In the meantime, you have a scout round indoors. If Debbie leaves her handbag lying about, have a nose inside, see if she has a number for the cunt.'

'Will do,' Steve said, keen to help, even if it meant betraying his beloved wife.

Debbie zipped up the large Adidas sports bag, lugged it down the stairs and put it straight into the back of her X5. She hid it under her yoga mat, then returned to her son's bedroom to check for anything important she might have forgotten.

Pants, socks, T-shirts, trackie bottoms, his new Reebok trainers . . . she'd even remembered to pack a couple of the videos and DVDs he'd specifically asked for. How she was keeping herself together, she didn't know. All she really wanted to do was lie on her son's bed, hug his pillow and cry, but she had to get his stuff together and out of the house before Steve and the girls returned. She'd been careful about what she packed. She didn't want to give Steve an inkling of what she was doing. If she took Charlie's computer, for instance, it would stick out like a sore thumb, so she'd left it there, along with many other things whose absence might be noticed.

Hearing the front door slam, she quietly closed Charlie's bedroom door and made her way downstairs to face the music with Steve.

'You all right?' he asked, hoping she was now talking to him.

'Not bad. Where are the girls?'

Knowing by the tone of Debbie's voice that she still had a cob on, Steve ignored her and chose to head to the kitchen for a cold beer rather than walk head first into yet another poxy argument.

'Don't fucking ignore me, Steve. I asked you a simple question. Where are my girls?'

Steve took a large gulp from his can, then took a deep breath to try to control his temper. It didn't work.

'*Your* girls. Your fucking girls? Are these the same girls you fucked off and left this morning, Debs, without saying so much as a bastard word to them?'

'You were here. You're their father. Too much trouble for you to have 'em for once, was it?'

'No, it weren't, Debs, but I had stuff to do, right? If you'd given me a bit of notice, I could have cancelled what I had on. But no, not you. You just fuck off and leave everyone to it.'

'I had things to do as well,' Debbie screamed at him. 'Important fucking things! And you still haven't bloody well told me where they are!'

'At your mother's, all right? Where else would they

321

fucking be? And if your important things included running round after that bastard son of yours, I hope you remembered to tell him he ain't welcome in this fucking house no more. I ain't having it, Debs I swear on my mothers grave, he ain't coming back in here.'

'Bollocks, you cunt, and you can leave my Charlie out of this.'

Steve stood up, his eyes blazing with anger. Pointing his index finger at his own forehead, he told her her fortune. 'See you? You're mental, a fucking head case. Leave your Charlie out of it! Are you 'aving a laugh? Your fucking baby boy is the cause of all this, and he'll probably be the break-up of our marriage as well. Why can't you see what's in front of your eyes, Debs? He's evil and he's scum. Everyone else can see it, why can't you?'

Screeching like a lunatic, Debbie lunged at him, hitting him as hard as she could. 'Because I'm his mother, you stupid bastard! Don't you understand that? I gave birth to him.'

Steve had never hit a woman in his life and had no intention of starting now. Holding her wrists, he tried to calm her down. 'Stop it, Debs, come on. I don't wanna fight with you, I just need you to see sense. I love you, for fuck's sake, that's why I married you.'

His final sentence jarred Debbie back to reality. She sank against his chest and sobbed her heart out.

'Shhh. Come on, don't cry,' he said, holding her tight and kissing her hair.

'I'm sorry, Steve. It's just everything. Charlie . . . Mickey, you and me. I'm going off me head with it all.'

Leading her into the lounge, Steve sat her on the sofa and headed back into the kitchen to open a bottle of wine. Debs could be the biggest bitch in the world sometimes, but he loved her dearly and always would. If she left him tomorrow, he'd never look at another woman, he'd swear to that. He handed her a glass of Chardonnay, put his own on the table and took her free hand in his.

'You've gotta stop bottling things up, Debs. You'll end up having a breakdown if you don't.'

Debbie looked at him and smiled through her tears. 'I know you're right, but please, let's not talk about it tonight. I can't face it, Steve. I've no more fight left in me body, I can't deal with it right now.'

Putting his big arm around her, Steve held her close. 'I won't make you talk about anything but me, you and the girls. How does that suit ya? Now ring your mum and ask her if she can look after Gracie and Rosie for a few days. It'll give us a bit of time on our own.'

Debbie handed the phone to him. 'You ring her, Steve. I haven't spoken to her since we came back from Centerparcs. You'll have to ask.'

Understanding her embarrassment, Steve made the all-important call. 'Sorted,' he said as he laid the phone on the sofa next to him.

'Did she say anything about me?' Debs asked anxiously.

'No,' Steve lied as he jumped up to put a CD on. Dimming the lights, he sat back down and snuggled up to his wife. They needed time alone, to try and repair the damage Charlie had caused in their relationship. Steve was determined to get things back on track.

Mickey rubbed Lois's back for what seemed liked the tenth time since he'd returned home. She'd been that ill, they'd brought a bucket into the lounge to save her from frequent trips to the toilet. She couldn't stop being sick, but seeing as she was unable to eat, had nothing to bring up but bile.

'Shhh. Stop crying, angel. Come on, Daddy's here now. Everything will be fine, trust me. I'll sort everything out and you'll be okay, I promise you.'

Wiping her mouth with a tissue, Lois turned to the man she'd grown to adore and forced herself to smile.

'I love you, Daddy.'

As he looked into his daughter's tearful eyes, Mickey felt his heart break in two. The poor little mite was suffering beyond belief. He would not rest until he got revenge for her. As he stroked her hair, he mused on whether or not to burn Charlie alive. He could quite easily set him alight and watch him go up in smoke. Telling Karen to swap places on the sofa with him, he headed to his shed to search for paraffin. He found some, took the cans round to the alleyway and, for the first time that day, allowed himself to smile.

A cremation was exactly what Charlie deserved, and Mickey was determined that was exactly what he was gonna fucking get.

Steve uncorked the third bottle of wine and danced back into the living room, doing an impression of Barry White singing 'My First, My Last, My Everything'.

'Sit down, you silly bastard,' she said, smiling at his antics. She'd enjoyed tonight even though she felt sad and empty after the shock of yesterday. In her heart, she knew it was time to let Charlie go and concentrate on the girls and her marriage instead.

'Thanks for tonight, Steve,' she said, her eyes almost closed with tiredness.

'You've welcome, babe. We should do it more often, eh?'

Receiving no answer, he realised she'd fallen asleep in his arms. Moving his left arm from behind her, he gently laid her head on his lap. As he noticed her handbag next to the sofa, he fleetingly remembered Mickey's request, sighed, and erased the thought from his mind. He couldn't do it. There was no way he'd be able to search through his wife's bag without her permission. It didn't belong in his rule book and as much as he wanted to help Mickey, there was no way he was going to ruin his marriage in the process.

Steve sat there for ages, deciding what to do for the best. As he watched Debs lying across his legs, he took in her pretty features and her gentle snores. His decision was made there and then. He just couldn't betray her. If Mickey wanted to dispose of Charlie, he'd have to do it alone.

Steve hated his stepson more than life itself, but not enough to kill him. How the hell could he ever face Debs again if he'd contributed to the demise of her only son? He'd break his decision to Mickey in the morning. He would still go with him and look for the kid, but once they found him, that was it, Steve was bowing out. What happened from then on was Mickey's call.

Looking down at Debs, Steve smiled to himself. He'd married her for better or for worse and he wasn't about to break his vows. Not now, not ever.

THIRTY-NINE

Unable to sleep well, Mickey rose early the next morning and by seven o'clock was raring to go. He realised it was far too early for Steve to be out of his pit so spent the next couple of hours pottering about downstairs, desperate to keep himself busy. Hearing footsteps on the stairs, he was surprised to see Lois standing at the kitchen door rather than Karen.

'Hello, angel, you're up early. How do you feel today?'

She flashed him a fragile smile. 'I'm a bit better, thanks, Dad. I feel hungry. Will you cook me some breakfast?'

'That's my girl,' Mickey said as he hugged her tight. Now, what shall I rustle you up? Beans on toast . . . omelette . . . or how about a full English?'

'Beans and cheese on toast, please, Dad.'

Mickey winked at her. She had a bit of colour back in her cheeks and he was relieved to see her looking brighter.

'It'll be ready in five, my little darling. Now, pop upstairs and ask Mummy what she wants.'

Half an hour later, with the breakfast plates cleared, Lois excused herself from the table and headed back to the privacy of her bedroom. She hadn't eaten since before the attack and breakfast had made her feel sick and lethargic.

'I was thinking, Mick. We should go and pick Alfie

up today. I miss him and it's not fair on June to leave him there any longer. Shall I give her a call?' Karen suggested.

The piercing ring of his phone stopped Mickey from answering his wife's question. 'Hello,' he said, recognising the number of his daughter's boyfriend.

'I've got the address for you,' Dean told him excitedly.

'Fire away, kid.'

Steve was in the middle of making love to Debbie, for the first time in weeks, when his 'I'm Forever Blowing Bubbles' ring tone spoiled their intimacy.

'I'm sorry, babe,' he said, reaching across to the bedside cabinet to turn the bastard thing off.

'Answer it, Steve,' she said, looking at the clock. 'I've got to pop out anyway, then I'm gonna sort the girls out and that.'

'Bollocks,' he muttered as he felt his hard-on deflate.

Mickey's dulcet tones telling him he'd got the address made Steve feel nothing but guilt. All of this was bollocks, he'd be glad when he was out of it. How could he be making love to his wife one minute then plotting the downfall of her only son the next? Thoroughly pissed off, he lay back on the bed for a minute.

'I'll see you later, Steve,' Debbie shouted to him.

'Where you going?' he yelled.

She hadn't been up ten minutes and had only just got out of the shower. Surely she hadn't gone out already.

Not getting an answer, he ran down the stairs in his birthday suit. 'Fuck, fuck, fuck,' he muttered as he peered out of the front door, just in time to see the back of her X5 disappear down the drive. Stomping back upstairs with the hump of all humps, he quickly got dressed, grabbed his keys and shot off to pick up Mickey.

* * *

327

After a quick stop at the bank, Debbie drove straight to Barking and pulled up outside the tower block. It's now or never, she thought as she glanced at her reflection in the mirror to see if she looked as bad as she felt. Checking that Charlie's sports bag was well hidden in the back, she took a quick look round to check that there were no thieves or druggies lurking nearby. Then, taking a deep breath, she strolled into the tower block, to rescue her beloved boy.

'Not left, you thick cunt. Right! Turn right.'

Steve sighed as he amended his mistake. His day was going from bad to worse and Mickey had been in a proper foul mood since he'd told him of his decision.

'How long have we been pals? I can't believe you, you cunt,' his friend had shouted at him.

'But Debs is my wife, Mick, I just can't do it. I'll come round to this Kevin's with you and help you find him, but then you're on your own.'

'Just fucking drive then, Judas!'

The rest of the journey to Harold Hill had taken place in silence, apart from Mickey's bad-tempered directions.

'Stop here. This is it, number twenty-four.'

Steve parked the motor and turned the engine off. Mickey ran up the path and within seconds had nearly broken the front door down.

'Wh-What h-have I done?' asked a petrified Kevin as he was lifted up by his scruffy T-shirt and slammed against the filthy wall in the hallway.

'Where can I find your perverted cunt of a friend?' Mickey screeched.

'It's n-nothing to do with me. I've told his mum every-thing I know.' Kevin could barely speak, he was shaking so much. His nan had popped round to the Co-op and when he'd heard the ferocious banging on the door, he'd

flung it open, thinking she'd had a fall or been in an accident. Trying to get his words out when he was nervous
wasn't easy for him, but somehow he managed to tell
Mickey that Charlie had been seeing his dad and was
probably at a tower block in Barking.

'If you're lying to me, I'm gonna fucking kill ya,'
Mickey said as he dropped the fat kid back on his feet.

Mickey ran back to the motor and leaped in. 'Andy's
flat, on the Gascoigne Estate, and put your fucking foot
down,' he barked at Steve. 'Oh, and by the way, it looks
like your darling wife has beaten us to it.'

Steve had had enough by now. He was sick of being
Mr Nice Guy. 'Whaddya mean, my darling wife? Don't
take this out on me, Mick. She's *your* fucking sister, you
cunt! You was the one that introduced us in the first place,
so don't take all your shit out on me. Save it for some
other mug.'

'Sorry,' Mickey said sheepishly. 'But if you'd have seen
the state of my Lois yesterday, you'd know how I feel.
Imagine if it were one of your two girls.'

'I know what you're saying, Mick, but you can't take
it out on other people. Charlie's the one to blame for all
this, no one else. Now, do you remember what number
Andy lives at, 'cause I fucking don't.'

'Not offhand,' Mickey replied, trying to rack his brains.
'But, believe me, I'll find him. Even if I have to knock
on every door in the entire block to find the cunt, I will
do it.'

Steve glanced at his pal. He'd never seen him as angry
as this before. He wouldn't like to be in Charlie's shoes
when Mickey managed to get his hands on him, that was
for sure.

'Now hurry up, Charlie. I'll meet you downstairs at the
car,' Debbie said, desperate to get away from Billy who

329

had spent the last five minutes trying to make polite conversation with her.

Once in the car, she was relieved to find all Charlie's belongings still intact. She started the engine, praying for her son to hurry up. She was desperate to get him out of the area and out of harm's way. She knew her brother better than anyone, knew that he was quite capable of finding her son and wiping him off the face of the earth, without so much as a second thought.

Breathing a sigh of relief as Charlie and Billy ran towards her, she ordered her son to sit next to her in the front.

'I'll drive you to the station ,then I want you to promise me you'll get the first available train to Glasgow.'

Charlie smiled. He was so excited about moving up North with his dad, he could barely believe his luck.

'There's a thousand pounds in here,' she said, handing him a white envelope. 'Now, what I'm gonna do, Charlie, is open up a new account at a different bank. Steve won't know about it, no one will. When you get to Scotland, all you have to do is open up a savings account, and that way I can send you money on a regular basis.'

'No problem, Mum,' he said. What a touch! She'd keep them in beer, fags and drugs. Result, he thought as he turned and grinned at his dad.

Mickey struck gold within five minutes. The third person he asked about Andy happened to be a heroin addict, dying for a fix. Snatching the twenty quid from Mickey's hand, the junkie gladly pointed him to the door of Andy's flat. Receiving no reply to his frantic knocking, Mickey kicked it down within seconds.

'Fuck,' he said, as he realised the place was empty.

'You check out the bedroom, Steve, see if they've been here. I'll case the rest of it.'

330

'Any joy?' Mickey shouted, minutes later.

The place was a tip, a shit-hole. Andy obviously spent the bulk of his life purchasing drugs rather than belongings.

'Fuck all in here,' Steve said, closing the door that hung ajar on the wardrobe. Just as he was about to leave the room, he clocked something bright blue sticking out from under the bed. He took one look at the Glasgow Rangers shirt and knew that Billy and Charlie had been there. Wishing it had been Mickey and not he who had found the bastard thing, he stood rooted to the spot, wondering what to do for the best.

Images of Debbie came into his mind. Her laughter, her temper, the lovely evening they'd enjoyed the previous night, their unfinished love-making this morning. Choosing his heart over his head, Steve opened the bedroom window and flung the Glasgow Rangers shirt out into the murky Barking air.

'Any luck?' Mickey asked seconds later as he stomped into the room to double-check Steve's search.

'Nothing in here, mate,' Steve lied, wondering if the guilt he was feeling was showing on his face.

Andy strolled along happily swinging his tenner's worth of Stella in a carrier bag. Billy had left him fifty quid as a thank you for putting him and Charlie up, and Andy had wasted little time in spending it. As Andy was permanently skint, purchasing crack, puff and a crate of lager all in one go was a fucking luxury to him. Having spent his money wisely, he couldn't wait to get home, stick on a bit of Hendrix, and get well and truly shit-faced.

'Oi, Andy!' little Terry Jackson called out. 'Don't go to your flat,' he said, pointing towards the tower block. 'There's two big geezers up there and they've booted your door in.'

'What did they look like?' asked a panic-stricken Andy.

'Dunno if they're old bill, but one's a big skinhead geezer and the other one's tall with dark hair.'

Dropping his beers so that he could run faster, Andy turned around and literally fled for his life.

At King's Cross, Debbie couldn't bear to let her son walk off without seeing him safely on to the train. 'I want a bit of time alone with him,' she said to Billy, urging him to make himself scarce. Billy took the hint and went off to purchase his sidekick and himself some booze for the journey.

Sitting down on a bench next to Charlie, Debbie held his clammy hand.

'Mum! There's people looking,' Charlie said, snatching it away. He felt totally embarrassed by her behaviour and open tearfulness. 'Why don't you go?' he said callously, as he looked around for his dad.

'Don't be like that, love. I am your mum. I just wanna say goodbye and make sure you get on the train all right.'

'I said I'd get on the train, didn't I? I ain't gonna leg it, am I?'

'Don't be nasty to me, Charlie. I love you more than anything and I've always been there for you. Don't be like this to me.'

'Sorry,' Charlie said. She was cramping his style now. He couldn't wait to get rid of her.

Hurt by his uncaring attitude, Debbie stood up. 'As soon as your dad gets back, go and sit in the carriage. The train's just pulled in and they're letting people go through.'

'Okay,' he replied, wishing his dad would bloody well hurry up.

'Now don't forget, Charlie, as soon as you get there, buy a mobile phone. I need you to keep in touch with me regularly and let me know how you're doing. If you're unhappy at all, or your dad's not looking after you properly, I'll come and get you, love. Things are bound to die down with Mickey in time, and you know you've always got a home with me.'

'Thanks,' Charlie said ungratefully.

His dad was walking towards them so he stood up. 'I'd better go, Mum.'

As Debbie put her arms around him, she felt empty and betrayed by his obvious lack of emotion. He seemed to feel nothing for her at all.

''Bye, Charlie. Take care, son,' she murmured.

'See ya, Debs,' Billy said awkwardly.

'Take care of him for me,' Debbie pleaded, tears streaming down her face.

Feeling momentarily sorry for his ex, Billy patted her on the arm. ''Course I'll look after him. Don't worry, he'll be fine with me.'

Debbie wept as she watched them get into their carriage and then, as the train pulled away, sobbed her heart out. Not knowing when she was going to see her beloved boy again was pure hell, but at least this way he was still alive. Packing him off with Billy was the last thing she had wanted to do, but it was better than seeing him cold on a mortuary slab.

Debbie headed back to the car park, started the engine and switched on her mobile. She'd kept it off all day, in case Steve rang her. She'd enjoyed last night and couldn't face lying to him. Dialling her answer-phone, the only voice that she expected to hear was his. The tearful messages from her mother she hadn't expected.

Debbie pressed Call-back. 'Come on, Mum,' she muttered, annoyed to hear the engaged signal. Heading for home, she kept on pressing redial. 'Whatever's wrong?' she asked when June finally answered.

'Oh, Debs,' her mother sobbed. 'I don't know how to say this, love, but . . . it's Gracie.'

'What's the matter? Has she had an accident?' Debbie asked frantically.

'No, worse than that. She told me something, Debs, something terrible.'

'Oh, for Christ's sake, Mum. Just spit it out, will ya?'

Debbie's day had been bad enough. The last thing she needed was her mother playing the drama queen.

June took a deep breath. 'Our poor little Gracie . . . oh, Debs, she's been sexually abused!'

Debbie swerved violently. How she escaped death then only God knew. She missed an oncoming lorry by inches.

FORTY

The day had started off pleasantly for June. Peter was out playing golf, the sun was shining, and she was surrounded by her grandchildren. At one o'clock, she put a tired Alfie down for a nap. A cooking lesson was next on the agenda. She helped the girls make their very first Victoria sponge.

'My stomach is so full, Nanny, I feel sick.'

June smiled at a pale-looking Rosie. She'd eaten half the bloody cake, no wonder she felt so ill. 'Go and have a lie down on your bed, darling. A little sleep will make you feel much better.'

For once, Rosie did as she was told.

As soon as the little girl had left the room, a concerned June turned to her eldest granddaughter. 'You've been very quiet the last couple of days. Is everything all right, Gracie?'

Chewing her fingernails, the child nodded and looked away.

June sat down at the kitchen table, and looked directly at her. 'You can tell your old nan anything, you know. Even things you can't tell Mummy and Daddy.'

Gracie's eyes filled with tears. 'It's a secret, Nanny. I do want to tell you, but I can't.'

'Why not?' June asked her gently.

'Because if I tell you, Rosie will be chopped up and killed.'

June kneeled down next to her. 'Don't cry, Gracie. No one will hurt Rosie, I promise you that. Now you must tell Nanny who's been upsetting you. Is it somebody at school?'

Gracie shook her head. Should she tell or should she not? Unsure what to do for the best, she decided to test the water. 'You know I was asking if Charlie did bad things to Lois?'

June nodded. She might have known this had something to do with her evil bastard grandson. 'Has he been nasty to you? Has he threatened you, Gracie? You must tell me.'

Gracie knew it was now or never. She desperately needed to tell someone. Averting her innocent eyes from her nan's, she stared into her lap. 'Charlie did bad things to me, too. He used to make me play special games with him. Is that what he did to Lois, Nanny?'

June took a deep, steadying breath. 'Tell Nanny what special games, darling, and I'll tell you if they're the same ones as Lois played.'

As she spoke, Gracie held her breath. 'He made me play the willy game, Nanny, that's what he called it. He made me put his dinkle in my mouth and kiss it until he told me to stop.'

June felt her blood run cold. Gasping for breath, she reached for the phone.

After her near brush with death, the drive back through London to her mother's seemed to take Debbie forever. Her head was all over the place and she didn't know what to think. She felt sick, ill and emotional, and just hoped there'd been a mix up somewhere along the line and a simple explanation would contradict the words she'd just heard.

Pulling up on her mother's driveway, she was relieved to see Peter's car wasn't there. Things were bad enough without him sticking his oar in.

'Oh, Debbie!' June ushered her daughter into the living room, her eyes red-raw from crying.

'Where are the girls?' she asked immediately.

'Peter's taken them out with Alfie. I asked him to, so we could talk.'

Biting her nails, Debbie sat down opposite her mother. 'What exactly did Gracie say to you, Mum?'

'We were in the kitchen, on our own. I'd been teaching her how to bake a cake when she started asking questions about Charlie. She wanted to know if he would be coming back, and then she asked me what he'd done to Lois. Well, I didn't know what to tell her, so I just said that he'd been a bad boy to Lois and he was in a lot of trouble.'

'Go on,' Debbie said, getting agitated.

June blew her nose and continued. 'She's been very quiet for days so I asked her what the matter was. It took a bit of persuading, but then she just came out with it, Debs. She said Charlie made her suck his willy! After I rang you, I gently asked her some more questions. She said when she was a little girl, Charlie played "special" games with her . . . used to make her touch him, you know, down there. I froze, Debs, didn't know what to do. I asked her if he'd ever touched her in a naughty place but she said no and clammed up. She didn't want to talk about it any more. Oh, Debs, our poor Gracie! What are we going to do?'

Debbie put her head in her hands. She felt like her whole world had just crashed at her feet. She'd spent years walking around in rose-tinted glasses, sticking up for Charlie – and now this. How could he do such a thing? Worst of all, how could he do it to his own little sister?

Snatching the glass of wine offered to her, she gulped it down in one then held it out for a refill. 'What time is Peter bringing 'em back, Mum?' She felt sick, cheated, and dreaded the questions she knew she would have to ask her daughter.

'I told him I'd ring him when we'd had our little chat.'

'Did you tell him what had happened? What Gracie said?'

'No, I didn't,' June replied firmly. 'I told him that you and Steve hadn't been getting along and you were coming round for a girlie chat.'

'Thanks,' Debbie mumbled awkwardly. 'You don't think he's touched Rosie as well, do you, Mum?'

June shrugged. 'I don't know, love. By the sound of it, the little bastard's capable of anything. He's never been right, love, not since the day he was born. It's a shame, but there's something seriously wrong with that boy.'

Holding her glass out for yet another top-up, Debbie sat in silence. She had to think now, and think quick. As she debated whether or not to trust her mum and tell her the story of Charlie's departure, she decided she needed to confide in someone.

'So that's it, Mum,' she said, ending her story. 'Him and Billy'll be halfway to Scotland by now.'

'Apart from hell, it's the best place for him.' June's tone was vicious as she thought about her no-good grandson. 'Listen, Debs, you can't have no more to do with the lad, not after this. You've got to wash your hands of him, you've no other choice. You've done more for that boy than any other mother in the world would have, and all he's ever done is throw it back in your face. Cut the apron strings, love. Let him fuck off with his scumbag of a father. They're well suited, them two. May God be my judge, they're a match made in heaven. Or, in their case, fucking hell!'

Debbie stared at the woman who had given birth to her. June looked old, all of a sudden, and Debbie could see lines of worry etched across her forehead. Determined not to cause her any more heartache, she spoke from the heart. 'I promise you, Mum, I'll never have nothing else to do with Charlie, not after this. But I need you to make a promise to me.'

'What?'

'I want you to promise that you'll never tell Steve or Mickey what happened in our home. Or anyone else, for that matter.'

'Surely you're not still trying to protect the boy, Debs?'

'I swear, Mum, I'm not. Charlie's history. If he's touched my girls, I don't care if I never see him again. Having said that, I don't want the police knocking on my door asking me to identify his body. And, believe me, if word gets out, that is exactly what will happen.'

June nodded reluctantly. A mother herself, she understood her daughter's dilemma.

With the subject closed, both mother and daughter turned their attention to the girls, discussing what to do for the best.

'Look, ring Peter now, Mum, and tell him to bring 'em back. When he gets here, suggest he pops out for a pint or something. I'm gonna take Gracie upstairs and have a little chat with her. You can have a gentle word with Rosie.'

'What do you want me to say?'

'Just talk to her, bring up Charlie in the conversation. Make it light-hearted, you know. Pretend he used to play Doctors and Nurses with you or something, and gently ask if he's ever played it with her. See what she says.'

June nodded and rang Peter.

'Mummy!' Rosie screamed excitedly when she saw Debbie waiting for them at Nanny's.

'How's my two bestest girls in the whole wide world?' she said, pulling them both close to her and hugging them tighter than she ever had before.

'I don't fancy a drink. I'm not thirsty, my love,' Peter said, as June attempted to get him out the house once again.

'Please, Peter, just for an hour.'

He grabbed his car keys and stormed out in a huff. *Dallas* had nothing on this bloody family! Guessing another drama was on the horizon, he felt like J. R. as he put his foot on the accelerator and left The Close at record speed.

As she watched Rosie playing Hide and Seek with Alfie, Debbie smiled at Gracie. 'Mummy needs a hand with something upstairs. Will you come and help me?'

Opening June's bedroom door, Debbie sat down on the bed and urged her daughter to sit next to her.

'Mummy needs to ask you something, Gracie. It's a very important something and I need you to tell me the truth.'

Gracie braced herself. She guessed her mum was going to ask her about Charlie.

'Me and Nanny were talking earlier and she told me that Charlie used to play games with you . . . touching games. Can you tell Mummy exactly what he did, or asked you to do?'

Gracie stared into her lap, shaking her head. 'I can't tell you, Mummy.'

'Why can't you tell me, darling?' Debbie asked tenderly.

'Because Charlie said that if I tell you or Daddy, something bad will happen to Rosie.'

As she took her daughter's little hand in hers, Debbie thought her heart would break. 'Charlie's not going to be living with us any more, darling, and I promise you that nothing bad will happen to Rosie. But you must tell Mummy what he said and did.'

340

Gracie still look dubious. Reluctantly she explained, 'He said that if I told you, he would chop Rosie up into tiny pieces and boil her in a saucepan.'

'He was only mucking about with you, love, winding you up. He didn't really mean it,' Debbie said, horrified.

'Really? Are you sure, Mummy?' Gracie asked innocently.

'Of course he didn't. Now tell me about these games he made you play?'

No longer frightened that her little sister was to be made into human stew, Gracie opened up. 'I didn't want to play them, Mum, but he made me.'

'What did he make you do, love? You have to tell Mummy. And after you have, I promise we'll never mention it again.'

'The game was called the willy game, Mummy. He made me hold his dinkle and kiss it. He made me put it in my mouth. He said that all sisters played the willy game with their older brothers.'

The horror that Debbie felt at that moment would live with her until the day she died. Her poor little girl, her and Steve's baby, abused by the monster to whom she had given birth.

'Are you okay, Mummy?'

Debbie somehow managed to hide her sadness and disgust from her daughter. 'Did he touch you anywhere, darling?' she made herself ask.

'No, Mummy, never,' the child told her. She seemed quite calm and looked as though she was telling the truth.

'When did these games happen, Gracie. Recently?'

'No, ages ago.'

'How long ago, darling? Try to remember.'

'When I was a little girl.'

Debbie squeezed her hand. 'Just try to remember a bit more, darling. Was it one year, two years, three?'

Gracie shrugged her shoulders. 'Don't know. More than two years, I think. It was when we were in the old house.'

'Good girl,' Debbie said, holding her close. 'Just a couple more questions for you to answer now, Gracie. Where did this happen? And where were Daddy and I?'

'You were downstairs, Mummy. I remember hearing the telly. Charlie used to come into my bedroom when Rosie was asleep.'

Debbie hugged her daughter as tightly as she could and kissed her on the forehead. Trying her best to protect her daughter's innocence, she chose her next words very carefully.

'Look, Gracie. Charlie was a naughty boy and what he made you do was very wrong, but seeing as this happened when he was younger, I don't think he actually meant any harm. I think he was playing Doctors and Nurses with you. It's not unusual. Even Mummy played Doctors and Nurses when she was a little girl.'

'Did you have to kiss Uncle Mickey's dinkle?' Gracie asked, surprised.

Debbie changed the subject quickly. 'Mummy promises you, darling, that you will never, ever have to see Charlie again.'

Gracie's eyes shone as she smiled up at her mother. 'I'm glad, Mummy. I hate him. He was always so horrible to me and Rosie. He said he was going to kill our ponies.'

Debbie took a deep breath. 'Honestly, sweetheart, Mummy promises, Charlie will never get the chance to be horrible to you again. Now can you make me a promise?'

Gracie nodded.

'What we've spoken about today must be kept a secret. It will be our little secret, just mine and yours. We musn't tell Daddy, or Rosie, or anyone else in the whole wide world. Can you promise to do that for me, Gracie?'

'Yes, Mummy. I promise I will never tell anyone. But Nanny already knows, I told her.'

Taking her daughter by the hand, Debbie led her downstairs. 'Go and play with Rosie and Alfie, darling, while Mummy has a chat with Nanny. Your nan will keep our secret, I promise you.'

Gracie smiled and let go of her hand.

Debbie dragged June into the kitchen and asked her the question that she'd been dreading. 'Did you talk to Rosie?'

'Yes, love. He hasn't been anywhere near her. Thank God.'

'Are you sure?' Debbie asked, frantically searching for more alcohol.

'Positive,' June replied, handing her a bottle of Peter's red. 'What did Gracie say?'

Debbie pretended to have a fight with the corkscrew. This was the last lie she would ever tell for her sick, screwed-up son and she didn't want the guilt to show on her face.

'It's not as bad as we first thought, Mum. He definitely never touched her or anything. He just showed her his willy a couple of times and made her kiss it once. Thankfully, it wasn't recently but ages ago, when he was younger himself.'

'How long ago?' June asked, not sure if she was being lied to.

Debbie took a gulp of her drink. 'Oh, yonks ago. Gracie said she was really young. Do you mind if we drop the subject now, Mum? I've had the day from hell and I just wanna relax for a bit before I ring Steve.'

June didn't answer but hugged her daughter instead. What could she say to the girl? There wasn't a word in the world that could comfort or compensate her for what she had just endured.

'Why don't you ring Steve, love, get him to pick

you up? You've had too much to drink to risk driving back.'

Debbie smiled at her mum, a false, sad smile that didn't even reach the corners of her mouth. 'I will, Mum, in a bit. I need to get meself together first. You go in there and play with the kids. I need to be alone for a minute, if you don't mind.'

As the door clicked shut, Debbie picked up her drink, wandered out into the garden and sat on the little wooden bench. She felt so let down, so stupid. So much time, effort and energy she'd wasted, trying to turn Charlie into a respectable human being. And, by doing so, she'd let down the rest of her family, the ones who should have been the most important to her. Looking up to the sky, Debbie prayed for forgiveness. She'd failed to protect her own daughter. As a mother, it was the most terrible crime she could have committed.

'Please, God, don't make Gracie suffer because of my stupidity,' she pleaded. She cried then and her tears fell heavier and faster than ever before.

As she spied on her through the window, June saw her daughter crumple. Dashing out to help, she held Debbie close while wiping away her tears.

'You can't blame yourself, love,' she said as Debbie's sobbing finally subsided.

'But it's all my fault, Mum. I sided with Charlie. I loved him too much. I even put him before the rest of my family and look where it got me. All of this is *my fault*.'

'It's not your fucking fault! Any mother would have done what you've done. I'd probably have done the same if it were Mickey. You have to forget about the past now, Debs. You need to lock all those bad memories away in a box and concentrate on the future. You have two little girls in there who need their mummy very much, and you have a husband who loves you dearly. All right, you've made mistakes, but haven't we all? Look at me – I chose Peter over you and Mickey, and lost contact with both of you. How do you think that made me feel? You have to move on, Debs, like I did. You've got to pull yourself together, forget about Charlie and concentrate on the rest of your life.'

'I know you're right,' she said gratefully. June's words were just the shake up she needed. 'Mum, can I ask you a favour? I'm not just protecting Charlie, but I'd die if Steve, Mickey or anyone else found out about all of this. Do you think we can keep it between ourselves?'

Holding her daughter's hand, June looked into her eyes. 'Of course. Look, Debs, in life there's a mixture of people. You've got your saints and your sinners. There's good people out there, there's mediocre, bad . . . and then there's pure evil. Me and you are probably in the mediocre category, but as much as I hate to say this to you, Charlie's in the lowest category of all. He was born evil, love, and that's not your fault, my fault, or anyone else's bloody fault.'

Looking at her mum, Debbie found that she could smile again. 'You're so right, Mum. I've wasted years trying to make him into the son I wanted. I've always blamed myself for his bad behaviour when really it's not my fault, is it? I need to move on, don't I, Mum?'

'That's my girl.'

June offered Debbie her hand. 'Let's go inside, love, and see what those beautiful little girls of yours are up to.'

Debbie stood up. She had two wonderful daughters, a loving husband and a great life. Realising just how lucky she was, she finally said goodbye to the black cloud that had haunted her for years. Charlie was the past now, dead in her eyes. As far as she was concerned, he could rot in bloody hell.

FORTY-ONE

One Year Later

As the cool sea breeze drifted against her skin, Debbie sat up, carefully folded over the page of her novel, and took a much-needed sip of the now warm lemonade in the glass beside her.

What a difference a year makes, she thought as she watched the tranquil waves lap against the shore.

This holiday in Tenerife had been Steve's idea. 'I'm thinking about taking my bitches on holiday,' he'd announced jokingly a fortnight earlier.

'When, Daddy? When?' Gracie and Rosie had screamed, jumping up and down with excitement.

Steve then put his hand in his pocket and surprised them with the tickets.

'Who's the Daddy?' he shouted, grinning at his daughters.

'You are! You are! You are!' they had both screamed.

Gracie and Rosie had changed a lot since Charlie's departure from the family home. They'd both come on in leaps and bounds and were far happier and more confident than they'd ever been.

'It's so much nicer here without him, Mum,' both girls had told Debbie on numerous occasions.

Many more stories of Charlie's unpleasantness had come to light after his departure. Nothing sexual, just bullying, threats and downright nastiness. It didn't take a genius to work out that he'd secretly led his sisters a dog's life.

Debbie had felt terribly guilty for ages, but as the months went by and Gracie showed no ill effects after the little conversation that they'd had, she had begun to feel better about herself.

'Boo!'

Debbie's thoughts were interrupted by Steve creeping up behind her.

'We got you an ice cream, Mummy,' Rosie said, handing her a half-melted cornet.

Sitting down opposite his wife, Steve polished off his Cornetto and smiled at her. 'I'm burnt to fuck, babe. The girls are getting a bit restless so I've told 'em we'll head back to the hotel. They wanna go for a swim in the pool.'

'Will you take 'em back, Steve? You don't mind if I stay here for a bit, do you?'

'You ain't met some fucking waiter and are planning to do a Shirley Valentine on me, are ya?'

Debbie giggled. He was a funny bastard, her husband, and never failed to make her laugh. 'I'd run off with any bastard, foreign or English, if it meant getting rid of you, ya tosser,' she joked. 'Go on, sod off. I'm dying to find out what happens in this book and I've only got three chapters left. You take the girls and I'll follow you in a bit.'

Patting her rounded stomach, Steve stood up. 'You make sure you look after me boy for me, won't ya?'

'Steve, I'm pregnant, not a bloody imbecile.'

He kissed her gently. 'Laters, sexy.'

Debbie smiled as she watched him walk away holding a daughter by each hand. The girls looked almost miniature beside his massive physique.

Debbie picked up her book, then put it back down.

She fancied thinking rather than reading, and sitting alone on an emptying beach was the perfect place to do so.

Her pregnancy had come as a complete shock to both her and Steve. Adding to their brood certainly hadn't been a priority in their lives. Steve was immediately overjoyed by their little mistake, though. Planned or unplanned, he could hardly wait for another addition to the Roberts clan.

Debbie felt differently and had been full of reservations since the blue line had first appeared on the test. Putting on weight, no alcohol, milk leaking from her tits, these were all of concern to her, but nothing was as worrying as the thought of giving birth to a son. The prospect of that happening filled Debbie with total dread. What if the kid looked like Charlie? What if he behaved like him? What if he tried to rape his cousin or nonce his fucking sister? She had done her best to keep her thoughts well and truly hidden. Not once had she mentioned abortion, although many times she'd wanted to, and she'd spent the first few months of her pregnancy smiling falsely while praying for a girl.

Two weeks ago she'd learned that her prayers had not been answered. Her five-month scan saw her leave the hospital clutching a picture of her unborn with the definite outline of a willy. Steve had been absolutely overjoyed by the news. Debbie was inwardly horrified.

Hence the holiday. Steve, being a big softie, had sensed his wife's unease and hoped two weeks in the sun might help her to get her head together.

As the beach ball landed at her feet, it interrupted Debbie's thoughts. Glancing around, she saw a little blond boy running towards her.

'I'm really sorry, Missus,' he said in a cute Geordie accent. 'My name's Sonny. What's yours?' he asked cheekily as he flashed her a toothy grin.

'Hello, Sonny. I'm Debbie. Where's your mum, love?'

'Over there,' he replied, pointing to a large woman in a striped swimsuit.

Seeing his mother wave and give her a friendly smile, Debbie carried on chatting to the lad.

'I'm gonna be a famous footballer one day and play for Newcastle and England,' he told her confidently.

Debbie smiled as he plonked himself down in the sand next to her. 'Are you gonna be the next David Beckham?'

He shook his head. 'No. I'm the next Gazza!'

Chatting to him, Debbie took in his freckles and cute turned up nose, and felt a slight maternal stirring. He was charming, friendly and gorgeous. Sonny was such an appropriate name for him. His smile seemed to light up the beach.

'I'm so sorry. He's not being a nuisance, is he? He doesn't stop bloody talking,' Sonny's mother said ten minutes later when she arrived to retrieve her son.

'No, far from it. He's wonderful company. You must be very proud of him.'

'Oh, I am. I'm Linda by the way,' the other woman replied, pleased by the compliment.

'Nice to meet you. I'm Debbie.'

'When's yours due? And do you know what you're having?'

'A boy,' Debbie replied. 'I've another four months to go. I already have two girls,' she added. Charlie no longer existed as far as she was concerned.

'Oh, how lovely. Your first boy. I bet your husband is over the moon.'

'He is,' Debbie said politely.

'My Sonny is the image of his dad, you know. Looks, personality, he even pulls the same expressions . . . two peas in a pod they are. Girls tend to be more like their mums, but boys usually turn out just like their dads.'

Debbie watched mother and son walk away. ''Bye, Sonny,' she shouted.

He turned around. 'You're my friend now. You musn't forget me.'

'I definitely won't forget you in a hurry,' Debbie replied, smiling at his mum who'd also turned round.

Debbie felt a sense of new optimism as she took a slow stroll towards the hotel. She hoped Linda was right and a son's making was all to do with his father's genes. Charlie was a ringer for Billy, that was for sure. Surely her unborn son would turn out to be just like Steve . . . On reaching the hotel, she headed straight for the pool area. Her family were easy to find, they were the noisiest by far.

'Mummy, get in!' Gracie screamed.

'Please, Mummy. Daddy keeps tickling us,' Rosie protested.

Steve swam to the edge of the pool. 'Is Mummy getting in? Or does Daddy have to fucking chuck her in?'

Debbie smiled. Finally, she felt ready to enjoy the rest of her holiday.

The traumatic phone call came three weeks before her due date. Debbie swore it was the shock of it which made their son arrive prematurely.

She had heard virtually nothing from or about Charlie since he'd upped and left with his father. He'd rung as promised in the first week, with his bank account details and new mobile number, and Debbie had been more than ready for him.

'I know what you did to your little sister. Unfortunately for you, Gracie has told me everything. Me and you are finished, Charlie. I've stuck my neck out for you for far too long. Now it's over. In my eyes you're dead, son.'

'What am I meant to have done? She's lying, Mum. I

swear I ain't done nothing,' Charlie whined as he tried desperately to protest his innocence.

'Don't fucking lie to me!' Debbie screamed at him. 'You and your father deserve one another. Now, do yourself a favour and don't ever contact me again.'

Twice he'd had the audacity to ring back, once begging for money and the second time just to abuse her. Debbie cut him short both times. 'Go to hell, Charlie,' she'd told him on the last occasion.

The day Debbie gave birth to her fourth child started uneventfully. She'd dropped the girls at school, Steve had popped home for lunch, and she was just about to do a bit of ironing when the phone rang.

'Hello,' she said, not recognising the number on the display.

'Debs, it's Billy . . . please don't hang up!'

'What the fuck do you want?' she replied coldly.

'It's Charlie. He's in big trouble. They've locked him up and apparently he's in a terrible state. I've been down tae the station, but the police wouldnae let me see him. I havenae got a clue what else tae do, Debs. I really need your help.'

She took a deep breath and asked, 'What has he done, Billy?'

'They're trying to charge him with rape and attempted murder. We need to get him a good brief, Debs, someone top-notch. I'd get one myself but I havenae the money . . . '

Debbie dropped the iron. 'I'll call you back in a minute. I need some time to think.'

Shaking, Debbie sank on to the sofa and held her head in her hands. Should she ring Steve? Her mum? She needed advice but didn't have a clue who to turn to. Staring at the living room wall, she noticed the pictures of Gracie in her tap-dancing outfit. As she glanced at the mantel-piece she caught sight of a photo of Lois. She was smiling brightly, with Mickey cuddling her.

'Bastard,' muttered Debbie. 'The evil little bastard.'

Charlie had already nearly ruined the lives of those closest to him and now some other poor girl had borne the brunt of his cruelty. Well, no more. Reaching her decision, she picked up her mobile.

'Billy, it's Debs. I've thought about things and I want you to give Charlie a message from me. Tell him that his mum says she hopes they lock him up and throw away the fucking key!'

Within seconds of ending the call, her waters had broken.

Steve was in the club with Mickey, going through the accounts, when he received a call to say that Debbie had gone into labour.

'I'll drive,' Mickey said awkwardly.

The relationship between Mickey and Debs had never truly repaired itself since the attack on Lois. Barely on speaking terms, they'd lost all the old warmth and love that had once bonded them together.

Debbie's action in sending Charlie away to stop him receiving his comeuppance was unforgivable in Mickey's eyes. He'd never been told exactly what had happened, but guessed that his sister must have packed Damien off, out of harm's way. Steve knew the score, Mickey was sure of that, but they'd been such good pals over the years that Mickey didn't want to spoil their friendship by backing him into a corner. Steve was in an awkward situation and, although Mickey would love to know exactly what had happened to Charlie, in some ways he admired his pal's loyalty. Debs was his wife, after all.

There were only two things that had kept Mickey sane over the past year. One was the thought of his delayed revenge because he knew that one day Charlie would rear his ugly head, and when he did Mickey would be waiting for him. The second was Lois. Thankfully, his daughter was now back to her old self, and seeing the improvement in her pleased him no end.

Dean Summers had been fantastic, a complete rock to her, and Mickey now admired him immensely. The memory of the day he'd turned up at Deano's house with the five hundred quid reward for tracing Kevin would stick in Mickey's mind for a long, long time.

'Leave it out, Mr Dawson. I don't want your money,' Dean protested.

'Take it. You've earned it. And please call me Mickey.'

'Then don't insult me, Mickey,' Dean replied. 'I love Lois and I wanted to help her. Why would I want paying for that?'

Mickey had looked at him in a special light from that day onwards. He'd even given him a little job at the club that didn't interfere with his training, and was in no doubt that one day he'd be honoured to refer to the promising young boxer as his son-in-law.

'I'd better ring June,' Steve said, aware that his brother-in-law was daydreaming.

Cursing the traffic, Mickey swerved to the right. 'You'd better ring Karen as well,' he replied, knowing that his wife was still extremely fond of his sister, even if he wasn't.

His wife was forgiving, unlike himself, and Mickey just hoped that little Alfie, who so far seemed to have his wife's temperament, would turn out to be more like him in the end. Karen was too nice, and he didn't want his boy to be trodden on in life.

The journey to the hospital seemed to take forever. As a frantic Steve rushed through the corridors, he prayed he wasn't too late to witness the arrival of his son. 'I'm the father,' he declared breathlessly when he reached his destination.

Baby boy Roberts was delivered at 6.15 p.m. exactly. A healthy baby, he weighed in at 7lb 2oz. He had a chubby face, a mop of blond hair, and looked very much like his father. With the birth being uncomplicated, Debs was moved to a ward shortly afterwards and Steve wasted no time in inviting the rest of the family to visit and share in their joy.

'Oh, he's gorgeous, Debs,' June gushed, gazing at her new grandson. 'Can I hold him?'

Handing her baby over, Debbie smiled at Peter. 'Do you wanna have a little hold of him?'

'I'd rather not, if you don't mind. Unfortunately I'm not very good with babies.' Peter secretly wondered if she'd given birth to another monster and didn't want to touch the thing, just in case.

'I am so fucking proud of him,' Steve said, peering over June's shoulder.

'He looks just like you, Steve,' Karen cooed as the baby was passed to her for a cuddle.

'Is Mickey here?' Debbie asked, realising that bar him, the rest of the family were all present.

'He's standing outside,' Karen said, nodding towards the corridor.

'I need to talk to him. Does anybody mind if I have five minutes alone with my brother?'

'I'll go and get him,' June said, praying that her offspring would finally kiss and make up.

'Do you want me to leave as well?' Steve asked, surprised.

'Yes, that includes you, Steve.'

Holding his hands up, he walked towards the door. He might be a big old boy, but he wasn't brave enough to argue with his Debs. She turned into a Rottweiler as soon as she raised her voice.

'Mick, your sister wants you,' Steve called as he traipsed out of the ward.

Being alone with Debs for the first time since the attack on Lois made Mickey feel anxious and awkward.

'Don't just stand there, come and say hello to your nephew,' she said, trying desperately to break the ice.

As he looked at the baby for the first time, Mickey couldn't help smiling to see the miniature version of Steve. 'He's a belter, ain't he?'

Debbie took the initiative. 'Look, Mick. I know we've had our ups and downs, but I think it's time for us to bury the hatchet and get back to how we was. I miss you so much, and it upsets Mum dreadfully that me and you are on bad terms. The girls are lost without seeing Alfie, and our weekends are crap without you and Karen being part of them. Charlie's history now, Mick. In fact, he's dead in my eyes. I promise you faithfully, he ain't ever coming back. Please let's try to sort things out, even if it's only for the sake of Mum and the kids.'

Mickey was desperate for some answers to the questions that had haunted him for the past year. 'Be honest with me, Debs. I know you sent him away. But where to? And who with?'

'Scotland, with his father. Unbeknown to me, Billy had moved back to Barking and had been seeing Charlie regularly. I didn't have a clue. I only found out after he attacked Lois.'

Knowing she was telling the truth, because of his conversation with Kevin, made Mickey feel less angry. 'Are you still in contact with him?'

'No. I've disowned him, Mick. And don't bother heading North to look for him either because I've just found out he's been locked up for attempted murder.'

Leaving out the words 'girl' and 'rape', she carried on. 'Billy rang me. Begged me for money to get him a good brief. I fucked him off. In my eyes, Mick, Charlie is no longer my son. I hope the evil little bastard rots in hell.'

As he looked into his sister's eyes, Mickey knew she wasn't bluffing. 'Well, at least in the end you saw the light.'

The baby's crying signalled an end to their heart-to-heart. 'Pick him up, Mick. You haven't held him yet.'

As he gently rocked the new addition to the family, Mickey smiled. He didn't feel a bit like Rodney Trotter this time round. He sat on the edge of the bed and handed his nephew back to Debbie.

'Look, sis. I will never forgive Charlie for as long as I live, and if I ever see him again I swear I will kill him. But you and me are a different story. Now you've come to your senses, I'm willing to give all the family stuff another go.'

Debbie smiled and ordered him to call the rest of them back in.

'Thank fuck for that,' was Steve's take on the matter.

'About bleeding time,' June said, determined to give her tuppence worth. 'Us East Enders are a different breed. We stick together, through thick and thin.'

Peter shot his wife a look. He loved her dearly ninety-nine per cent of the time, but as soon as she changed into a Pearly Queen, his love quickly turned into a form of hate.

'Come on, June, we must be going. It's not fair to leave Lois with the girls any longer.'

''Bye, Mum. 'Bye, Peter. Bring the girls up in the morning,' Debbie said, waving them goodbye.

''Bye, sis.' Mickey kissed both mother and baby before turning to Steve. 'And you, you fat bastard, owe me a night out, to wet the baby's head.'

'Tomorrow,' Steve said, ushering his best mate towards the door.

Breathing a sigh of relief that he finally had his wife to himself, Steve took Debbie's hand in his. 'We're gonna have to decide on a name, girl. We can call him Bobby after Moore, Geoff after Hurst, Trevor after Brooking. What's it gonna be?'

'Sonny,' Debbie said immediately, 'I want to call him Sonny.'

Steve was surprised by his wife's quick decision. 'Why Sonny, all of a sudden? You never mentioned it before when we were discussing names.'

'It's a long story, Steve, but if you don't mind I'll tell you another day. I feel so tired all of a sudden. I can't keep my eyes open.'

He bent over and kissed her gently. ''Bye, darling.' He turned to the baby, ''Bye, Sonny. Daddy'll be back first thing in the morning.'

Debbie smiled to herself as he left the room. Steve was like a dog with two tails and she was glad, after all the shit they'd been through, that she'd managed to make him so happy.

Turning her attention to her son, she noticed him gurgle. He was an absolute cutie, and thankfully she'd bonded with him immediately. He couldn't be more different from Charlie to look at. His tuft of blond hair stood out like a sore thumb and his chubby red face looked angelic somehow. The door opening disturbed Debbie's thoughts.

'Hello, I'm Nurse Chimbonda. I'm just checking if everything is okay or whether you need some help?'

Debbie smiled. 'I'm absolutely fine. I'm so happy. I've got everything I've ever wanted.'

Gas and air, the nurse thought as she smiled politely and left the room.

Lying back on her pillow, Debbie pondered the words she'd just spoken. It was the first time in her life that she could truly say that and mean it. Steve and the girls had always meant the world to her, so had the rest of her family, but now she had the one thing she'd always craved.

A son to be proud of.

A son who was capable of accepting and returning her love.

And, most importantly, a son who had not been born evil.